BORN IN REVOLUTION

Patriot or Traitor

A Reluctant Comrade

To die for what purpose

Russia Circa 1900

MASTERO

"Born in Revolution" is a fictionalized representation of well-documented non-fiction. The truth of inhumanity is well-known.

The(true)Mastero.com
Masteropublishing

Dedicated to Grandpa Max

To my muse, my eternal soulmate…the cherry on top of what has been a delicious sundae. We filled the bucket and then some.

To my family, those at my core, remember your roots as you would childhood.

Grandpa Max

…was born in Riga, Latvia, in 1888—a time when the curse of tyranny was stirring such suffering that it bred revolution and war.

I thought Grandma was just tired, she was always old, but when she woke and saw I was there, she mustered what little life she had, managed a nod, then a smile from trembling lips, but her gaze reached somewhere deep into my soul. "You should know this about your grandfather—He wasn't a coward. If he put up a fight, he'd been shot." She struggled to breathe. "If he surrendered, he'd be sent to war," a sigh, "A foolish war only to defend an evil czar from a more evil Kaiser."

I thought Grandma was lost in a nightmare. As a kid growing up in the fifties, comforted in the cocoon of privilege, a child's innocence still intact, and whether it was The Lone Ranger, Bonanza, or war movies, they were fables, knights slaying dragons, death no more than pretend.

I turned to my mother. "What is this about?"

My mother put her hand on my shoulder. "A czar and a Kaiser were bad bullies who hurt people for no reason."

Grandma groaned, "Chased by the Cossacks, tried to escape, slipped and fell on the ice..."

My mother held me. "Cossacks are mean bullies. It was winter. The roads were covered in ice and snow. They chased after your grandfather on a horse-drawn sled and ran over his leg. The injury made him worthless as a soldier, left him with a limp, but saved him from going to war."

Grandma reached for my hand. I remember—her hand was cold when she took mine in a gentle squeeze— "Not a coward. Kill or be killed, for what. He'd be sent far from home to save an evil tyrant."

I started to cry. My mother told me to kiss Grandma goodbye.

On our way home, she explained: "I told her you were being bullied." She was worried about my temper. I got in fights. Kenny Fox beat me up for not giving him my cookie at lunch. I'd wake up in the middle of the night and crawled into my mother's bed, always the same nightmare, Kenny was chasing me.

"You need to be careful about what you say and how you act. If someone is mean, get away. You mustn't fight. Avoiding trouble is not being a coward. It's being smart."

Backstory – Empires and Tyranny

From the dawn of civilization, royals married royals; daughters were traded for alliances, and regardless of temperament, the eldest son inherited the throne—unless life or death detoured down a different path.

The British Empire spanned the globe, but when their king died, there was no male heir; only the king's eldest daughter had sufficient blue blood to claim the throne. Born in 1819, Victoria was crowned queen in 1837.

The princess embraced nobility by marrying a prince and dutifully bearing nine children. Her eldest daughter followed suit and also married a prince, but a botched birth left her newborn with a withered arm.

Ashamed of the imperfection, she was desperate to try anything to fix the handicap, including torturous therapies that twisted, pulled, imprisoned, and inflicted humiliation and abuse on the fragile boy. She forced him to hide his arm, told him to keep it a secret, to be a soldier, and, regardless of the punishments to body and mind, his damaged spirit was bolstered by the noble's spell that God empowers royals as if gods.

Prince Wilhelm was an unholy child, but when his grandfather and father died the same year, he inherited the throne at twenty-nine.

He was under siege by socialists and a Congress that questioned the monarch's right to rule with absolute authority. Demands for reforms enflamed an already volatile temper. He was bred to rule as a tyrant.

Czar Nicholas II was born in 1868, the younger brother who thought his older brother would be czar and he'd be free to live as a playboy, but in a twist of fate, his brother died at 20. His father, Czar Alexander III, a giant of a man, ruled with threats, exile, and executions. He was bred to believe God himself anointed him. A tyrant was not to be questioned—and silenced his Congress. He shamed his average-sized son with humiliation and abuse. Insecurity and doubt were not permitted. He cursed his heir for being more interested in poetry, games, romance, and partying. Told his son that czars were to be feared warriors, not act like girls.

At the turn of the 20th century, Europe was held in the grip of two young royals who believed being a cruel tyrant was a test of manhood.

Wilhelm and Cousin Nicholas would meet while attending family celebrations. They'd eye each other with suspicion, if not contempt.

The family tree comes with a pecking order measured by palaces and warships, and a long history of family disputes and ambitions that spill into wars. Queen Victoria's tree had branches reaching from Moscow to London and hosted endless celebrations to honor her nobility. Wilhelm and Nicholas watched Grandma's armada sail up the Thames—they wanted to be as powerful as their grandmother.

Grandma Victoria once said of Wilhelm, "He had little heart or tact – and ... his conscience and intelligence have been completely warped."

She said of Nicholas: "Russia! I wouldn't wish that for any of us."

Between the cousins lay the Habsburg dynasty. The Austrian emperor could trace his noble lineage to the thirteenth century. An empire steeped in sophistication: Opera, Mozart, ballet, artists, wealth, academia, and an imperial army that fought for honor, but lost to the Prussians in 1871.

Emperor Franz Joseph of Austria ruled Hungary, Bohemia, Croatia, and Galicia with an iron fist. A long reign. Crowned at eighteen, the eighty-six-year-old monarch died a year before the war he started ended his family's six-hundred-year-old dynasty, but he would have known he was the end of the line. His imperial army was laid in ruins.

Nobles were under constant threat. Franz wore a steel collar and rode in an iron-clad coach, precautions that saved his life. But tragedy followed him. His younger brother, Maximilian, was executed by Mexican revolutionaries. His wife and nephew were assassinated. His son murdered his mistress and then committed suicide. Questionable motives stemmed from vengeance to fear, heartache to ambition.

Bishops, ministers, and generals owe their fate to their monarch. Loyalties tested, trust easily lost. Tyrants depend on the loyalty of generals as dogs to their master. Empowered to send millions to their deaths to defend their throne and the rule of tyranny.

Just as the warm Mediterranean was home to the Greeks, Persians, and Romans, the frigid Baltic was home to the Vikings, Huns, and Livonians—the warrior Norsemen who seized Rome.

At the eastern edge of the Sea lie Latvia, Estonia, and Lithuania, where it would take a few days under favorable winds to reach Sweden, Norway, Finland, Denmark, Poland, and Germany, but would face dangerous currents, storms, and hidden sandbars. The sea floor was littered with shipwrecks.

The Danes and Swedes dominated the Baltic until 1700, when Czar Peter the First turned his army from Moscow to march three hundred miles west and seized the Baltic States. Peter showed no mercy as he swept through the pastoral Swedish-ruled settlements. A battle plan of terror that enslaved the conquered farmers, hunters, and families who thought the wilderness was their fortress. They built his seaside capital, to which he boasted— "Who but a Saint could manifest such a heaven in life." The victorious tyrant christened this monument to his ambition, St. Petersburg.

Latvia lies at the center of the Baltic's eastern border. Its capital, Riga, is an ancient city with a long history of foreign masters. The seaport possessed the tools needed for civilization to flourish: a safe harbor, a river, freshwater lakes, endless forests, and fertile soil on a foundation of stone—the raw materials needed to build palaces, forts, and cobblestone roads.

The city is divided by the broad and deep Daugava River. On one side stood the nobles' palaces and grand cathedrals. The river was their moat and border. The soldiers kept the bridges and ferries under guard to protect their paradise.

On the other side of the river were factories, mills, and villages of the subjects filling the coffers of the nobles. Riga was a cosmopolitan city of a few hundred thousand: German Lutherans, Polish Catholics, Russian Orthodox, and a congregation of 30,000 Jews.

Survival depends on assimilation. Jews took on roles as peddlers, tailors, blacksmiths, printers, bakers, butchers, and skilled tradesmen who built homes, tended to the factories, crafted tools, and created remarkable machines. But it took bribes and favors to be an owner. Assimilate, retreat, or flee, for if given to protest, you were exiled or executed.

Only the favored were allowed to become lawyers, doctors, teachers, politicians, or landlords. To get ahead took risks measured in grave danger. Trade in salt, sugar, tobacco, alcohol, perfume, and trading in the sins of gambling and prostitution could reap big rewards, but only the most daring or skilled seized the gold ring. Jews held no monopoly as victims of prejudice; all have to find a way to survive.

Wealth is power, but nobles hold the sharper sword and thicker shield.

Talent and fame carried their own risks. Plato to Shakespeare, actors, writers, and artists expose the truth of human nature, embody the spirit of their times, but must skirt censorship to preach reform.

Diversity is a spectrum of beliefs: atheists to zealots, assimilators to anarchists, socialists to libertarians—segregated as strangers, divided by language, tradition, and custom.

Capitalism requires Democracy, but Capitalism does not always serve democracy. Democracy and capitalism don't tamper with the traditions of inheritance and sheltering wealth. Capitalists place faith in free enterprise. Inequities are justified: “You reap what you sow.” A mandate to reward ambition and greed. Survival is left to your own devices.

Socialism seeks to balance inequity by distributing wealth and empowering labor. Karl Marx and Friedrich Engels envisioned a world without borders, masters, or religion.

“From each according to their abilities, to each according to their needs.”

A dynasty sprouts from the seed of ambition. A wolf is ordained by the almighty to lord over a flock of lambs. Tyranny is a sacred tradition started by a pharaoh who convinced the people that building a pyramid was God’s wish. The pharaoh as God.

Tyranny is the opposite of nature. It wants to seal Free Will in One vision—One brushstroke—One path—the will of One master. Tyranny is a world of black and white.

Freedom is the spectrum of color. We paint our path with the random brushstrokes of Free Will. Our imagination sets us free to explore endless paths. Emotions filter logic to create art that stirs a spirit, not just tools of utility. The price of diversity is diversity.

We defy the laws of physics with Free Will. We are creators with the power to manipulate nature. Convert wood to heat, mass to energy, use tools, invent instruments, able to fly—able to convert dreams to reality.

Mother Nature is a strict mechanism of growth and decay manned by invisible mechanics that build, repair, and revise the universe in an eternal process of growth and decay: the black and white process of evolution—but with the brushstrokes of a most remarkable artist following strict rules, but endowed by its creator to create heaven and earth.

CHAPTER ONE – *Home* – Oct. 1898

My grandfather's story…

A shtetl is not a village. A shtetl has no tavern, no strangers, no general store. You survived as a farmer, hunter, and peddler, and rarely reaped what you sowed. Faith was hope for mercy. The reward was sharing in joy and neighbors bringing comfort when in misery. We were bonded by loyalty, but they'd bicker over what was right, sometimes with a swat from a hurtful temper, but trust was unquestioned, and a blessing soothed the debate.

Depending on what trouble you found, our home was a week or more east of Moscow. Three days west to Riga if at a good pace. It took sunrise to sunset to reach the Count's tavern, inn, church, and general store. We faced harsh punishment if his tax wasn't paid.

As a boy, I was shown to turn at the elm with four branches, follow the elm until reaching the spruce, and then over the hill to find the pond. The pond was where Uncle Moshe gathered his family and friends in their shtetl of four shanties.

We didn't live near the pond. Poppa thought hiding in the forest was safer, with more hope than faith that our wilderness was a fortress. Our home was almost a hundred paces down a hidden path. Uncle Moshe argued to be close to the pond. "Why have to fetch water so far?"

Gramps and Poppa were bred by a fox. A fox is more cunning than a dog. A dog foolishly barks and gives chase without regard for the prey's tricks. The fox hides, sets a trap, and only hunts defenseless prey. Gramps called his older brother a smart dog—quick to smell value and loyalty, but prone to take a foolish risk for an easier reward.

Uncle Moshe and my cousins Joshua and David also wanted out of Riga and followed Gramps to settle in this wilderness. They put their shanty between a patch of spruce and the pond. His trading partners, Mr. Hirsch and Mr. Kornicker, brought their wives and children to help with the harvest, and they also appreciated our calm and decided to stay.

It was a summer day. Warm enough to bring thirst with little effort. No dark clouds to suggest a storm was brewing, but the wilderness didn't whisper those familiar sounds of nature, as it should. My older cousin, David, was setting traps near the patch of birch. He knew every critter, every path, and realized the unfamiliar sound was neither wolves nor bears and raced like a deer through the forest's maze to warn us.

Poppa grabbed my arm and gathered the family to hide behind a wall of spruce. The storm was a fast-moving echo of thunder that shook the ground and our fears. Our escape came without a moment to spare.

Mr. Kornicker, whose violin can make you weep or dance, held his daughter, who was also my best friend. Ruth was two years older, never scared, and took me on adventures with her dreams.

Aunt Esther was an artist, and her husband, Harold—who preferred to be called Mr. Hirsch rather than Uncle Harold—showed little patience, more like a professor who taught us lessons by sharing his books and scolding us for not paying attention. He treated my little cousins, Mordecai and Ezra, like misbehaving dogs, but as the beasts descended on our paradise, he too was softened by fear—crouched to his knees, held his frightened boys and their mother for dear life.

Mamma took me in a hug, her hands covered my eyes, and whispered, "Don't look!"

A wet summer thickened the spruce into a wall of prickly pine, but we were so close to the shtetl that a cough would give us away.

Cursed by my unmindful nature, I peeked between her trembling fingers, and through the tangle of branches, I was only able to catch a glimpse—and discovered that the Golem was not a fable.

I was six when Mamma cried out in horror— *Golem!*' A word I had never heard. She was shaking so bad that it scared me to come out of hiding— "What is a *Golem*?

Mamma said I was cursed, "*Possessed* by curiosity." I would spy on their grown-up talk, and while I didn't understand all of what they were saying, I knew groans were worries, tears meant sadness, and laughter was about foolishness. She spanked me, not hard, not as if I was bad, but more like she was sad. "Her lie trembled in a whisper, "Golem is a fable." But she said *fable* the same way Gramps said, "The forest is our fortress."

I thought the Golems were bears or wolves, but as they came closer, it was five thick men wearing their skins. The warriors trampled our four shanties, slid off their horse and slashed what was left in the rapture of hate. The branches, skins, and straw that made a home were kicked away in search of plunder and tossed aside treasures whose worth was more in sentiment. The battle went on until they surrendered to our poverty. Cursed for having no gold or silver, they harnessed the one cow that didn't run off, tied six goats to their horses, and then eyed our patch.

They came as predators trapping prey. We held our breath; so close, swords ready to cut through our wall of spruce.

The quiet before the storm was distracted by a nearby war cry.

Shouting came from near the pond.

Still holding our breath, Mamma still covering my mouth, they celebrated what we didn't know but returned with no regard for seeking out worthless prey and showed their hate by setting torches to the rubble.

Czar Nicholas II was crowned six years after I was born and thought Jews and immigrants were a poison infecting his White Russia. Gramps said, "He rightfully suffered in fear of assassins." He lost his grandfather to an assassin, and his father died while the playboy was enjoying the rewards of being an irresponsible younger prince. His older brother was to be czar but died of sickness at twenty. Nicholas took the throne at 27.

Even if the ransom were paid, Jews could no longer trade in alcohol, and why my family of bootleggers moved to the secrecy of the wilderness.

The pounding hooves faded as the cloud of smoke choked our breathing. Took a moment for the bonfire to wake us to the nightmare. It was an inch to sunset when we saw what we already knew. I discovered that Golems aren't spun from fable, and that the forest isn't a fortress.

Poppa read our minds— "What sin did we commit to earn such a punishment?"

Gramps suffered to find a reason. "Paid the tax! Was it not enough?" He looked for a verdict, but all were too frozen in shock to pass judgment.

Bubby put her hand over his mouth to quiet his moan of pity. She preached a valuable lesson: "God's mercy is in the blessing that our lives were spared."

Held together under the fever of loss, we gathered before the coffins of ruin. Only the stumps and the hearths remained. We searched the ashes to find charred treasures that demanded we mourn their loss.

Aunt Esther found her box of memories, but the photos, her trinkets, crafts, and diary were ashes. She held up the blackened cameo her grandfather carved. Tears dripped onto her sleeve as she tried to wipe off the scar, but the reflection was gone

Brass keys were all that was left of Mr. Kornicker's violin.

Uncle Moshe's menorah had lost its holiness. He cried over the loss of its antiquity, "It was too old to know how old it was."

Wilted leather covers were all that was left of Mr. Hirsch's prized collection of our favored stories. Tales of injustice by Russian and Jewish authors, stories of romance being sold for a meal or shelter, warnings that poverty and wealth were a curse. Lessons that mocked life's journey as traps of greed were put before friendship.

The burnt offering infected our throats to find our souls. We recited prayers while Bubby repeated the blessing that our lives were spared, but even her tonic could not soothe the loss of books with lessons yet to be learned.

Uncle Moshe's sermon: "God's lessons can seem harsh, but He is reminding us that truth often needs to be taught with punishment to learn."

A half-moon cast the burnt offerings into shadows, as Poppa led our procession past the pond to the winding trail that leads to our cabin, a hidden home made with thick logs and a slate roof.

Mr. Kornicker gave a blessing of thanks to Poppa and Gramps—"You knew," placing his hand on their shoulders, "Takes a fox to know the pond was a trap. You're beavers. Built a strong nest."

But as we passed the pond, our footing was hidden in the shadows of night. Poppa stumbled over an unfamiliar log, poked his boots into the weeds, leaned over, looked down, and tried to push us away.

Another memory that won't be erased by putting ink to paper—a headless Albert Lapinsky.

Gramps paid his respects— "Fought with a sickle against five with swords and muskets." He was a friend fifty years ago. and thought by chance that he met my grandfather at the tavern where Gramps comes every summer to fetch supplies. Mid-summer is when bottles, sacks, seeds, and tools are plentiful. The feeble warrior followed him home from Riga as if an orphan.

Bubby never trusted the 'Pirate,' as she called him. "The thief blamed everyone for his misery but the thief himself. Why did he attack?"

Gramps sealed his verdict, "He died as he wished. A warrior."

Gramps met Mr. Lapinsky at fifteen while delivering bottles for Bubby's father to Mr. Shapiro's tavern, where Albert swept the floors. He blamed the friendship on envy, "I thought him a Viking warrior because he showed no fear to risk." My grandfather's parents also showed no fear.

Their misguided journey taught a hard-earned lesson about peddlers who trade deceit for profit. He learned as a boy that if you had anything of value, you're prey. That the wolf's intent is known. And watching his parents set their bait with kindness, he saw them as liars setting a trap.

Their friendship ended at seventeen, when girls were all they thought about, and my grandfather questioned the sacks of treasure Lapinsky said were earned by some hard-earned chore.

My bubby, Augusta Blum, was raised by her mother to be a seamstress, a cook, a healer and a fortune teller, taught to share only those cures and premonitions that brought comfort. Bubby Gussie's inheritance was also the secret recipe for tonic. She once told me, "Tonic has been a Jew's trade for fifty generations."

Gramps courted Gussie by sharing tales about foolish neighbors who suffered and celebrated the punishment and rewards of romance. They'd take long walks that ended with fishing by the river, but he couldn't summon the nerve to snatch a kiss, let alone propose, a shy boy held by fear of losing her friendship—believed that if she thought he wanted more— *friendship would be desire's victim.*

Albert seduced girls as if a contest. The pirate had little use for a heart. The cocky thief needed to prove he was the better man. Not all his fault. Few girls could ignore Albert's good looks and a liar's charm. He liked to stir the flutter in a girl by showing desire.

By tradition, a marriage would be left in the hands of the matchmaker, but Maximilian Gutlian already had Bubby's parents' blessing. Their regard for the trustworthy young man was obvious, but her mother knew better than to arrange a marriage. She knew her daughter would be tempted by the bait of scheming pirates. Gussie had a rebellious streak, and her mother knew good men like my grandfather were too respectful to woo passion. She hinted to her daughter to spy on Albert Lapinsky, and it didn't take long before she saw the lying charmer stealing another girl's heart.

Gramps was counseled by her wise mother, "You will win her heart. I know your sort. I'm still in love with such a man."

Nervous, scared, fearing rejection, dreading a "No," he proposed with a simple note— "Please marry me."

Bubby kept that brittle note in her hutch as her most precious treasure. She'd take out the yellowing paper with the slightest excuse.

Bubby's mother died too soon after she married Gramps. Some got sick, others didn't, those with the fever died. Her father died a week later. His heartache was brought to peace by his wife's tonic and the white flower.

Gussie discovered that in the privacy of marriage, romantic passion was kindled by an honest man's desire. She gave birth to a screaming, fussy, and fawned-over baby girl, that they named Selma, after her mother.

We left Mr. Lapinsky's headless body by the pond, too weary and too dark to bury, but prayed for his soul to be taken to heaven—a Kaddish.

We took comfort from the nightmare by sharing meals, chores, prayers, and beds. Gave blessings to Poppa for hiding our livestock behind a fence of bramble sealed with vines: two cows, ten sheep, nine chickens, eight goats, and Ilyich, our mule.

My cousins Joshua and David tracked down two of the five cows, seven of the twenty sheep, only five from the herd of goats, but felt fortunate to find most of the forty chickens.

Bubby gave another blessing—hunger wasn't to be another punishment.

It took from early August to the week of harvest to chop down four trees, move the stones from the hearths to the new homesites near our cabin, and by early October, we had cobbled together four log homes. But the cloud of fear hung low.

Haunted by the beast's ghosts, worn by the labor of rebuilding and the toil of harvest, there was no fervor to be found in Uncle Moshe's service for the Holy days of Yom Kippur, Rosh Hashanah, and Sukkot. The call to find faith only enflamed a tested temper. Shook the Old Testament as he cried to heaven, "Faith needs Hope in the Lord's mercy."

Keeping busy helped heal the wound, but I was held in the grip of the beast's spell. Mamma said to write a story. I thought about being a brave warrior slaying beasts. She told me that putting such a story with ink to paper would take me to a world of my own making.

Poppa's sermon surrendered to a heartfelt lesson: "*Bubbe's potions and a mamma's hugs might soothe a nightmare,*" and then he confessed, "*We gave you comfort in a child's dream of fables and fairytales, but now you know that we live among beasts*."

CHAPTER TWO – Leaving Home – Oct. 1898

I woke to their bickering as if it were a storm.

Mamma was worried, “You should go,” with a poke to Poppa.

“Too much to do.”

I didn’t understand why her fussing was so angry. I peeked from under the blanket. The candle lit familiar shadows.

“They’ll take him.” She opened the tin, grabbed a handful of flour, but in such a fever, she made a cloud.

Gramps poked the embers of the hearth. “I need the boy.” His hand on his back, hunched over. “Don’t know how many more harvests I got in me. “Ten is old enough to help, and too young to pay any mind.”

Mamma hit the table with the rolling pin, “The road isn’t safe.”

Gramps told her that taking me on an adventure to Riga would help to cast out the spell.

Poppa stopped rubbing the blade. He banged the table with the special rock used for sharpening, “Your father will take good care of Max,” stood up to face Mamma, “Czar don’t want some ten-year-old twig as a soldier.”

All I heard was, “I could be a soldier?” My dream to be a warrior.

My bed was tucked in the far corner, furthest from the hearth. A good bed of wool stuffed in good cloth and off the ground on a frame. Between the beds and the hearth was a long table and my bubby’s hutch. My father made it with all kinds of drawers to store her magical herbs.

Gramps tugged on my foot and dangled the prize. “You’ll earn your way, but the reward is to see Riga.”

I dreamt of palaces, bridges, a harbor, from drawings and stories of the Czar’s kingdom. In battle between fear and excitement, “Now?”

“Now.” Gramps shook his head with a laugh, “Harvest won’t wait.”

”You said I had to be thirteen.” Thirteen seemed far from ten.

“You’re as smart as a thirteen-year-old.

Mamma taught me how to write by copying her letters, but I didn’t understand why I needed to learn so many different letters to make words in so many different ways, only to say the same thing? Hebrew and Yiddish didn’t look like Latvian, Russian, or Polish. The ancient and holy letters were too fancy for me to draw like hers.

She held me tight with a look of worry— "You need to know what a stranger is asking, otherwise you can't tell them what they want to hear." The lesson took me deeper into a dark tunnel. I was raised without needing lessons to learn all the different ways to say the same thing. My family argued in Yiddish, complained in Polish, would pretend they were Russian, and peddle with our neighbors in Latvian.

I learned to count by what was in the egg basket, and when I was seven, Bubby had me helping to make her tonic. It started by counting and peeling potatoes, then I learned time by how long to stir the mash, and after three years of helping, without knowing, Bubby had handed down my inheritance. A lesson as valuable as knowing which weeds heal and which made you sick enough to die. She'd give me a spoonful to soothe a cough or calm a fever, a fear, and sadness, but she'd warn me over and over— "Too much makes you sick, and if taken too often, it makes you, its prisoner."

My schooling was chores. Hunting and setting traps had me think like a fox. If I weren't paying attention, Bubby would use the stirring stick, and Mamma would swat me with her broom. Poppa's lessons carried danger, so he'd smack my head to make me pay attention before cutting off a finger or hand—those chores were sharpening an axe, a knife, and a sickle.

My grandfather didn't need a broom, stick, or smack to prod me to help him unravel the puzzle of how much to value a trade. He'd have me add time, value the effort, and mull over the dangers and rewards, a lesson to teach me how to find a worthwhile profit.

Hebrew was kept holy. Gramps said that a wise man conjured Hebrew to conceal God's messages. "A secret code to protect from the pharaoh's many gods."

Yiddish was spoken at home and with those who shared the bond of Abraham. Gramps said that Yiddish bonds us to like-minded. '*Chutzpah* says so much more than a warrior's courage, *tsooris* is worry, not sorrow, *mishagos* is more like a fable as nonsense, and *mishagunnah* meant you're aware you're so wrong as to not be worthy of more talk. Such words are meaningful descendants from our ancestor's spirit."

A good year of rain filled with 20 bottles for trade, but we'd always keep the first two jugs for the family. If it were a dry summer, we'd need to clean the scum of the pond with a good cloth or dig the well deep to just get 10, but Poppa didn't fret, "Tonic's value equal to grain in times of plenty or scarcity."

As soon as the potatoes were ripe, we'd swing the sickle against a row of barley and wheat, and then Bubby would add those weeds and herbs that grew wild by the pond to give the potion its dreams. It takes weeks to make tonic. Poppa or Gramps take to the road to trade with the farmers they know. Flour was safer than tonic for trading in Riga

Bubby and Gramps's marriage was a partnership made in heaven—peddler with a well-regarded product, but if not for Bubby's mother, their union would never have happened.

Uncle Moshe taught me Russian with the warning— "If you don't understand your master, "You'll be held under suspicion as a thief or worse, a heretic."

CHAPTER THREE – Saying goodbye – Oct. 1898

Gramps pulled me out the door, "Time to go."

While I hitched Ilyich to the wagon, Gramps pulled a few nails, and lifted the slats to reveal the wagon's secret, a fake floor.

I heard the clink of glass bottles coming from between the trees. Poppa hid the bottles between the boards, nailed it back down, and hid under a blanket of hay. Cousin David's canes and rabbit skins put on top as bribes to avoid a thief's prying eyes.

Gramps whispered in my ear, "You be a man now. Go tell Mamma you're all excited to see the city—you do this for your Mamma."

I did as I was told, even though I was afraid of leaving home, but filled with the dreams of seeing Riga, curiosity came with a cure from Mamma's infection of fear.

She hugged me until I couldn't breathe. "Come right home." A warning to her father. "Don't need to see everyone from here to Riga."

Gramps climbed on his throne of a buckboard, but when I went to sit beside him, he pushed me down. "Ilyich had his own mind. You need to take the mule by the harness and show him the way."

Mud made it hard to get up the hill. The path began at our cabin, went past the pond, and into a path through the forest known only by the sign of which tree marked another turn. As we made our way, I saw my cousin Herman milking a goat among the shadows. Herman joined the family three years ago when he married Sarah, Ruth's older sister. He called out, "Good luck and safe travels."

Uncle Moshe, even with the cane, struggled to take a step.

We got a bit further before Ruth called out, "Where you going?"

"Riga."

Ruth said she was going to be my wife, but being two years older, and a head taller, could swing the sickle longer than me, but a girl didn't get to go anywhere, except to the Festival. I think she wanted me because I'm the only boy she knows besides her brothers Mordecai and Ezra, who were just seven and five. Mamma said, "Ten is a boy with only the itch to be a man. A girl of twelve is already a woman caring for the home and family."

She won't let go. Stronger than me, Ruth would've been a better helper.

There was the clanking of my cousin's razor-toothed traps forged by the blacksmith in trade for pelts. David and Joshua's dream was to catch enough mink to make a coat worthy of a noble, but in a whole year, they'd only trap two or three. Mink could fetch a good saw, axe or shovel.

David ran to catch up. "Heard you're going to the city." Gramps stopped the wagon. David placed his hand on my head, "Lord, keep watch—safe and prosperous. You're a lucky boy. Such an adventure." My cousin had God's ear. He looks older than twenty because of pocks and long scraggly hair and wispy beard cut with his knife into patches. Looked like a scarecrow.

David and Joshua spent most of their time in a tree. They'd sleep most of the day and watch the critters roam about at night.

While he'd be waiting, David liked to carve a worthless branch to look like the last critter he trapped. If he favored someone, he carved their face. He made me a cane for my birthday and said it was supposed to be me, but it got me worried, I looked like a mouse. David pulled my ears. "Big ears, big nose, big eyes," and laughed until he choked. I made Bubby take out her treasured mirror, and as if caught in his spell, I was a mouse.

Joshua is the opposite of David. Same blood, but it didn't make sense that they were brothers. David is Uncle Moshe's son, a saintly possum, who can talk until you fall asleep, but Joshua never said much. He never came to Shabbat supper, even though his father was our Rabbi, Joshua prayed to critters and birds.

Because of all the rain, the ground was sticky mud. Ilyich was working hard, and my boots kept getting stuck. Cold pebbles rubbing my feet to be hardened according to Bubby's lesson.

Samson wanted to follow. He'd bark if there was a good critter and would retreat if it were a bad snake. Snarled if a wolf was near. I thought he'd protect us, and asked, "Gramps, can Samson come?"

"Needs to keep watch here." And Gramps had me shoosh him away. Leaving him behind was a new kind of hurt. Took yelling at Samson to make him stay behind.

CHAPTER FOUR – A muddy path - 1898

The wagon's wheels dragged, and I pushed while Ilyich pulled, but Gramps had to climb down from his throne to give us a hand. He spat, then mumbled a curse in Russian to make sure the curse reached the Count and swore out loud. "This land should be ours."

The curse echoed until I realized it was news, "It's not ours?"

He shook his head. Spilled a secret. Looked to the heavens to find the answer. "We've been blessed to tend to it, but it's not our kingdom. I'm not a king, and you're not a prince. The Count lets us tend to his land."

This truth was soon forgotten in the stew of a child's mind that gives little thought to the troubles of the grownups.

The path to reach the East-West road meanders through a forest of prickly pine that gives no sign of a village at its end. Without knowing the signs, you'd be lost in a trap of wilderness. Knowing the signs was knowing the trees. A lesson I learned from the punishment of being lost.

Poppa thought to soothe my fear and carved me a knife. Had me throw it at a rabbit. I missed by a good pace, "See if you can hit a tree." Took me fourteen tries to get it to stick, and twenty-four before I hit a rabbit, and that's when I got lost by chasing after a deer.

Fortunately, Mamma got worried when I wasn't begging for supper. Fortunately, Poppa was as good at tracking as David and Joshua.

He hit me hard but then realized that a spanking wasn't the lesson I needed. The next day, he took me back to where I got lost and explained, "Trees are like people, no two are alike. It's all about the skin and limbs." He rubbed his hand on the tree's skin. "This is birch, white with black pocks." Took his knife to slice off a strip— "There's hard wood and soft, with chestnut and oak being the best for a solid table to work on."

He showed me that when we reached the giant oak, if we turned right and followed the patch of white birch, we'd get to the east-to-west road.

My boots were pulled off by the trap of mud, and I begged Gramps, "Let me ride in the wagon," but complaints only draw sermons. "Need you to push." My grandfather didn't listen to my fussing, just preached from his throne. If I complain about hunger, he'll tell me some proverb about how *hunger is a whip for doing a chore.*

I heard the loud 'caw' and knew a hawk was watching. David said, "A hawk and owl are a bad omen for trapping, but it's the silence you need to fear— quiet is the sign of a wolf or bear." Nearing the fork in the road, getting dark, and Gramps decided, "Stop here for the night."

I gave one last hard pull on the mule's harness, but she was done for. Gramps climbed off the wagon, groaned, bent over in a bow, hand on his back, went to the mule's ear, sweet as can be— "More hay for supper." Ilyich is under his sorcery and pulled the wagon over a hill to have us hide among the bramble.

He took out the sack, broke off a handful of challah, dunked it in the soup, but then waited for my blessing. But I'm thinking God already heard Gramps, and he never answered me, anyway, but I was too tired, thirsty, and hungry to stir another lesson, and just murmured, "*Baruch atoi adonoi*." I sucked off the soup with little bites to make the challah last.

"A good day," my grandfather said as he crawled onto the bed of straw, shifted about, took another swig from his flask, closed his eyes, and before I got settled, he was snoring with that sort of sniveling snort.

Leaving home and traveling the road excited my fears, but Gramps wouldn't make a fire. "We mustn't put temptation on the wind to give notice to others we are here."

The chill of the night was spun by the wind, and I was glad Mamma had Gramps bring my coat. Making the coat was a lesson in stitching together rabbit skins and stuffing the sheep's wool between the fur and a deer skin. When I asked her why we were making a winter coat in the summer, she answered with another lesson. "Good to plan ahead." I poked myself with the needle, and she showed no sympathy. "That's how you learn."

The wind stirred the wolves, who I believed were hiding. A night without stars or moon. A blind man's darkness.

I wasn't supposed to go on this trip until I was thirteen. "You'll stop being scared when you fight fear as a man." That night, I wished they had waited until I was thirteen.

I heard something scratching under the wagon, "It's a wolf!" I nudged Gramps, then dared to wake him— "You hear that?"

He just grumbled and rolled over.

I was scared. I pulled on his arm, "No, really."

He sat up. Spit over the side. Leans hard against my chest to look around. "I see and hear nothing. You're a foolish boy scared by the wind.

Go to sleep." He squeezed my arm. "Silence your childish thoughts. Who but an owl could find us on such a dark night?"

I wanted to believe he was always right, that he knew everything.

"Close your eyes. You can't fall asleep if you're noisy with worry."

I closed my eyes and squeezed them tight, but that invited the nightmare, so I opened them. Through the branches, I searched for God, but there were no stars to light heaven. When I asked Gramps, "What does God look like?" he told me, "God looks like me," and then pretended to get really tired, moaning— "He must look really old and be really tired from all this mishigas he created."

I pray to God even though I can't see him. I beg him to protect us, but I don't think he knows I'm here. I knew he'd get mad, but in fear, I risked his temper. "Gramps," and leaned in closer, "Tell me my story."

He rolled to his side. Looked me in the eye and then with a groan. "Your story!" loud enough like he's meaning to shove me out of the wagon.

"The one about the boy who isn't scared of anything."

He was a good storyteller, and that's how he taught me Polish. Would repeat the words in Yiddish.

Gramps takes a sip from his tin, "What is the story about?"

"A warrior is not just brave but pays attention to learn valuable lessons. Better to be smarter than the beast. To stay safe, you need to plan, to think ahead, and not fight the beast with only a sword."

"Tomorrow, when I ask you to clear the field, remember our brave warrior. Remember that we will work hard to earn a prize that will feed us all winter. You will also be quiet, and you'll learn how I trap a dragon.

CHAPTER FIVE – Harvest – 1898

Sleep came without warning, but then soon after, from somewhere close, I heard Gramps calling for me. "Max!" in a temper meant to punish. "We won't fill these empty sacks by sleeping all day. No more stories."

I sat up expecting a smack, but he just warns me, "Better I should leave you here."

When my grandfather made me angry, I wanted to run away, but then I got scared imagining what if I got lost and never saw him again.

I beg for sleep, asking, "Just another minute."

"Sleep is for the dead," he says as if it's true.

I try to hide under my cap and turn my back to him, but he won't let me escape and kicks me, "Lazier than the mule."

Our journey is a book of lessons. We follow a well-known path carved by horses and wagons since the time of the Vikings. He told me it was the same road that Czar Peter marched his army from Moscow to take Riga during my great-grandfather's time. Peter was the czar long ago—the grandson of the first czar."

I looked down on a path that seemed to go on forever, and that stirred a new worry. "Poppa said we'll be a week going but less coming home."

Gramps shook his head, "Time on the road depends on how long it takes."

Later that morning, we followed a path that made itself known by the marks of wheels and hooves. and found a field not much more than ours.

My grandfather waved to a man of Poppa's age. The farmer wore the black suit of the pious and a wide-brimmed black hat of the Orthodox, and I'd have thought he was fancy dressed to go to shul. He waved back with the smile of a knowing friend. "Maximillian, only you'd brave the mud."

Gramps took a bottle from under his throne and gave that nod. I was told to stay by the wagon, but I needed to take a piss. I liked to drown the ants crawling toward my boot.

I'm close enough to hear their talk, mostly of miseries and mitzvahs. The warming sun was halfway to overhead, and the chill of early autumn was warmed by the time he called me over. "Time to give battle, grab your sword."

I grabbed the new sickle Poppa made special for me and followed Gramps into the field. "Need to clear two rows."

The sharp blade made a clean cut, but I was put into a sweat before I cut away twenty paces worth of a field that seemed to grow longer.

I hear the memory of my pledge not to complain and be a good partner. I took a deep breath and cleared another row as my grandfather cleaned the whiskers of grain and filled two sacks— my old chore.

Day ends when sunset darkens the field.

I tie Ilyich to a tree and grab an armful of hay.

"You were a good partner. Tomorrow, I will teach you how to value a trade. You keep your ears open and listen to the wants of the farmer. I'll offer less, they want more, and I might walk away, but in hope he'll call me back if he believes my price will be his best offer."

Gramps dunked the challah as a reward and gave it to me. "But profit isn't known until we leave the baker. First, the farmer gets his share, and the mill is paid a ruble or more to turn the grain into flour. The sacks are another kopek but deserving. It takes a loom made at great cost to work the straw to burlap. The price of flour is all about how good the harvest is. Better year, lower price. For a lighter sack of wheat we might trade for six rubles, oats a ruble less, barley sometimes more." He ponders, "A three-ruble profit per sack would be fair. Four is better."

Poppa always told me, "If it's sugar or salt, or such a thing of desire, you get more for the trade."

"You listen. Salt and sugar are traded by only the most favored of merchants. Salt is dug from a secret tunnel. Said to be somewhere in the furthest hills of Poland. Trade goes through Warsaw, then to Vilna by those Jews who are loyal to the salt mine's owner. A sugar crop is something I know little about, except that it needs to be grown where it's warm all year, so it must be far away. Those who manage to avoid being killed or robbed while bringing it north can make a fortune, but the risk is equal to the reward."

In the shadows of sunrise, I found an opening in the stone wall to give us an easy path out, and on the other side was an open field where a young man with the strength and size of two is cutting grain. Gramps called out, "Interested in selling your harvest?"

He didn't look up, but stopped, then spat in our direction.

Gramps doesn't give in so easily. Grabbed a bottle from under the buckboard, whispered to me, "Let's see if I can tempt him."

He acts all friendly and greets the farmer in Latvian, puts on his disguise, and sprinkles flattery— 'Fine crop. Care for a sip?"

I watch from behind the wagon.

The young man raised his pitchfork—"I won't drink your Jew tonic," making jabbing motions.

Gramps hurried back to the wagon. "Not worth the bother." Took a few sips and nodded for me to sit beside him. "You take the stick." He looked back. "That farm used to belong to Horace Stein. What happened to him, I don't know." He shook his head and grabbed my hand. "Blame his spirit on only knowing punishment. Czar punishes us for what sins, I don't know."

He told me it wasn't always like this. When he was a boy, Jews were respected—for trade, law, medicine, numbers, theatre. Jewish scholars filled the libraries. "When my father was your age, there was a woman czar—a German princess married to a weak czar. Some say she poisoned him to take the throne. Queen Catherine, and then her grandson, Alexander II, let Jews attend school—if only to convert them. A giant of a man, he punished all who weren't Orthodox. He wanted a pure Russia, and his son, Alexander III, another giant, avenged his father's assassination. Thirty thousand Jews were exiled from Moscow.

We left the forest. "Your grandparents were Galician," Gramps said. "That land lies between here and Palestine. Good farmland. But a battleground—Czar against Sultan, Prussians, Germans, Russians."

A dark cloud of dirt comes at such a pace and with the roar of thunder, that Gramps took hold of me with hope over faith—"They won't be interested in an old man and a boy with a small wagon." I feared that the pile of straw wasn't enough to hide six hard-earned sacks of grain.

Two strong horses, a heavy wagon, three men standing tall, eyes full of suspicion, bears clad in fur, black hair flying like their horse's mane. Two had the rifles, but the threat was their wagon owning the road. I held my breath as they flew past. Gramps whipped Ilyich to hide in a ditch.

It took some time to catch our wits. Gramps handed me the hammer. "Check if a bolt came loose." Two bolts hold the wheels.

I searched through the mud and wished Poppa were here. He'd be doing the fixing, and I'd be on my grandfather's throne of wool with springs that soften bumps. Poppa would walk alongside our mule. He couldn't sit still. Poppa told me, "The chores of the journey are in equal measure to the chores of being home."

No sooner had I finished hammering in the bolt than he hit Ilyich with a sharp snap of the rod. The mule struggled to pull the wagon out of the ditch, my boots slipping. Gramps had to get down. Heard him mumble a lesson to cool his temper, “Mud and hard work are good for the soul.”

Struggling long enough to work up a sweat, still in the ditch, when two well-armed men climbed off their horses and gave us a hand. My grandfather offered a cane as a reward, but they laughed.

“Chasing after a wagon driven by three men.”

“Not far ahead.” Gramps nods, “Moving fast.”

We returned to a road that’s awakened by the sun drying the mud. The road comes alive with a parade of carts, wagons, and horsemen.

A cart rattling with the clanging of iron, pulled by two young men in black suits, wearing round fur hats, blocks our path. Their devotion is made known by the payaos of curls dangling over their ears. Their poverty is shown by patches and tears in the thin cloth of their black coats and white shirts. Bubby would want to mend and wash. “Likely coming to trade pots for grain.” His hand on my wrist.

The young men stopped to peddle. “Are you interested in a trade for pots and pans?”

My grandfather shook his head. “Have all we need.”

"We can save you the trip to Riga.” Recites a prayer of good fortune as a sign of brotherhood. “I have valuables to trade. Do you have grain?”

Gramps paid his respect by stopping. The bold young man held up a frying pan, then waved his other hand— “Have very nice pots and pans. You know what sort of blacksmith you’d need to find such a thing. Fire and hammer all day. If so blessed, your mother or wife will thank you.” He studied our wagon, smiled, “You trade in hay?” With a grin.

Grandpa would argue with Uncle Moshe about the charity of the Hasidic being in want of a trade or favor, and with a snap of his cane to the mule’s rump, we left the pots and pans behind.

CHAPTER SIX – Peddlers – Oct. 1898

The village had a tall church, big barns, a long field of cows, pens of pigs, chickens running free, boys my age playing with a ball, and a long row of men sitting like crows on the perch of a strong fence. A village like Vladistok. I asked if it belongs to our Count.

"Not our Count, but a man who has the favor of the czar. This all belonged to the Shulman family, a good customer, but no more."

"What happened?"

"If your business shows its profit, the Russians take it."

"The goyim have so much, and we have to beg to trade pots, pans, fur, tonic, and grain with such labor, yet they sit on a fence and have such bounty. Why be a Jew?" I ask Gramps, "Is peddling to be my life?"

"Everyone is a peddler. Even the czar must trade rewards for loyalty. But if you're asking what it takes to have the wealth of a Count, you must be clever with no regard for others. Your scheme must be without charity. A cold heart. Show no want. Be certain with intent."

I look back to see a long home with boys playing with a ball and not doing chores. "What is this about? What's this place?"

"A school."

"School?"

"Lessons of what I don't know."

"What do they learn in school that I don't learn from you and Poppa?"

"The ways of their church and the czar's laws."

Gramps kept his stick to the mule—his smile was no more. "Come sit beside me. As you know from the festival, Jews are not always welcome. We suffer for not having faith in the Christian belief that God sent his son, Jesus, to teach us the lesson of brotherhood. And while his lesson is born from the Torah, the Jews of his time thought him a heretic for preaching against the rabbis who wouldn't stand against the Roman czar, who was as our czar, harsh in judgment on Jews."

The thunder of a blacksmith is hidden from behind a wall of shrubs. I look back, "We need a new bolt."

"The Goyim blacksmith is not anyone you bargain with. He's in service to the nobles."

The smell of pigs roasting over a bed of embers stirs my hunger to beg Gramps to stop. I longed to eat pig, but told it's not kosher, not allowed. The rule is another I don't understand. Bubby said, "It makes you sick."

I didn't want to hear Gramps giving me another lesson, but I didn't understand, "The Czar and Goyim feast on pigs,, a church with gold Saints, homes with windows, a school, What do we have?"

My grandfather turned so quiet I could hear the wind as we turned the corner and lost sight of the Christian's golden Eden. "Who to blame for our misery? A neighbor feasts. We struggle. Who is to blame? Laziness? Foolishness? God's Will? Does God make a good or bad crop?"

The road flattened. We passed farms and pastures where lazy cows spend their day chewing grass. Gramps liked to say, "Cows live the easy life and don't deserve pity." We traded tonic and furs for a cow. We wait until the cold of winter to butcher, the cold keeping it good until spring. Gramps said if all went well, we'd trade for a cow.

Butchering is a hard day's work—cutting the hide, sawing limbs, knowing what's good from the cow's insides. To make it Kosher by draining its blood, and reciting blessings. I remember being fascinated by the brain, thought it was a nest of white snakes. My father said it's where God stores our soul—so to ascend to heaven as death turns memories into messengers that ascend to heaven as if smoke." You burn your skin off when soaking the hide in the brine of fermented vinegar. Poppa told me to be thankful. "Leather and a full belly, what more can we ask for."

A wagon with five young men came upon us, waving as if they knew Gramps. Their clothes were ragged: white shirts yellowed and torn, frayed black pants held by the poverty of rope for a belt.

They had no mule or horse. They pushed a cart loaded with crates of chickens. They were about to pass without stopping when one of them held his stare on my grandfather. The young man let out a loud hello, "Shalom!" He nods, "I believe we've met?"

Gramps squinted. "Not that I recall."

"You were kind and generous. You gave me challah, and we shared your fine tonic." He laughed. "I'm Ira, Ira Ben Cohen." Came closer, whispered, "A fine tonic." Been some time." He smiled, "I forgot your name, but it wasn't kindred."

Gramps replies, “Maximilian.” Gramps rubbed his beard. “Yes. You were a boy. Not yet with a beard. But you remember my vodka,” he smiled, a handshake with a proud laugh.

He pulls my grandfather close, a smile, “A bottle for chickens?”

“Have only my flask.” He looks to the sun directly overhead. “A good time for a rest.”

“We’ve deserted.” The young man confessed his escape. “Taken to serve as slaves, not soldiers. Held at gunpoint to steal and drag our people from their homes.” He leaned closer, “If you protest, you’re not welcome anywhere. Called us anarchists. The Czar is the anarchist.”

The one with glasses was most anxious to tell their tale. Held up a book. “Can you read German?” Handed it to Gramps, “A new bible for those wanting freedom.”

Gramps only needed to glance at the first page before shaking his head, “Karl Marx.” A snort. “That all men should be equal and share in the bounty of the land. A dreamer.”

“We won’t be taken prisoner,” The young man’s Yiddish was flavored with the pride of importance. He pulled a sword from under the blanket. The other two showed pistols. “We fought for our freedom. Protest cost us five brothers. We hope to make enough for passage to America. Democracy has no czar.”

That dream put thoughts in my head. Was there someplace where there was no master?

My grandfather scolded Poppa when he talked of sailing off. Gramps told him, “Such a thing is foolish. To cross an ocean to what? Their manifesto is the capitalist’s god of money. Call them police or Cossacks, owner or noble—tyranny is greed.”

The one with the scar across his cheek was angered. “I was to be a doctor, but the magistrate said he had enough Jewish doctors. You’re the fool to think we can hide as sheep from a wolf.”

I’m pulled to sit beside him. Gramps tapped Ilyich, we ride off, but my grandfather called back, “May your prayers be answered.”

He shook his head, and groaned, “There’s no place where greed doesn’t rule. We’re taught to survive with suffering. I was boy your age put to work building a castle. Learned about the pulley.

I remember when Poppa drew a picture of how a pulley works. “It’s a wheel wrapped with a rope. Such a simple thing, but it gives one man the strength of four.”

CHAPTER SEVEN – The Mill – Late Oct. 1898

After a long week we finally reached the mill where the grain is easily ground to flour for a ruble. We're close to Riga. Roads became crowded. The villages have two, three or more churches. We passed a synagogue that was as big as barn. Gramps had me kneel beside him to give a blessing for a safe journey. "Bubby knew this was a good time to go."

The mill is owned by an old man dressed like a Count; his authority was guarded by two costumed men with rifles by their side. The rocking chair as his throne, a young princess filled the silver goblet.

We drove the wagon to the tall stone tower that has a wooden wheel dipping into the river. The giant wheel turned as its buckets filled.

A boy not much bigger than me, but made of thicker stock, came from inside the tower to help me load the sacks.

The mill was as my father had drawn—the waterwheel, the tower, and the giant stone wheel was connected to the wheel by a pole and gears.

As we watched the grain ground to flour, I asked the boy, "Do you live here?"

He laughed, "To live with the Count would be the end of me. No amount of work satisfies the old coot." He shoveled the flour into sacks, "I'm Kermin," and we formed a kinship of sorts. He was eleven, a year older, and also liked fishing. "The Count is an angry man. Nothing pleases him." And then came close, "There's talk of a chest of gold hidden somewhere under his house. Said it's protected by a thousand skeletons. Thieves punished for trying to steal his treasure."

Kermin shares what he knows about the mill's legend. "Before he was the Count, before there was a mill, he had a plan to build such a thing by tempting fools with promises of wealth. He sent his boys into the wilderness to cut this large block of granite from a distant mountain. Must have taken a hammer and chisel some time and sweat. It's said that after all this labor, just as they were setting the wheel in this mill, his three sons were killed when the wheel fell over and crushed them."

We left the mill with six sacks of flour. I looked back with envy at Count Malenkov's palace of a thousand stones, and the second-floor porch held up by tall white columns, with too many windows to count and chimneys in each corner. A palace made grander by a garden of shrubs cut to shapes.

I asked Gramps about the dungeon, skeletons, and treasure.

"A miser without a heart. A royal without royal blood." Pinched my ear with that grin, "A golem."

"Then I want to be a golem. He has a treasure in his dungeon, a wheel that grinds grain without leaving his throne," and I argued, "He's a czar who sits on a fine throne while all do his bidding."

Gramps turned to me with a frown, "He has nightmares. The rich and nobles are like any man. They suffer from sickness. Know pain. Fear death."

"The boy said he promised his sons this treasure, but that they died under the stone. Is that true?"

"That's what I heard." He told me the story of the Count. My lesson on the curse of inheritance. "He was an orphan who put a spell on a lonely, widowed Countess. She died soon after the marriage from what ailment we don't know. The inheritance goes to the husband or eldest son, depending on treachery. True for the czar as it is for a peasant. A timeless custom from the time of the pharaohs that poisons the path for family and the eldest son. The Countess had three sons from before she married this pirate, Melenkov. Whether the sons died by accident or murder, the truth was buried under the stone."

"A thief rewarded with a life in this heaven?"

"The Count has no family, no friends, no one to care for him out of love, so he must pay people to tend to all the chores. There's no Bubby or Mamma to do the cooking and give comfort. Everyone is after his fortune. Must always keep an eye on his treasures."

My grandfather clung to Judaism and justice as though tied to the great stone. He questioned God, scolds God for his punishments, but won't abandon God. I often heard his confession, "To do otherwise would make me a fool in life and suffer forever in death." He'd sip his tonic, "I'm a peddler who gives honest labor. My only sin is doubt."

CHAPTER EIGHT – Riga – 1898

Home was six long days behind us when fields, forests, and the nest of a village grew into towns of swarming bees. Gramps is fussing. Says we need to be mindful. But greed is on our side. The soldiers, sheriffs, and thieves are lured by heavy loads needing four strong horses to pull.

With each mile, the river widens. There's a large raft with a shack, its chimney billowing black smoke. Paddle wheels turn the water, just as what drove the stone wheel at the mill. Gramps gave me a lesson on 'Steam' engines." Boiling water does the work of four men with poles."

The fishermen's boats are pulled and pushed by the wind or current. Their labor is lifting nets. I watched in envy as they hauled in a barrel of fish. No need for bait or waiting, but then I thought, this makes fishing no longer heaven but labor. No time for dreaming under an afternoon nap.

The closer to Riga, the boats grow from one to two sails, then see boats the size of a village with chimneys the size of trees that could hold more than two wagons filled with a field of grain, or a barn of fifty cows.

In the distance, steeples come into view, but my wide-eyed study was captured by a harbor where men ride machines with iron claws that lift large crates packed with what I wouldn't know.

Poppa's drawings were true reflections of what I beheld, but even as fine a picture and story as he told and drew, this was so much more.

The city is a forest of steeples. The Church Crosses touch heaven. The homes are so grand that I asked Gramps, "Are these all the Czar's palaces?" Bigger than barns, taller than an oak tree.

Wagons, carts, and men on horses crowd the road, but then my rapture turns to fear as the smoke and noise of an odd-shaped wagon comes rushing toward us. It moves about like a rabbit. A wagon with no horse. A fancy man behind a window, hands on a wheel, with a woman wearing a fancy hat beside him, and two nobles sitting high on a throne behind them. The magical wagon passes by in a blink. "You told me of such a thing, but to see it."

Gramps laughs. He nods with a grin— "It's like that ship in the distance. See the smoke? There's a hearth inside that boils water to make steam that moves the gears and pulleys."

"Why have I never seen this in Vladistok or on the road? Are they only in Riga?"

“Only nobles have the treasure to buy such a thing. No farmer or peddler we know has such a fortune.”

The dirt road is now made of stone cut into squares, and we enter a canyon cut between rows of homes painted in colors, and of such size that they must be nobles’ palaces. Two or three homes are stacked on top of one another. The sun reflects off glass windows. Some are made of brick; others are smooth, as if made of clay. The doors are scrolls of black metal on carved wood. The roofs are red, gray, or black slate, and others have thatch so thick they must have the gatherings from a hundred haystacks.

We rounded a corner and came upon a church so grand it outshines all others. Its steeple is a golden egg with a pointy tip. “Gramps explained that this was the Czar’s church,” and pointed to the gold cross with its two bars across the pole, and a third tilted at the bottom as if to hold the pole up.

When I asked why we don’t have this cross? Poppa told me, “Different signs, but all pointing to heaven.

We followed a maze of canyons made of tall homes and entered an open field, Gramps called “The Central Square.” We’re scared to a halt by more of these Motorwagen carting around finely dressed nobles and their queens. The wagons are regal, all painted white with gold scrolls. The driver sits on a throne, wearing a top hat. I asked, “They be czars?”

“No, but in the Czar’s favor.” Gramps steers clear of the Square.

Everywhere, soldiers in fancy blue uniforms, some holding silver-encrusted rifles with a long knife at the tip. The horses shine as if they were bred from a fable, as black as night. The fancy soldier’s white uniform is made even fancier with gold fringe and a silver helmet topped with a tall row of feathers, “The czar’s warriors.”

I recall that moment as if it were yesterday, when my childhood nightmares of Golems as bears became confused by warriors as knights.

Gramps stopped before a magical tower watching over the Central Square. Made of red bricks stacked and whittled into all manner of shapes. Heavy wooden doors with scrolled metal bars held by brass hinges. Above the door was a stone figure of a warrior slaying a serpent, and half-naked black slaves serving that master.

He pulled me by my chin, “This is the guild of the Blackheads,” said with anger. “It’s where the best artists and craftsmen come to work and trade with nobles and the rich. But only for the Gentiles. The better trades are all taken by the Goyim.”

A boy my size came at us, waving a stack of papers, and blocked our path. Gramps shook his head and waved the boy away. Whispered to me as though someone was listening, "Their newspaper stirs trouble, and no matter if it speaks truth, it bodes no good." Gramps snapped his stick on Ilyich to move from the Square, but then turned to me to explain, "A newspaper used to be announcements of birth, marriage, death, and had warnings of pestilence, drought, or cold. It does no good to speak ill of the Gentile, be they a shopkeeper, preacher, noble, or Czar. Such stories only invite trouble."

Gramps knew Riga like a fox and kept to the narrow alleys that left behind the fancy home. "Peddler can't have their cart or wagon seen on their roads. Stone roads are owned by those with fancy clothes."

I picked up the scent of the baker's shop before turning the corner. "The baker does not bargain," a lesson, "He counts on peddlers like us to feed his ovens. Horowitz will be more than fair."

A man as big as Gramps and me, if put together, greeted us, full of smiles. "Maximilian! Of course, you were first to the harvest. Such a fox."

The terms of trade are set with a whisper and a handshake. The baker lifts two sacks to throw over his shoulders.

Gramps grabbed my ear, "Don't just stand there, take the smaller one."

The room has two large metal boxes with drawers, and underneath is a fire of red-hot embers. A zaftig bubby is rolling out the dough.

I put down the sack and stared with longing at a shelf lined with sweets. She's as big as the baker. "I'm Mrs. Horowitz," and the nice lady greeted me with a cookie topped with what looked like brown butter.

That first bite casts a spell that could last a lifetime. "What is this?"

Mrs. Horowitz laughed, "It's called chocolate. A seed from farms that are far away."

The cookie sent me into a fever. I ate it so fast that it only had me wanting another. "Can I have another?" begged.

I got a smack from Gramps. "That cookie was a gift, now you must pay. Do you have a ruble?"

I couldn't leave. Sweet chocolate drove me to madness.

Mrs. Horowitz shook off Gramps, took pity, and handed me another of the magical cookies. I think I cried when he dragged me out.

We continued our adventure down a street of more treasures. Behind large glass windows were the gold trinkets of nobles. The signs were in

Russian, so I struggled to read them. At ten, I knew only a few letters and fewer words. "What do they say?"

Gramps gave the lesson with a moan and a shake of his head. "And why you need to pay attention when we teach you how to read and to speak Russian." He pointed as he taught, "Jewelry and Clocks." The fancy store has a door carved from dark wood and a window trimmed with lace curtains. Inside were tall clocks, paintings of nobles on a horse or with their family sharing a meal in a garden. His lesson took on that same voice as when he cursed the Count. "The greediest of traders. A trade for these most precious treasures starts with a desperate seller, willing to take crumbs. The shopkeeper has enough money to wait for a buyer rich enough to pay more. I knew the man who owned this store. He was a cart peddler who sold or lent you what you needed, but you only paid a small amount. Some call these peddlers a shylock. When you're rich enough to lend out money, the Goyim call them a banker."

The streets of these fine shops were crowded with such fancy-dressed nobles. Gramps whispered, "If he knew you, Shlomo would take a few rubles each week until you paid him all you owed. He made enough to buy this store, but before he went from cart to shopkeeper, he changed his name from Shlomo Canter to Gustav Smirnov and his God was changed to Christ." Gramps pulls me closer. "Jews need to change their name and God to have a store on the Gentile's street." I didn't understand this lesson until a few years later, when I understood the price of trading with these nobles.

The next store had more gold jewelry, rings, and necklaces, all made finer with colored stones. "That was Albert Weisman. He changed his name to Vladimir Gostkowski. I knew him as a boy selling salt and sugar. The story of how he came to such a precious trade, he wouldn't want to say, but would confess to those he knew, "The rich want costly things that have no purpose but to be admired."

My adventure had me forget fear until a soldier dressed in that fancy blue uniform ordered his two men to inspect our wagon. Gramps bowed, lifted his cap, "I know. Sunset coming. We'll be on our way."

The noble held him with a raised rifle. The other soldier looked under the straw with a knife at the tip of his musket, but they were too late. Shown God's mercy. The last two bottles of tonic weren't found. Gramps paid the ruble as ransom, and we were waved on.

Gramps smacked Ilyich with his stick harder than I'd ever seen, and with a jolt, our mule lurched from the soldier. "Peddlers become Merchants by knowing how to curry the favor of nobility. The rich are fools who will spend more for a table if it's carved with fancy edges, and ten rubles for a hat if it has lace rather than the warmth of wool. You must know how to read the rich. Their want of such treasures is only to make others look on them with envy. Mr. Horowitz can pay me more for the flour because he makes more by being among the goyim.

"I'd say he makes more by having chocolate."

I was under the spell of wanting to be a rich man, but as we waited for the giant raft to take us to the other side. If Gramps and Poppa can't make enough treasure to be rich, how could I have such hope? I looked back and saw a boy my size shoveling dung into a cart. If I left home, would I be chained to a broom and a shovel, never becoming anything more?

I realized even at that young age that all poor suffer. No prey is spared from a hungry hunter.

Lamps are lit by a man with a long pole holding a candle. My excitement about crossing the wide river was to behold the marvel of Riga being lit by such lamps that it was as if lit by the stars of heaven.

We join a dozen other peddlers' carts on this raft with a chimney blowing smoke. Crossing was more than an adventure. I'm under the spell of being awake inside a dream.

The harbor keeps busy. Under the light of lamps, an army of men are loading crates, livestock, timber, and machines onto the giant steamship. Another ship, with the giant wheel on each side, was unloading people.

Before we reached the other side, I heard the tumult, smelled the smoke of frying, but not enough to cloak the foulness of manure.

We left the ferry. Not a stone road, but a peasant's dirt road. The wagon was shaken by ruts, rocks, and holes. The homes are not painted. There were few with glass windows, but as we entered the village, we turned onto a street with stores and homes made of logs cut smooth to planks. This Central Square was lorded over by a grand temple with glass painted as stories from the bible, but Gramps thought it a sin. "The Orthodox have no shame." A groan, "To build such a thing as if a church."

I heard loud talk in Yiddish, not Russian or Latvian. The women's heads are covered with shawls, and almost all wear the heavy, dark dresses of the pious. The rich Jews show off with fancy shoes, black suits without patches or frayed edges, and proudly show their wealth with the gentile's bowler or wide fedora, but most are in rags and a peddler's cap.

I think of how the Gentile's stroll about at a calmer pace, less hurried in their stride, less cautious in their glance.

The Hasidic are fewer. They show their piety with longer coats, the belt of tzitzit tassels swaying at their side, and the long locks that dangle by the ear. Gramps nods to the Hasid as we pass by as if they know each other. "I would be Hasidic if made to choose. I seek spirit, not pride of a fine suit to stir envy." Riga has many Jews, but they are not all as one."

My uncle Moshe told us about their ways, he said, "Too certain. Too set in their ways. Endless rules and rituals. Monks who believe life is meant for prayer to find some paradise I didn't understand, but found great wisdom in their bible called the Kabbalah. He tried to explain why God wasn't merciful to the Jews, while being so favorable to the Goyim, "Hard lessons need to be earned to be appreciated."

My grandfather steered the wagon away from the tumult, but as this day of dreams gave way to night, the adventure left me wanting more.

We left behind the noise and lights of the busy markets as we ventured into the dark. My need for tumult got worse. I longed to go back for cookies and the salted dumplings, but he broke my longing when he pointed to a good-sized barn alongside a well-lit cottage. "Mr. Levin is a friend from long ago. We'll be staying there tonight."

He didn't tell me. Gramps liked a surprise. "A home and bed? Not the floor of the wagon?"

Two boys and a dog greet us before Mr. Levin comes rushing out and gives Grandpa a loving hug. I'm introduced to his sons, Myron and Joshua. They ask me my age and then tell me they're nine and twelve.

Their home is a palace of five different rooms, and there's a barn beside the house giving off the sounds of cows, chickens, and goats.

The mother called for us to come inside. We sat down to a supper of the easiest to chew cow meat taken from the ribs.

After dinner, I'm pulled outside by Joshua. Under the light of two lanterns, he kicks a ball over to me. "Kick it back."

I slept beside Joshua and Myron on a soft bed made with wool stuffed under a sheet, but I couldn't sleep. I didn't want the day to end. I had more joy on that day than on my best day of catching a good eating fish.

But Myron threatened to send me to sleep with the goats if I didn't stop talking about chocolate cookies.

CHAPTER NINE- Mr. Dayan- 1898 - Oct.

I woke at sunrise and nudged Joshua awake, begging him to go play with the ball. He shared my fever for the game, but it's not long before Gramps put an end to my holiday. "Long day ahead. Mamma made me promise not to dawdle."

Misery comes in all ways. Punishments can be harsh, but leaving my new friend was a new test of heartache.

He lured me to the wagon with a well-buttered challah, and Bubby's pot was refilled with Mrs. Levin's soup of noodles, cabbage, and onions. Like a critter to a trap, bait was set with a wedge of her sweet and salty cheese.

I looked back and wanted to jump off the wagon to stay with my new friends and this family. The toilet, bath, and sink were inside the house. Worked with a pump you only needed to push up and down to deliver water. When I asked Gramps how Mr. Levin became rich, he smiled, "Before I left Riga with Poppa, we taught Mr. Levin our trade. His ambition and courage were greater than mine or your father's. I've told you before, if you want to be rich, you must take risks or be born to it."

The wheels shake, and we return to the village of Jews. Our first trade was with the blacksmith for new bolts. The large man stopped hammering. Gramps handed him a flask. I didn't know that he had Mr. Levin pour the two bottles we had left into eight smaller, tin flasks. While they shared a toast, Gramps asked his old friend the blacksmith, "Why so few soldiers? A safer journey I've never taken."

"The Cossacks have been sent in all directions—pogroms in Lodz, Warsaw, and Odessa. The large factories and mills owned by those rich Jews are feared as armies. Success and good fortune are breeding envy among the czar and Goyim, and workers want more of a share."

"A moment of peace bought with a good harvest and trouble elsewhere."

We left the blacksmith and stopped at a shoemaker. Gramps surprised me with a new pair of boots. "I can't have you giving me half a day of work on account of your feet hurting.

The shoemaker handed me the new boots, but they were so big they fell off. He stuffed a wad of wax inside to make them fit. Told me, "At your age, you'll outgrow a shoe in less than a year, so when it becomes too tight, take some of the wax off until your foot is big enough to fit."

I put on the new boots and strut about as if a noble.

Our entrance to the Jewish quarter was met with the cackling sounds of women frying dumplings and potatoes behind clouds of smoke. No matter that my belly was full, I was under the spell of onion, garlic, potatoes, and noodles, same as the cookie. The peddlers laughed when I asked for chocolate. The carts and bakeries on this side of the river aren't fancy. Bread, matzah, challah, rolls. Their cookies are what Bubby makes: baked dough with honey or berries.

I noticed a woman dumping a bucket in an alley lined with outhouses.

Most homes were like our shanties. Cobbled together from scraps, few have doors, and only the general store, temples, and the privileged have windows with glass. A roof of more than boards or thatch has the prize of slate.

Ilyich needs me to guide him through roads crowded with peddlers protecting their carts and wagons, until we leave behind the hive to come to a pasture with eighteen sheep. Their village has a shul with the star on its door, but I heard an unfamiliar sound coming from inside—men and women at long tables with small machines hammering needles into cloth, put through the sewing machine to stitch pants, shirts, and dresses—shelves stacked with rolls of cloth.

"Getting a gift for Mamma and Bubby." Gramps traded a ruble for thread and needles while I studied this magical machine, stitching cloth so fast it would do in a minute what would take Mamma an hour.

The matron smiled at my wide-eyed wonder— "Never seen a sewing machine?"

Our next stop was down a hidden path to find a barn at its end. "Said to be a good furniture maker. I need to make a trade with my bottle maker. I think he'd appreciate a new throne more than rubles or tonic."

Inside a barn large enough to hold a dozen cows stood a tall man who looked like a warrior. Thick black hair, dark brows, and a handsome face shaved clean. He was in battle, but not with a sword, but by pushing a log through a giant round saw driven by a machine attached to the saw with pulleys that could slice a log into a thin board. His uniform is a leather apron with many pockets holding a hammer, knives, and tools I didn't know. The smock covers the torn overalls of a peasant.

To the side is a bench with a man's face carved into dark wood. The carving is as good as my father's drawings. Looked like a regal noble with a twirled mustache, wearing the fedora of a prince, and smoking a pipe.

He took the board and stepped back to study his creation. He finally noticed us. "Can I help you?" But I didn't understand the words. Sounded German.

Gramps answered in Yiddish. "I'm Maximilian. A mutual friend, the blacksmith, Heinrich Wisotsky, said you might be interested in a trade of rubles for a chair." Gramps peddles the trade as though he'd be doing this craftsman, who I thought to be of Poppa's age, a favor.

"Mr. Dayan." He took a quick study of Gramps. I'm given a nod.

"I see you make fine furniture." The barn is stacked with chairs, a long table, and a hutch that speaks to the taste of nobles. His craft was a skill I had no idea how to do.

Gramps pointed to a chair, its proud legs and arms carved. "How much?"

He squints, as if struggling to decide on its price: "Five rubles."

Gramps turned around to open the secret of the wagon and grabbed a fur hat that was hidden between the five remaining flasks. "Perhaps this nice tin of tonic, and a warm cap."

Mr. Dayan put on the cap I watched Bubby make. She used good deerskin and rabbit fur. He hands Mr. Dayan the flask, "A taste."

A moment later, with a smile, "You have more?"

"Next time."

Mr. Dayan lifts the chair from the stack and onto the wagon.

Gramps looks at three logs no bigger than me, "You can use chestnut? Oak?"

The craftsman nods, "Always."

"Maybe next time."

Our last stop was a tent with a big hearth. A man is holding a long pipe. I watched him blow a bubble as if by magic. My grandfather explained, "Sand is melted to glass and becomes gooey like thick honey, and until it's cooled, you can blow it as a bubble, or if so desired, put in a mold that shapes it into whatever you want, in this case, a bottle."

He left to meet with the owner while I watched the blacksmith forge glass over hot coals, not with a hammer to iron but with a strong breath into a long pole. He blew a small bubble, and another man clamped two iron molds to squeeze it into the shape of a bottle. The hearth was hot enough to feel its heat from outside the door.

The owner favors the chairs enough to load our wagon with three crates. Gramps had me show off my skill in math when he asked me, "How much is 12 x 3?"

"That makes thirty-six bottles."

We left Riga behind, and I was invited to sit beside my grandfather. He put his arm around my shoulder. "So many lessons. What did you learn?"

My mind swirled with all that I'd seen. And after I went on and on about the cookies, the dumplings, and playing ball with Myron and Joshua, he interrupted, "My little bubbalah, "Enough with the rewards, what did you learn?"

"Need to know the value of a trade. Know what the customer wants and what they're willing to pay."

There was so much joy in his kiss to my forehead.

CHAPTER TEN – Home – Riga – 1898-1899

Two weeks since we left, and the trees had changed from color to bare branches. The tall fields of grain were now flour for bread and feed for the livestock.

I heard his bark and knew we were home. Samson was the first to welcome me with such longing as to knock me down.

Ruth was picking chestnuts of the ground, saw us, and let out a cry. Came for me like Samson. Her hug took away my breath. "I need stories." Suddenly, my misery at leaving Riga behind was warmed by love, and I realized I was missing them without knowing it.

I joyfully left behind my worn-out Gramps and a mule whose pace was slower than a turtle, and joined with Ruth and Samson in a race home. I waved when we passed Uncle Moshe and Mr. Kornicker, busy skinning a deer, but turned from the chore when they heard Ruth shouting, "Max is back!"

My cousins, aunts, and uncles appeared from everywhere to give me blessings with prayers of thanks. All were in want to hear about the journey.

Gramps rolled past, but his greeting was barely a wave before he disappeared into our patch of forest.

I was in such a hunger of heartache to see Mamma, Poppa, and Bubby that I cut short my tale of Riga being magical, and going on about chocolate, and ran off with Ruth clinging to my arm. Samson was still pawing me as we ran down our path, ran past Gramps, and burst into home.

Bubby dropped the ladle into the kettle, crying, "My bubbalah," and after a punishing hug, she stood back, pinched my cheek, "The leaves told me that you were blessed with a safe journey," and poked my stomach. "I bet you earned a belly of sweets."

"Chocolate cookies! Such a treat." She knew.

Mamma heard and came racing through the door. Pushed Bubby away to choke me to death against her soft pillows.

When she finally let go, I turned to ask Bubby, "You knew about chocolate?" and then I showed off my new boots. "It would be so wonderful if we lived in Riga," going on and on about the towering steeples of the cathedrals, the palaces for homes, cobblestone roads, fancy stores with glass windows, and then Poppa showed up while I was going on about Joshua and Myron and the Levins' big home. I told my father, "There's a carpenter who carves as well as you can draw."

"He must be an artist, but did I hear you're going to move to Riga?" Took me by my shoulders, "Grew another foot," laughed. Gramps finally showed up. "I see you brought Gramps home in one piece," and my father pulled me into a hug."

Their love was as great a joy as my discovering Riga.

Gramps held up my hand— "My best trading partner, ever."

But after going on and on about the journey, and my want to live in Riga, Poppa decided that I needed another lesson. "Seeing a city for the first time is a memory we don't ever forget, but city life is different than farm life. We wouldn't have enough land to grow what we need." Pulled close to capture my attention. "The dream of a foolish boy who hasn't had to make his own way, and thinks Riga is cookies. We earned that trip with our labor, planning, and turning potatoes into Bubby's potion. You'd shovel manure and sleep in an alley."

I thought of the boy shoveling the horse manure. My dream was to live in Riga, and with every day as a holiday of treats.

When I asked Gramps about staying with the Levins, he told me, "They move around a lot." I wondered about the man who makes fine furniture— "Maybe I can learn to make fine furniture like this man we traded for chairs."

"You will starve." Poppa pointed to Bubby's hutch. "I made this. It serves its purpose. Fancy furniture!" Poppa laughed, but as a curse. "Need a rich customer." Poppa held up his whittling knife. "Furniture maker needs saws, hammers. A craftsman's tools are dear. The blacksmith would have his hand in your pocket."

My grandfather had the final word. "We harvest a field of wheat and trade the milled grain. Even a craftsman must have a mind for making a profit." Poked at the log in the hearth. "Go be something other than a peddler. God bless." He handed Bubby the new scissors, thread, and needle, "but know that our teachings are to make money by reading a customer's want, to make a profit by knowing the value of what you offer in trade."

Bubby smacked my behind. "A dreamer doesn't bring home such fine gifts and a pocket of rubles." She hugged Gramps. "Don't want to hear what this scissor and needle cost," and then she came for me. Took the scissors to my curls. My curly hair had grown over my eyes and ears. "You look like a beggar."

Mamma took my wrist in a firm grip to make me listen, "A visit is not the same as living someplace. You need roots to hold you."

Ruth had been sitting quietly, but the thought of me leaving brought her to a fever. "You can't leave!"

I want to go deaf and blind to their lesson and return to my dream of a bakery with all the chocolate I want. "That furniture man didn't seem hungry to me. He had chairs as thrones, and a hutch with drawers for silver and racks for dishes. Carved a bench for a noble's palace."

Poppa stopped whittling and scratched his dark beard. "He must want good chestnut and oak."

The next day, my dreams of Riga filled me with longing for Mr. Levin's pump while I was fetching water.

Poppa had conjured a new crop for trade. Hearing about the furniture maker and thinking he's prosperous, he took me to the wheat field for the chore of cutting down the big oak. He looked up, rubbed the bark. "This furniture maker would prize oak. Much of the good oak around Riga was cut down long ago to make the nobles' homes."

The next day, Poppa handed me an axe, "This tree is shading too much of the field." He hoisted me up to the lowest branch and had me chip away with the axe.

My cousins, David and Herman, helped trim the top branches.

With a shack's worth of thick branches, my father turned to the three of us, surprised when he asked, "Who wants to go to Riga?"

"Now?"

"A few weeks, as soon as the mud freezes. I'll make this a sled, and then we'll slide down to Riga."

"I'm in. Been wanting to set traps closer to the river, but what's this about? Bringing oak to Riga?"

"I want to see what our furniture maker is willing to pay for good wood. If he isn't interested, the trade for good wood must have a price."

Poppa made the sled, and no sooner were we ready to go than of course, Mamma made a fuss. He repeated for the hundredth time that the trade in wood could help.

Whipped by a biting wind, Poppa, Herman, and I kept the sled moving. I was thankful for my new boots, but it was the warmth of a new pair of wool socks that kept my feet from freezing. We all gave David a blessing for the gift of a beaver that Bubby sewed into my coat of rabbit and deerskin and made warm gloves and a hat for everyone.

The journey was an exciting adventure. My father hammered nails into a thin plank that we wrapped under our boots.

The river was busy. Hauling cargo on sleds was a long-standing practice. Sleds were loaded with everything from wood to stone. Too slippery for a horse, so no thieves or soldiers were out to demand bribes. We slid into Riga in three days.

Mr. Dayan offered a good chair that would make a noble proud in trade for the oak.

Poppa admired the craftsmanship. He appreciated the value of the trade. "I have no one to sell this to."

Mr. Dayan wanted the oak and reached into his pocket. "How about five rubles now, and come spring I'll pay another five?" The deal was made, but Mr. Dayan was disappointed that we only had our flasks of tonic, no bottles to put into the trade. He called into the Barn, "Yitzhak, I need your help."

A giant of a man, but with a boy's face, came from the barn. Mr. Dayan pointed to the load. The bear lifted the thickest branch that took both my arms to wrap around it, and both Poppa and Herman to lift it into the sled.

We were invited to share a meal, but Poppa turned the furniture maker down with an apology and the gift of a tin flask of Bubby's tonic. "Next time. Want to make it to my friend's home before dark."

CHAPTER ELEVEN - Amber – 1901 - Fall

Over the next three years, I went to Riga six more times and fell deeper under the spell of its magic, especially playing ball with Joshua and sleeping in Mr. Levin's fine home with a pump and good beds.

Each time I returned to the isolation of home, it stirred a longing to live in the beehive of Riga, a city so full of honey. My father would make it a point to take me down those alleys where homeless orphans shovel manure, ice, or snow, for bread and little else.

I turned thirteen but didn't feel like a man. I was still a twig. More, I was confused about God. Poppa and Gramps told me that a Bar Mitzvah was a tradition and a pledge to follow the Commandments, but I didn't understand why the goyim were our masters. Was this why Jesus also had doubts? If we're the chosen, why aren't we the masters?

That summer, a bad drought forced us to dig our well deeper than ever. The pond was no more than a swamp. Not much of a crop. A sack of onions, two sacks of potatoes, skinny beets that gave us little to ferment into sugar and yeast. A great effort was needed to make just ten bottles.

Poppa saw this as a mitzvah, "The price will be more than double for everything. We'll trade ten bottles for maybe thirty rubles. My father improved the secret hiding place by sealing the floorboards so close they looked as one.

We were two days on the road, just past the Gentile's village, when a new breed of thieves stopped us. The drought turned farmers and shopkeepers from saints to sinners. Poppa was prepared, paid the ransom with rabbit pelts and David's canes. They didn't see the bottles hidden between the boards.

With the poverty caused by the drought bringing everyone into a panic, we knew there'd be trouble, but at thirteen, I didn't understand the danger of my father taking such a risk. Greed had him under the spell of the risk bringing a great reward. The Czar forbade Jews from the trade in alcohol, but I had faith in my father's new secret hiding place. There'd be no stops to trade for grain since no one was selling, everyone hoarding what they had. We were going straight to Mr. Levin's. He'd sell the vodka. I begged to come along. I wanted to spend time with Myron and

Joshua. I knew my way home from Riga and promised to visit and return for spring planting.

We were a day from Riga when we saw the long line. Found out the road was blocked by a gatehouse manned by twenty soldiers on horseback, their rifles aimed at the long line of carts and wagons, an endless migration of all seeking salvation from barren farms heading into the city.

Poppa was determined. I was surprised we didn't turn back. He said he had faith we'd be okay. "They'd have to pull apart the wagon to find the bottles. I have a ransom of three rubles." I admired his courage even though I didn't understand why he was taking the risk.

The soldiers delivered their threat with the bodies of ten bootleggers piled by the side of the road. If caught, you'd be shot without a trial. Not exiled or sent to prison.

We arrived in Riga the next day. This was not the city I knew, but a battlefield of suspicion, fear, and threats. We raced through the ghetto to get to the Levins, but when I ran to the door and yelled for Joshua to come on out, a Russian general appeared, followed by two soldiers, all with a pistol or rifle at their side.

We were threatened at gunpoint to reveal where they went. My father was relieved they escaped but not surprised. "Friends. Their boys play with my son." My father went to the back of the wagon. Pried open the back floorboard and held up a pair of fur gloves and hat. "A gift for my friend. I trade in fur."

The general took the hat and gloves, but then had his soldiers search the wagon. I didn't breathe again until they shook their heads and went back inside.

My father was determined to sell the ten bottles. It was dark by the time we reached the edge of the city and came to a cottage hidden among a swampy wilderness.

Ira Shapiro had been a friend of the family since his father's tavern had sheltered Mr. Lavinsky. Ira was overjoyed. "My rubles are worthless. They took my tavern but not my customers. Vodka has greater value than gold." Ira Shapiro was also taught by a father who knew that tomorrow isn't promised, to save his money. Thirty rubles were a fortune.

My father split up the coins. He hid twenty in the wagon, and then put two in each pocket, two in our boots, and two more where, if searched, it meant he had been stripped naked.

We kept to a path hidden by a dense forest and went miles out of the way to avoid the Gentile's village. We heard the pounding of galloping horses, but it was too late to hide. They came on us as a wolfpack, six farmers turned thieves, with rifles and pistols pointed at our heads, snarling, in fever.

Poppa waved his hands over the wagon, "We have nothing."

The elder knew a peddler's secret and had his gang pry open the floor. He found the first purse of twenty coins. "What do we have here?"

He put his pistol to Poppa's neck. Under the spell of madness, the younger man wraps his arm around Poppa's throat— "What else are you hiding?" Pushed to the ground. A kick. Then, with his knees on my father's chest, the elder grabbed me by my neck, "Boy, going to pay?"

Poppa begged, "We're all under hunger's spell." The two young men find the four rubles in Poppa's pockets. "Greedy kike."

Desperate to help, I kicked the elder, but he smacked me with the end of his pistol so hard that I fell asleep in the darkness without dreams.

I awakened to such pain, I didn't know if this was death. Poppa was on the ground. He was crying. Then I realized they had taken Ilyich and the wagon. Poppa was sick in anger. His pants were around his ankles.

"I have the two coins in my boot, and the one in my heel that Gramps said is gold and valuable."

"It's not enough." Cursed God, then turned on himself. "Should have given what was in our pockets." More regrets. "Greed." All through the night, I heard him muttering, "Need more…not enough…too late."

The moon made the forest a nightmare of shifting shadows. No sleep. "A punishment for what sin?" He searched for an answer, but heaven was silent.

I didn't understand. "Why didn't we stay home? Couldn't you have sold the vodka in Vladistok?"

"They know our tonic. We'd have been arrested."

"But why take this risk?"

"There's a tax." Finally, the truth, a confession I didn't expect. I knew of the tax. The festival was last week. "We didn't have enough?"

"The Count wants our land. Told we had to pay twenty-five rubles or leave." Desperation brought him from anger and regret to the temper of a peddler needing to find profit. Anger to determination. He steps on a rock. Studied it. A plan? "You've always wanted to behold the sea."

"The Baltic?" I had only heard stories about the endless lake.

"We're going to hunt for treasure."

I shook my head, "The sea has treasure?"

"Say a prayer." Always the fox. "We can't go home until we earn another fortune. A beaver don't quit."

He pulled me back to the path. His pace quickened, "There's buried treasure to be had."

Poppa headed north from the east-west flow of the river road to the wilderness, and by the next afternoon, the dirt turned to a new manner of dirt that was as soft as flour. The air smelled as if baked in salt. He led me over slippery hills where the ground shifts under our feet, and I followed him across a path hidden by sprouts of tall grass.

It was more than I could imagine—as great as when I first laid eyes on Riga, but this was Nature's magnificence—an endless pond stirred by movement, breathing, coming and going, the rhythm of life. Lured by thirst, I opened my palms to cup the cold water as it rushed over my feet. Brought it to my parched lips, about to quench my painful thirst, when I heard Poppa yell— "Not good. It'll make you sick," calling down from the hill of sand. "Forget thirst, we have treasure to find."

But I'm taken by the spell of the sea, didn't listen, pulled off my boots, rushed across the cold sand, and splashed in the water. It was cold as ice, but as it rolled over my naked feet, it healed my dried-out body. I had to taste. "Salt?" My father was hidden in the tall brush.

I looked out on the endless coast of sand, and in the haze of early morning, not far from shore, were six boats as a village of fishermen, their harvest is spent tossing about on a rough sea as they lift a net filled with a bounty of fish. Farmers with no regard for the drought. Their crop would keep Riga from starvation.

Poppa had no mind for anything but digging deep into the dune. I pointed to the fishermen. "Time to hunt. The treasure is found by digging." He handed me a shell. "Dig. And as you dig, feel for a rock."

All day and into the night, we dug up the sand like gophers. We'd move after the hole was too deep. He searched deep into the shrub. Stamped down the stalks and got down on his knees, digging with care.

At first, I found only sand. I'd hear his curse from another empty hole. But he wouldn't give up.

"Max, come see." He woke me, crying tears of joy. Held the glassy orange rock to sunrise. And its color matched the orange of the sun.

He handed me the stone. “Hold it to the sun.” The brownish-orange glass-colored stone glistened. “These stones are most precious. Much more than grain, tonic, or wood.” He’s in fever. “Dig! They hide under the sand.”

Suddenly, he’s on top of me. “Stay down,” he whispered, and pointed through the tall grass. The fishermen were coming ashore. Some distance away, but Poppa told me in a whisper, “Can’t be caught.”

We crawled some distance until we found a new patch of tall grass to hide. “You keep digging,” and he passed out.

I dug fourteen holes as he slept, and found four stones, one bigger than the next.

He didn’t awaken until the sun was a foot from sinking into the sea, but when I showed him the four stones, he wiped his eyes, “A dream?” and held the rock up to the sunset. “The best I’ve ever seen.” Hugged me, trembled, stared into my eyes as if pouring all his love into my soul. “My good luck charm. We can go.”

I’m pulled to a path heading away from the sea and sand into the marsh and a spindly forest. He confessed the lesson, “To dig for amber is forbidden. The stone’s value is equal to the punishment. We’d be thieves for stealing the Czar’s treasure.”

“Czar owns all this?”

“Even the sea.”

“He has ships with cannons that say he owns the sea.”

“Why are these rocks so precious?”

“The Czar sets their value. His magic turns worthless stones into precious jewels.”

“How did you know this was here?”

“Inherited my curiosity. When I first came to Riga, I needed to explore. I heard tell of the sea and had to see it. There was this man hiding in the tall grass as we were, and I caught him digging. He blessed me that day by confiding this secret. “Dig deep and don’t quit.” He discovered the treasure by accident. A fisherman digging holes to find crabs, worms, anything for bait, and found the precious rock.”

“Why did he tell you? What did you offer?”

“I offered nothing but hunger. I pledged to keep his secret. He had a heart for charity.”

CHAPTER TWELVE – Home – 1901

We sneaked toward Riga under the cover of night and then circled the city to avoid checkpoints. It was past sunrise when we reached Ira Shapiro's home.

Over a welcome meal of chicken stewed in Mrs. Shapiro's salted broth, the amber was judged equal to the lost thirty rubles—a value set in sentiment as much as hope. The price takes a noble's desire, not need.

I woke in the soft comfort of a bed to hear a biblical rain pounding against Mr. Shapiro's slate roof, and celebrated by turning over to return to sleep, thinking it would be a day of needed rest—every bone ached, but Poppa shook me from the dream.

"Get up!" he rejoiced— "The storm's fury will be our shield. Thieves, soldiers, and sinners will surrender to the comfort of shelter."

The crusted earth turned to mud, then a stream, and by the time we were halfway home, each step was a test to slog through an endless shallow pond, but Poppa kept me going with his spirit of this storm as our salvation, repeating its blessings for soothing our thirst and that of dried-out streams, ponds, and rivers.

We only needed to cup our hands to collect God's mercy.

Day three, and our shield of rain and mud became ice, snow. Winter's cruel bite came as suddenly as a summer storm. We passed the Gentile's village without fear. Poppa was right; all had taken shelter at home.

It was midday when we reached the pond, full, frozen, a salvation, and turned onto our path, surprised to find everyone gathered in front of our cabin. Stricken from exhaustion by Mamma's wailing, "They came for the tax!"

Gramps was holding Bubby. "They came yesterday morning. We gave them what we had. Nine rubles. The Cossack said, "Not enough."

"I told them you went to trade furs." Gramps handed Poppa his flask. "Couldn't use tonic as a bribe. That would be our end."

With a proud smile, Poppa held up the sack of rubles. "We can pay."

Everyone celebrated with dancing and hugs as Poppa shook the purse. Mamma suffocated him with kisses. Relief the best of joys.

I caught his look but knew to keep our trials a secret. He rehearsed our story; I agreed to not speak of our adventure.

The next morning, Poppa left for Vladistok.

The Count's tax Collector took his time, rubbing the seventeen silver coins—is this all?"

Gramps set the lie with a cup filled with half a truth. "Bad harvest has everyone trapping critters. All anyone has is fur to trade. I'm giving you all I earned."

In pride and joy, anxious to get home, he slept for days, no one disturbed a much-needed rest.

Winter forced more rest. It snowed until we couldn't dig out, so when spring came it was a grateful celebration, but harvest was months away and hunger was settled deep. Paralyzed by a winter without mercy, unable to hunt, critters and beasts suffered as we did, saved not by mercy but by Poppa knowing to keep the ten rubles from the tax, He left when the snow had melted enough to clear a path to Vladistok and traded for six chickens, a rooster, and four goats, keeping five rubles for a future that always had unknowns.

He returned to find Uncle Moshe with his head bowed the jacket and pants stained in blood.

"Wolves." Moshe moaned, cursed, shook, "There were too many. Maximilian took the worst. Gussie and Selma were gathering herbs to heal Kornicker. He's sick, near death." He chokes on the tears, "They were attacked."

Poppa raced down the path.

David and Joshua tried to hold him back. "Go no further, will steal your heart," but he pulled away.

I was with David and Joshua when their screams pierced the air. My mother's leg bled, Bubby's arm torn to the bone. Wolves dragged Gramps into the forest. David kicked one off, chased two others with a branch, but Joshua's leg got bitten before he slit the wolf's throat.

That night, Bubby, Mamma, and Joshua were suffering from the bites. Uncle Moshe knew the curse, "Rabies." The poison of a cruel fever before the mercy of death.

By morning came the madness.

Poppa gave in to their pleas and mixed a potion from the flower I was told to never eat—the pretty white petals. Nature's evil side wearing a disguise.

Bubby was grateful when Poppa fed her the potion but was tortured by the poison's hell. Herman held her down and with a nod from Poppa he put their hands over Bubby's mouth. Poppa found the strength to put his hand over Mamma's mouth and nose; Moshe did the same for Joshua.

Ruth held me as I suffered in a place of misery that had me cursing God as merciless and lost hope in faith.

Days of wailing.

Uncle Moshe chiseled their names, day of birth, date of death, and three words of testimony to their kindness. "A Loving Soul."

Poppa ran off after we buried them. He wouldn't say Kaddish. Such was his anger toward God. It was left for Herman and David to cover Gramps, Bubby, Mamma, and Joshua in the blanket of dirt.

Ruth stayed by my side, but we both needed more comfort than we could give. Her father recovered, but Mr. Kornicker suffered guilt upon hearing that the women had gone to the pond to gather his healing weeds.

Days were lost under the spell.

Poppa sat huddled in the forest under a cloak of fur and drowned in Bubby's vodka. He held his axe in want of revenge. When I sat beside him with my axe, he murmured, "Leave me be."

I was lost, numb, my thoughts twisted from stolen sips of tonic.

My uncles, aunts, cousins, and our family did all they could to bring comfort, but it took weeks of being frozen in mourning before my father returned home. Seeing my suffering, he awakened to realize that his son needed a father and took me in his arms. "Death is certain, only its time is unknown. We must accept this our fate." He shared a sip from the flask. "They had a bountiful life with a fair share of blessings. I must be a mensch. You stayed by my side, didn't quit, dug until you found the stones. A great test. It should have been our time to die. You've seen all of life's good and bad. Remember, no matter the suffering, whatever the test, each day is a gift—some with pain, some in joy. Don't ever quit. This lesson is for me as well."

The vodka warmed me. A lesson from Bubby: drink with sips, "Only to soothe, not to get lost." Gramps, Mamma, Bubby, and Joshua were not gone. They were inside us.

Ruth wanted to give me comfort. "I want to watch the stars and think of heaven with you. To die having shared our joys and our miseries." Her holding me had a want for more, but her kiss scared me for its stirring. I confessed my truth. "We should be married, but I'm not a man in that way. I'm so lost and confused, it's all I can do to get out of bed."

She pulled me close. There was that softness of her lips pressed to my forehead.

"I don't know how to hold a girl as a wife. I know nothing of what it means to be a man. I have no way to care for you."

She suffered for a moment but then kissed my cheek with a smile. "Someday. But don't make me wait too long."

I'm lost between anger and the pain of wanting her, but not knowing how to find the right path, I went to find my father.

I confessed my stirring, "I don't think I'm a man?" I asked him about marrying Ruth. "How do I join with her as a husband? Isn't it to make a baby? I don't want a baby."

His smile was a sign that my mishagos was helping him heal. "Ruth is a good woman, but she's two years older, and the difference between almost fourteen and going on sixteen is like ten years when comparing a girl to a boy." A deep breath. "This is not the time for such thoughts. You have more to learn." He wiped his eyes. "These tears are imagining you one day being a father." A true smile. "But you marry when your heart won't let you do anything else."

I couldn't think of Ruth as a wife. I loved her like I loved family.

CHAPTER THIRTEEN – Riga – 1902 - Spring

Heartache was lost to the chores of spring, but our curse found a new spell when Mr. Kornicker returned from Vladistok, waving a notice. "These were posted on trees all along the road."

We stopped turning the soil. "There were four hangings. Markowitz was one of them."

Poppa stabbed the dirt with the spade. "The Count wants it all. He'll be here soon enough. No tax will be enough. If we told him the truth and offered up our vodka, we'd be his serfs for life."

Moshe gave him a sermon on the sin of alcohol and its temptation. "Better to be out of that business."

The next morning, my father woke me with his revelation— "You should live in Riga."

"What?"

"If he'll have you. We'll bring him oak. Better you make furniture than tonic."

"What of you? What will you do in Riga?"

"I'm staying here. I'm going to be a farmer and give up the road. You must go. There's always a need for a good carpenter."

"I can't leave you."

"It's only May, we have a long summer of waiting until harvest. If not to your liking, you know your way home."

Uncle Moshe sided with Poppa. "Meant to be."

Ruth wasn't having it. She cried, held me, wouldn't let go.

Poppa pulled her off, "Ruth, stop this now. You're a woman. Max just turned fourteen. He's not ready to be a husband. He needs to learn a paying skill."

She finds her wits from that truth. She ran inside her house and came back with a sack of matzah and berries. "You'll always be in my heart," and ran off.

"I can't go."

Poppa pulled my arm, "She'll be okay. She knows better."

We loaded a cart with short logs so as not to be a burden.

Thieves had no interest in oak, but as we neared Riga, we were stopped at the checkpoint. The soldiers were only interested in food or rubles.

The noise and smoke of Motorwagen were no longer a fright, but the tumult awakened me to why I wanted to live in the city.

We passed Mr. Dayan's neighbors of tailors and seamstresses and turned onto the hidden path of bramble. At first sight of the familiar barn, I'm suddenly taken by the fever of fear. What am I doing here? How can I leave my father?

My spell of excitement turned to the pain of fear when I realized I was going on a journey without my guide, "I can't leave you," seeing through his eyes, suffering as I am, "Let's go home."

"I'll be fine," with a forced laugh. "Lucky if he'll take you, an honor, he's a craftsman."

Poppa was lost—a ghost.

"I have taught you all I know." He wouldn't leave, stood by the door, and waited forever until Mr. Dayan noticed us.

"Moses Gutlian, more oak. What do you want in trade today?"

"You have my son under your spell. We know this is too much to ask of Riga's finest craftsman, but we are here to ask if you'll take my son on as an apprentice. He's smart—a hard worker."

The carpenter was tall, strong, and struck the pose of a confident elk. He's not as Poppa and me—he's a Viking. His Yiddish was flavored with Prussian. An educated man who wears a peasant's leather apron over a worker's torn cloth overall, but it couldn't disguise a warrior's spirit.

He studied me with those dark eyes. "Is this your wish or your father's?"

"It's been my wish since the first time I came to Riga."

He invited us inside.

Poppa admired the wall of tools but was captured by a bench carved with the outline of a noble posing with a sword, a costume of medals, brought to life with proud eyes, a beard, and a twirling mustache. My father was held breathless, "I cannot draw as well."

"I hadn't thought of taking on an apprentice. Such a responsibility." Mr. Dayan came close. A head taller, he leaned down. "How old are you?"

"Fourteen." Poppa took me by the arm— "Max has seen all of life's misery."

"What do you think God looks like?"

I was shaken, confused, such a question, but the seriousness of his tone drew me to confession—"I thought he looked like my grandfather," and laughed. I didn't need to struggle to conjure my truth—"Now I think

God is not a grandpa, but a storm, the sun, trees, creatures, and a pond. God is merciless and merciful. Nature is merciful and merciless. Would a kind grandpa have created such beasts?" Poppa's words. I broke our first rule. I hadn't looked through the eyes of the customer. What's the value for him in this trade? "We brought oak. Show me how to make such a thing," pointing to the bench.

The master didn't give any hint. Not a smile or frown, but he didn't turn away or smack me for heresy.

"You speak Russian?"

I nod, and boast in Russian, "Enough to sell fur and grain for rubles. Less of Hebrew, more of Polish," and then in Latvian, "I could be thought Latvian for knowing their ways and talk." I knew nothing of him, but as the sunlight shone on the warrior's eyes, I thought I found a kindred spirit. "I want my teacher to think highly of his student. I've been taught to be a beaver and never quit. A fox to think ahead. But I must confess, I'm cursed. My mother thought I was possessed that I was too curious. That I had to know everything."

His verdict was given with a broad smile. "I can show you how to use the tools, but only you can decide if this is labor or passion. We'll give it a try. Do you know your way home? Have a few rubles to not starve?"

My father handed me four rubles, "Can't spend a kopek on a cookie," and a handshake for Mr. Dayan. My first test was to show my strength and unload the logs. A chore that Poppa must have planned for, because the logs were cut to a size I could handle.

He put his hand on my shoulder, "A new test for both of us. You have to learn a paying skill, and I have to find my own path back to life." He turned to leave, but Mr. Dayan held him back.

"You must stay the night and break bread. My wife won't forgive me."

"No," stumbles, pushed Mr. Dayan away. "I must go." A backhanded handshake, a quick hug, "Trouble in front is easily seen—look behind and to your side" – and pulled away. Took a few paces and turned around. "Be a mensch."

Mr. Dayan understood. "Next time."

He pulled the cart at such a pace that by the time I realized this might be a mistake, he had turned the corner.

He thinks I'm a man, but I'm a foolish boy who didn't realize that his heart was going to suffer for saying goodbye, but as my father left, I also suffered the pain of losing my right hand, half my heart, but knew he wanted this for me, “A mensch knows that the right path is not the easy path. We’ve taught you all we know. It’s time for new teachers.”

Mr. Dayan pulled me into his workshop. The giant of a young man, who was the size of a bear, lifted a heavy log onto a table that feeds the round saw. Thick brown hair to his shoulders. All work. I’m ignored, but Mr. Dayan wouldn’t have it.

“Max, this is Yitzhak.” A hunter would back away if this bear turned on him. He nods but gives me no more than a glance. Yitzhak returns to the chore of pushing a thick log through the saw to slice it into thin boards.

The barn was crammed with a fine cabinet, four chairs, a table, but I first noticed the shelves stocked with all sorts of fabrics, tools, and odds and ends of buttons and studs. There’s the wall of tools that Gramps would value as a year of labor to earn. I imagine there are names for all the tools. Too many saws and sharp knives to know their exact purpose. I count six hammers, but each is different.

My lesson begins with a broom. Sawdust as snowfall.

But my heartache over missing Poppa was lost when an angel came through the barn door. “And who are you?” Her question is warm, not asked as a stranger, but as if she were expecting me. It was impossible not to stare.

The top of my head came to just above her shoulder. She has long, wavy, brown hair that isn’t held on top of her head like Bubby and Mamma, not in long braids like Ruth, but as a groomed horse’s mane flowing down her back. The layers of a peasant’s cloth can’t hide a shapely figure.

Mrs. Dayan placed her hand on my shoulder, “Aren’t you a fine-looking young man.” Her welcoming and excited nature took me by surprise. “I’m Etta,” but then noticed her husband’s harsh stare, “Mrs. Dayan.”

I looked down at a floor covered in sawdust. I was too shy to look at her, let alone speak, but she lifted my chin and shook her head to pull me from shyness. “What’s your name?” Her Yiddish is also flavored by German.

Mr. Dayan noticed my shyness, but with a smile that knew a boy’s mind, he helped to soften my embarrassment. “This is Max. His father traded him along with the good oak for lessons on carving wood, and for your cooking.”

She laughed, "Good oak and a good young man for my sausage."

"I think you'll find Max a willing student. You can fill his head with your stories. He knows Russian, Latvian, and some Yiddish."

"How old are you?"

"Fourteen." I looked up to most people and had only skin and bones under my clothes. My curved nose and curly hair marked me as a poor Jewish boy. Except for Ruth, no girl had ever paid me any mind.

"It's late. Time for supper." She took me from the barn along a curved path to a cottage that was hidden by shrubs and fir. The home has a pipe for a chimney and a window with eight small windows. There's no sign of Mr. Dayan's craft to show pride in this peasant's shack.

The room is larger than my family's cabin. Five paces to cross, but ten or more paces long. A farmer's table long enough to seat three chairs to a side, with one at each end. Only the hutch filled with children showed his craft. I looked closer, the children are sculpted from magic that brings wonder. I needed a moment to tell if they're real or sorcery. In the corner is a stove of black iron, not a stone hearth.

Mrs. Dayan had me sit at the long dining table, and then placed four tin plates, metal forks, and knives.

Yitzhak and Mr. Dayan entered a moment later. Supper was goat sausage. "Good Bavarian food," Mrs. Dayan said with pride. "Do you know where Bavaria is?"

"Germany. I know a lot about Germany." I was anxious to impress her, "My father has a book with maps and pictures along with the story of its history. There's the mountain kingdom of Bavaria, and the cities of Munich, Berlin, and Frankfurt. I've seen pictures of Berlin. Much grander than Riga."

"Very good. Berliners are true Germans. A great city. Many scholars. Study of the mind, the nature of the universe. They are tolerant of Jews but not always welcoming. Easier for a Jew to get an education than a girl. I was fortunate. The professors at the University would let me listen in on their classes. My home was a morning's walk from Berlin's best university. My father was a lawyer." Her voice turned soft. "He passed some time ago. Mr. Dayan was the handsome young man who took me from mourning to start a new chapter of life here in Riga."

Mrs. Dayan put a small loaf of bread and cheese on the table and asked me, "Is the sausage to your liking?" as if my opinion had meaning.

"This is a feast." Heavily salted, the sausage is a treat.

Mr. Dayan and Yitzhak ignored us and discussed plans for a cabinet.

Mrs. Dayan loved telling me all about Germany, but then she tested my Russian with the same question as her husband had asked. I answered in Russian, thankful Uncle Moshe kept on with my lessons. "Did you ask if I believe in God, or did you mean trust in God?"

"Very good. Could be either. Which for you?"

I needed a moment to search for all the words. "Russian is the hardest of languages, but I'd say I believe God is nature, not a grandpa, and we're his puppets. I lost faith when our shtetl was burned. Then my mother, Bubby, and Gramps were killed by a pack of wolves. That was a few months ago. So if there's a god, it's merciless, just like nature."

She lit another candle. "I'm so sorry to hear." The warmth of her stare cast a spell. "I'll need to make you a proper mattress."

Mr. Dayan turned to Yitzhak. "Max will sleep beside you in the loft."

Yitzhak nods. He kept silent, but I noticed his glance.

Mr. Dayan said goodnight and hurried me out the door, "We need our rest."

I followed the bear back to the barn. "We're up there." Climbed the ladder to a bare loft.

His bed had more wool than what Bubby stuffed in mine. I'm on the floor. He turned away, but told me in Yiddish, "If you snore or move around too much, you'll sleep below on the table. Don't sleep on the hay, it's got vermin."

It took a long time to fall asleep. I couldn't stop thinking about Mrs. Dayan until a rat raced past, and then a cat gave chase. That had me wanting to hide in sleep.

CHAPTER FOURTEEN – Riga-School – 1902-03

Yitzhak woke at dawn, kicked me from sleep, and hurried to the cottage as if being chased. The orange glow of sunrise casts a faint light through the window on Mrs. Dayan. I had to look away before the spell of her charm made me feel more foolish than I'd already struggled to hide.

She filled a tall mug with warmed milk as I wandered over to have a closer look at the dolls of little boys and girls, looking so real that I needed to touch one of them. She set out a plate of crackers, as sweet as a cookie, and placed a sausage beside it.

Meat with milk? A cookie for breakfast? No observance of Kosher. Bubby served meat separate from milk, butter, or cheese, but that was deemed enough reverence for a rule she would explain as, "Tradition." Mamma said it was a waste to feast on both when milk, cheese, and butter are good for an early meal, and meat is better as dinner's reward after a day of chores. Uncle Moshe interpreted the rules of being Kosher as lessons learned from being poisoned,

I ate the sausage, drank the milk, and enjoyed the cookie, but the hauntings of a heavenly master still lurked in the shadows of beliefs clouded by doubt, and I struggled to ignore guilt.

Mrs. Dayan asked me to write a list of things I liked and didn't like, "Start with food, and then tell me what chores you like and don't like, but write the list in Russian."

I was surprised that she wanted to know me. I was scared of her. She stood tall, certainty in her manner, and I wanted to impress her and tried to make the letters fancy. Wrote 'cookie, chicken, eggs, and mostly bread.' I thought about how I liked helping Bubby make her tonic, but that was a secret, so I wrote down 'fishing' and 'hunting,' and then I saw her collection of books in the magnificently carved hutch, the only furniture that showed such craftsmanship. Wrote down the Bible and anything to do with history.

She glanced at my list, surprised, "Were you schooled in Russian?"

"My family mixed up words, but my uncle grew up in Moscow before being exiled to Warsaw, and my mother taught me how to read and write most everything else." I thought of showing her the twenty pages of my diary and my father's drawings that I packed in the sack with my clothes, pen, and paper in the barn, but Mr. Dayan didn't ask what was in it.

She whispered something to Mr. Dayan. He nodded. "You'll take Max to school."

I was in shock. "I'm going to school?"

Mr. Dayan put his hand on my shoulder, "There'll be plenty of time to learn how to carve wood. First, we need you to go to school."

He commands Yitzhak with a grin, "I know you're cursing me and vowed never to go back, but Max needs to know their ways."

"I thought I was to be an apprentice. What will I learn there?"

"You'll learn about the Russians."

"I know enough Russian to do a trade."

Mr. Dayan kicks my chair. "Max, you're very smart for fourteen, but this isn't to speak Russian, but to know Russians. You know nothing of life under these masters. You need to know."

Yitzhak is as upset as I am. "Why today?"

He shook his head, stared down at Yitzhak, "Don't argue with me."

Yitzhak was in as foul a mood as I was as we left the seclusion of Mr. Dayan's cottage and barn and made our way through the familiar neighborhood in silence. It was a long walk to the river. The path was always crowded with peddlers' carts—each with their own treasure—latkes frying, dumplings, chicken, eggs, milk, shirts sewn, leather cut to boots. The Jew's village was a long row of stick houses and stores without windows or doors. Each street had a synagogue offering its own blessing. There were so many living in the small shacks that I couldn't imagine living among them as a stranger. Even from the street, the baby's cry and a family's arguing left me appreciating my home shared with only Bubby, Gramps, my mother, and father in peace and comfort. But then there were the bakeries. A sweet smell I struggled to resist. I knew to hide the four rubles in the floorboard of the barn.

The soldiers and Cossacks roam the street on horseback and on foot to make their threat known. We knew to cross on the Jew's ferry, the bridges under guard.

I wanted to stop and watch the ships in the harbor, but Yitzhak had no patience for my curiosity. Our ferry passed beside the Czar's bridge of iron and stone. Gramps taught me on our first visit that the Jews can cross to the Gentile's side and must return before sunset.

There's a line to get on and off the ferry. Yitzhak paid the kopek, but we were stopped by three soldiers in the policemen's uniform of a fancy blue coat with brass buttons and given the Czar's authority with a red star on their caps. Mrs. Dayan warned us, "You'll be stopped, questioned, but tell them you go to the Russian school. Say the Czar wants you to be Russian."

They eyed Yitzhak as a threat but let him pass. I'm stopped. "I go to the Russian school."

We stepped off the ferry and onto a long wooden dock. I breathed their side's sweet air as we crossed their Central Square with its cathedral towers, rows of stores, and homes painted in different colors. Shaken by the belltower's seven gongs. The bell hidden in the Town Hall steeple rang loud enough to reach the end of the world. The clock's hands are as tall as Yitzhak.

There was so much construction going on all around us that we were invisible to the soldiers and well-dressed. Yitzhak pulled me through the same back alleys as I did with my father and Gramps. We knew to avoid prying eyes. You'd be chased for daring a glimpse.

Even the trees are trimmed by an artist to craft leaves and branches to appear as if a ball on a stick. A soldier with so many medals that he must be a general owns the road on a white horse. The sun shone off his helmet. He waved his sword to lead a parade of fancy, uniformed troops in white coats. They marched into a spring garden of flowers, not potatoes, beets, or cabbage.

The Czar made the city a fortress of something so grand as to humble all in reverence. The river is a moat. The bridges watched. All roads are held by the Czar's beasts. The Cossacks strut about to earn a ruble by threat alone. The wealth of the faithful was made known by the nobility of a city carved by magicians.

Riga is a maze that meanders about as if meant to confuse. Yitzhak left the paths I knew, turned the corner, and we came to a gate blocking the courtyard of a large brick building. A tall fence of bars, bars for doors, protects the windows. "This is a school?"

He finally looked at me and told me, "Also a prison and hospital." He would pass as Russian or Litvak, but it's his size and strength that command regard.

From behind the iron gate, I heard groans coming across the wide courtyard, and I saw inside, men in white coats stained with blood. The guards ask if we're students, and with only a nod, we're allowed entry.

My insides turned to fever as we crossed the long courtyard to hear the moans, crying, screams, and could see inside the long row of beds. Above the hospital on the first floor, the second floor was the school. The third-floor windows were boarded up behind bars.

A flock of girls dressed in well-pressed white aprons, protecting a blue striped smock, rushed by and entered the first floor.

Two guards stand beside a man in a suit, and we're asked if we're students. Again, Yitzhak is given a nod without further question, while I'm asked in Russian, as a test, if I'm a student. I answered correctly.

We were given access to a staircase, and a teacher asked which class we're in. Yitzhak knew to answer, "Lieberman."

We entered the dark hall with rooms to the left and right. Yitzhak knew his way and pulled me into a room crowded with boys, some younger, some older.

He told a big boy in the far corner of the back seat to get up. When he said "Nyet," Yitzhak lifted him from the seat and took it. That boy, in turn, bullied the smaller boy in the seat next to him and saluted Yitzhak.

I'm given stares by thirty-six prying eyes, and sat behind Yitzhak, but on the floor.

The teacher entered a few minutes later. I was surprised to see this professor was an elder with a gray beard, bald on top, wearing thick spectacles held by wires. I would've sworn he was Jewish, but in a Russian school.

He marched about as though in a rush to get somewhere, paced back and forth, as if waking from a nightmare. Dropped his leather bag on the table, and books fell out, loose papers floated to the floor. Wiped sweat from his forehead with a rag. Tugged on a poorly groomed beard and let out a groan that brought the rowdy boys to silence. He coughed, then rambled on in Russian, asking questions about the workings of a telegraph. He went on to explain electricity. I struggled to understand. "There are tiny particles that are invisible but inhabit the air."

It wasn't long before Yitzhak pulled me out of the room.

"Are we leaving?"

"You can stay. I've had enough."

I wanted to stay, but Yitzhak wanted none of it. I wouldn't think of not staying by his side, not in fear of getting lost, but to show loyalty.

We returned to our side, and Yitzhak picked up his pace, no longer needing to sneak about. We were passing the Hasidic temple and crossing to the shops along Central Square when we heard the thunder of hooves entering the square from all sides.

The beehive of bees peddling, preaching, building homes—didn't have a moment to escape before they came on us as a storm of hornets. A dozen more from the other road. The Cossacks wrapped in the skins of badger, fox, wolf, lashed out with whips and clubs without regard for child or elder. Those who were too slow to get out of their way were kicked by hooves or the Cossacks' tall black boots or staring down the point of a pistol pulled from a wide belt still carrying a curved sword.

The cavalry came with wagons. Their fancy gold buttons and a tall hat of braids put them in charge.

We were in the middle of the road, blocked by peddlers rushing to hide their carts. Yitzhak grabbed my arm, but he was too late; a whip wrapped around his chest, and when the horseman tried to drag Yitzhak by the neck to the dirt, he was pulled off the horse—Yitzhak had stood his ground—the bear against a wolf.

Two soldiers slid from their horses to force Yitzhak to the ground, this by the threat of a pistol to his head. The one he pulled off the horse kicked him, but Yitzhak grabbed his leg, showed no fear for the pistols aimed at him, and used the Cossack as a shield to roll out of the way just as a wagon driven by a madman, waving his whip, snapping at the soldiers, came racing into the square.

Yitzhak was forgotten as they gave chase to stop the wagon.

Surrounded, the madman jumped off. Stood defiant. A rebel, inflamed by hate, aimed at an officer but was shot in a hail of bullets before he pulled the trigger.

A Cossack slams me against a wall, a thick scar, a beaten nose, a few teeth, not much older, a snarl, I'm no more than vermin, "Not worthy," tossed to the ground, turns to find new prey, and snaps his whip to bring down worthier prey.

No regard given for the pious. Grabbed the boy's long tails of hair dangling in front of their ears, the payaos, and tore off their long black coats, tossing aside their wide-brimmed black hats.

The whip wraps around the tallest boy's neck. Another was kicked to the ground, and a third waved his arms to summon God's wrath, but the Cossacks circled the flock.

Their Tzadik, the Hasidic czar, showed the courage of faith to march between the boys and the beasts. His holiness is made known by the tall crown of mink and shiny black robe.

The Tzadik raised his hand to call on God.

Yitzhak grabs me, forcing a path through the crowd, anxious mothers, shopkeepers, tradesmen, mules, horses, carts, and wagons. Yitzhak cursed, "Not our battle," and I followed as he retreated to the barn.

Mr. Dayan was talking to two beggars in tattered suits. They noticed us coming up the path, and the smaller of the two waved to greet Yitzhak. They exchange nods, and Yitzhak reports on what happened.

"Hasidic to warrior?" the one with a beard and long hair let out a loud laugh. "A Russian army of Jews converted to soldiers," nods to the big man next to him, "The Czar is a fool."

I'm judged with suspicion. The two strangers pull Mr. Dayan aside. They shake their heads, hide their conversation, and leave with a nod to Yitzhak.

Mrs. Dayan came down the path, smile to a frown, "What are you doing back?" accused Yitzhak, "Did you go to school?"

I want to defend Yitzhak, "We went."

"It was nonsense," but her stare sends Yitzhak to the barn.

"Tomorrow, you'll go alone." Mrs. Dayan commands respect.

The thought of going back to that madness, the fear of being beaten by soldiers, "I don't want to go. I want to learn how to make furniture."

She shows me a softer side. "You need to know how they think, what they believe." Mrs. Dayan held me with a firm grip, "You'll be careful, but we can't be afraid. Only a worthless fool hides in a cave."

"You know the wilderness, the ways of trade, taught to be wary, you'll be fine." She took my shoulders in her strong hands. "We need you to tell us what you learn. We need to know what they're teaching."

Early the next morning, she pushed down the path, "You should be in school. There's too much to learn to waste time."

I crossed the bridge in fear, but I'm an invisible child. Overnight, a village of fifty tents appeared as if by magic. The soldiers wore red uniforms, brass buttons, and feather-plumed helmets.

A young Russian with a temper entered the class. “Sit still or be punished.” He’s young, tall, with a goatee, carefully dressed in a suit, holding a long stick. The class bully, the one who Yitzhak shoved aside, calls out to the professor, “What happened to the old Jew?”

“Hands on the table,” and with a quick snap of the stick, he smacked the boy’s hand hard enough to shame him, but he held back a cry and stood against the teacher. “Go to Mr. Breznivski. Tell him you require punishment.”

There was a moment of defiance, “Come for me, and it’ll be the last thing you do before prison.”

Suddenly, there’s silence. All become statues. “I’m Mr. Shmirnov.

I was sitting on the floor between desks, near the back, but he noticed me. “You are Polish? Jew? Litvak?”

In a whisper, knowing a lie was not going to be believed, I confessed to the truth, “Litvak, Jew.”

The teacher hit me with the stick, “Go be a Jew someplace else.”

I’m torn between wanting to stay and learn, but relieved to have an excuse to spend my days learning woodworking. To satisfy Mrs. Dayan I listened from outside the door and snuck a peek to see what the teacher was going to teach.

He called on a boy to recite what he had written on the board.

The boy stuttered. I heard a smack, the boy’s cry, and the teacher asked another, but there was only silence. He yelled loud enough to be heard in the hospital, “A class of fools.” In anger, he turned back to the board to point to the Russian alphabet. The few who couldn’t read were sent from the class after being hit with a stick and told, “Go be a soldier.”

Riga was under guard by police, Cossacks, and soldiers, but I knew my way around and returned to the barn. Mr. Dayan and Yitzhak were carving wood.

“It wasn’t the Jewish professor from yesterday, but a young Russian. He told us we wouldn’t be learning about electricity or how a telegraph works, but how to read and write in Russian, and that we’d know the Czar’s laws or be sent to be soldiers. When he saw me, he hit me. Said a Jew didn’t belong in his class.”

He nods. “What else?”

“I hid in the hall and listened in, but he only wanted to teach Russian.”

Mr. Dayan hit the table with his hammer. “As I thought.” He handed me a tool. “You’ve done well. You’ll learn about Russians from Mrs. Dayan. You have a good ear. A smart boy. I heard you counting nails and measuring the wood. I will teach you my craft, but better we teach you about life.”

Later that night, after Mrs. Dayan had me read from a book about Russian history, I went back to the loft. Yitzhak was whittling, and I risked interrupting with a question that was nagging me, “You look Russian, not Jewish, yet Yitzhak is a Jewish name?”

“Mr. and Mrs. Dayan took me in some years ago. She named me Yitzhak after a cousin who was a warrior and died fighting Muslims.”

I finally had a woodworking class. Mr. Dayan sands the wood with care. “The wood needs to be smooth.” It’s a long day. My arms burned, the skin of my hands rubbed raw. I asked for leather gloves, Mr. Dayan laughed. “Soon your hands will be leather.” He rubbed his hands on the back of mine. I thought of Bubby, “Old boots harden feet.”

He had a commission to make a soft couch and asked me, “Do you know how to sew?” I nodded. “For now, you will stuff cushions,” and handed me a wad of wool.

Another lesson from Mamma I complained about. Taught to push the needle straight through the fringe and space the circles of thread. I asked as I did whenever she gave another lesson, “What do I have to know this for?” She’d say, “So you don’t become a helpless fool.”

My reward wasn’t carving wood but spending time with Mrs. Dayan. After supper, or those days when Mr. Dayan and Yitzhak were gone, only told, “Finding work,” we’d spend precious hours teaching me German by reading ‘The Communist Manifesto.” She knew all about the author.

“Karl Marx was Bavarian, bred German, well-educated. His father was born Jewish but converted to Christianity. As you know, this is a lie needed to open the door to a good school, but it wasn’t school that taught him the most valuable lesson; it was being in a city of factories and mills, where he was inspired to consider the plight of the worker. Marx was humbled by poverty. He came to depend on the charity of his wealthy friend Friedrich Engels. Engel's father was a rich industrialist. He’d tour the factories, return home to their palace, and struggled with the inequity.”

CHAPTER FIFTEEN – Riga – Dayan – 1903

The year passed in a blur of chores. Kept the tools sharpened, sanded the rough edges smooth, and stitched cushions together. There was less time spent with wood and more time spent preaching for the overthrow of czars and priests.

Mrs. Dayan surprised me with chocolate cookies for my fifteenth birthday.

My curiosity and faith in heresy set loose a willing spy to sneak about courtyards, to listen under open windows, as a ghost overhearing a science class, hidden in a hedge to listen to Ministers plotting paths to riches, and my reward wasn't sausage, noodles, cheese, and cookies, but the countless hours with Mrs. Dayan who held me under her spell.

She fattened me from twig to branch and was eye to eye with Mrs. Dayan.

I felt guilty for not visiting home, but my father came months after I settled in and broke the news to me that "Ruth married a good doctor." Without Bubby's potions and the pond running dry, waves of migration from Moscow brought Uncle Moshe, Mr. Kornicker, and the others to Vladistok to manage the Count's well-respected doctor's large home that he converted to a school, an inn, a shul, and a hospital.

My father apologized, ashamed for not bringing wood. Tried to hand Mr. Dayan a ruble.

"No need. Max is a hard worker. He earns his way."

He was no longer proud, but a beggar—almost a stranger. Without the trade in tonic and under the spell of mourning, he lost his way.

Mrs. Dayan came rushing to the barn to beg him to stay. "A good meal. To talk. We must get to know you."

He pulled away. "What's the hurry. You must stay."

He stumbled about, eyes avoiding mine.

She pulled him close. "You raised a brilliant son. We've been blessed to have him," her eyes spoke as a proud mother, took his hand, "Max also struggles to let go of the past." I shared his tears with a hug.

"You should be proud of your son. A fine young man."

"You've given me a great gift, but I should come home."

He smiled, "I'm fine. A hermit's life. Not for you. This is better. A life with purpose." He stayed the night and earned their respect. My father was a welcome Marxist. Even Yitzhak found sentiment in stories of my family's trials.

I worked with passion, not the labor of a serf. My hands were hardened to the promised skin of leather. My shoulders widened; I was stronger. I bought ink and paper with the rubles Mr. Dayan rewarded me with for my fine work. I write most of what I think in secret. They wouldn't understand my doubts and fears. I keep those pages under the floorboard. Yitzhak is like a brother for his protection, but I feel as if I'm being watched, and yet I cling to faith that I'm trusted.

Mrs. Dayan doesn't keep Kosher; there's no Shabbat, but they donate furniture to Rabbi Frank's nearby shul, which serves as a temple and as a home for the homeless. The young and liberal-minded rabbi welcomes a congregation of the poor, and Mr. Dayan preaches Marx to the lost. "I was raised Orthodox, but lost faith as a young man. Religion turns neighbors to strangers over foolish rules."

Mrs. Dayan willingly shares her memories. "I was raised by a Jewish father who was exiled when he married a Christian girl for love. He wouldn't attend church or temple. My father celebrated the tradition of a meal and enlightened conversations to bond family and friends, but it was all taken away when they removed him from court. A lawyer unable to defend his own was too much for him…" but couldn't finish.

My father hadn't visited for almost a year. I was worried and wanted to go home, but Mrs. Dayan made the excuse, "He told you that he's fine as a hermit. A visit would only stir up heartache."

There is always a parade of comrades. Some come to organize protests; others bring Lenin's newsletters to distribute. The prophet preaches to injustice. They come from as far away as Berlin and Odessa. A network of missionaries spreading the gospel. Their ruminating is over what lesson was needed to convince the nobles of their evil. The most fervent Marxists are bred in the Ukraine—the Tartar cities of Odessa and Kyiv. The Teutonic Poles of Vilna, Minsk, Warsaw and Lodz are bred to serve. I know nothing of their plight, but what he preaches.

Mr. Dayan spends precious rubles on drink and meat to convert the pious to comrades. Good reason to be fearful all the time. Familiar territory. I was an apprentice to a family who taught me to have eyes in the back of my head. Fear is tempered by a heart scarred by terror, hands and feet hardened by harsh chores, and the nightmare that beasts roam the wilderness. I struggle to ignore the thought of punishment. Not exile, it wouldn't be prison. Few are given the reward of bread and shelter. If believed by even the whispered breath of rumor of stirring trouble, there's no trial, but a swift execution.

I hand out Lenin's broadsides from the shadows, for if I'm not with Yitzhak, I'm hit; the newsletters are crumpled and thrown in my face. Most see it as heresy to argue against the holiness of czars, priests, and rabbis.

Mr. Dayan shows great courage to preach at the quarry, factories, and mills. He preaches to those coming and going from their labor. Some over a furnace, more breaking rock, a battle with shovel and picks, slaves for no more pay than heat, bread, and ale. He's a preacher whose pulpit is the shadows— "Break the shackles of tyranny. You are sheep in surrender to the beasts." Few give oath. Labor is what life is about.

I want to believe. I want to have faith in his dream, but I'm lost in doubt: Jews, Christians, farmers, everyone with different wants. Miners and factory workers are another breed. Ambitious Jews convert to Russian to be favored citizens. Only Gentiles are welcome by the Guild and Courts. The Hasidic follow their secret map, but it's not of this world. The success of a few Jews will be our undoing. Rothschild, Hirsh, Poznanivsky, bankers, industrialists, moneylenders, the builders of pyramids pay in ale and bread, not a fair share of the bounty of their feast.

Mr. Dayan's temper is aroused by those known as 'Assimilators.' The learned, the scholarly. They preach to banish the outdated traditions of a sacred past and embrace the sins of the 20th Century. The educated and enlightened are known as Haskalah. To be enlightened is to be respected as 'Maskilim, a *Maskil.*'

Mrs. Dayan and I need to sneak away from Mr. Dayan's eyes if we want to read books by Voltaire, Descartes, and Spinoza. She's opened my mind to God being an excuse for our ills, not our master. Her favorite quote— "Ignorance is the ally of tyranny." I've learned about the nature of electricity and how it powers motors and telegraphs. I understand how atoms are invisible planets that build our universe. I conjure a future in which politics and religion are converted to the exacting rules of science. But science is heresy to Mr. Dayan. He believes that the Maskilim are a distraction to the conversion of pious into vigilantes, pirates, and anarchists.

Yitzhak embraces me as a brother, but his passion for the cause is orthodox, born a vigilante. I guard my thoughts as well as my new pages.

Mrs. Dayan is German to her soul. I'm jealous of the time she spends with comrades with German roots, but I learn German as Germans speak. She and Mr. Dayan disagree over Wilhelm's intent. She believes the Kaiser to be a forward thinker who embraces enlightenment, preaching unity of purpose to build a new world.

Her sermon defends the Germans for having no respect for backward Russians, Catholic Poles, fanciful French, and pagan Serbs. Mrs. Dayan agrees with Kaiser Wilhelm II. "To reach the goals of Marx and Engels with education, science, engineering, and embracing technology." Mr. Dayan argues as I'd never seen. "The Kaiser is a petulant child. Queen Victoria's grandson envies grandma's wealth. He wants her colonies. Doesn't want to pay pirates for sugar, tobacco, rubber, spices, and silk. The new barons are the wealthy, but the Kaiser sees too many Jews among their ranks. Their wealth needs to be channeled into his vision of a pure German empire."

Mrs. Dayan's loyalty to her husband was tested when a male cousin she knew from childhood sought her out.

Heinrich Shultz is a proud German banker. He was passing through Riga on his way to St. Petersburg with the intent of meeting the Czar. "The Kaiser is Europe's best hope. He's building a new Germany. His vision is a future that embraces reforms to improve the lives of all. To make Germany as industrialized as Britain. If the Czar would open his mind to the Kaiser's vision, the workers would share in the profits."

Mr. Dayan's temper is strained. "Wealth only feeds the bourgeoisie and nobles."

Shultz shakes his head. "Jobs lift all out of poverty."

He's on fire. "The workers are left homeless because you don't want to run a factory for their benefit, only for yours. "You say you bring jobs by loaning money to the factory owners. You admit to loaning to the Mayor. Riga is his prison. Profit is the seed of greed."

He pushes Mr. Shultz out the door. "You take his business when the gambler can't pay." The gold cow had only one commandment: Profit!"

Her loyalty tested, silence is her shield, her sword is preaching with the certainty of equal justice.

Mr. Dayan's faith in revolution is forged in revenge. Monthly meetings measure time. His comrades are given great respect. She's at odds with her husband's talk of burning down the palace, but her love is so great that she hides her doubt—as do I.

Her favorite four disciples invite Mrs. Dayan to a rally that is disguised as a play. Mr. Dayan argued that putting on a show to ridicule the powerful will not recruit warriors, but she holds him under her spell. Mrs. Dayan gave me the nod. I hid my excitement.

I know them as writers. They wear the disguise of a beard, scarves, glasses, and, depending on their audience, dress as a peasant or in tailored suits of the bourgeoisie. Their mannerisms keep me guessing as to who they really are. She's dressed as if in mourning. Wears a black dress that has no bustle or fringe as her favored disguise.

Anton leads us down a flight of stairs. It's musty, dark. I can smell the audience's breath. We're in a basement without windows.

I count thirty-five young men. Two are Orthodox. The rest are ragged alley dwellers earning a ration of bread as pick-pocketing thieves.

Only an orphan would give thanks for the warmth of the potbelly stove. There's the stench of a toilet that is no more than a box with the top cut open.

The writers are wearing the costumes of a priest, a policeman, a merchant, and a peasant, and for the next hour, they ridicule the police as thieves and priests as cowardly lambs fighting off the wolves with fables. Laughter is in anger, but hearing there's no bread or ale, no shelter in this cavern, only three take the pledge to fight as comrades in the revolution.

Mrs. Dayan believes that to recruit three is a win. She pulls me from the hall in rapture. "This is how we'll stir reform. A play opens minds to change. To get someone to read the Manifesto," she sighs, "Impossible. Books are only read by those who already know what is wrong. Better to stir things with a story."

She turns to me before we reach the path to the barn with an angry confession: "I was upset that he argued with Heinrich. The revolution needs the bourgeoisie."

CHAPTER SIXTEEN – Home – Riga - 1905

Mr. Dayan holds me to a higher purpose; he's always in a fever, workshop forgotten, his comings and goings kept a secret, but I know he's preaching for a reign of terror.

I'm confused by my friendship with Mrs. Dayan. In front of Mr. Dayan, I'm treated like a boy she likes to tease with chocolate-coated cookies. Still, when we're alone, we're students on a journey into the depths of knowledge, her access to literature, philosophy, religion feeds a hunger to turn our doubts to faith. I'm entrusted to speak my mind with the four professors, but we're poisoned by doubt, lost in our search for a path where the promise has the glimmer of truth.

Anton is a writer of some reputation. Dignified by his portrayal of the all-knowing narrator, he casts an illusion with a gifted actor's reflection. His stories mock the greed of thieves and the laziness of beggars. Sickly, his coughs alternate between painful breathing that stains cloth with bloody spit. His tales are about familiar families who fuss and feud. Stories about thieves who seduce with charm, infirmity, deceit, and disguise. The corruption of society by distrust. The tyrannical father is the Czar, the demanding wife, his dutiful empress, but a mother who breeds wolves to unite as a pack on weak prey." Warnings about giving your trust to posers with outpourings of attention. We look down from a perch where we dream in nightmares and spin tales, the author as master of his world.

Mrs. Dayan is under the spell of this penniless writer who struts about as if a noble but always in need of a ruble. Fyodor's characters duel over cruelty, cheating lovers, godless and god-fearing, but all believe in the god of money. "How else to teach the fool that the fire of this hell is lit by a Midas casting spells with a gold torch."

She's humble. A role hardened by Mr. Dayan, but she once confessed to me while under the influence of a peasant's wine, that she plays the role of a blushing schoolgirl, "Charm is one of my shields." She recites from the most romantic of poets—Pushkin, but her heart is torn, and she laughs when he's around at such notions of romance, only to cry in her pillow.

His characters engage in quarrels over politics, greed, ambition, and religion as both the pious and the anarchist. The four professors preach for vengeance on those stealing their soul with suspicion and fear, to sparking the hope for some place to escape, some way to change their destiny, a path of hope. "The test of loyalty requires faith in the promise of hope."

A dry summer made for a poor harvest, and anything worth eating is hoarded by those who have been bred to do such things. A ruble is worthless if the farmer is hungry. Only the threat of death commands a trade.

The bad harvest made winter even crueler, and by March, a healthy horse is eyed more for its meat than its use. Cats and dogs are long gone.

The request came from the Count's Sergeant to make the Count's sofa. Sixty rubles is hailed as a great honor, and told by the noble's guard, "A well-deserved reputation."

What would take a month, we created in two tireless weeks.

It was a work of art. "This is worth a hundred rubles for the artistry of your skill." The carving around the border told the story of a king's victory. There were twenty horsemen carved in the frame.

Yitzhak and Mr. Dayan set it down in the parlor as I stare in wonder at the chandelier that has a thousand crystals. The hutch is a masterpiece. Paintings cover the wall. Gold trims the walls and doors. A thirty-foot ceiling is the sky of a heavenly sunset. The palace is a treasure chest.

There's no greeting, no admiration, no nod of thanks as a fitting reward for the artist, nor a purse with sixty rubles. The Sergeant sends us on our way with a promise of being paid when the Baron returns.

Three trips to the home over the next two weeks are met with the same promise. "They are traveling," repeated each time. Yet the truth is in front of all our eyes. Mr. Dayan holds back Yitzhak. He doesn't challenge the lie with the truth that the Baron can be seen driving about Riga in his motorcoach as if the Czar himself.

Mr. Dayan pulls Yitzhak aside, "Not today."

The next day, six armed police, the ones with a gold star on their silver helmets, came to the barn. The Captain holds out a purse. "The Baron has this for you.".

A quick count. "Twenty!" Mr. Dayan throws it to the floor. "I will take back the sofas."

The sheriff's men aim their muskets. "You are fortunate to be paid at all. And such a handsome fee. I thought they were worth only five. You will be shot if found on the other side of the river."

Mr. Dayan kicks two unfinished chairs and pushes over a hutch needing doors. "We will burn his palace."

Mrs. Dayan blocks the door to stop him. "You are known. Won't make it across the river. There will come a time."

His savings are gone. The landlord can show no mercy, "Most goes to the tax Collector." A patch for a garden, no field to plant a crop. No traps. Borrowed to buy the fabric, wood, and nails.

He's taken to such a temper that I fear for Mrs. Dayan—and spy through the window to make sure she's safe. I've seen a naked woman, but this is not my mother, not my grandmother or cousins, she's not the unknown girls and women bathing in the pond or river. She's a woman I should only know as a mother, but who has captured my heart. I am seventeen, and my awareness of such things no longer comes as a surprise, but as the yearning festers, I'm losing mastery over my needs.

In such a fever, I head to the alleys to trade a ruble for a woman's flesh. Too nervous, I drink until I'm in a fog, but as I stumble through the tavern, past the shadows, I find the backroom where the girls flaunt their bosoms, bare legs above the knee, and the doll's face is painted with thick red lips, black marks darken her eyes, with a hive of dark hair all fluffed about. "Three rubles."

I think of what it took to earn five. All I saved, but for the four coins I can't spend. I measure her value to food. She smiles, but my fear is aroused by ignorance of coupling. I hear the echo of Poppa's warnings about the risk of trading in sin—and its sickness of pox and fevers.

Mr. Dayan was making plans to torch the rich man's palace. Yitzhak would be by his side. Mr. Dayan told his comrade that he needed her to stay behind. "You will spread word of this deed. A martyr for the Revolution."

My role in this plot? Lookout? Light the torch? Murder? I have but one excuse—as a preacher to spread the word.

It's been a year since my father came last. I need his wisdom in such things. Every day I expect him to show.

Mr. Dayan is caught in a trap. He's under watch. A plan to go into hiding. Yitzhak brings me to the cottage. It's late, between midnight and sunrise, a bag on the floor, Mrs. Dayan filling another sack. He looks down on me. "You are a comrade, yes?"

My silence stirs his temper. He paces about the table, clouds the room with the fog of a peasant's tobacco, but his smoke is less than the poison I feel stirring in my belly for having to hide my heresy of doubt. A lamb to a warrior's soul. A blacksmith's strength to a child's weakness. A mask of devotion. He has no trust in cowards. Yitzhak will stand by his side and slay me if told. If I spoke my truth, Mrs. Dayan would understand, suffer heartache, but if forced to choose between her husband and me, she'd pull the trigger.

I look down to hide my doubt, study the grain of the table, and follow familiar paths marked by pits, scratches, and knots, but the grain shows only paths leading to the dark knots of traps. I hide in the memory of when Poppa and I brought the oak that made this table. Thirteen was another lifetime. Mr. Dayan blessed the table— "This tree has the honor of serving as the pulpit on which patriots gave birth to the revolution."

There's a squeak from the stove door. He feeds the legs of the chairs he smashed. The embers flare into flames that cast a haunting shadow of the Golem. And as he comes close, his hands on my shoulders, I'm pressed into a chair, demand my sight, and with a foreboding stare, he asks for the second time— "My comrade?"

To take the oath is to follow him into battle, thievery, and murder. Truth is the punishment of exile, or if deemed untrustworthy, execution. Gramps would say, "Vengeance only breeds revenge."

Picks and shovels against a swarm of locusts armed with rifles, cavalry, and cannons?

A fable that David slayed Goliath with a stone, for I know it takes more than a well-thrown rock to fell a deer, let alone Goliath.

Mr. Dayan's faith has the fever of a messiah on a mission. I'm a grateful apprentice, foolish to think I was an adopted son, but he has no regard for anyone but a comrade willing to die for the cause.

The greater price for my exile will be the punishment of a broken heart. To lose Mrs. Dayan's comfort. But she is his most trusted comrade.

Yitzhak is Cain to my Abel, but he's my brother, he's my father, she's my mother, our bond as family. What more is there to die for?

"I believe," my oath said as truth—*I believe that tyranny is darkness and brotherhood the light.*

He slides the copper-tipped pen and tin of ink across the oak table. Hands me precious parchment. Holds up his bible, the Manifesto. Raises his fist to bring me to devotion— "Write your oath. Write it in Marx's German."

I would argue that a church and temple spread brotherhood with charity, that a congregation shares the load of misery, and a safe harbor to soothe pain. The church and temple provide valuable lessons from our past—the evil of a king's greed and ambition. The lessons of yesterday still speak to the suffering of today—a bond with faith in brotherhood.

His grip is strong enough to lift logs, but made stronger by a mind clever enough to carve useless wood into something useful— but it's vengeance that stirs this father's blood. Mr. Dayan teaches with the manner of a demanding father, but he is the wolf to my family of sheep.

He takes a twig to the embers and brings the torch to the table to light the candle. I need to hurry before the candle is lit. Can't hide my doubt in the shadow. I put ink to paper. There will be new paths on the other side. Tomorrows are more precious than truth.

"Read it." He demands.

"Death to the beasts."

Mr. Dayan looks right through me. "One day you will face the beasts, but not today. For now, you will be my eyes and ears. I am taking Mrs. Dayan to Berlin."

CHAPTER SEVENTEEN – Home - 1905 - May

He crafts a trunk with a hidden floor to hide his favored tools and goes into hiding. I'm put in charge of selling what is left of unfinished furniture, wood, fabric, and nails and commanded to raise enough to book passage by train to Berlin—the fastest path to escape.

He has a peasant's mind for value. I raised double his expectations. I know the shopkeepers and peddlers. They understood the value of such fine work, materials, wood, and the giant saw.

We meet at a farmhouse at the edge of Riga. He counts the fifty-three rubles. My reward is five. I swallow my disappointment. I would ask him for more, but he'd accuse me of being a greedy peddler. I had prepared my protest as an investment. "I will be a trusted spy."

Mr. Dayan knew my mind. "Go home. Make tonic. Time will come when we'll need comrades outside the city." Not absolution, but he knows my spirit is a preacher, not a warrior.

She pulls me close, and I tremble. Her love burns. I need to pull away. Need to hide my tears, but she doesn't let go—the whisper in Yiddish. "You are the son I dreamed of. Find your path." Etta's love is branded into my soul beside my family but it's better that we're separated.

Yitzhak never shows regard for sentiment. He's charged with recruiting comrades and waiting for word from Mr. Dayan to come to Berlin or lay siege to Riga. I'm shocked when he comes for me with a hug.

CHAPTER EIGHTEEN - Riga – Hasid - 1905

I only needed to stop at one home to realize that preaching with doubt will not convert even the most hateful of the czar's tyranny. No sooner had I asked a stranger to trade his dream of tending his farm and family for a dream of brotherhood as a comrade sharing the bounty of his farm than I knew, a minute into preaching, that this was too much to ask. My doubt showed through. A peddler needs to preach with certainty.

The birch with the four branches still points the way, but it's not long before I'm pained to see that our secret path is now a long stretch of stumps, and the dirt trail has ruts dug by heavy wagons. No doubt, a sign of trouble. I feared the worst. Cursed the Count in Yiddish, spit in revenge, and sealed the curse in Polish to pay my respects to my grandfather. I passed the pond and looked ahead, surprised to find our shanties now four fine homes, made from the trees that had been our fortress, now tombstones cut into planks of wood.

"Who goes there?" He appears from behind the closest house. I remember this Russian. He was a tax collector at the festival.

"Mr. Ivanisevic, it's me, Max. Max Gutlian. Maximilian Bloomberg's grandson. Been a long time, I'm Moses Gutlian's son."

He squints, not from the bright sun, but to find the memory. He draws his lips to pucker, thick mustache pressed to a broad nose, and lowers his head, "Not that I recall."

A moment later, two others come from the cabins. Strangers, also of Russian stock, both holding rifles.

"Moses? Yes. He was here. Found him by the pond, dead. Looked like a snake bite."

"Dead?"

"Rattler or maybe spider, could've been anything I imagine."

The Count's servant is a known liar. "Where are the others? My family? Poppa said they were in Vladistok."

Shook his head. "The doctor married that girl from here." His arrogance is a mask of deceit. "Shame to have lost him. All Jews were exiled. Maybe Lodz, Minsk, Vilna, maybe Warsaw.

The three men circle me. Ivanisevic comes within a pace, "Can you make this tonic?" He holds up a bottle. Handed it to me with a nod and put his hand to his mouth to mimic a swig.

To stay here as his brewmaster? To remain on the bloodied soil of my family. To suffer each moment in memories. I took a sniff and a swig to help the lie. "Very good. Yours?"

Holds my eyes with the stare of suspicion. "Yours!"

"I left here as a boy." Take another sniff. "Yes, it's the potion my grandmother gave me when I was sick." I suspect that they took the land. My father would've put up a fight, but if everyone had left? I didn't need to ask if our home was gone. Any sentiment would fall on deaf ears. It's enough that they believe I don't know the recipe. To ask to see his grave, to see our home, to ask if there are any possessions left behind, would only invite taunts.

I notice that the pond is suffering. Well must be dug deep.

A pack of children runs at us from the fields but stops at the sight of a stranger. They look at me as if I'm a ghost. I was that child living in isolation, seeing a stranger would have sent me to hide behind my mother and bubby. Leaving home as a witless boy was not far from the truth.

They have no want for another mouth to feed. I leave without trouble, but I'll never know if it was Poppa's refusal to make tonic, a snake bite, or the infirmity of sorrow that brought him to take the flower to end it.

My mourning is felt as the hollow ache of an orphan.

My stomach is in knots, got those painful cramps, can't go, then go too much with dark water pouring from my bowels. My mind won't stop punishing me. Gramps would be telling me to move on and make my own life. Poppa might've passed on his dream to venture across the endless sea. Bubby would want me to find peace in knowing that they had a life in which the blessings outweighed the troubles. Surviving was a test, but with each test, they wanted another tomorrow. Family was their heaven.

Not sure how long it had been, but my dreams were broken by the murmurings of sheep. I climbed over a stone wall. Tall fields of corn prove the value of a good farm. The dog warns its master that I'm here. I'm about to run, but the farmer is wearing the black suit of the Orthodox, calls out, "You lost?" in Yiddish, and waves.

"Lost? Maybe."

Without hesitation, he places his hands on my shoulders. "What misery has you under its spell?"

A sorcerer or a Holy man, he's read my mind. "All gone." I'm shaken by talking to someone who isn't a ghost.

"Come with me." He calls for his children. An older boy and a younger girl stop tilling the good-sized field.

The boy looks to be about my age but has a full beard. Mine is just tufts and patches of hair. He puts down the hoe and greets me as if I'm a friend. The two girls, not yet teens, both dressed in long gowns of patched cloth, but I can't see much of their faces, being hidden under large straw hats. They wave, then return to clearing the rocky soil while her older sister carves furrows with a hoe.

"You lost?" His kindness unlocks the grip of my misery. "I'm from Riga. Apprentice to a craftsman. Learned how to make a decent chair, hutch, table," I say with no pride.

"A worthy trade."

I'm well fed. The mother lays out a plate of chicken and potatoes, but the greater reward is the father's comforting. "It's not how long a life, but that it was a life worth living. That we have enough to help others is how we serve Hashem's will."

A full belly, a good night's sleep, and a healed bowel, but it's his faith that gives him hope and calms his fears that has me realizing my loss of faith has left a hole that needs filling. Karl Marx, no matter the truth of what he says, only digs the hole deeper.

Thought only of returning to Riga, but not to find Yitzhak.

CHAPTER NIGHTEEN - Riga – Church – Hasid.

Soldiers everywhere, twenty-five guard the bridge; they give no regard to a long line waiting to cross, and the toll is whatever bribe or treasure they choose. A farmer is entitled by custom to keep a male and female, but the Captain threatens to take all three.

Motorcoaches, wagons, horsemen, bicycles, and carriages are like blood flowing through the city's veins. Early afternoon, and the square is alive with the bustle of commerce. Stone and lumber feed the construction of palaces, homes, shops, churches, and roads. The tentacles of growth feed the wealth of nobles and favored bourgeoisie—the Czar's two-hundred-year legacy. I pay tribute to the artisans. The masons and carpenters should deserve a share of this treasure. It was their skills, strength, and fortitude that manifested a noble's dream, but paid in kopeks. Why are the Gentiles deserving of the greater rewards?

I never thought to enter St. Peter's Church, but I'm unable to resist. If I'm caught, there'll be trouble. I climb the ten wide steps and peek inside, only to be overwhelmed by its grandeur. I need to catch my breath, step back from the door, and look around in fear that I'll be seen trespassing, but everyone is watching the soldiers terrorize the peddlers.

I look back inside and realize no one is in prayer. I don't know the day of the week, but midafternoon isn't a time for prayer unless you're a Muslim or it's a holiday, and there are no holidays this time of summer.

The church proudly displays its treasures. A towering ceiling held by sculpted beams and columns. Could there be anything grander in heaven? Under the spell of such magnificence, I'm brought to kneel in reverence, but in fear of being caught, I hide between pews, but can't help peeking over the top. The pulpit is draped in purple satin, behind it is an organ with a hundred pipes, and rising above is Jesus nailed to the white cross, and he's staring at me. Has he called me here? I rub my eyes. He's in such pain.

Every creak and groan cause me to imagine someone is behind me, about to be arrested for this trespass, but as I soak in the spirit of this remarkable cathedral, I measure the risk to its reward, and believe the price will have been worth it, such is its spell of being in God's heaven.

I count 33 rows on either side and wonder whether that number has any significance. Jesus is too far for me to tell if he's real. I need to get closer and crawl under the pew to go one row at a time until I reach the first pew. I look up to realize he's carved from wood, evidenced by cracks in the paint. His hands and feet are nailed to the cross with spikes. So thin and pale, wisps of a long beard and hair, flesh covered in a cloak of white cloth, held as a prisoner to the cross. Was this punishment for the sin of doubt or certainty? Why would a father punish his son in such a manner? A czar's threat to bring his subjects to heel? Stained-glass windows show Jesus healing the sick—healing potions or God's judgment? Christian love and charity are only for each other? He was a Jew, so why not us as well?

The altar is wood twisted into scrolls as if a garden vine. Given flourish with gold leaves and silver flowers. Nestled among the vines is a robed woman holding a lamb. Her gentle eyes watch over the flock. Does her warmth soften his pain? The columns touch heaven, and my spirit is held by Jesus.

There's the smell of holy smoke. I turn in panic. Someone is lighting a candle. I'm not alone. It's an elderly woman hunched over a long table with a hundred lit candles. Their Sabbath? A mourner's candle? Do they mourn as Jews? How not? A caring soul needs to cling to the departed.

I want to pray, light a candle, give a Kaddish, but would that be sinful? Am I a stranger trespassing on their house? I would ask Jesus why no mercy? Would Jesus answer a Jew? My God doesn't answer, why would theirs?

"You there, what is your business?" The priest appeared without warning. My heart stops, can't breathe, about to be punished, but I turn around and I'm relieved to be comforted by a kindly stare and a pious face shaved as smooth as a child's. He's a small man hidden under a black smock, but made larger by the crown of a cone, and made holier by a gold Jesus dangling from a gold chain, leading me to believe I'm in the presence of God's messenger.

My heart stops, in panic, and in fear of being sent to prison, I think to race out the door, but he holds me with a firm hand, "Are you lost?" asked in Russian.

I searched for the word 'prayer' in Russian but didn't know it. I study his face for clues as to his heritage, but he looks more Jewish than a tall Litvak; there's no sign of a Russian's thick bones, and I dare to ask the Priest in Latvian, "Will he listen to the soul of a Jew?

The priest smiles, “You’ve been called to Jesus?”

“Have I? Can he hear my prayers?”

“Why else did Christ summon you here. What is your prayer?”

“I have no faith. My God is not merciful. Is yours?”

“Jesus died for our sins. Most merciful, most forgiving. You’ll be given absolution if you do penance and your sin is temptation and not evil.”

“Absolution? Penance?”

“Penance for your sins and absolution is forgiveness.”

“Penance?”

“An oath, a prayer, a confession that recognizes the act as a sin.”

“Is doubt a sin?”

The priest nods for me to sit beside him. “Doubt is not a sin, but a hole in your soul needing to be filled.”

“What if my sin is that I want revenge? But as soon as I asked, I feared that such an admission confessed too much truth, that he’d have me arrested as an anarchist. Revenge? Revenge for what? Not for hate. Not to murder. “Is it a sin to have improper thoughts of a married woman?”

He places his hand on my arm with a smile. “Oh, yes, temptation, but improper thoughts are not a sin unless you commit the deed itself. But understand that such thoughts need to be confessed and ask forgiveness.”

“Do you light these candles to give comfort to the dead?”

“And to comfort the living.”

“Can I light one?”

“You are a Jew!”

“I was. I don’t know anymore.”

He holds up a Bible. “Read the New Testament. Learn our ways. Attend mass. Give confession to a priest. Admit your sins, and when your soul finds faith, you will come to me, and I’ll baptize you.”

“Baptize?”

“You have no soul until you accept Christ as your savior.”

“Jesus won’t listen to the likes of me.”

“You must be ready to listen.” With a skeptical squint, he hands me the book as if it’s a treasure. “Read. Go to the church on your side of the river. Not the Polish Catholic, only the Russian Orthodox. Go this Sunday. Pray. Know that Christ is our savior.”

I had read passages with Mrs. Dayan, and all spoke to Christ's mercy, charity, and kindness. I say without thinking of the Priest's values, "They will let me into their Service?"

Moments pass as he studies me with new interest. "Your Russian is very good. You are troubled by doubt. Take our path and find your way." Sniffs, my rags that carry the stench of the road—" We invite all, but bathe and wear clean clothes out of respect."

Gramps explained the story of Jesus. The Rabbis at that time were as nobles with authority over the congregation. The ruling Pharisees clung to traditions and shunned Jesus as a rebel. They were challenged by the assimilating Sadducees, who spoke from both sides to appease the Romans. "Jesus thought poorly of the Pharisees. They ruled as nobility. Christ was a revolutionary, but not an anarchist. Neither patriot nor traitor. Gramps said, Jesus is just like this Karl Marx, a messiah preaching God's message of brotherhood."

Their glass window was painted as the God I conjured in my childhood. A grandpa, a bearded old man. His throne is within the clouds of Heaven. His love extended by the tip of his finger touching his son's. "Is God the Father? The Czar to his prince?"

The priest pressed his hand down on my shoulder to make me kneel. He holds up his hands, "God is Jesus and all that there is," touches his finger to his forehead, and then shifts his hand across his chest. "My dear Lord, reach out to this lost soul and show him your light."

I feel the pain of Christ. His blood is the sweat on my palms. My feet burn from the nails. "Is Christ calling me?"

The priest takes me by my chin. "Open your heart and let in Jesus."

I look to the pulpit. "He feels my suffering?"

He wraps his warm hands on my head. "God feels everything."

"Can I be saved?"

"If you find faith."

"Faith in the Czar? It's not a sin to kill his enemies?"

The priest lets go. His grin is no longer comforting. He stands. "God has a plan. Our Czar is God's messenger. His priests are your guide. We are in service to the Czar."

My doubt is caused by confusion. The Czar as Jesus? To die as a soldier for Christ. Jesus wants war. A czar as God? This is his heaven, not mine. A Jew has no soul? Was my family without a soul? Can I kill in the name of the Czar? This can't be. No God before me. Is Jesus another God?

Why aren't we all brothers? Lenin is right. This is a fable—a trade without value to give my life for a master's bidding.

I drop the Bible on the pew and race out of the church to run from the spell of their cathedral's magnificence, but I don't know which way to go. The bourgeoisie and cavalry take notice of my escape.

An Officer orders his men to fetch me, "What are you doing here?"

I respond in Russian, "I'm a carpenter's apprentice looking for work."

They rub their hands against my coat, against my pockets, and over my back. I followed Poppa's rule, one ruble in the pocket. The nine I have left are tucked where they shouldn't search unless of that sort. If they are, I'm at their mercy, no matter Poppa's trick.

He forces his hand into my pocket and takes the four kopeks. Shows it to his comrade. "Good enough."

I cross the bridge to our side, giving thanks to Poppa for the lesson of a bribe. I envy the soldier's day. Their only chore is making threats. I think to enlist. I wouldn't be given a rifle or sword. I'd have a shovel to load a cart with their foulness, haul stones, butcher, pluck chickens, chop wood. Would they make me a warrior? So great is my confusion that I want to be the beast. But as I study these men, I realize my delusion. Never have I seen a Jew an armed soldier. Only those bred from David's branch of the tree, a Yitzhak, a Mr. Dayan, can pass as a warrior. We're not from one seed. My branches are the soft wood of a birch.

Mr. Dayan warned me, "The greatest sin is to die in battle for the czar's want of another kingdom."

Congregations are divided by what we eat, how we speak, act, dress, and the shape of a nose. The priest warned me not to be Catholic. The Christians are as divided from each other as they are from the Jews. I soak in familiar smells, the familiar howls, our side is not the quiet manner of gentlemen and ladies, but a fervor for laughter and suffering, this is not a Christian's home.

I'm pulled to the heart of the ghetto, lured by the comfort of its noise, smells, someplace familiar, and I wave to those who know me. I'm eyed with regard by Mr. Katz. He still has Mr. Dayan's giant saw on display in front of his general store. Paid fifteen rubles, but the greater profit is earned by being able to lay out the money and can afford to wait.

Mrs. Esther calls out, "Maxala!" She makes latkes just like Mamma and Bubby. I inch closer to her cart, dizzy from the smell of frying onions and potatoes. I can already taste the salted potion. She looks like my bubby, with her dark ankle-length hair braided into a wall across her brow—the full cheeks of a dumpling. Mrs. Esther hands me a latke and refuses my offer of three kopeks.

I can't wait for it to cool and burn my tongue in haste. The pain is worth the reward.

I stumble against Mrs. Shreiter's cart. The seamstress eyes my ripped jacket and offers to sew it back together.

I wander in memories and embrace the Jewish quarter as if in a dream. The familiar faces have me feel at home. My sadness is soothed by the noise and fury of its tumult. The stirring of the city distracts from my misery. I hear my miseries when in the quiet of the wilderness.

CHAPTER TWENTY– Riga – July – Lina - 1905

By sunset, the peddlers are in retreat from the roads and streets. Is it Shabbos? I've lost track of time, but I know we're near harvest. Could it be the Holy Day of Yom Kippur? Maybe Rosh Hashanah?

They hurry and change from rags into black suits, fedoras, shtriemel, and the dangling tzitzit. The pious join in a parade to the Synagogues to be made holy by communion.

The Hasidic congregation is greater than the length and width of their prideful cathedral. The honored elders wear the black Bekishe, thick fur-fringed hat of a shtriemel. The young men keep their fingers busy fidgeting with the knots of a tzitzit. The holy strings dangle from their pants to soothe worry and focus thought. Prayers are kept in a small black box strapped around their arms or forehead. They mingle and greet each other with a warmth and friendship I envy. They parade in rapture. I want their fervor. They must have God's ear.

His dark brown eyes study me through thick glasses. "I know you?" 'Know'—said as if, can I trust you? The Hebrew of a scholar.

Their synagogue is as if the goyim's Cathedral.

He shakes his head. "You look familiar. Were you once of our Court?" His breath has been cured in brine.

"No, but I'm from Riga." We may be counted in the thousands, but we're bonded by heritage as neighbors in Riga's ghetto. Most faces are familiar. We meet over a dumpling from a cart or by trading with the same peddlers, shopkeepers, and tradesmen.

"A peddler without a synagogue?" A question that asks if I'm less a Jew and more a pagan.

"Not of any temple. Had my Bar Mitzvah." I share his attention with the procession of boys to men bonded by their black suits.

"You read what passage?" His glance turns as he needs to give blessings to the well-wishers, "Shabbat Shalom."

"King David. Where he asks, where is God's mercy."

He returns to study me. "What do you know of us?"

A test? Pride takes over. "I know the Zohar, Kabballah, and can read Hebrew."

The Rebbe is surprised. "What do you know?"

"That to find God's light, I need to study your maps. To open my soul to heaven, I need to leave this material plain."

"How old are you?"

"Seventeen."

The congregation forms a strict line. Front-to-rear, decided by the rule of age. The last to arrive are the youngest.

The Rebbe returns his stare. "You are educated by a Rebbe? A Hasid?"

Is this a sign that God is drawing me from that priest to Hasidism? "My uncle Moshe was of your flock in Vilna. He was my Rebbe."

I overhear two boys, and discover that it's Saturday night, but also the end of Rosh Hashanah. Only women, girls, and young boys can do chores. "Come with me." He's of Poppa's age if judged by the salt of gray hair. His beard is trimmed, not as an elder, yet he has an elder's confidence but shows me the kinship of a father.

I'm led to a courtyard. It's lined with stacks of wood, barrels, rows of crates, a chicken coop, and a small garden. We passed through a narrow tunnel behind the temple. There's a large house. Two floors. Home to a hundred or more.

He opens the door and guides me into a beehive of women, girls, and Bubbies, all buzzing about in the chore of cooking a feast. They glance at us but quickly turn back in obedience to their work.

I count sixteen children of all ages running about. Five babies are crying in the corner, the cribs lined in a row. A woman has one in her lap, with her breast covered as she feeds it. No matter the heat from ovens, all but the children are covered head to toe in heavy black cloth, scarves wrapped to hide their hair.

In the middle of the room, the older woman scoops out noodles and vegetables from large kettles. A feast is being placed on a large table. The bowls and plates are tended by sixteen women, ranging in age. The hearth is as wide as a man and gives off such heat that it turns the cool night air to summer. Only one of the dozen windows is glass.

"We can use your help."

Three girls are manning the pots. Four are mixing noodles and cheese in big bowls. Five girls are cutting and dicing cabbage, broccoli, onions, none pay me any mind, but as I turn from his gaze, I notice a girl my age scrubbing a heavy kettle. Her stare lingers as she studies me. But her stare also catches the matron's eye, a hawk watching prey. The crown of white hair is done in a braid tied into a bun, and she quickly crosses the room and is about to smack the girl with a stick that she wields like a sword, but the Rebbe nods to the matron as if to ward her off. "I know you're shorthanded."

He turns to me. "You can help keep the fire fed and fill the buckets with water."

She takes my measure. "You are Jew or pagan?"

"I am a good Jew who observes the Commandments." I peddle the heresy to gain trust as I believe truth would mean exile, and I'm too hungry for a portion of the noodles.

"You live in the dark." Said with certainty. The Matron takes my arm with a firm grip. "Go fetch wood and split more if needed." But her attention is drawn to two young boys struggling to clean a heavy pot.

She waves her stick over the frightened boys. "Leave the pots and go pluck chickens."

The matron hands me a heavy pot, and I follow her to the well in the middle of the courtyard just outside the kitchen. She hands me a wire brush. "You'll cut wood after cleaning the pots." There are two other boys half-heartedly peeling potatoes. The matron smacks them, "Lazy, no good," and shushes them away.

The girl, the one with the kind eyes for me, brings me another pot. "What's your name?"

"Max."

She stirs her finger inside the pot and offers me the bite. "My favorite is the noodles, but best with the browned cheese. Our reward." She tells me in Polish, "Go ahead, the scraps left in the pots are the best of a meal."

I scoop out a mouthful.

The matron has her eye on us and chases the girl away.

I clean the pots, but she allows me no rest. "Gather wood and feed the stoves."

I grab split logs from a pile of wood. The girls back off from the stove as I feed it. I hear the murmurs of cursing me like I'm a stray dog. I look smell my rags to remember the priest's warning.

The girl who keeps her eye on me comes out to find me. She has another pot. She's different than the other girls. She wears a thin cotton dress that is not as heavy. She's a few inches shorter than me, has the face of a girl, but the bosom of a woman. I'm taken by her large brown eyes and round cheeks. She is not like the other girls who are slaves to the matron. She has the temper of a rebel.

I took the pot. She ignores the warning and mocking to follow me back to the pump. "I'm Lina," in Polish, and without permission, breaks off a chunk of browned noodles, and surprises me by holding it as bait, inches from my mouth.

I'm embarrassed. Scared to stir the matron's wrath, but I'm captured by her boldness, and take the offering in one bite. Lina reminds me of Ruth for her show of affection.

I turn away from her attention and avoid showing my shyness by peeking around the side of the doorway. Ten well-dressed women wearing shawls of lace take the platters down the hallway. I hear the men howling chants of prayers or sermons and sneak behind to follow.

There are ten men of a grandfather's age, long white beards, seated as kings around a long table on chairs that are carved with such detail that Mr. Dayan would admire the craftsmanship. The elders are paid respect by men who are closer to my father's age. There is an order as to who serves which elder. A ceremony that would have me think these grandpas are noble. Their high-backed chairs are a throne.

A Bharucha in appreciation for the meal. The grandfather, at the head of the table, waves his hand to ring a bell, and the parade of the finely dressed women serves him first from the full platters of chicken, cheese, bread, and noodles. A feast that Bubby would be proud to serve.

The displays of wealth would have Gramps grumbling. Gold holders for the candles. Gold trim on the silverware. Bowls of salt. No want for food. I can't help but wonder what their trade is? How to earn such riches? I rarely see a Hasidic at labor. None have carts on the street to peddle wares. How do they earn?

A finely dressed woman notices my stare. "Be gone," frowns at Lina, sniffs in disgust— "You don't belong." I didn't know she followed me.

We return to the kitchen, and the matron gives us both a smack from her stick. "Where've you been?"

Lina doesn't cower. "Cleaning pots and cutting wood."

"You don't go anywhere."

Hits me again with that stick to my behind. "With such a smell, you must stay in the courtyard."

Lina is handed a broom. The bell rings from the dining room, and the matron hurries down the hall.

Lina pretends to sweep. She wants my attention. I fetched an armful of logs to pose as if doing a chore. She leans toward me with the broom sweeping my dirty boots and whispers, "They have no end to their gluttony." I'm a stranger. She must see me as an ally to show no regard for the pious. "We're their slaves."

"You trust me. Why?"

"An outsider. A rare sighting. But more for confessing to me when you said, "I wish I had their faith." She laughs. "A fellow doubter as am I." She pulls closer. "The Hasidic believe themselves above even the Orthodox. Their Rebbes profess God has ordained such rules."

This girl is no peasant, not from the street, but a young woman of perhaps fifteen, if judged by her sharp tongue, and would better suit the liberal congregation of the Haskalah. She's enlightened to more than just the ways of the Torah and Kabbalah. Wise to secular thoughts. "Why do they keep you here?"

"A prisoner of their injustice." She doesn't whisper. The courtyard is ours, but their stirring is just beyond. "You learn your place, or you're punished with the stick. My pity for the boys who have yet to have their Bar Mitzvah, or have no mind for scripture, for they will have to fight over the scraps of what is left. Noodles without butter or cheese, maybe a cooked potato for the weak. A girl's only reward is working in the kitchen, as we take the first share, but I pray for exile."

The matron returns with her flock. Lina gets busy sweeping, and I feed the fire. But a moment later, the matron returns with clothes. You must wash," and holds out a clean white shirt and the black pants. "Change into this after you clean off." Hands me a scoop of lye.

I do as I'm told. I take off my clothes, wash under a pump, and change under the shadows of the courtyard.

The kitchen is once again a beehive. The girls and women clean and sort the dishes.

From some distant room, there's the echo of a violin playing with a spirit as none I'd ever heard. The music stirs my soul. The violinist holds each note until it reaches deep within. But it's not long before the spell is broken by silence, and all return to chatter and chores.

The matron approves of my following her orders to clean up, and with a quick sniff, she waves for me to follow. "Only male," she hands me a cart, leads me down the hallway, past the dining room, and stops before the entrance to a very large hall that is as tall as it is wide and long.

The room is two floors with its middle open. The wall is finely carved with a picture of Moses holding the tablets of the Testaments. The windows are painted glass, telling stories from the Bible. A column of ten heavy pillars has been carved to look like vines.

The matron guards the door to a temple she's not permitted to enter, and tells me, "Clear away the empty bottles. When you're done, return to the kitchen." There's that stare of punishment, "Do not wander."

When I return to the kitchen, the matron is waiting. We're alone, the hive silent. "Put the bottles on that shelf," pointing to another hallway. "Where are you from?" She speaks only in Hebrew. I need to earn her trust or be sent away, but is this my fate? To be a Hasid?

I tell her of my miseries, and her mood changes from master to mother. "You'll finish the chores in the morning," and as a mother's reward she spreads butter on two slices of challah, and then with a glance toward a burlap sack stuffed with chicken feathers, the matron informs me— "Eat. You'll sleep there," and I'm left alone.

Their charity soothes a hunger, but I know enough of their ways to wonder if my doubt can be converted to faith.

I clean the hearth and put away the bottles, and as their holy kingdom finds quiet, I return to the sacks of flour, and sleep takes me—until the rats come out from hiding and grab the broom to protect the food. A chore that she didn't mention.

A kick to my side awakens me, with open, tired, burning eyes. I need sleep, but when I see its Lina, I sit up. "Sorry to wake you."

"I make the bread." She opens a tub of flour. "Are you wanting to be Hasidic?"

"I don't know." My shyness gives way to curiosity. I have no experience with a girl besides Ruth, but I learned about romantic desire from Mrs. Dayan.

"I'm in misery." She sits beside me. I'm shocked by her boldness. "My father sent me here to be married and make babies. As if I'm a cow."

"A Cow?"

"You speak Polish."

"You said to be a cow?"

"I'm to be married off. Most likely to one of these old men, but it wouldn't matter. They are all masters if you're a woman." She can't sit still and goes to the trough to fill a pitcher with water. "Whoever it is, must be someone important." She mixes the water with the flour. "Most likely the Tzadik."

"The king? Are you a princess?"

She laughs as she kneads the dough. "Yes. I'm cursed to be a princess."

"Not an honor?"

"A prison sentence. I've been here a month, but it feels like a year," shakes her head, "I stay only for my father's sake, but his grip is weakening."

I don't understand. "Who is your father?"

"A Tzadik. His temple is in Poland."

"You don't know who you're to marry?"

She's angry, "They tell me nothing. Treat me as a servant." She moans, "I cursed them. Punishment is to wear me down to obedience."

"You're Polish, but from where?"

"The past five years we lived in Lodz. Do you know it?"

"I know of it but have never been further than here."

"My first ten years were in Minsk, but kept prisoner, so I wouldn't know the difference between here, Lodz, or Minsk." She looks around, and in a whisper— "My marriage is meant to join our two Courts." Lina is bold in that she tells such truths. "My uncle was a Tzadik, but he was exiled for being outspoken in the ways of the czar." She snorts, "They demand ignorance of the outside world." Lina's eyes locked on mine. Her long nails grip my arm. "Look into my soul. I don't want to be a cow. They think that by fifteen I should have had a brood of babies."

The matron and her flock can be heard coming down the stairs. A dozen girls and women spread about the kitchen. The Matron eyes us with concern. "Where is the bread? What have you two been up to?"

"I'm making challah."

I fill a dustpan, "I'm sweeping out the ash. Bottles cleaned and put away."

"Go get wood. Tend to make a fire."

I'm pushed by a pack of four boys racing through the courtyard toward the kitchen and knocking the load of wood out of my hands. "Who are you!" The boy pushes me away.

I calm my temper and gather the wood, but when I return to the kitchen, the same boy is pushing a girl from the table to grab sheets of matzah. I don't understand this behavior. Where is his piety?

Two older boys, at least old enough to have the fuzz of a beard, make it known that they are married to the two girls with the big bellies. The girls are younger than Lina, maybe thirteen or fourteen. The husbands rub their wife's belly with pride, letting it be known with boasts of touching the belly that this is their baby.

Moments later, there are too many in the large kitchen to count—men, women, boys, girls, elders, all coming and going. The boys know only to take the matzah. Only men have the right to have challah. The girls butter and honey their bread. The elders are served scrambled eggs.

The pimply faced boy who had pushed me aside grabs a matzah, then boldly takes a fresh challah, cuts a thick slice, and puts on a wad of butter. He struts about to show his privilege. When he notices me in the corner, he comes closer. "You! New boy! Who are you?"

"I'm Max."

"A fitting name for a dog." He is maybe my age. His payos dangle below his ear. The strand of hair curls against a shaven face. He's skinny, small as me, but acts as if a king, "You aren't Hasidic?"

"Don't know. Maybe."

"Peddler or farmer."

"Craftsman of fine furniture."

The boast is met by a stare. He studies me, but our meeting is interrupted by a thickly bearded man who pulls me away. "The Rebbe wants to see you in his office."

I'm led from the kitchen through the dining area, through the temple, and into a hallway lined with room after room where boys of all ages are listening intently to their teachers. At the end of the long hallway, he opens the door and nods for me to enter a room lined with shelves of books. The desk has four sides. As if four desks joined together and wish Mr. Dayan could see this strange creation.

The Rebbe, who invited me into his kingdom, waves me in, and smiles as he nods, "Our charity of shirt and pants, imagine you have a full belly, and would ask if we earned the trust of our newest member?"

I'm lost in confusion. Lina has me turned around. What choice do I have? What life can I make? Find Yitzhak, and what then? Revolution?

"What do you know of the Kabbalah?"

Lessons from my family keep coming to my aid. "Yahweh's guide for the most learned to find the true path?" My uncle, grandfather, and even

Mr. Lipinsky taught me all about the Hasidic ways, but much of it I didn't understand.

"You are a curious young man, aren't you. But you answered in the form of a question. You have doubt."

He can read minds. "Taught to question everything. I blame my grandfather and Poppa."

His smile has the warmth of being with family. "My father and Grandfather were also my Rebbes. My family name is well known. Do you know of the Tzadik, the most learned Rebbe Abramowitz?" Said with a hint of pride that is wiped from his brow when I shake my head. He picks up a paper, I can see it's written in Hebrew. "Please, if you would, read this so I can know which class you would belong to, if you were to join our flock." His tone is as if dangling a reward. The letters are scribed by a hand skilled in drawing the difficult-to-remember Hebrew letters to be as art.

I study the page and recognize enough to know the chapter. "King David." But then I stumble. "I know this passage."

"No value as a test, then is it." A nod of respect. "Good to know you're not a goniff. You could have easily cheated." He picks up the bible and opens it to a random page. "Read this."

I take a deep breath, not for the test, but the greater question of whether this is where I'm meant to be. Uncle Moshe warned me about getting lost in the Hasidim's maze. "Great value in joining a kingdom of learning where loyalty and devotion can bring comfort, but the Tzadik is as their czar. The flock is divided by rank, as if in the army. I can tell that this Rebbe is more of a scholar than Uncle Moshe. He can read minds, so I suspect this means he must be closer to knowing God. Could he deliver me to faith? Curiosity pushing me forward to remember Poppa's lesson—*Knowledge is more valuable than a ruble if there's truth to the lesson.* The fog of not wanting to prove myself lifts, and with the focus of wanting the prize of being invited in, the letters take form as words. I look at the page and need to press my mind to search for the memory of Hebrew, and recite a few lines.

"Enough." His grin is that of a teacher confused by a student's wisdom. He ponders my verdict. "Some will never learn. Some are blessed to have a mind able to learn." He comes around the desk to study me further. His hand on my head to read my soul. "You have a mind to learn."

Not asked as a question, but I easily answer with my truth, "I do."

“To banish fear.”

Is he a wise man or a sorcerer?

“And when the fear is gone—to slay the beasts or convert them?”

“To be King David and have my soul freed so that I could sing of the beauty of life as a poet. But I must confess that I think of felling Goliath with a stone as a fable. I have tried. I think it would be best to be King Solomon and possess the wisdom of knowing the value of a trade.”

His eyes sway as he studies me. He paces, takes a long draw from his pipe. “The Hebrews are a long chain joined by the links of the father teaching his son. To know our history is to understand the strength of brotherhood. How else has our flock of lambs survived longer than the pharaohs, Assyrians, Nebuchadnezzar, Cyrus, the last of the Babylonians, and yet we are still here. Their kingdoms have long since turned to dust. We survived because our souls are connected, and our flock is spread across the fields of many kings. No matter that a thousand of our lambs are eaten, our souls are joined in an eternal brotherhood, sons to Hashem.”

He goes to the shelf lined with books of some age for the withering. “The Zohar is a guide that gives meaning to the laws of the Torah, but to know the Kabbalah is to understand God’s soul. It is a path with guideposts that lead us from a mortal life to the eternal universe of heaven. To lift a student from darkness to the light. You are blinded by misery. It is only by transcending our ignorance that you will find God’s light.”

He reads minds to cast the spell of certainty. He knows my fear is from doubt. A man of great wisdom, but is his wisdom truth? Or is he a dreamer stirring faith with hope? “Curiosity is the greatest of my cravings, but can a foolish boy who needs to see value, find faith in such a path?”

He put down the pipe. “The journey takes discipline and patience. To learn to play a violin takes much practice, much patience, and then you must be blessed to transcend the manipulation of strings to bring out the instrument’s spirit. To climb a mountain so high that you reach the clouds. Such a journey takes great courage. To turn the fear of death to the enlightenment of your place in God’s plan takes the certainty of faith.”

“I want to teach my hands to play the violin with spirit. I want to learn.” I take the oath not from faith, but as I did with Mr. Dayan—A lie spun in my doubt of ever finding faith in a certain truth.

He pushes me out of his office. “We will see about your fate.”

I turn at the hallway to the kitchen, and there are hundreds of boys and men divided by age. The girls and women are treated as serfs. Lina said women are no more than cows with their bellies and lives as a cocoon, nest, and enslaved to tending to the needs of boys to the elderly. Are the Hasid no different than the pecking order of czar, noble, bourgeois, and peasant, but the Rebbe holds us by dangling a trade of labor and loyalty for the reward of a family in communion. Is the Kabbalah a puzzle without end? Or a path to find certainty in faith? If I follow the Kabbalah's map, what heaven is my reward? Will I float in clouds? Is the sky warm and blue? Do we float above the sweet scent of flowers? "Life is meant to be a cruel test to appreciate its joy." His lessons etched a deep groove. He led me down a path to believe that life is to experience all its wonders, good and evil. Our reward is eternal sleep, and not a boy's dream of a pond with endless sweets, willing fish, and no chores, but as he'd warn me, *Perhaps an endless night without day, but no matter its kindness, if it's without answers, it's just more of our darkness.*

I pass through the temple, down the hall, but before reaching the kitchen, I'm pushed to the floor by that pimply boy who believes that he's a prince but reminds me of the beasts for his cruelty. He breaks my spell of pondering mysteries without answers. He walks off with a laugh, and I return to the kitchen.

The matron is my master, and my chore is to split wood and tend the hearth. My reward is that after each swing of the axe, I get to stop to watch Lina through the kitchen window. Her chore is to work the dough and braid it into challah. All the girls spend their day cutting, slicing cabbage, beets, potatoes, and I wonder what farm supplies this bounty. Riga's ghetto surrounds its kingdom, a garden less than Bubby's.

I carry the load of split wood to the hearth and have my first moment since this morning to talk to Lina. "Are you okay?" but she looks at me with a grin, not a smile, and a shake of her head as warning.

We are near each other all day, but she keeps her distance.

Night slows the pace. The three girls who are lowest on the pecking order finally finish their chores and leave.

I go to my bed, protecting a sack of flour from the rats, and as the candles are snuffed for fear of fire and the hearth left to embers, she appears from the shadows, having hid in the closet where they store sacks of grain.

Surprised to see her standing over me, I ask, "Why didn't you talk to me?"

"I was warned you'd be punished," she sobs, and then sits beside me.

"Why?"

"I'm promised to one of these dogs." You'll be exiled.

"What can I do?" My heart hurts. I want to hold her. I want to save her, but to go where? To save her for what? I don't understand what I'm feeling.

"Is Riga safe?"

"I don't know if we're any better off beyond these walls."

"Whatever I'll face is better than being their cow." She has Yitzhak's courage.

We're startled by the matron's call.

Lina sneaks away.

The matron storms into the kitchen— "What goes on here! Where is Lina?" She lights a candle.

"I saw her leave some time ago."

"You are not to speak to her—or any of the girls."

CHAPTER TWENTY-ONE – Lina – August 1905

The day passes into night. My dreams are spun with memories of lessons by my family, to the nightmare of beasts, but the stirring in the hallway wakes me from my sleep's careless wanderings.

I sneak across the darkness of a kitchen lit by the last of a candle. I peek from the edge of the doorway to where they store the pickled vegetables and breads and spy on a dozen boys with their fingers in jars.

The pimply boy catches my glance, "What are you looking at!"

The boys form behind this czar in a show of loyalty. "I don't know why you're favored by the Rebbe, maybe for pity. A test to convert pagan trash. I told him the likes of you aren't worthy of such trust. I know you. I saw you that day. You and your giant ran off. Escaped thanks to the loss of my three friends. They should have taken you two instead."

I thought of that day and how Yitzhak saved me. I search for the right words in Hebrew to show him I'm more than his equal—more than a schoolboy. "I trade grain for tools, tools for rubles, rubles for what I need. I know how to set a trap like a fox. I can labor as a beaver and have been trained by a master craftsman to make a chair and desk worthy of a Count. I've read the Torah, can read and write in Hebrew, know Yiddish, Polish, Russian, Litvak, and German. What do you know? How long would you survive if not for this cocoon!"

The boy studies me. His laugh is false. Turns to gather respect from his friends. His stare is meant as a threat. "I know the Kabbalah, the Zohar, and the meaning of its teachings. I am closer to Hashem than you to me. I have no want for a peddler's trade." His temper is not a scholar's. He has the arrogance of the bourgeoisie. "You're no more than a mule."

I understand Lina's fear. To marry her? Two earners to soften the cost of making a home. I'll make furniture, she'll peddle whatever has value.

The Matron overheard my argument with the prince, came between us, and pulled me aside. "Get out!" I'm pushed into the hallway, stumble against a teacher, who grabs me by my arm, notices the Prince—"What goes on here?"

The Prince steps forward with the temper of a king, "He's a heretic posing as a Jew for want of our charity."

The teacher studies me, “What do you say?”

“I’m a Jew by birth and recited my Bar Mitzvah. I’m here to be enlightened by the Kabbalah.” I don’t confess that I would ask why Yahweh is not merciful to Jews?

“If this boy is to find the light, we are blessed to show him the way and in doing so, we serve our purpose.”

Uncle Moshe taught me about Hasidism, but I worry that my soul is that of a rebel, that I’ll forever be unable to cast aside doubt.

Lina is shackled to the chore of baking; no way to talk to her, so I take my doubt to the hidden shadows of the courtyard. I’m surprised when one of the Prince’s group sits beside me, and whispers for my attention, “He treats us all the same.” He reveals that the prince is the Tzadik’s eldest son. “His father is the Rebbe Abramowitz.”

The Hasidic are strict about following aristocratic traditions, passing titles and privileges to the eldest son. He leans close. “He saw how she went to you. He’s jealous. Lina is to marry Yisrael, but she wants no part of him. He’s a fool with girls.”

“That’s Lina’s prince?”

“This is why they punish her. To bring a rebellious princess to task.”

She’s in the kitchen cleaning a pot and I slip her a note.

She looks at it. Eyes wide and tucks it under her apron.

I’m feeding the hearth. She’s carrying a full pot, and I use it as an excuse to help. “We need to talk.”

The Prince is watching, anger boils, comes for me, kicks me, tackles me to the ground, choking me— “What have you done! Who told you? You told her!”

Three guardians pull him off. Lift me from the floor. “You must leave – you will leave now.” Yisrael’s followers push me out the kitchen door and into the courtyard.

“What goes on!” The Matron cries out. She’s holding Lina by her wrist with some force. Beside her is the elder, Rebbe Abramowitz. He’s followed by an entourage of outraged disciples.

The Prince calls out, “He told Lina I’m to be her husband.” Yisrael eyes me, “I saw them talking. How else could she know?”

“Did you tell Lina that Yisrael is to be her husband?”

“I told her she shouldn’t have to marry anyone if she didn’t want to.”

The Rebbe turns to Lina. “You will marry whom we choose.”

“I won’t marry that pig,” her glare is aimed in anger at Yisrael.

The matron smacks her hard.

The Rebbe grabs her wrist. "Foolish girl. You are blind to what is best for you. You will marry Yisrael, and God willing, give him many sons—what more is there to know."

I feel helpless. I want to save Lina, but there are too many.

Rebbe Abramowitz is the Tzadik's brother. He faces me, a smack to my face. "I invited you into our home, and this is how you repay me."

I'm caught in the middle of a storm.

Lina pushes the matron away, kicks the girl who tries to grab her, "Let me go!" A big girl tears the back of Lina's long black dress. Her temper unfurled, Lina kicks her away.

"You will pay!" Yisrael throws a punch, but the smack to my chin hurts him more than me. A frail boy without muscles.

Lina escapes out the kitchen door. I push him away, easily break free, and his brothers are paralyzed in shock.

I race off to follow Lina into the courtyard and gain ten paces as a head start before Yisrael's disciples are commanded by their prince to give chase. Lina forces her way through twenty or more onlookers. Mothers protect the children. A dozen men and boys stand frozen, confused.

I set a trap by kicking over a pile of split logs. Lina is a few steps ahead. She unbolts the gate, looks back, sees me, waits a moment, and I follow her to the other side. The kingdom is surrounded by a stone wall flanked by an iron fence.

Our escape enters the frenzy of wagons, carts, horses, and crowded pathways into a harsh wilderness of manmade storms, lightning, and thunder—a battlefield guarded by beasts wielding swords and pistols.

Lina's face was scratched. There's blood smeared on her cheeks, but her smile is the smile of freedom.

Blocked by the bustle of wagons, riders, and peddlers, only a few paces from the stone wall and the heavy metal gate that guards the kingdom, I turn around expecting to suffer more of their attack, but the command of Rebbe Abramowitz holds them. Unwilling to expose his Court to the shame of chasing after us, I look back to catch the glare of the Prince. His eyes spew fire. Between the waves of wagons, riders, and carriages, I feel him casting a spell with a mystic curse.

We become lost in a fast-rushing river of wagons, men on horses, the horseless carriages racing about, belching smoke, scaring a path with horns blaring.

In the midst of the tumult, uncertain of Lina's intent, I argue my defense in leaving the sanctuary of Rebbe Abramowitz. His charity, his intent to teach me the Kabbalah, the Zohar, not as Uncle Moshe tried with explanations that only confused me about other worlds and mystical paths, but as an invitation to find faith in God with study, prayer, but I disrespected his family name. I blame the prince, but what about Lina?

Lina pulls me from confession to find absolution in her appreciation. Every other breath is a gesture of thanks. She's a warrior set loose, who dares the motorcoach, waves her hand to dodge a parade of carriages, and any doubt that this was a sacrifice of finding faith is lost in the fever of her spell.

She disregards questioning stares and takes my hand with a smile that testifies to her desire for my partnership.

With courage born of freedom, she pulls me into an alley without looking ahead. She startles a horse. It lifts its front leg, a warning kick from its hoof, not an arm's length away. The driver slides off his bench in a fit of temper, waves his crop, spews a curse for getting in his way, and yells at us, "What goes on here!" His eyes darting back and forth to her torn dress, bloody cheek, "You've attacked the poor girl?"

Her round cheeks bear the scars of battle, stained with blood. Her torn dress reveals the flesh of her back and arms. The nest of long braids came loose to become a tangled strand of a mop. She grabs the man's arm, "He was saving me from my mother and father's temper for wanting to marry him."

She takes me by the hand, and we race off into the sewer of an orphans' alley. I peek to see if we're being followed, but there's only the homeless picking through the trash.

"I hate them. I hate them all. I'll be no one's slave." Lina catches her reflection in the cobbler's window, spits on the ragged edge of her sleeve, and wipes the blood from her cheeks. "I'd have killed him before being his cow." She leans against my shoulder. Anger vented to shame, "I've brought shame to my family," but cried in revenge. She kicks the dirt as if to declare her freedom. "I told them I wasn't going to marry. My mother wanted to set me free, but my father sent me to them like I was a cow with a rope tied around my neck."

Her plump lips, round brown eyes, are the soft shell of a hardened rebel. "You're my knight. So brave. You saved me—our escape. A kiss on my cheek warms me. "Where is your castle?" She laughs. Shame turned to the joy of freedom. “Show me Riga. All I’ve seen is the inside of that prison. Locked between my room and the kitchen.”

She looks like a child’s doll that had been dragged through the street. I feel a stirring that begs to hold her in my arms, but she’s in search of discovery, pulls us into the peddlers’ market of Gravnovsky Road, caught in the spell of a woman’s clothing shop. A moment to soak it in, “I want to make hats.”

CHAPTER TWENTY-TWO – Lina – Sept. 1905

I see through her excited eyes and remember when Gramps introduced me to Riga's endless temptations. I thought it was a magical wonderland. I want to find courage in her courage, hope in her hope, but I've come to realize that Riga is not a wonderland, but a harsh test of survival. She's an innocent to the ways of the wilderness. I'm the fool who knows better.

But it's a day like no other. Her wide-eyed excitement makes me stop every few paces so she can imagine another dream where it's her store full of her creations.

Mrs. Esther waves from behind a cloud of boiled dumplings.

I introduce Lina, and my adopted Bubby gives a welcoming hug, but didn't miss a breath before asking where I've been.

I don't have the heart to confess that truth. She'll suffer if told. "Been working the harvest and met this poor girl who stole my heart." Lina kisses my cheek, "My hero. Saved me from servitude."

Lina's disheveled state is an understandable infliction of poverty and earns the charity of dumplings filled with whatever was scraped together.

A warm sunny day that sparkles from within. A day that is like no other. I'm a guide, her teacher, and she makes me feel like a man and not a mother's son.

The trance was broken when Lina asked, "Where will we stay?"

I feel the nine rubles in my pocket. It's enough for a few nights on a bed in someone's home. A room at an inn comes at a price only the bourgeoisie, adulterers, gamblers, thieves, and merchants can afford. Nine rubles will buy a week of bread, cheese, and kraut if given without profit from my favored carts.

We pass shops, bakeries, taverns, and restaurants, and I ask about a room, or if they have a need for a carpenter, but everyone is already sharing a bed with strangers, under siege by an endless stream of migrants in exile, and the trade of fine furniture for a bed and bread doesn't find a match.

I surrendered to the inevitable just before sunset, but the barn doors are closed. I wanted to believe that I'd see Mrs. Dayan in her flowery dress tending the garden, and she'd look up with a smile from under her straw hat.

We inch closer to the cottage. The door is sealed with a board and nails, but as I turn to confess to Lina that the best I can offer is a bed of dirt, I'm startled by his yell—

"Max!"

"Yitzhak?" Where was he hiding?

"Max!" I look up. He's on the roof of the cottage, and like a cat, he slides down fast and lands on his feet.

I want to hug him like a brother, but he'd pull away. I think to shake his hand, but that's not his way, but Yitzhak surprises me with a rare sign of kinship—he takes me by my shoulders, pulls me in for a hug, and shocks me with sentiment, "My long lost brother."

Lina boldly introduces herself, "I'm Lina." He's surprised by this small girl wanting a man's handshake. "Max saved me, and while you appear as if Goliath himself, I can see you're a friend, not a beast."

Yitzhak shakes her hand. "My Polish is poor. Max, who is this?" asked in Russian. He studies Lina, stares at the scratches, the torn clothes, the mop of hair, and says with a grin. "The blood of a warrior."

"Yes, she's a warrior. You've met your match. We need to catch up." I nod with a glance toward the cottage.

Half a moon cast enough light into the room to see its bare. "Have you heard from them?"

Pulls me close, "We threw a torch into his parlor," a smirk, "the couch was kindling." Welcomes my hand on his shoulder, "They're gone."

He pries off the board and opens the door.

"You both look like you could use a drink." He opens the stove and takes out a bottle. "To the Revolution!"

I take a swig and hand it to Lina. She shakes her head, "What's this?"

"Supposed to be ale."

She smells it, shakes her head, but then takes a taste, "Whew, burns!" Another, this is a long swig, "Oooh."

Yitzhak wanted to know if I recruited any comrades. I told him the truth. "Got lost in the misery of losing my father. Family all gone. Home taken. It was all I could do to breathe until I found Lina."

"We'll strike the spark," he grabs the bottle, "To the revolution."

"To freedom." Lina reaches for the bottle.

"What is her story?"

"My story," Lina confronts Yitzhak in Russian, "Do you only speak Russian?

"I know a little of all languages."

She comes closer and purposely strains to look up to him. "I wanted you to know I was listening in." She stands back, and in Russian mixed with Yiddish, Lina tells Yitzhak, "I was a prisoner of the Hasid, promised to this boy, but I will die on the street before being that fool's cow."

"Lina's father is a Tzadik in Minsk."

"I was sent here to marry their prince, who is no more than a pig."

Her act of courage stirs Yitzhak. Their eyes meet for the first time, and Lina puts him under her spell. He puts his hand on her shoulder, "A warrior."

Lina hugs him. This puts him in shock, me in envy. He forcefully pushes her away, "We are comrades, but no more."

"Comrade?"

"More than a friend. Loyal to death. What are your skills?"

"Seamstress, baker, perhaps I can make hats, dresses, and suits."

I'm torn between the risk of partnering with Yitzhak or retreating to some room and searching for a job, hammering nails or sawing wood. The Guild holds the trade in its grip. Unless of a noble's favor, few customers will spend for fancy cabinets, chairs, or sofas, and there are too many skilled in carving wood into fine furniture. To find work in a trade, a father taught his son how to lay brick or stone, bred by an artist, a fortunate son born to a mason with a patron, it's a long road to move to the front of the line. All else are slaves paid in crumbs.

Yitzhak shares bad news. "Stravinovsky will be here in another week to move in with his family. I'm supposed to be gone."

This was no longer home. Nothing left. All sold. Mrs. Dayan's children that she brought to life with locks of her hair and painted so real they came to life as the most fetching boys and girls, all dressed in clothes made with buttons and fringe. I sold the clay she shaped to make her children. I sold her precious books to Hiram for four rubles, a bargain that made me cry. The hutch, chairs, and table were the treasure that earned the fare to Berlin.

Yitzhak had no sentiment for such things.

We sit on the floor and share memories, matzah, cheese, and finish a second bottle of this fiery ale. I would tell the brewmaster to cook longer.

Lina falls under the spell of alcohol. After a long speech on injustice, she passed out.

Yitzhak nods toward Lina, "Are you sweet on her?"

I'm embarrassed. "What girl would want me?" I laugh to hide the fact that I'm in love. I've seen the girls chase Yitzhak, and how Lina stared at him, but Yitzhak never pays girls any mind.

"You are a fool with girls. You think yourself not worthy—or is it that you fear being made a husband?"

"What of you?"

"It is easier to bring a girl to bed than to get them to leave. We need to forget such foolishness and recruit, but I have only a few rubles left. Labor that pays more than a few kopeks is owned by those who wield the power. I have a plan to rob the Baron."

He scares me into making the decision I dread. Its risks are as great as its rewards. "I have a way. My bubby gave me the recipe to make money." This or be shot as a thief. "I'll need a kettle, a barrel, and a pipe. A ruble for potatoes, another for sugar to make a good mash." It takes me only a moment to conjure the plan. "Mr. Shlotsky. You remember, the baker. We made the cabinet and the table. I noticed he had a kettle hidden behind the oven."

If caught, a fine, prison, or exile to Siberia. A risk to even ask. The next morning, I lure Mr. Shlotsky to the back room and point behind the crates and sacks of flour to let him know that I've seen the kettle. I confess my plan. "My bubby taught me how to make the best."

His fear is as great as his need for money. The big man shakes his head, moans, "Everyone with their hands out." We both argue against taking the risk, "I owe taxes, bribes, and the price of flour is double."

We surrender with a hug, "We will share equally."

"I will only boil on a night when there's no wind to carry the scent." He has the yeast, the sugar, the ingredients. "I'll need two weeks for the mash to ferment, then another few days before it's cooked and then we'll need bottles. But it's all about who we sell to. Does Ira Shapiro still have his father's tavern?"

Mr. Shlotsky shakes his head. "Taken by the generals."

The next night is calm. He helps me with the yeast, sugar, and potatoes, while Yitzhak clears away the sacks and crates, to lift the heavy kettle through the trap door, down the stairs and into the basement.

I put the pipes on and assemble the still.

Lina is in the fever of a dangerous mission, keeping a lookout.

Two days later, the mash is sealed in a barrel and left to ferment.

I search for a buyer, but sneak about, and only talk to the few I can trust. Those with money don't want the risk, those without can't pay until they're paid, a trade I've learned to avoid.

But we have befriended the baker, and in exchange for going around and finding the best price for a sack of good flour, he keeps up well fed.

For the two weeks while waiting for the mash to ferment, I went to war with Yitzhak. He wants to do battle, I ask for patience and preaching to recruit an army. Lina is beside Yitzhak. Not interested in talking about a future where we have a store selling fine furniture and hats. She only sees me as a comrade.

Her curiosity is as great as mine. She has me read the Manifesto as if it were a Bible. She sneaks us into the theater. "I learned to sneak in with my mother." I discovered it was her mother who made her daughter a rebel. Her heart wanted to free her daughter from the life she resented, but she didn't have the courage or see a path to escape. "My father forbade theatre, so she played her role as the dutiful and devout. "I'd have been shunned, sent penniless into exile."

"My poppa would say a fortune or being penniless is the only way to buy freedom, but not so with the Orthodox, they close their eyes and pray.

Lina shows friendship, but not desire. Yitzhak only wants to talk about converting lambs to warriors. Lina is a willing comrade. She soaks in his preaching.

We sneak about at night to round up bottles.

Two weeks later, I start the boil and soften our fears by digging a hole to vent the fumes. By the second day, I have something close to what Bubby would approve, only when it cools do I add the tincture of thistle, dandelion, and honey to make it Bubby's.

Lina helps me fill the twenty bottles, and by the end of the chore, we leave with our share: ten bottles, each one sold for three rubles to the one Jew I could trust. Mr. Horowitz had sold the giant saw, was grateful, and had money.

We snuck back to the cottage, and rewarded ourselves by celebrating with the one bottle that we'd keep for ourselves.

"I have a comrade I trust. He said he'll pay me three rubles." Yitzhak rushes out before I tell him I have a buyer.

Left alone in the room where I dreamt of being with Mrs. Dayan as her husband, Lina being silly under the potion's spell, and romance comes easily. In fever she pulls me in for a kiss, but this is my first taste of this sweetness, and it's not long before I've rubbed her lips to the point of soreness. Lina takes my hand to her bosom, but I have no clue what to do. She reaches into my pants.

I suffer for the embarrassment of the sin, and more for not knowing what to do next. Lina swirls in the potion's spell, but a moment after lifting her dress, she vomits and passes out.

CHAPTER TWENTY-THREE – Lenin -Sept. 1905

I leave the cottage to clear my head in the cool night air and find Yitzhak in front of the barn talking to four men. I recognize the two who are almost as big as Yitzhak. They were frequent guests of Mr. Dayan. Balkius liked to mock me. He's Lenin's ghost, a Mr. Dayan, a Yitzhak, and I'm under suspicion, "Comrade or coward?"

Yitzhak is in high spirits and introduces me to the two strangers. He's middle-aged, about my size, and is wearing the brown suit of a teacher. I think he's a Jew, not only for curly hair, but for the scholarly posture. The other stranger seems familiar, but the thick, long hair and gray beard could be a disguise. He stares at me through wire-rimmed glasses, and I need to escape from the spell he casts with gray eyes that see into you.

We follow Yitzhak to the cottage. He whispers to me, "How is Lina?"

She was asleep on the floor but woke up when we entered. I had wiped up the vomit and put a pillow of flour under her head. She tries to stand, but is wobbly, and sways into the arms of Balkius, who takes great joy in hugging her in his big arms.

She pulls away with a curse in Polish, I don't know.

"A Polish girl." He bows, "I'm Comrade Balkius."

The one with the disguise studies me with some regard, comes close, and asks me in Russian, "You were the apprentice to Mr. Dayan."

I nod. There's something familiar about him. The eyes, his voice.

"You will give us the honor and join us. We are meeting 'good comrades.' You will be welcome."

Yitzhak pulls me close, and in a whisper, "He's the Prophet."

He leaned in close enough to overhear— "The prophet is it," and lowered his beard to reveal his truth. "The Dayan's apprentice." He places his hand on my shoulder, "A smart boy," and holds me in a commanding stare, "You will join us."

Before I answer, Lina tugs on my shirt. She's excited, "May I please join?" Grabs Yitzhak, "I won't be a bother."

The men laugh. Balkius teases Lina, "A pretty little Jewess like you in a tavern?"

"But protected by six knights." I'm not surprised Lina is so bold. "Let me come. I'm a comrade." Lina turns to the Prophet, "You will want women by your side"— Her seduction is spun from a hunger for rebellion. A feral cat set free from under the master's bed.

"What do you know of comrades?"

"I'll be no one's cow. I want to be free."

His grey eyes hold her in sentiment, not lust. "My wife also believes this. My Nadezhda. She took the oath. Told me women are braver than men. Said, we are tortured in birth, only to suffer with men as dogs." Everyone laughs, but he holds up his hand, places it in on Lina's tangle of hair, she calls her spider web, "Lina will be our Joan of Arc." His blessing spoken with the reverence of pride, "Such a warrior. Yes, brave women, not mothers and daughters, or a wife in servitude, but a wolf in sheep's clothing, our daughters of the revolution."

Balkius puts his hand on Lina's arm, "Comrade," as if to lay claim. Balkius is a Viking like Yitzhak, but romantic in spirit. "How did you happen upon this path?"

"God's Will. She shows no mercy." Their laughter is out of respect.

Yitzhak pays his respects, "She read the Manifesto. Lina escaped from a Hasidic prison because she wouldn't be the prince's cow. She is a true comrade."

Balkius is smitten. "You are from somewhere near Warsaw. I'm from Thrun?"

"When I was a girl in Minsk, I would escape now and then with my mother to see shows about cruelty and romance."

Lina is a month shy of sixteen, but a woman by her manner. Balkius lures her to sit beside him on a haystack. I overhear her telling the bear, "I was a princess, but my mother wanted me to free myself." The men are held captive. "I was a prisoner locked in a library of all that is known, but I only had my mother's trust. My father commanded me to be Hasid. They believe themselves to be God's chosen, but it's because they're blind. They live inside a cell of their making. They are guided by a map, but it's not of this world. They had no answer when I asked: then why did God make the evil beasts our master?"

The Prophet studies Lina. "What do you know of Karl Marx?"

"He speaks the truth." She turns to me. "God isn't coming to save us. We must take down tyranny."

The Prophet takes off his beard and wig and reveals his truth: "The manifesto is a map. The path will be revolution, patriots with the courage of a lion. Only war will bring the lie of royals as gods, that there's a God's mercy for the pious and dutiful, preachers who threaten the flock with hell when this is hell. Taught to be thankful for a life in servitude. We need warriors to convert lies to truth." He savors another swig of my tonic. Nods to me. Knows I'm the brewmaster.

"My father was a liberal thinker. My teachers taught the truth of tyranny. My sister and brother were hanged for telling this truth. They paid the price for questioning tyranny." He takes Lina's hand, "You are a child with the wisdom of an elder. The Manifesto is only a map. We'll need your courage to find our way." He sips the tonic and nods in approval. "A toast to our Saint Joan," takes Lina by the arm, "You will come with us."

Balkius passes around the open bottle. Everyone nods in approval. Yitzhak grabs two more precious bottles, is in rapture, and forgets our hunger by giving charity of our precious vodka.

Lina admires such men. She has their passion for revolution.

I hear her tell Balkius, "I will never again be locked in a cage. My map says I want to find the path for vengeance."

"A true comrade." Balkius takes the lead. He guides us through a maze of familiar streets, always with a long look in all directions at each corner. Studies the wagons and horsemen before they pass, in search of ghosts he suspects lurk in the shadows.

No moon or stars to light our path, the road is marked by candles lit for a father, son, husband, a long day at the forge, mill, cart, shop, or with pick or shovel, looking to find his way home for supper.

Yitzhak was not blind to my desire for Lina and warned me many times, "She looks like a child's doll, but is a warrior, and won't be a wife to any man." I knew, but my heart couldn't let go and it burned to think how Lina was so cozy with Balkius, the familiar pain of heartache.

We cross a field of overgrown shrubs and follow a dirt trail through a patch of forest until we find a stone cottage. There are two small windows set high enough that Yitzhak needed to be on his toes to see in.

A middle-aged man greets us with blessings in Yiddish. Excitedly, but with respect, he takes the Prophet in a hug, then bows to Balkius, and repeats his greeting of gratitude in Russian and Polish. He stops to look down at Lina. "Who is this?" The shock of a girl in our midst.

"A true Comrade," Balkius uses any excuse to claim her.

He opens a bookshelf that serves as a secret door, leading to the outside. We follow a short path to a barn with dozens of cows and seventeen men sitting on haystacks, a long bench, and crates. Four in the corner are smoking pipes, the rest smoke cigarettes, and when we enter, toasts are made, all stand, and hold up their mugs.

An elder grips the Prophet's wrist, "Bless you for coming." He's handed a mug and clinks to the toast.

The elder takes the pulpit. "Before you preach to setting us free from this misery, I want to share my journey. In my time, we had respect—we were in charge of the Post. I was trusted to deliver mail. Alexander is assassinated, and his grandson, Nicholas II, has sworn to purify Russia. Either we leave or remain as serfs with debt. No end to taxes. The Count, Mayor, and council are rich from what they've stolen!"

The elder's son adds his lament, "Priest or Rabbi sell us hope for a ruble in tithe."

Balkius stands, "I was a Count's tax collector," he smiles at Lina, and repeats in Polish to pay his respect with the flirting of a suitor. "My birth name is long forgotten. My father had ambitions and traded his Jewish soul to be Russian Orthodox. In the trade of a soul for a job I was made a tax collector, where I learned the tricks of smuggling. To know which cloth was French, Italian, or Russian. Tariffs on anything foreign. No regard for whether the woman's dress or the man's suit was all they had. Protests met at gunpoint. No mercy. I did what I was told. I, too, had a gun to my back. Always someone watching. There is only one path from tyranny, and it's to be as cruel as they are."

He scratches his goatee, lifts his worker's cap to rub his bald head, and works his spell, eye-to-eye, one-by-one. "We will lure the wounded, the deserters, and heroic soldiers who fought the Sultan and lost to the Japanese who sank the czar's fleet. We must preach to a flock of sheep and wounded warriors afflicted by defeat, labor as a peasant, dig coal, iron, feed a forge, and wake them to the truth that tyranny exists only because they've surrendered. When the time comes, when opportunity presents, we will be the tyrant and rain down thunder and lightning." He holds us in a messiah's grip. "We will stir the embers with the kindling of speeches and strikes. The Czar will try to soothe with crumbs and vodka. The priests and Rabbis will soothe with promises of heaven to keep the flock as lambs. We must throw logs on the fire if we're to wake the sheep from sleep. We will choose the battlefield and the weapon of our choice."

I glance over to find the source of that rotten tobacco. The pipe-smoking scholar takes off his glasses, runs his hand through his thick curls, scratches his beard, holds his hand over his eyes, and shakes his head, as if to force himself to silence. I cannot read his mind, but I believe his fever is infected with another plan.

Yitzhak is in rapture, "I lit a flame, next time I'll blow the palace after I put my knife into his neck."

There was no report about the fire, but when I snuck past the Baron's palace, the corner room where we left the sofas, the walls and windows were freshly painted, and the evidence was quickly erased—the power of a noble to make truth disappear.

I'm held to doubt. I could preach that the Manifesto and the Bible are fables, but a brotherhood with no masters, no beasts?

The prophet stares down at the professor. "David's stone struck flint, and that spark brought down Goliath to ignite an army. We will be the flint and the hammer. We must burn down the kingdom."

The professor closes his eyes.

They drink my tonic with a thirst that has no limit.

The prophet raises his voice, "America, France, Italy, all began with no more than flint. The sparks were: Washington, Lincoln, Napoleon, and Garibaldi. The most courageous of warriors are the first into the fight. That is why they are the most honored." His glance to the scholar, "How can a worthy crusade be otherwise?" preached to his disciple.

I want to have faith, but a revolution will burn down the kingdom, but as Anton said in his play, *Revolution will burn the fields, and if left without tending, there will be no farm. Washington won the battle, but it was as President that he won the war.*

Balkius raises his fist, bows to the Prophet, and rules the pulpit with the certainty of a believer. "He has the ear of the Duma, haunts St. Petersburg, our party will be known as the Bolsheviks. The proletariat will be the majority. The Prophet is everywhere."

Yitzhak and Lina are in rapture "From the palace flames we will light the fire of Communism."

Balkius lifts the shirt of his friend to reveal a back that's been whipped into scars. "The Czar makes soldiers thieves for his want of another castle, but here is the soldier's reward—a back whipped to submit to battle. To lose an arm, a leg, their face, more, their life. Do we die for the Czar's pleasure?" he lifts Lina to stand on a crate, "Or as Saint Joan told me in her oath, To die for purpose."

Lina is twitching, in rapture, her eyes wide. I was beside her when she swore not to be the cow for that arrogant prince. I surrender to my dream of her as my wife and mother of our children. Jealousy tears at my belief I can be a comrade and cry out without thinking, “What of America? Their revolution brought a civil war. Workers get shot if they go on strike. What has revolution won but tyranny as slaves to greed and hung by bigotry. ”

There’s silence. I want to run. Will I be shot as a traitor? The Prophet shakes his head and laughs, “Capitalism is not Socialism. Who among the rich doesn’t take a hundred rubles to his worker’s one. You are right. America is evidence that capitalism is another brand of tyranny. Merchants are the most ambitious of thieves. The rich are nobles. The companies, kingdoms. They own their workers. Their government is run with the same bribes, threats, and judges on the side of the rich as all nations. Fortunes buy a mayor, a sheriff. The rich are Czar. They go to war before paying a fair share of tax. America’s rich are jealous of the Czar. Jealous of tyranny without consequence. Greed to satisfy envy. Lincoln’s fable of freeing the slaves was a preacher being taught the lesson that beasts are merciless. Slaves still pay the price. The rich deny that their fortune was made on the sweat, wisdom, and sacrifice of their workers.”

The Prophet puts his hand on my shoulder. “There will be souls converted by preaching, but if we’re to awaken an army of sheep from the slumber of labor, it will take more than a sermon to turn Masters’ into brothers. A strike is a hollow army against the master’s golden cannons. The worker has nothing if a paycheck is missed. The master has a long sword and wide shield. We will decide what is the battlefield.”

The professors sneak away on horses. The Prophet hugs Yitzhak and Lina and then takes me by my arm, “Doubt is a wise man’s curse, find faith that from the ashes I will lay a foundation on which the workers will be the masters.”

Balkius tempts Lina to come with them, but the Prophet put an end to his disciple’s plan, “They will stay in Riga. The revolution needs comrades everywhere.” He grabs Balkius, “We have our own path.”

CHAPTER TWENTY-FOUR – Beasts – Oct. 1905

Lina is beside me. Her legs shake, twitching about in a fitful sleep. I get up and go outside to take a piss on what was Mrs. Dayan's carefully nurtured garden and suffer for her being gone. I didn't see Yitzhak after he kept on the path to Riga while Lina and I returned to the cottage. I'm left alone to argue my doubts, but I'm distracted when I hear the echoes of hammer to rock. Need to find your way through the maze of wilderness to reach the Czar's treasury of granite—his prison with punishing labor.

I try to keep the creak of the door from waking Lina, but the rusted hinge sets off its alarm and awakens her with a fright. She looks around, her head turning each way, and it hurts my heart when she asks, "Where is Yitzhak?" as if her comrade had left for the revolution without taking her.

"I don't know."

Lina is a beaver. She needs to keep busy. Leaves the floor to crank the pump, fills the copper pot that Mr. Blum loaned to us, and then opens the stove door to feed dying embers. The flame shines through the thin black cloth of her torn smock. I watch with desire as she takes the knife to chop cabbage and onion with the potatoes I kept from my mash.

As with Mrs. Dayan, I'll guard our friendship as reward enough.

Lost in doubt, I don't give any thought to the howls of dogs or the nagging crows. I don't heed the warning of a rustling twig or scratch of boots against the stone path. My back is to the door, but I know from Lina's look of horror that the storm bursting into the room is not Yitzhak celebrating in rapture. My nightmare finds its way into the day.

The beast has the feared uniform. Gives a hard tug to choke my struggle to submission, drags me out of the room, through the door, boot pressed against the back of my head, shifts it about to rub my face into the dirt. Everyone knows the Chekas by their uniform of a long black leather coat, boots to the knee, a sash with pistols, and a Cossack's curved sword. They are masters of the whip, like to snap their leash around their prey's neck. All are commanded to watch their hangings.

The general stands over me with the stare of a hungry wolf. Almost the size of Yitzhak. A thin patch of whiskers, not a scar to prove battle. Whip wrapped around my neck, and when I try to turn to find Lina, I'm made to face my inquisitor in this hell of Mr. Dayan's unholy dirt.

The gold eagles on his cap signal his authority. The elder's white mustache is neatly trimmed. They are Moscow Russians, disciples of the Czar, authorized as god's executioners.

I hear her howl, then a curse of hate. There's the kick to her side, and he lashes out with a strike to his cheek. She screams as loud as a wolf and lashes out with her sharpened claws that draw blood. Her attack is met with a brutal smack to her soft cheek that knocks her to the ground.

His boot against her chest, pressing down to invite torture. My punishment is to stand witness. Her torture is my punishment. Guilt or innocence won't soften his fury. There'll be no mercy. He already knows our truth.

"Where is Lenin?"

His question gave me the answer. We weren't hidden in the shadows. His scent was fresh. They were on the hunt. We were given up by a spy, a traitor, or a beaten man who thought his suffering would end with a confession. Few dare to stay silent. Yitzhak is known. Our whereabouts were easily traced. His name was never spoken, but we knew.

The threat doubles. Two come out of the barn, waving the bottles.

I feed a peddler's spoon of a lie mixed in a glass of truth to stall execution. "We delivered chairs to a Jew. I don't know him, but perhaps he is this Lenin?"

Possessed by hate, Lina has no fox in her. She strikes as a cornered badger with purposely sharpened nails to tear another scar to the inquisitor's hand.

His smack to her face is testimony to the pain she inflicted. "You're sickened by Lenin's pox," curses, spits, and kneels between her legs, rips the dress from neck to thigh, demands surrender—lashes out with smacks to her soft cheeks, curses her mother, "Kike bitch!" Unbuckles his belt. Her punishment to be his reward. "I will make Lenin's whore mine," and asks me again after he smacks Lina into sleep, "Where is your prophet?"

Another lie is needed to earn a moment more of life. I twist the lie with truth. "The Jew had a big barn. It was a nice home near Vronsky's mill."

He laughs, "No longer," and tears at her stockings. His punishment wakes her. She's a badger with a snake. He grabs her by the wrist, twists it, another howl, but a mercy in the punishment of a punch that has her head fall to the side, with eyes closed to the escape of sleep.

The devil stares at me to send a message of fear. "Where are your comrades?" Looks around. His three guardians search for ghosts.

"Comrades?" I know he knows. How long had they been on Lenin's trail? How many are dead in Lenin's wake? Lie or truth, our punishment is the same. "There were ten, maybe more. I knew one from the tavern on Stanislav Boulevard." A decent lie.

His cry came from above the barn. "To your death!" Yitzhak leaps from the roof, rolls, needs only two strides to make ten paces, and snaps the closest Cheka's neck. The bottles dropped. He turns as quick as a heartbeat and throws his knife to find the second soldier's heart, but my guard, the third beast, his boot pressed on my chest, swivels his pistol from my head to Yitzhak's, but before he can blink, Yitzhak pulls a pistol from his belt, hear the shot, and look down to see the Cheka's blood splatter on my shirt.

The final showdown. He's straddling Lina. Had a second while Yitzhak attacked. Bent to kneel above Lina, grabs his whip, snaps it to lift the gun from Yitzhak's hand, and takes aim with the pistol.

I want to be a warrior. I want to save Yitzhak. I should take the bullet. He is a warrior. I'm a useless lamb. My courage stirred by revenge for all the beast's evil, my respect for Lina and Yizhak, my only faith is in doubt.

Aiming straight at my head, I bump my shoulder against the soldier's leg. He pulls the trigger, but his aim is lost to the dirt, inches from my foot.

Yitzhak was already on the attack, no regard for the pistol, leaping over me to tackle the beast, two warriors locked in battle. Hands on throats, legs kicking, bodies twisted, a bear to a wolf. Yitzhak matches his strength to the wolf's temper, and wraps his powerful arms around the beast's chest, lifts him like a sack of oats, throws the Czar's leather-bound policeman to the dirt, kneels on the general's chest, boots kicking, but Yitzhak grips the chin to force his prey to stare at his victim eye to eye.

The Cheka is held by pride to not beg for mercy. Yitzhak pressed down harder with his knee to the chest, "You will deliver a message to the Czar. The sheep are now wolves. When you come for revenge, I will know it's you. The scars of an angel have branded your ugly face. Now I'm going to make you a beggar. You'll walk with a limp." In an instant, Yitzhak stands, bends his knee, holds it above the leg, and releases a full measure of his fury to break the leg like a twig. The swallowed cry is testimony to the soldier's courage. "Never again will you snap a whip." His knee bent, pulled the trigger, and stomped on the beast's hand. "A stump for a hand," but again, the general grits his jaw, won't surrender.

"You will never again know a woman. Blood for piss"— Yitzhak doles out a crueler punishment than death.

Lina looks to her hero with the regard I wished for me. Bloodied, half-naked, beaten, she's lost to a hopeless struggle. A whisper to repeat her pledge— "For the revolution. For you." A twitch of a smile before the mercy of death.

Yitzhak nods, "My comrade."

I pull her onto my lap. Selfishly, I ask, "Don't die. Let me take your place. You are worth ten of me."

Lina was born with a rebel's soul. Took Lenin's oath with passion. Her faith was cast by the spell of Lenin to be his warrior. She swore to never surrender.

"A true comrade." Yitzhak's testimony is the eulogy he wants. No sentiment for mourning, he takes a moment to scan the battlefield with pride. "We will make our stand here." His search finds direction, but it's not mine.

I'm shaken but find our purpose. "Her death needs to be honored. Lenin must know of this. We will find Mr. Dayan in Berlin. Tell him of your victory. Of Lina as a martyr for the Cause. Our Saint Joan. We must tell Lenin of Lina's courage. Her sacrifice must be honored." My misery needs to believe she died for a greater purpose.

"You're right."

But the sound of hooves and whistles put Yitzhak in another temper. "First, we'll kill as many as we have bullets."

The four bodies lay in a path between the cottage and the barn. The Dayans' home is set back a short distance from the nearby village. Our neighbors—a congregation of pious families earn full bellies from trade in cloth. We will be shunned for this blasphemy. They might suffer our punishment for simply being neighbors.

The road was lined with a forest converted into cottages, barns, and villages, but the shrub of bramble and a thick patch of birch and spruce hid the barn and cottage from the road.

She looks into my soul. The stare of death finds me. I suffer in guilt as a coward.

Yitzhak has no heart for such sentiment and carefully studies the beast's arsenal. "The pistols have a clip," counts, "three bullets," grabs three more from the general's belt. Loads the clip and finds two more clips. Eyes the whip, the knife, the rifle.

The whistles and pounding of hooves are close.

I'm imprisoned in the hollow of darkness. I have no faith in God's heaven or this dream that holds Yitzhak in its spell. I'm certain that our battle pierced the ears of Riga's peddlers, but they'll be silenced with a lie of anarchists being killed.

The whistles shout the alert. I press my lips to hers—our second kiss, the first kiss was under a spell. This kiss is goodbye. I try to pull on the loose threads to cover her nakedness. I want to surrender to death. My mind is changed by guilt. I brought her to this. "We'll die here." Death will be a blessing. Torture to live with this memory.

He grips my arm, "No, not here. They'll bury us to hide this victory. A palace must be our battlefield. This story must be told."

The soldiers appear at the end of the path. Shots are fired from fifty paces. Too far for their skill. The distance between us is no more than a few seconds in a brisk stride.

Yitzhak fires two shots to warn them we're ready to fight.

The two soldiers shoot at us from behind the spruce. Yitzhak empties the pistol to open a path. Puts in the extra clip. They duck for cover, and we race from the barn behind the bramble. Bend to sneak along a ditch fouled by the refuse from the rows of shanties. Our escape is along a path so tangled by the web of homes, factories, and shrubs that even a native would lose their way.

Riga is an ancient village tangled in a web of roads. Only a church or temple to tell you where you are. Each direction leads to another danger. West to a wilderness guarded for the treasure of its granite quarry. South leads to the Russian-held farms. The Levins were one of those victims. North is Riga and a certain death by hanging. East would take us along the river, eventually to the lost homes of my family's ghosts.

I think what a blessing that the Dayan left just weeks ago. Mr. Dayan would never have surrendered.

Riga is no longer home, only memories of moments I thought would be forever.

CHAPTER TWENTY-FIVE – Wilderness- 1905

I suffered to leave Lina to wither in a ditch. I suffered for the guilt of having brought evil's misery to our innocent neighbors. I heard the echo of Comrade Lenin's call for revolution — "All is a battlefield, no innocents, all are soldiers." No time to beg forgiveness from those we've cursed.

We make our way along paths of ditch and bramble to an unknown destiny. Riga has no signs to help a wanderer find their way through tribal villages, industry, and nobles' kingdoms.

Where to run? Maybe to hide? But who can we trust? Sickened by guilt, I follow Yitzhak, witless and without direction. We sneak along a dried-out ditch that was last year's flowing creek, surprised to come upon a minion of ten Orthodox huddled on the steps of a peasant's temple.

They want to take no notice of two blood-stained boys. Had they heard the shooting? The distance is measured by the minutes since our escape. A temple will offer no shelter for heathens. The Orthodox don't want to know of pistols or rifles. Their door is closed to heathens who invite trouble.

Clouds of dust are stirred by wagons. The dirt hasn't seen rain for some time. Drought is only good for vultures.

The storm of the chase follows with whistles, shots, and the thunder of cavalry, forcing a path without regard for the innocents. We climb over barrels filled with wool to a solid thatch roof and watch the aimless rampage, police in the fever of revenge, the thunder of cavalry causing a wagon to tip over, and a captain's motorcoach to weave into a road clogged with peddlers' carts. The two little girls were saved at the last second by the courage of a mother's lunge.

The police swarm. The army was ordered to trample with no regard. There'll be beatings, a noose, and another excuse to purge all who are not in the nobles' favor.

We wait for dark and climb down. The race is now a search. Yitzhak sneaks through a maze of clothes hung across rope, children with sticks battling it out, the ones with a nearby mother carried inside, the clamor of routine disrupted. We're not strangers to those we pass. The ghetto has been home. We reach the edge of its border, where roads and streets of homes and businesses darken to the silence of poverty, our path through shanties held together by little more than hope. A trail that dares trespass by any but the rats who can sense a cat. We cling to shadows.

They peer through cracks in a wall or door that offers no protection other than as a sign for no trespass. There'll be no shelter, no sympathy. Everyone heard the whistles and gunshots—innocents and thieves in hiding.

The Russians protect the favored who pay a hefty tax and kneel before their authority. The shopkeepers, bourgeoisie, landlords, merchants, and priests have sidewalks and roads made of stone and not splintered wood or fouled dirt. Their homes are guarded by iron fences, bolted doors, thick shutters, walls of brick, windows with glass—a cocoon purchased with a trade of bribes, but it's a fragile faith that they've bought security.

Thunder alerts patrols. We sneak behind Levi's butcher shop. My boots are stuck in the muck of his cows. I purposely slip toward the trough to dunk my arms and wash off the unholy blood. Bubby would smack me if I drank this fouled water.

"North or south?" Yitzhak turns to me, as if I have the gift of prophecy.

"I'd need the wisdom of Solomon to make such a choice. North will take us through the hives of the gentile bourgeoisie, and the southern path is held by those orphans who are as feral as vermin."

"Find Mr. Dayan in Berlin, and honor Lina. We'll go south."

"Easily lost in the wilderness of Lithuania."

"Follow the coast through Prussia?"

We hear the echo of the cathedral's bell tower strike five times. There are no safe paths—one road out in each direction. The river is the czar's moat, the bridge a gate. The beasts will search for us throughout the city. The wilderness is Nature's test—a forest of the devil's making held by thieves in the disguise of hunters.

Mr. Dayan sold it all to make the long, risky journey by fast train. To leave the station at the center of Riga and arrive at a grand station in Berlin. I think of my family's migration from Warsaw to Vilna. "South to find comrades in Vilna?"

"If not there, Minsk, Lodz, maybe Bialystok?"

It doesn't matter to me. I can't escape Lina's ghost. Only execution would end my nightmare.

"South it is." Yitzhak turns to the river road.

I pull him back. “Checkpoints. How do we explain the blood?”
“Tell them we’re butchers.”
“Better if we keep to the farms.”
We stand on the mounds of the buried and hide behind their tombstones. A cemetery for Jews is an honor only given to those who pay a steep ransom. Most Jews are buried in trenches beyond the ironworks. I suffer more guilt for not giving Lina a proper grave.
Patrols race past.
“We’ll follow the coast. My father showed me where to find precious amber. It’s hidden under mounds of soft sand. Fish instead of grain and vegetables.”
“A boat. Taken on as fishermen and sail to Germany.” He nods as if considering the idea. “The sea can take us anywhere.”
“What do we know of sailing?” I hear my poppa’s warning, “Coast is held by prospectors and soldiers. No more than thieves.” I shake my head. “The sea will show no mercy.”
Yitzhak counts a handful of rubles. “Eighteen,” and turns to me.
I slip my hands into empty pockets. “Left behind.”
We look across a harbor teeming with a dozen schooners and steamers, but we’d be trapped. The dock is heavily patrolled. All passengers are questioned. I remember when Gramps sealed my inheritance in that new boot, I asked if it could buy passage to freedom. “Need more than a silver sovereign,” he said with a moan and grunt, only to realize from his confession that he was saddened that he couldn’t buy passage for us all. He took absolution by telling me, “Wherever you go, life will be a test. The reward is to find joy in nothing and have ambition for something you can believe in.”
The Baltic schooners leave from Riga, and if they go due west for two or three days, they’ll find the Viking’s home of Sweden but risk the czar’s navy. Norway and Finland are said to have the fiercest of wilderness.
Yitzhak has but one dream, “South through Vilna, then west to Berlin.”
“It will take luck to find Mr. Dayan in such a large city.”
We argue over a plan. I would never confess that my dream is to be back with Mrs. Dayan.
We watch the cavalry ride past with torches marking their path.
“Our tale won’t be allowed to spread. Few will learn that four beasts were killed. Defeat is never mentioned. Only our neighbors will know that

evil had visited. To speak of such things is an invitation to exile or execution. The murder of the Czar's guardians will arouse investigation. The Mayor will learn. The Czar would know. Losing four of his palace guards will stoke his majesty's prideful embers to flames. A bribe will be paid to those police bold enough to extract a ransom, or more likely, they'll be shot. The police know us. "Dayan's apprentices." In time, there will be posts with our likeness. But our crime will be as thieves, not murderers. We served Lenin well, but the truth is that a reluctant comrade helped light Lenin's match, which will be his secret. Stealing has the same punishment as murder. We'll be on lists.

I look back and feel sickened. I leave Riga not with a full purse and the pride of a craftsman, but as an anarchist in worn-out boots that hold a pitiful inheritance. I don't need to wonder what my family would think.

Our pace is forced to a crawl. The wilderness looms as a dark shadow on a nearby horizon, and with each step closer, it grows more foreboding.

The wind stirs the fir and spruce, casting hauntings. We leave the road, make our own path through a field of overgrown straw, and enter the forest as blind men.

Pricked by dangling branches, my legs are burning sticks. The day's nightmare tortures my heart. "I need to rest."

Yitzhak shows no regard. I follow out of loyalty for another mile, but festering in heartbreak, I surrender. Let him boast of lighting the spark for revolution without me. I search the stars of a moonless night for God's answer. No matter my oath to forget such a fable, the grandfather I imagined as God is summoned by a mind spinning with doubt—that this foolish boy wants to believe in a merciful God. I search for the brightest star. The one my Bubby had me pick. "Everyone has their own star." I believed her when she told me, "Yours is the brightest, and it always leads to the north."

My wishful prayer was soon lost to a gust that brings the forest's shadows to life. Branches twitch like the scratching of vermin. There's an owl's murmur, and the nasty cry of crows.

Yitzhak's soul is hardened by hate, unaware for the moment that I surrendered to rest, but he won't leave me in peace and turned back to remind me that I swore an oath to exact revenge and laid down beside me.

Even though it was a lie, I swore in writing to sell my tarnished soul to the revolution. I have little faith we can slay all the beasts, but I was willing to sacrifice my life to save her. I was ready to take the bullet for

Yitzhak. I can hear Lina telling me, as if she's beside me, *Go do battle and not have pity or guilt for my fate. What better death than serving a righteous cause.* I found courage only from the desire to save my friends, but it was lost the moment she left my side.

What is her reward? To be forever frozen in the vengeful stare of a soul lost in darkness, or the glory of God's blessing for a rebel's courage.

I want to find a path forward, but to what dream? Poppa calls down from a nearby heaven: "You'll starve if not a patient trapper."

Need a good pond for bait. Forest offers no charity, no mercy.

The city tempts with desire. It struts about in grandeur. Homes, churches, temples, the nobles' towers full of pride, and the bourgeoisie's stores of treasures that excite greed.

I'm a peddler, not a warrior. A peddler is better suited to tell the story of her sacrifice. I would explain to Yitzhak that I will earn honor as a preacher. To lead the exodus not as a warrior but as a teacher. He will think of me as a coward, so I say nothing. I will follow him because he's guided by passion in faith, full of hope, and it's my hope that passion will rub off on me.

CHAPTER TWENTY-SIX-Wilderness, Oct.1905

Not long after the glow of sunrise softens the shadows, the mask of silence is ripped by thunder as bullets strip bark from nearby trees.

"Hunters?"

"Cossacks?"

We race from our bed of leaves. I stumble over mounds, ditches, rocks, and roots, and look back to find only shadows. He's as nimble as a deer. I can't keep up, but can't argue to slow down, he'd curse my despair.

He stops to press his ear to the wind. "We lost them?" Slows his pace. The fear of chase fades into a battle with the forest.

"We keep going. There has to be a village or farm." He kicks me hard enough to get me off resting on a fallen tree. We climb a hill and reach the peak—only to discover this wilderness has no end.

We wandered lost without a sign of life, for three days we hadn't found berries, mushrooms, or Bubby's healing weeds. Not a lake, river, or pond that hasn't turned to muck. But Yitzhak is driven by an oath of vengeance; there will be no surrender.

But I know the ways of the wilderness. "Need to find a stream, a pond, and set traps. Can't be stirring about if we're going to catch anything."

The labyrinth of pine, spruce, and fir. A drought's brittle needles poke, bite, and scratch.

By the fifth day, we're familiar with the test of hunger, but thirst is another depth of punishment.

God's mercy, luck, or fate, day six, and we're rewarded by a shallow pond. A handful soothes the pain of thirst, but a pond has many rewards. I found the sweet nectar of ripe blueberries. The pond is too shallow for fish, but it's a wellspring. I search for a snake, a frog, a rabbit, any critter worth eating.

I snap my hand quickly enough to snatch the frog. Find three more. This is my heaven.

Yitzhak is on the prowl while I soak my crusted skin under the pond's healing mud, and crawl onto the bank to find, by some divine mercy, a peaceful sleep that gives me rest from the madness.

Yitzhak is intent on a better prize. He follows known tracks. Finds the rabbit's hole, but as he works hard to dig it out, he freezes at the sound of the rattle. It slithers from the hole, coiling around his boot.

He strikes first and grabs it by the neck. The rattler shakes the beads of its tail to make its threat, opens its jaw wide, bares its fangs, but Yitzhak wraps his fingers around its neck, a twist, battle won.

He stacks a pile of kindling, takes my flint, strikes his knife, and draws a spark to set a fire. He gives no regard to being found.

I was taught to know poison from the good. The frogs are green, not the bad brown toads with spots. Frogs are better eating than the snake's bony flesh, but we trade hunger for a welcome stomachache. I know the cure and pick thistle, dandelion, mushrooms, and Bubby's good weeds that soothe a stomach put back to work.

He wants to leave, but I beg Yitzhak for another day to prove the pond's worth. I show him tracks, "Racoon."

He studies the prints, "Maybe a badger. Beaver?"

"A pond is a good lure. Traps will keep us fed."

Yitzhak is restless for battle.

I want to stay here as a deserter. I need to prove this is paradise and dig a hole as deep as a rabbit's and then balance a heavy rock with a thorny stick. Worms and the skin of the frog as bait.

But before I set a second trap, Yitzhak returns all excited, yells, "Come!" He grabs my arm to lead us along a path worn by wagons into deep grooves.

Hidden behind tall grass, we reach a clearing of trees cut to stumps. Each tree was evenly cut to just below a tall man's hip. At its end is an opening carved from a wall of spruce. Not knowing what trouble might lie on the other side, we spy through the branches, surprised to find a circle of white cottages—as if from a dream or fable.

Yitzhak climbs an old elm for a better view, and I follow. From our high perch, I count ten cottages made holy for having five sides, each with a red door topped by a triangle at its peak—a sign only these pious would understand. The village is brought into communion by a church at its center. Their faith in Jesus is made known by the five spires, each topped with a Catholic's simple Cross, not with the extra branch or the tilted leg of the Russian Orthodox.

Between the forest and the cottage, there's a pasture of tall green grass dotted with sheep and goats. We climb down.

“They’re pious. We should be welcome.”

“I don’t see anyone.”

We crouch, slink our way between the sheep and goats, slowly, calmly, and cross the pasture. When we reach the nearest cottage, our gaze is distracted by a small square window set so high that Yitzhak needs to stand on his toes to look inside. Says in a whisper, “A gentry’s home.” Taken to mean it shows comfort.

We turn the corner. Another window, also set high, and painted with a ghoulish devil ruling over sinners from a throne of fire.

There’s music coming from the church. No one is outside. All must be inside. Sunday? We cross to the southern side. A godly grandfather painted on the glass. “Catholic? Christian?”

Moments later, a joyous hymn gave way to the sound of children playing. We crouch down. Peer around the side of the house with caution. Watch a parade of families. Mothers and daughters are draped in gowns of well-loomed cloth as golden-haired angels. The fathers and sons wear matching white tunics that hang from shoulder to hip. Norseman. The light-colored hair and posture of Germans.

Two proud women, of the age when hair is white, stand tall beside two elders made wise by beards as long as their years. The elders are given honor with longer robes, tied at the waist with a red sash.

A boy, half my age, but already a man’s size, spots us. Brave or foolish, he comes running without fear, arms flailing, and lets out a yell as if to rid a ghost from their home.

Yitzhak emerges from hiding, takes a few steps toward the boy, and says in Latvian, “Friends, no trouble.”

Boy stares—says nothing.

We’ve drawn the attention of the fathers, and one calls out to the boy, who retreats without lowering his stare, inching backward.

I join Yitzhak, “They’re pious,” I want to think, “Charitable?”

I offer a trade to the fathers in Latvian, “We can pay.” I tell Yitzhak, “Hold out a ruble.”

We’re two mongrels stained in mud and blood. The women push their wide-eyed children toward the cottages.

The fathers stand guard.

Yitzhak brings the same fear as a bear.

The priest wears a regal, long white robe. His tall crown is trimmed in red and gold, with a gold cross studded with a five-sided amber stone. The symbol of piety dangles on a gold chain. The Priest clasps his hands in reverence. “Man’s blood?”

Yitzhak shakes his head, “Vermin,” and turns away, murmurs in Russian, “Threat would be better,” spits, and I see his hand reaching for his knife.

The Priest peers into our souls. “Repent your sins before you ask kindness from the Lord’s servants,” said in German, and he turned his back to enter the holy church.

Yitzhak’s temper holds him captive. He calls after the priest with a curse of his own— “What sort of god shows no love for the needy?” Repeats his curse on the fathers. They have no sympathy for pagans.

Yitzhak lifts the bucket from the well. Takes a sip. He’s about to pull his knife, but I beg, “We’re not to win any favors with a threat. They are pious. Women and children. I poke his tunic. “Blood stains are a curse— “Hard enough to earn trust.”

“Blood or not, the pious give no love, save for their own.”

I argue on behalf of the pious— “You have given them reason.”

An explosion. The sheep scattered. He lowers the pistol. The shot was meant as a threat. His grin is pursed as a warning.

Yitzhak chases after a lamb, but there’s another shot. The men have pulled their guns from beneath their tunics. “Let’s go.”

He surrenders in retreat. The field gives way to a border of spruce. No matter the blue sky of a cool fall day, Yitzhak makes it impossible to enjoy the blessing of nature’s freedom.

Another poor farm. The farmer and his three older sons guard their two cows with rifles and pitchforks.

A peaceful sleep under the stars.

Awake rested, bowels are more content to push out the meal of frogs, snake, and plants without suffering, and take a decent piss from that pond water.

The forest gives way to open fields, and by midday, we came upon three shacks that are no more than a hovel for critters.

Four children take turns throwing rocks at the crows. An ageless woman in layers of black rags sits with her head slumped. Her tattered shawl, ripped jacket, and torn dress bring pity. She doesn’t look up from the throne of a well-chiseled stone step. The shanty’s holiness is made known by the ghost of a cross over the splintered door. She holds out her hand to beg.

"Give her a ruble."

"A ruble gets them nothing but another day in hell." Yitzhak has no sympathy. "She needs to move on."

But on the other side of this shtetl is another manner of hell. The scarred remains of a forest burned by the curse of lightning. Nature as cruel as the czar in doling out punishment.

We don't stop until well beyond hell's grip.

The next day, there are open fields of flowers and weeds that show traces of once being tilled, and on the other side of a dried-out stream, we come to a wall of heavy rocks piled as high as Yitzhak is tall. He stands on his toes to see what's on the other side.

"A palace!"

I fear he was heard, "Quiet." I search for guardians on patrol.

Yitzhak shakes his head— "A hundred cows, a hillside of sheep," climbs higher— "A lake!" without regard for being found

I warn him, "A prince would have an army."

He climbs the wall. I panic and pull on his boot, begging him to stop, but he kicks me away. He takes hold of his knife. "Better to kill this prince!"

"A coward and warrior against an army?"

"I don't see an army." He points toward the lake, "We'll die of thirst while staring at a sea."

"And for lack of a ruble, we would starve at a tavern while others feast, such is the law of ownership that takes only one side."

Yitzhak's rage was forged as a boy raised as a mule and dog, and from the prophet's preaching, his hate was riled to a rabid comrade. "We'll wait. Dark soon enough. We'll take a lamb. Meat for a week."

"Let's go a bit further. If there's no stream or pond, we'll come back and take our chances." I wonder which of us is the fool.

Yitzhak shows no sympathy for my ills and fears.

The lake was a good omen. Not a mile down the path, and we come to a stream that flows under the wall. We follow its path until we need to hack our way through a web of bramble until we find a pond.

While drowning our thirst, we can see under the clear water, good-sized fish. I'm all excited and try to grab a fish, fall in, swim after, but the fish scatter. I climb out and think of fishing with bait. The ivy's long stem will work as a string, but I have nothing to make a hook.

Yitzhak carves a spear and jumps in.

While he lunges and curses, I think of Poppa's trick. I take off my pants, tie the bottom, wade in, and tell Yitzhak to hold one end, "I'll hold the other. Maybe one will be curious enough to swim in?"

Our feet sink into the soft mud bottom, dragging my pants as a net. A few more tries, but the fish know better.

"Let's be still." We stand like statues. They're lurking about. He's about to give up when one comes close. Yitzhak argues to spear it, but I tell him in frustration, "Give this a chance. It can work."

Patience is rewarded. I slide the pant leg and grab it shut, trapping a good-sized fish. I can just hear Gramps's lesson on patience.

Yitzhak sparks a fire. He knows nothing of risk, but only the reward.

"A better trap will be to weave a basket and load it with bait."

As the fish cooks, I start pulling on vines and tall grass and weaving the basket as I was taught.

A good fish cooked over a fire. I feel at home and enjoy a restful night's sleep.

The next morning, all excited, I dig up the worms and shove the four wigglers into the long basket, add the rock, and sink it into the pond.

"This is my dream of heaven."

Yitzhak holds no regard for my dream of heaven and wanders off.

I jump in fully clothed. My curiosity sets me off toward a far end covered by what I thought was a fallen tree, but as I get close to the mound of tangled branches, the water starts to churn. Dark shadows swim toward me. The fallen tree is a dam. I've trespassed.

I know the beaver's teeth are as long and sharp as knives. They're fast. I'll lose the race to the shore. I have one chance to bluff, but I must do so with certainty. I smacked the water and kicked about, and thankfully, the beaver retreated from my bluff.

Yitzhak had seen the battle and was sharpening his spear. "Stay there. You'll be bait."

I ignore his taunts, slip off my jacket, pants, shirt, and Long Johns. Clean off the remains of blood, and dive under to retrieve the basket—break water, celebrate, "A fish." The trap worked. A funnel the fish can squirm through to get in, but it becomes a spear when they try to get out.

While I bask in paradise and imagine this becoming home, Yitzhak is in a hurry to find the revolution. He argues to leave. "This is the life you dream of. No purpose, no cause to battle for."

“Maybe not forever, but winter is coming. We’ll trap the beavers. Fur coats, meat, and a pond of fish. What more could we want?”

A grim stare. “To just survive. We’ve been called to revolution.”

“One more day.” He puts me to the test. I’m at a fork in our road. I’d take this one. Beaver, fish, eventually deer, raccoons, any critter living near here will be coming by. But I also know the forest has beasts. Beyond wolves or bears, a rattler or vermin, this generous pond might belong to the prince or a trapper. Am I trespassing?

“You took an oath. You lied?”

I followed Yitzhak, maybe in loyalty, perhaps fear, but it wasn’t for revolution; my bait was the lure of city life. I can taste the dumplings, latkes, bread, butter, eggs, salt, sugar, and tonic with good meals. My curiosity is stirred by the tumult, quenched by books and respect for the skill of craftsmen. The city as art. It pained me to give up heaven.

I dry two fish over the embers, pick mushrooms and find patches of dandelions and weeds, but in a rush to take along a store of food, I pull on the wrong weed. The three-leaf poison is held by a long vine. Without studying, I pulled a leaf, about to eat it, but I was saved when I heard Mamma shouting, “God forbid you even touch the weed with pointy leaves of three.” I looked at it. I was about to eat Poison Ivy. I quickly rub off the poison with a hard rub using dirt. I pick dandelions and thistles to rub in their healing potion.

The wilderness gives way to fields shorn of the summer crop. On the horizon is a small stone church, made holy by a simple steeple topped by the white Cross.

CHAPTER TWENTY-SEVEN – Vilna – Oct.1905

We follow the westerly current of a river that widens and deepens as we leave behind the generous pastures and farms worthy of a noble to shrink with each mile to no more than rows of small homes with barely room for a garden. The dirt road widens from a trickle of a few peddlers to cobblestone boulevards. The tumult takes a spirit calmed by isolation and leaves it to struggle with a squirrelly fever.

Vilna is more forested and hillier than Riga, less a busy port, although a wide river divides the city. Riga has ever-changing neighborhoods, while Vilna has pushed poverty to the outskirts. But its cobblestone streets and painted homes, brick and plaster, are a reflection of the city I miss, and would call home if not for the troubles. Vilna has more Poles, Germans, and Lithuanians thriving as a well-traveled path at the crossroads between Warsaw, Berlin, Riga, and St. Petersburg. It's a holy city of colorful spires reaching the clouds. Poppa once said, "Vilna's Litvaks are as bees. They never stop buzzing about in search of pollen to make honey."

Uncle Moshe said Vilna was a battlefield of piety. Christians, Jews, and Catholics declare themselves to be the most pious in the face of the Czar trying to convert all to Russian Orthodox. Tithe as a tax. Poppa wondered how the Hebrews survived this millennium-long migration from Egypt, reaching as far north as Vilna, Riga, and Moscow. To have survived the Ottoman Muslim empire, even to have flourished for a time in Constantinople, and always to have migrated north. Kiev, to Odessa, through Galicia to Warsaw, spreading in all directions, he asked, "Are we pioneers in search of greener pastures, fleeing prejudice, or pursuing opportunity?"

The Czar wants the tithe, and lures with the bait of grander cathedrals topped with fanciful domes tipped with swirls of green, red, and gold. His Central Square is marked by the cathedral and bordered by two- and three-story palaces trimmed by craftsmen with the skill of Mr. Dayan. The central square is a hub with spokes leading to different neighborhoods. Store windows proudly display treasures—watches, frilly hats, polished shoes… Nobles strut about in finery. Their homes and carriages show their wealth. Vilna is more than Riga.

Yitzhak argues against this show of wealth, as would my family. "Should be owned by the craftsmen who made such a beautiful home. What does the artist get? A few kopeks a day."

A patrol of five well-armed police pushes us into the alley. The officer with a twirled mustache and trimmed beard gives orders in Lithuanian and repeats in Russian— "To your side," thinks himself a prince, and poked by bayonets through alleys until reaching a wooden bridge.

We follow a procession of workers and peddlers over the narrow peasant's bridge made of wood. I can't help staring in awe at the Czar's bridge of iron and stone. Sundown, Jews forbidden on the Gentile's side. A rule known from Riga. Men and women, children to elders, wheel the carts with the wares, food, and clothes that didn't sell.

Our rags stand out against the Hasidic and Orthodox wear the pious uniform of black suits, white shirts, and show their pride with the round fur of a shtriemel. Fedoras made holier with wide brims. Yiddish and Hebrew warm my ears. So many that Vilna becomes a homeland.

A bookstore is crammed with more books than the Russian school's library. Its peddler sits in the shelter of a stall. I read the posted broadsides—a synagogue's desire to be the soul of the community.

I'm drawn to a shelf stacked with gold-embossed leather covers. The Russian books are familiar, from Pushkin to Dostevesky and Chekhov. The German books are about science, medicine, and the history of Greece and Rome. The longest row of books is the familiar stories of a Jew's misery and joy.

The bearded clerk is rabbinical, a professor, wears a tattered black suit, and an Orthodox fedora. He asks me in Hebrew if he can help. Yitzhak had snuck in behind me and had me ask, "Marx?"

The clerk studies us. Shakes his head. "Don't know of this?" but there's a grin, a nod, "We have only what the Czar permits," and turns to help another customer.

The cathedral of a temple commands the entrance to the ghetto. An elder with a lifelong white beard and the longest locks of payos that dangle from the round fur hat, but it's the shinier and longer black suit of a rebbe that is his declaration of pride that he's a Hasidic of importance. Through round glasses, he stares into my eyes. His white beard is also a nest of snow speckled with crumbs. He pulls me to his side. A firm grip, surprised that he takes my wrist, and then motions to the heavens to call to

God—“Awaken this lost boy’s soul to your Light.” The missionary won’t let go. “Come with me.”

Yitzhak pushes him away with such a temper that he scares the preacher, “Only fools have faith in otherworldly dreams. Go pray to your merciless God for answers when the Cossacks burn your temple.”

The row of peddlers tempts us. Yitzhak knows my weakness and pulls me away from the bakery—tempted by the joy of cities bought for a coin over needing to match wits with the wilderness for hard-earned meals.

Pious to pagan, rich to poor, all keep to their own, segregated by language, worship, poverty, and wealth. A city of hundreds of thousands, brought to communion by commerce.

A parade of the pious Jews passes by. Yitzhak mocks with a curse—“The czar’s sheep!”

The Chasidics protect their holy spirit in isolation but flaunt their identity with the headdress of a towering shtriemel and dangling their piety with the payot—God’s laws interpreted as a tailor and barber.

The Orthodox favor a wide-brimmed black hat. The more prideful of the flock wear a bowler with a bowtie. We turn from the Square’s temple I thought was a cathedral, and hear Bubby’s lament, “Not to show your treasure.” Is there a bribe or trade for such a sanctuary?

A better neighborhood shines with a row of homes made of brick or mortar over stone. They would laugh at Yitzhak—I warn him to calm his preaching— “Won't convert a full belly to go hungry as a comrade.”

Yitzhak pulls me into an alley, “We need to go to the factories and mills. There’s no hope for these golden sheep.”

We sleep among fellow wanderers, thieves, and orphans, but Yitzhak’s preaching against the Czar and master finds no recruits even among the hungry and hateful. He’s mocked for such a dream. “Why would we kill the bear to face a fox?”

I plead for the only job offered, and shovel manure to earn a ruble. It’s enough for a small loaf and a slice of cheese. But Yitzhak is intent on preaching to the factory workers, who ask if being a comrade earns bread and ale.

On the third day, the fancy man who does the hiring each morning, I learn had earned the noble’s favor with a contract to clean the roads of manure and convert dirt to a paved road, promotes me from shoveling manure to hauling stone.

At the end of the day, I join the line to receive my coin, but the fancy man makes me beg for the ruble. Yitzhak was watching while trying to recruit the laborers and noticed the shame. I catch him out of the corner of my eye and race to keep him from beating the fancy man to death. "He is not worth prison." The man's top hat comes off to retrieve more coins.

At night, thieves disturb our sleep, but Yitzhak only needs to stand tall and show his size to end the threat.

Women prove the better thief. They tempt with no need for threat. Yitzhak keeps me from spending the hard-earned ruble. "A whore is no more than a thief." I would have gladly paid to learn the ways of sin.

A synagogue of such artistry, having just been built, the last of the bricks put on just two years ago, and I look inside. A church of pillars, pews, a towering ceiling, and a wooden pulpit carved by a Mr. Dayan. The members are polite, a nod, their pride hidden, humble, bonded as comrades, and their blessings won by trading loyalty to the Czar for the freedom of prayer, have me longing to be a comrade in their congregation. They have faith in the future, but such splendor is only pride, not hope.

Our skin is scarred by the vengeful of bedmates: ants, spiders, and lice. I argue to spend a ruble for bath and lodging, but Yitzhak takes pride in the scars.

By day four, we've crossed the city's length and breadth and searched for comrades among the Polish villages. Catholics and sinners both come with the same argument— "With what cannon, what musket? And then who will be our master?"

That night, we thought we found a reward of soft grass and the serenity of the city's noise muffled by distance. Lost, exhausted, we fall to sleep in an instant on a well-groomed patch of soft grass.

"Move it!" kicked awake. Rousted by hard smacks. "Holy ground." Lit by his lantern, we realize we're in the garden of a church. The two soldiers wear the cross as a badge on tall caps, and pistols in their grips.

I take him by the arm before he can reach for his knife. I repeat the pledge— "Not worthy. Not here. Not tonight," and bow to explain to the guardians of this Holy ground, "Our mistake."

Only the alleys between mills and factories are allowed as beds for the homeless, orphans, and sinners. A battle between drunks and fearless rats to stake a bed of dirt.

Day five, we continue our search for comrades but turn to the Czar's mill and forge. Workers shuffle past on their way to labor. Yitzhak asks if a day's labor will fill their belly or provide a bed. Their eyes show that they're comrades in spirit, but we're forced to surrender our preaching by bayonets and cavalry.

I return to earning a ruble for laying stone over dirt. "Thirty stones cut clean," and the bulldog of a beast hands me a hammer and chisel.

The new road is opposite a fine inn, so the chore is lessened by pretty maidens serving meals to the gentry. The shikhas willingly bend to display their bosom for an extra coin.

To chisel thirty rocks into a block needs a good pace, but I'm slowed by the distraction of the barmaids. The man beside me chips stone twice as fast, laughing at my carving as if I were sculpting a statue. "Put that thought away." Nods to the inn, "That'll be four silvers for the meal, warm bath, and bed. She'll want at least a gold coin to take you upstairs and make you a man." His laugh riles me to work faster, even though my hands hurt from new blisters. The softness caused by weeks on the road without chores.

Yitzhak wouldn't take on labor. Preaching is his labor, but his arrogance, short temper, and threats earn no willing comrades. He calls on me to take up the chore. I find no shortage among my fellow mason for want of revenge, but lose the lesson when asked, "To fight with what against so many." My doubt remains, but I'd ask, we kill the beasts, but then what? Who will chisel the stone?

It's the end of the day, about to be paid, our crew of ten had added another ten paces of cobblestone to the dirt road, the bourgeoisie nod with regard, the barmaids smile, toasts by the fortunate, the fine carriages struggle against the cliff of stone to dirt, when we hear a loud chant coming from around the corner of the inn.

Nine sturdy men are banging hammers against chisels, cursing threats—coming for our line of ten, the master retreating behind his two thick guards.

"You've taken our job!"

'A strike!' Yitzhak looks at me in shock. "We dishonored a strike!" He pushes away the two Russian guardians, grabs the master who rules our squad of laborers, and with his hands to the middle-aged fancy man's jacket collar, he vents his rage— "You made us the scum of thieves!" The guards grab him, but he manages to push the master into the arms of the nine men whose job we took.

Whistles in the distance. I pull hard on his arm and point to the crowd.

"The Police have been rousted."

Yitzhak pushes me away. He lets go of the master and turns to the nineteen workers. "Comrades. We make this our battlefield!" The workers are caught between Yitzhak's war cry, the threat of guardians, and the oncoming herd of police. His temper boils. "Are you sheep or men!" The police are soldiers, like cavalry, rifles drawn, galloping down the boulevard, not a moment away. They're a squad of six, four on horse, two racing at us with pistols raised.

Yitzhak calls on the men, "Unite as brothers and burn this unholy city!"

They look at him as if he's a madman. The biggest stands against Yitzhak, "This is our home. We're masons," said with pride, "Another silver coin is all we want."

The prince bows to the leader. He sees no profit in war. "You are indeed masons. These are peasants," looks down on our crew, the ten paces deemed a meager return on investment. "An extra silver."

We're surrounded by the soldiers, strikers, my crew, the prince, and the shocked bystanders.

The Prince throws our wages on the ground. The ten silver coins roll about. He laughs as we scramble to pick it up.

The police aren't satisfied. They want blood and begin to kick and hit us with clubs. I would argue that we're innocent; we were doing the master's labor, not the protest of strikers, but Yitzhak poisoned the well.

My fellow laborers suffer the taunts of the master, the striking crew, and the police, and retreat down the unpaved boulevard.

A peddler shakes the handles of his cart of iron pans and calls to Yitzhak, "And who will bury us!"

Another night fighting off the rats in the alley of orphans and thieves.

CHAPTER TWENTY-EIGHT – Road –Oct. 1905

There is one well-traveled road from Vilna to Berlin along a dangerous path through the Prussian wilderness. Poppa was a keen student of history and warned me about this journey with stories of this feudal kingdom whose early ancestors pillaged Rome. Surrounded by enemies, their sons were bred to be fierce Teutonic warriors. A possession of the Austrians, they were forced at the turn of the 19th century to unite with their German cousins to defend against Napoleon and the Russian czar.

Yitzhak's fever for revolution has me long for the routine of laboring with a shovel, chisel, or broom. I side with those who see only death in protest. Gramps would say, "Rid us of one beast, and another will follow." I was bred to be a peddler, but my dream is to have a bakery, find a good wife, and pass down my lessons to my children. I should have married Ruth and kept our farm in the isolation of the wilderness. We'd gaze upon the stars at night and spend our days baking cookies and bread.

We were at the western edge of the city when we were greeted by a farmer who plays host as a tavernkeeper in front of his barn. The middle-aged Lithuanian expresses no love for anyone—"I curse all I serve as beggars and thieves. I ask for a silver and get a kopek if lucky." He lends a comrade's ear to Yitzhak's talk of revolution but shows us a worried glance at the mention of a journey through Prussia. "South to Warsaw would be where you should go." The Innkeeper has no love for Russians or Marxists, only for two silver coins for the two pints and a basket of bread. "Road to Warsaw is a parade of crows in migration." He leans close, "Warsaw has comrades. I hear of protests, strikes, and murdering Russians. No bank, cart, or store is safe from thieves."

We were given his nod to sleep on the floor.

I won the argument, "Better to find the revolution in Warsaw than die on the road to Berlin." Yitzhak's excuse was calculating the odds of finding Mr. Dayan in a city with hundreds of thousands.

The road from Vilna to Warsaw is busy with wagons, carts, and soldiers on horseback who threaten for a coin. It's not long before finding another village, a little further, we'd see a shack, a wife, mother, daughter, children, peddlers serving ale and bread. An hour or so later, there'd be a church nestled among farms.

A week without suffering anything more than spending rubles on bread, cheese, ale, meat, bed or floor, a butcher, a baker, a general store, and the master's fine home at the edge of a sprawling farm. Nearby would be his sheriff's jail. The height of the church steeple marks prosperity.

We're getting close to Warsaw as the pastures get smaller, villages come sooner, and the road is crowded with travelers who only want to beg, trade, preach, or steal, but none want to hear Yitzhak's preaching.

Homes are inns run by the mother setting the rules, a wife doing the cooking, daughters pouring the ale, and boys cleaning up and serving chicken or pig, cow or deer, with bread, and cheese, while the fathers and grandfathers watch for trouble. They answer Yitzhak with the only question they want an answer to— "Less tax if we threaten revolt?"

Closer to Warsaw, and he draws a louder crowd. More curses for a sheriff, mayor, or noble, but none take Yitzhak's oath. Pistols drawn by loyalists owing their full purse to the grace of nobles.

Days went by spoiled by hot meals with another coin gone.

Down to our last few coins, I ask the Catholic innkeeper if there's anything we can do to earn a meal, but as with anywhere, sides are drawn by faith, custom, and hunger.

At the edge of the city, we find a village of Jews with two taverns, a row of rooming houses, and a synagogue as long as a barn and as narrow as its eighteen rows of pews. Eighteen being a good number.

I whispered to Mr. Kietzel, the tavernkeeper whose village is a congregation of Orthodox, "I'm a grandson taught the recipe by my bubby. Hid the bottles between the two floors of our wagon." The secrets to the recipe earns kinship and trust.

I build the secret drawer inside a cabinet, wedged under the bar.

Yitzhak takes the axe to a tree.

The greater reward than good vodka, ale, and a bed stuffed with wool was that Yitzhak's fever was cooled by a full day of chopping trees and working up a sweat.

CHAPTER TWENTY-NINE - Warsaw - 1905

The steeples are mountains in the distance. They give notice that Warsaw is the grandest of the Czar's capitals. Checkpoints are manned by regal troops and collect a toll if going over the bridge to the nobles' boulevard. There's a line of wagons, workers, peddlers, and motorwagons waiting to cross a wooden bridge.

On the other side of the river are brick mills and factories of such size as to hold a hundred horses and cows if a barn. The towers are chimneys blowing black smoke. Warsaw is both Vilna and Riga combined.

The fishermen stretch out big nets between two boats. Two pull hard on long oars while four hold the net.

A captain has a hundred men under his command. He gives orders to roust, threaten, and fleece. Forced to stand in a row. He's a regal officer with the gold helmet of nobility that gives him the license to dictate a man's fate. His lieutenants perform the inquisitions, and by some rule decreed by the Czar, a verdict is made as to who will be loaded into one of three wagons. The livestock of boys and men is kept under guard.

But there's a protest by a pack of five workers. Their faces are darkened by whatever mine or fire they work over. They stand as one, sharing the spirit of protest; when threatened, four more join.

The officers' uniforms are aristocratic. Red, blue, and bronze helmets with plumes, the soldiers wear brown. Their rifles shoot six bullets from a clip. The shots will come fast and straight. We've seen it in action.

The band of young men are wearing gray or blue overalls. They stand tall against bayonets. Their leader cries out, "We work at the Czar's forge as his serfs, what more can we give."

The crowd backs away. Yitzhak and I watch at the rear of a long line of workers and wagons.

The general on a white steed with the authority of a gold helmet, waves his crop with a flourish. "Send him to hell." The lieutenant shoots the leader.

The regiment aim their rifles at the eight remaining strikers. They raise their hands in surrender.

Two soldiers lift the body from the road and throw the young man into the river. The current washes him away without regard. I thought that he'd be caught in a fisherman's net, but I watched in shock as they lifted their nets, leaving him to be swept away as if he never existed.

Any protest is quickly silenced. The wagons are led away.

The men bow and dutifully pay the toll.

Yitzhak is shaking, mutters, "One was willing to die. One!"

We leave the main road and wander behind a row of stores. Crates line the alley, and we're surprised by four good-sized young men. They wave their guns, but only to scare us off.

Yitzhak startles them by pushing the crate aside and staring down the thief behind the pistol. "Did you see what just happened?"

"Punishment for the murder of the mayor. We all pay."

"They were taking conscripts?"

"Some to the army. More likely the mines." He warms to Yitzhak with a lightened grin. "Jews go to a mill or a factory." A silver Cross dangles on a chain. The three others lower their gun.

Yitzhak preaches revolution, to which the gangster replies, "Our cause is treasure not to be shot for some dream."

So many miles on the soles of our boots that my coin will soon be revealed. But saved by cobblestone roads worn smooth.

A boy waves a newspaper.

Yitzhak looks over my shoulder, "What's it say?"

"A Jew murdered the Mayor's tax collector." I read the report. "Said by a Marxist."

"We've found our comrades."

I'm sickened. Warsaw is cursed. I turn away and look at a river cluttered with barges. I count three with trees, two with grain, and one with coal. A mile of docks, men unloading the cargo onto wagons. The city is the mill and forge receiving grain and iron.

Fancy horsemen give no regard for the motorcars—all in madness.

Our day is a journey from the ghetto to trespass into their mountains of palaces, cathedrals, and grand homes. Who but a Czar can bend God's creation to their will?

The cavalry owns the boulevards. Poland suffers from being surrounded by the ambitions of Austria, Germany, Prussia, and Russia.

Yitzhak stops a man in the gray overalls and asks in Yiddish if he's a comrade. Hearing 'comrade,' he quickens his pace, the same as Riga and Vilna. The people are devout only for gold and silver coins, paper money, and dumplings covered in onions. A bitter ale costs double in this city.

Everything is much more expensive. Even the pious Hasidic can be seen hustling between shops, peddlers plying their trade for what I don't know.

We dodge fancy buggies. The bourgeois strut about dressed in finery. Noble women parade by as if on a mission in wheel-sized hats, bows and feathers, satin not cloth, a tangle of ruffles. Wealth is everywhere. The rich wear high-starched collars, ties rather than bow ties, and the shopkeeper's bowlers more than the Orthodox fedora. They dwell in the heaven of a gilded world.

Need to navigate against a current of Hasidics to Orthodox who own shops that are tended by merchants showing their pride in success with fine suits, with glass windows and fancy signs. A grand temple made of large stone blocks occupies one corner of the Central Square. Across is a palace of four stories that had such a congregation that I needed to cross the busy road of trucks, wagons, carts, and motorcoaches to realize it wasn't a synagogue, but a giant general store like I never could have imagined.

It's a palace of a store so grand that even Yitzhak can't resist taking a closer look. We sneak inside under the cover of women's dresses and hats that bulge and billow.

The suited shopkeepers peddle from behind fine cabinets inside this nest of dark wood carved into paneling. They wear the same fancy clothes as their customers. I listen in as angels dangle treasure, but mindlessly, I bump into a cart. Not my fault. She purposely set out the tray of candies to tempt a sale. Her cane was held at the ready. The matron smacks my wrist to let me know there'll be no thieving fingers.

I'm pushed by the flow of shoppers toward fur coats hanging on racks. The fur is the best of a trapper's season: beaver, fox, and mink.

They smell like flowers. I smell like the dirt of a long road.

Noticed and not welcome, the young nobles confront me as vermin, a rat in the store. Gallant warriors need little courage to be a lady's hero.

I crouch behind cabinets to sneak my escape through the maze. I find Yitzhak in a far corner, caught under the spell of wooden ships, painted soldiers, and men's toys of compasses, watches, and telescopes.

I plead in a whisper, "We need to leave."

The policeman comes fast, waves his club in one hand and a pistol in the other. Yitzhak awakens to join me as we rush to join the flock of feathered ladies heading out the door.

But we're caught in a trap. The soldiers come from both directions. Four of them poke our backs with long bayonets to force us to the shadows of an alley. The officer questions our business.

I'm quick with an excuse that would be my dream. In Russian, "Carpenters hired for millwork but couldn't find the man who hired us."

The fatherly Russian softens his grip to warn me, "Past sunset."

The same law everywhere, but our trespass had been a worthy risk for such a feast.

The Policeman points to the streetlamps, "Need to be gone before they're lit."

The alley is a well-groomed dirt road tended by tailored groomsmen and carriage drivers. The wide path is between the backs of palatial homes. Even the stable doors are carved by craftsmen.

The peasant's wood bridge has no toll or questions when going back to our side.

Warsaw is a maze within a storm. Grander than Riga or Vilna but spun from the same cloth. A wilderness of beasts and vermin chased by gods and warriors. Strangers shunned or pay dearly for a favor.

We return to the ghetto's central square, and a congregation of Hasids on one corner, the Orthodox on the other, but at the center is another of these grand stores, dressed down for Jews bred to bargain.

The side streets are lined with proper homes, and when we ask about the cost of a room, the fee ranges from 3 to 7 gold sovereigns.

Need to leave the bourgeoisie Jews and find our side of the ghetto.

Our journey continues through a patchwork of boundaries marked by Yiddish, Russian, or Polish.

We pass a shul, boasting its faith, with stained-glass windows set into the walls of plastered masonry. I'm stopped by nine holy men needing one more for a minion of ten. The Rabbi sees into my poisoned soul and asks if I'm Orthodox. He shows no interest in Yitzhak. "Come inside for Hashem's healing and shelter."

I yearn for the comfort of faith, but Yitzhak tells the Holy man, "Fables blind you. Open your eyes."

The Orthodox elder ignores Yitzhak, but holds my arm, "Respect for our hosts. They want what we want: food, home, and the blessing of family and friends."

CHAPTER THIRTY - Warsaw – Nov. 1905

Yitzhak pulls me from the pious to follow him from this path of hallowed prosperity to the desperation of poverty. Cobblestone to dirt. Alleys of stench and foulness, not flushed into sewers.

There's the echo of angry cursing, and Yitzhak drags me inside. The walls are loose boards. The dirt floor is slippery mud. Either from vomit or spilled ale or by a thatch roof that is so full of holes it wouldn't stop a drizzle. Not even a barn fit for livestock, but a bench with bottles, tables with the rowdy, and we've found a factory man's tavern.

Six long tables. The closest table has sixteen men of various ages and sizes, all wearing gray overalls marked with the scars of factory work. Eight on each side in a heated argument. One side curses the czar in Polish; the other curses in Russian.

The next table has four on each side. One side wears the peasant suits of the poorest of Jews; the other side has four men who seem familiar.

The one puffing a pipe is in a disguise of thin wire glasses, an oversized worker's cap, and a scarf that hides all but his mouth and eyes. They argue in Yiddish and Hebrew. The one beside him has no hair but an eyepatch. Imagined him as a bearded, curly-haired bohemian. He stands on the bench to gain attention, "The strike served notice. The furnaces are as welcome a reward as the master's bread and ale."

Behind the bar is a beast of a man giving watch to his row of bottles and a barrel of ale. Behind him is a wall with two shelves lined with mugs of all sizes. Most are short pints made of tin, the larger pint is glass, and six handsome steins with decorative art sit proudly on their own shelf.

The tavernkeeper slides a smaller tin mug of foam toward Yitzhak, "Never seen you. Where are you from?" Asked in Polish.

I answer for Yitzhak, who has taken on the role of silent observer; such must be his fever for having found comrades. "North." Yitzhak knows more than he lets on. I know Mrs. Dayan taught him Polish. I'd catch him preaching in Russian or Polish, but with languages jumbled in the other's words. He didn't like it when I questioned this act of secrets.

"You're a Jew?"

Yitzhak steps to the bar. He reveals his secret. "What of it?" In Polish.

"Don't serve the pious!" The pig stands up to the bear.

Yitzhak stands taller. "I don't believe in a merciless God. And I don't hold any regard for a coward who hides behind Jesus."

The top of the tavernkeeper's mane of hair is only as tall as Yitzhak's nose, but his shoulders are broad and he has the belly of a pregnant woman. He hasn't cut his reddish hair or beard in years. His mane is a woolly bramble of gray, red, and black. Turns to look down on me. "You're a Jew," he spits, "And not much more than a boy. You must be the shylock who has your bear shake the tree if it don't drop apples."

I need a moment, want to laugh, but Yitzhak, "I'm the shylock. I trade cowards for comrades. He's my fox, sniffs out liars." Yitzhak laughs as I haven't seen. He puts a kopek on the crate, with a nod to me, "My comrade."

The pig looks at me with a stare— "Comrade?"

He boasts, "Took our oath from Lenin himself."

The four men who I swear are familiar had snuck over to a corner booth. The room becomes quiet.

The tavernkeeper grabs two of the large tins and fills them with ale. "To Lenin himself." Pounds his chest, holds up his fist, "Comrades!" The men rise. They all raise their mugs, bottles, fists. "Comrades!"

Yitzhak is overcome in rapture. He loses his snarl. "We've been tested in hell." Not a boast, but a lost soul believing he's found paradise. "It's taken a long journey to find the revolution." He sips the foam. Studies the room. Finds the preacher. "Are you warriors or cowards?"

The men crowd around Yitzhak. "I am your Comrade, Jakob!"

They all raise their mugs. "A toast to welcome our comrades!"

I don't take the mug, don't toast, but slip away, want to be forgotten. My heart sinks. He's found the battlefield. He's found his army.

Yitzhak and his comrades are too busy taking turns giving the oath to notice my retreat. In trade for their oath, they receive a pour. Bond in threats against the Czar, curses for the bourgeoisie. They toast to revenge, but hold out their mugs to Jakob, thirsty for free ale.

Jakob drinks more than his share. He could fit two of me inside his belly. He eats sausage but offers none. Jakob celebrates Yitzhak as Goliath. "All are comrades. No White Russians. No pious." He complains loudly in a peasant's Polish as he pours another mug of ale. "Spit on the czar, then slit his throat."

I inch closer to the booth in the far corner where the four whom I can't place have gone to retreat from Yitzhak's celebration. I peer through their cloud of smoke, squint to picture who is under the worker's cap, behind the scarf, a disguise. Enough to keep me from knowing, but when they mention Yitzhak by name, glance down to give me a nod of notice, and overhear their murmurings in Russian— "Coincidence or did he find them?"

A boy is hidden under the booth. No whiskers, but his stare is not meek but probing like a sentry. I crouch on the slick dirt. His sorrowful eyes are a mirror that reminds me of myself. I imagine he's another twig with the spirit of a lamb.

Bold in greeting, he offers me his handshake, "Hiram."

"Max."

The boy tears off a chunk of bread, nods toward Yitzhak, tells me in Yiddish, "Jakob respects your bear."

"Why are you here?"

"Jakob gives me chores for bread and this home," Hiram explains that Jakob turned his tavern into a bund the day after the four above us showed up a week ago. "Only comrades."

Hiram's home has a small tin mug filled with crackers. There's a blanket with more holes than cloth, but I'm taken by a picture of a well-dressed man and woman, nailed to the wall. He notices my stare. "My parents." He looks at the picture. "They shot my father for something I will never know, but why my mother?" He's hungry for comfort. "I was hiding under the bed. Stayed there long enough to give in to hunger and thirst. Escaped, but only to wander in hell until I was found by Jakob in the alley out back. Has me run errands."

He is weakened to a mouse. "I know that fate." We mourn nightmares in silence.

I hear the four above arguing softly in Russian over what to say.

The clouds of smoke sink beneath the table, infecting my breathing.

Yitzhak is in rapture. He earns great honor by sharing our story. Everyone toasting his courage, "Killed three Chekas," boasting, "Left one alive to report to the Czar that the sheep are now wolves. Then his tone turns somber but proud. "She'll be remembered as Lenin's Joan of Arc." Finally, her story is told.

In all our time on the road, he'd never talk about that day. They toast Lina. I can't help but suffer in that nightmare, forever in mourning.

The cheers return to cursing the Czar.

Yitzhak looks around. I crawl out before his search finds me in hiding. I stand on a bench, nod, "To our fallen Comrade. Hail, Lina."

The men turn to study me. Jakob comes at me. "Who is this lamb you keep for a pet. How is there this friendship for the likes of a bear to defend a mouse?"

Yitzhak pushes Jakob aside, comes beside me, and holds up my arm. "Max took his pledge before Lenin himself."

I recite the oath out of loyalty. To do otherwise is to confess to being a traitor. "To die for the purpose of revolution! My brother! My comrade."

The night wears on with revelry until Jakob closes the tap and corks the bottles. Celebration fades to the slumber of drunks.

The four in the booth divide, each taking a cushioned bench for a bed. I no longer wonder what earned this holy privilege. It's them.

A hurting wind blows through the slats of wood that barely hold up this barn.

I can't sleep for the hauntings of this tavern are a nightmare. Jakob huddles with Yitzhak. I think to confront my neighbors, but Yitzhak grabs me to join. Jakob offers a mug as an apology. "We had a strike at the iron forge less than two weeks ago, but we were forced to retreat. These men were there. They'd be shot if they showed their faces at the factory. We need you to go. Let the men know our time is here." He holds Yitzhak by the wrist. "You are truly the messiah's warrior. This is your destiny. You stir men with your courage." He takes Yitzhak by the wrist. "You are who we've been waiting for."

He looks into my soul. "You must stay by my side. We fight for a noble cause. We have found the revolution. Revenge! Our battlefield. For Lina, your father, for the most righteous of reasons."

Jakob set out our mission. "Go tomorrow to the forge. Tell them you're experienced in making molds in metal. Yitzhak, you tell them you know how to sharpen. Once inside, you'll raise our army."

My coward's soul is stolen by loyalty to Yitzhak. I let him drag me from the tavern in the middle of the night, without sleep, to make our way to a brick fortress. The giant mill by the bridge where we saw the soldier shoot the protester. The tall chimneys belch black smoke.

It was sunrise when we reached the bloodied cobblestone path by the front gate. We learn from the dozen men already waiting in line, "The General ordered the blood not to be washed away."

We're taken one by one into a large room lined with books and boxes of papers. The officer sits behind a grand desk flanked by six soldiers on either side.

Yitzhak tells the Officer, "I work with metal," having learned from Jakob the lie needed to get a job.

The General has a brass helmet, and studies Yitzhak. "Better a soldier," and waves to his guards.

They grab Yitzhak, but he stumbles, bends over, and pretends to act out an infirmity. "My back was broken fighting off thieves. I'm no more than a lamb. I can't shovel or use a pick. Can only grind metal to a sharp edge."

The General studies Yitzhak, but doubt gives way to Yitzhak's posture. "A ruble if you grind three hundred. This will be your last day if less."

Jakob had told us what to say, what to expect. "You'll be conscripted unless you act infirm. Tell them you grind metal. A finisher allows for moving about."

Nervous, I face the General. "I make molds."

The Officer laughs, "Give the Jew a shovel and take him to Josef." Jakob told us that they need to replace the strikers. "They'll take you in."

The soldier leads Yitzhak, me, and eight others up a steep flight of stairs. At first, it's the smoke, the clouds, the smell, the darkness, and we've entered hell. The endless floor of beams, columns, and a solid wood floor is infested by the heat and fire of the ovens. Sparks fly from grinding metal as lightning. Stamping machines bring the thunder as they smash iron sheets, and from out of the thunder come weapons and tools.

I hear Poppa and Gramps— "The factory is the harshest of a serf's trade."

I'm put beside a hairless beaver of a father's age and manner who is hunched over a worktable. I nudge closer to look over his shoulder. It's as if I've returned to Mr. Dayan's workshop. Josef is a craftsman carving a block of wood. He uses a hardened tool with a grooved blade. Intense focus. The splinters fly off from the block to form the shape of a bayonet.

Minutes pass before he wipes the sweat from his brow. Turns to grab a tool of tongs, notices me, and introduces himself with a kindly manner— "I'm Josef. You must be my helper. You'll feed coal to the hearth and use this blower when I hold a mold over the embers to make it red hot."

My sickle is now a shovel made heavy from the weight of coal. But this is not a field under heaven's sky but darkness and smoke that tests my resolve. Life on the road, no matter its toll, was never a prison with brick walls and windows covered with bars and boards.

Yitzhak is ten paces away at a machine that spins a wheel of stone. His focus is not on grinding metal, but studying the rows of men at similar machines, eager to preach to recruits.

The Cossack watches from a high throne. He's an armed beast. One of many stationed at the end of an endless line of long rows. Ten men to each row of grinding machines. The molds are poured at the far end. It's my job to feed the furnace, then take the rough-molded iron that Josef poured into the molds, cooled on racks, and wheeled down the row, handing out blades to be sharpened.

Yitzhak gives no regard to turning out his three hundred blades. He comes behind me as I shovel another load of coal into the hearth. Hands me a poorly sharpened blade, "Ask the blacksmith if this blade is sharp enough to kill a Cossack. Ask him for me. He must be Polish."

I show Josef the blade, ask if, "Sharp enough," but I do not ask if it'll kill a Cossack.

He runs his finger along the edge, shakes his head with a frown, "Not good enough."

Yitzhak has that look, "You'll not recruit if you don't ask."

"He doesn't know us. Need to earn trust. Give me time."

"Ask him how much he makes."

I ask, but Josef just stares at us. Shakes his head and goes back to carving another shape of a blade into the mold. I think this skill is what Mr. Dayan trained me for. If not for the heat and smoke, I could have a passion for this labor of carving molds.

The Cossack comes down from his throne. A rifle in his hand, pistols in his belt, and in the other hand is the whip. Pokes Yitzhak as a threat.

Yitzhak goes back to grinding but keeps an eye on the guard.

My cart needs more coal. I wheel it past Yitzhak, and hear him yelling over to those nearby— "What do you earn for this mule's labor?"

One answers, "A ruble for three hundred." He has the ear of the four who are also grinding metal. "And how much does he make?" Nods toward Josef.

"Mold-makers earn more."

"A ruble for this day of labor makes us no more than serf."

They shrug their shoulders and go back to grinding metal."

Midday, a flock of boys brings around bread and ale.

Josef is kind enough to share his loaf. I'm only given a slice. He asks me if I'm from Warsaw, "Your Polish is good, but it has a different flavor." I told him I'm from Riga, but my family was from Warsaw. He tells me that all this land was covered in forest when he was a boy. He proudly points to the beams that hold the floor and tells me that his father cut the trees that made this fortress. "The river turns a paddle wheel that used to grind seed into flour, but now turns the pulleys to turn the grinding wheels." The pulleys run the length of the floor. I think of the Count's mill and the magic of such labor.

The mold-maker is a Poppa and Gramps. Josef likes to talk about the past. "My father worked at the old grain mill. And when they made this to a forge, I was a boy," laughs, "Too many years ago." He shares a chunk of cheese, "The czars' ambition turned farms and forests into factories. Who else but a czar could make such a thing happen?"

I appreciate Josef's pride. But it's his regard for how the Czar made all this happen that leads me to believe Josef won't be a willing comrade. I feel a kinship from our talk. He's Poppa making the chore a lesson. There is the reward of a thick strip of pig to put on my bread.

Will Lenin order his comrades to build such a thing? What will he pay? Will he open the windows and let in fresh air?

Josef overhears Yitzhak's preaching. He looks at him with a squint of regard and lets out an angry snort. "Grind my metal." Josef stops engraving and goes to tip the heavy cast-iron bucket. He carefully controls its tilt, knows just how much of the molten stream to leak down into the center of each mold until full.

I look away from the blinding light of sludge to see the Cossack stuffing a chunk of bread in his mouth. The pig of a man then takes half the wedge of cheese in one bite. He swills the ale as he marches down the narrow aisle to show us his reward. He pokes the men to pick up the pace. None dare to fight against a musket and whip held at the ready.

Needing to lean over the hearth to set the molds, Josef hides inside a mask to stare into the hot coals, waits a moment for it to boil, and lifts the tray out. He nods toward a pair of gloves. "Put them on and carry the tray to the rack."

I study his mask. "I've never seen such a thing,"

"Let me show you." He puts his mask over my head, and then pushes my head over the hearth's red-hot embers. I'm blinded as if staring into the sun—made to suffer to prove his point—but the lesson is learned. The leather protects me from fire, and the painted red glass shields my eyes from going blind, but the heat inside this coffin causes my breathing to be pained, boiling sweat burns my eyes, and I pull away, take a deep breath.

He turns to me, "A needed lesson to know why I make more."

He holds the mask with pride, "A gift from my wife when we were first matched by her mother. She asked why I'm hairless, and when I told her of my craft, she wanted to save me. She took the skin of the cow before roasting the meat, tanned the hide, and stitched together this mask."

Josef grabs a red glass plate from a tray of them. "I used to have to hold the glass to my eyes with one hand, but then I had only one hand to tilt the bucket. I cut the slots and added red to the sand when I blew the glass to make the lens."

I look around and realize that most of the men have a similar mask, but they cut away the sides. A needed fix so they can breathe, but not Josef, he wears it as his wife made it.

Josef boasts, "One by one, they came over and asked why the master only graced me with this prize. When I told them this girl I was courting made it for me, they asked if she could make them one.

He then confessed that the mask became a cause for revolt. "I told them it would cost a few rubles, and they got mad for not having rubles to spare. I had them ask the master to pay to have more made, but they were beaten back to word.

I think of Mrs. Dayan. She would have done such a motherly deed. "I wish for one day to be blessed with such a wife."

"She still makes them, but I charge only what a man can spare."

Gramps would have charged at least two rubles. Poppa maybe three, the same as a glove or cap. For Josef and his wife, the masks are about the value of kindness and blessing. "My wife works at the textile mill, as does my three daughters. After a day's work is done, they stitch the leather on the good sewing machines. No matter their labor is the same long day as ours—they will do this so that no one should be without."

Josef's charity is who he is. "Jesus gave us the true path—Charity, mercy, labor, and forgiveness."

Walking back to the tavern in the dark, after the harsh but rewarding test of the day, I argue to quit. Yitzhak won't have it.

When I asked Josef, "You get an extra portion of bread and cheese?" He answered, "For those who carve the molds." Josef poked my ribs. "You will watch and learn."

I thought of a life tending to the oven and carving molds. I wondered if this hell could be made to my heaven as it has for Josef. A wife, daughters. Pride in his work. Carving wood or metal? The hearth being a blessing in winter, but what of summer?

He asked if I was homeless. I confessed my trials with only the better half of my story. "A poor Jew from a small shtetl who learned the craft of peddling but found trouble in finding work and was lured to Warsaw with the promise of opportunity." And then let it slip without thinking, "I sleep on the floor of a tavern with those who share in the Cause.

Josef asks with some concern, "What Cause?"

I realized my mistake the moment I said it. Josef spoke of his faith when he shunned Yitzhak for preaching Socialism. "Jesus will save us." I disavowed knowing Yitzhak as no more than another man I met in line.

"The cause of being Jewish," sweetened the lie, "My Polish is not so good— 'not our cause'—meant, 'my faith."

He breaks off a wedge of cheese and hands it to me. "I know where you can have a dry room for a few kopeks. A clean wood floor, and the matron includes bread." I'm surprised he doesn't shun me for being a Jew.

I thank him for the offer and flatter his cheese even though it's bitter. Not as Bubby or Mamma would make.

The day passed with shoveling and learning the art of mold-making.

Yitzhak tests my loyalty as we walk back to the tavern. "These men were poisoned by the strike. Made them fearful cowards."

Jakob convinces him to go back. "Invite them here. I'll sweeten the trade with a free mug of ale and bread."

Yitzhak drags me from the tavern before sunrise. I follow, knowing my reward will be a warm hearth against this cold. Josef might have another chunk of bread, cheese, and his ale. I take on the mission only for another day of having found my poppa in Josef.

We wait at the gate along with the hundreds, maybe thousands of men, women, and children. We crowd the river road. Too many to count. Six factories and mills all lined up in a row.

Josef sees me. He's with four women. Comes over and introduces his wife. She's a woman as tall and strong as Josef. He waves to gather, "My daughters," three girls, each taller than the next, plump red cheeks, and hair the color of straw.

I smile, "You are truly blessed."

"We live some distance, edge of town, forest for a neighbor to one side. Our walk takes us past my church." He pulls me close. "I have my own home—a garden with guardians. My dogs were born as wolves. Took them as orphans when I shot their mother for stealing my chickens. I taught them to guard my home and not eat us."

Josef introduces Yitzhak to his family.

The eldest daughter proudly tells Yitzhak, "I fix the looms at the textile mill."

His wife reaches into her sack and hands me a small loaf of bread, saying, "For you and your friend."

Yitzhak asks if his daughters are married.

Josef gets angry. He scolds Yitzhak, "You'll have nothing to do with my daughters. "They'll marry no worse than a Catholic man with a proper trade."

CHAPTER THIRTY-ONE – Warsaw - Dec. 4, 1905,

Asleep in the familiar nightmare, I imagine it's the beast's sword stabbing my hip, but it's not a dream; it's the nightmare of a day I hoped would never come. I couldn't convert him from this fable where all workers rise against the beasts, united in brotherhood.

"Let's go!" Yitzhak is in my ear. "Wake up!" A harder kick. "Today we fight for liberty!" shouting for all to hear. My comrade is in haste to make this day from the same cloth as my nightmare.

His comrades curse his war cry because they suffer from drinking Jakob's poison, but I know these beggars and thieves will forgive the pain as easily as they forget their sins. It won't be long before they demand more ale in trade for loyalty.

Yitzhak accused me of not preaching. He doesn't listen to my lesson. "We need to curry friendship before you can open a mind to such sacrifice for an unknown reward, but he has no patience for revolution."

As the fog clears, I squint through tired eyes at an empty mug that's pressed under an unworn sole. The four preachers don't recruit by working alongside the proletariat. I doubt they've been inside a mill or forge. I imagine they stirred the strike from the comfort of this booth as their pulpit. I took a seat beside Leon. I don't confess, no need, his nod confirms the actor's role.

Lenin's disciples give no name. They want to be known as: "Artist, Philosopher, and Writer." They are men of an age to be warriors, yet they pose as wise Rebbes. They speak of hardship, but their faces show no scars, their hands are soft, not calloused. They recite the prophet's manifesto as if it's the Torah. I show respect. I know to hold my doubt in silence. I don't question their preaching but retreat into the silence of a coward.

I stand on tired legs and wave away the professor's cloud of smoke. Behind the fake beard, worker's cap, and thick black glasses is the one who was beside Lenin on that fateful night. He knows me. I'm an honored comrade. Last night, he pulled me close, whispered with a grin, "You have done well." Leon took off the wig and beard. He'd cut off the long curls, shaved off the beard, and changed his glasses from wire to wood frames.

The tavern provides barracks for their army. These recruits have little to lose but another day of misery. Some are here for the warmth of the stove and another mug of ale—revenge for their misery of having been fodder for the Czar's wars. Many tell of how they lost their family to the injustices of tyranny. A few bear the scars of punishment. Their souls were stolen by war, prison, and hunger.

They honor me. Yitzhak has told them our tale, but Yitzhak knows doubt is my only faith, and yet he's done the better job of converting me to his side with a plea of loyalty. "You have been with me from before Lenin made us comrades, to when you swore to Mr. Dayan." Last night he pulled me aside, "Do not lose faith now that we're so close."

I envy Yitzhak's passion. He never wavers— always steadfast. A believer. Has certainty in the righteousness of the Cause.

"When the beasts are slain, the reward will be life as heaven."

Yitzhak has the faith of a preacher, but the soul of a warrior, so when I confessed my doubt in the hayloft after another night of sermons from Mr. Dayan, he told me, "You are a peddler looking for profit. But a revolution's profit is not rubles. With faith comes courage."

Leon points his pipe as if to give me a blessing, but I feel no kinship from his blessing. The learned preach as proletariat, but they smoke fine tobacco, a bourgeois prize. We are no more than kindling.

I slip from a bed of dirt, made to mud from spilled drink and vomit. Yitzhak has no patience for my struggle and grabs my wrist to lift me to his side. He pulls me from the tavern, and I follow in dread. Yitzhak imagines stirring a thousand men with the promise of liberty and leading the workers as his army. He tells me, "We'll strike fear in the beasts." His boast, "The Cossacks will stand aside, or we will slay them all."

I have little faith there will be such warriors among our factory's proletariat, or that beasts will lay down in surrender. Poppa would say, "One wolf owns a thousand sheep." I believe today is our execution.

I follow Yitzhak but tread carefully, mindful of foul tempers.

Jakob snores loudly under the blanket of a wolf. He speaks loudest for stealing from the bourgeois— "For the cause." Under his wolf's skin is a second coat of sheep's wool stitched to deerskin. I would ask him what earned him the right to two coats when my thin coat is a rag of rabbit.

An hour until sunrise, and the cold fights against faith in staying loyal. Streetlamps unlit. We keep to the alley. The regiment is camped between the Czar's bridge and palace. Winter has Warsaw in its grip.

Yitzhak hurries, but the alley is littered with foul things that slow my pace. Bones waiting to be eaten by scavengers. Jews, peasants, and anarchists kept to our side of this fortress—bourgeoisie, nobles, and gentry on the other side of the river—another world.

My coat hardens to ice. Winter is as cruel as fire, but Yitzhak gives no thought to such things as cold. I struggle to follow and slide across a path of frozen muck, only to stumble against a mound covered in snow. I fall, and as I push down to stand, my hands break through a thin sheet of ice, and by the light of a full moon, it's the face of a ghost staring to heaven.

I pray my comrade goes on without me. I'm ready to set myself free from this unholy oath. But it's as if I'm attached to his heart, and he returns to lift me from surrender. "Today is the day. This is to be our battlefield. Our sacrifice will be heard." He confides in me the big secret that Jakob revealed last night. "Lenin declared December 5th as the day to ignite his revolution." His note was read with great reverence by Leon—"We will break the yoke. The Czar will know the sheep are wolves." An echo of Yitzhak's message to the Cheka executioner.

Lenin made heroes of striking workers. Seventy-seven were killed in Lodz. Poland's treasure chest of Jews empowered to manufacture. The Czar promises reforms, but it's always a lie. Why pay a fair wage and provide fresh air when a threat works better.

The workday begins at sunrise. Soldiers keep watch from fidgety horses; their rifles are held high; their threat brings order to the thousands who come each day to add another block to the Czar's pyramid.

I sneak away from Yitzhak to hide against the fence, hidden by the shuffling crowd. The gates are open, but I'm lost in the current of the river. It glitters in the colored light of sunrise. I dream of sailing away. "Rivers are nature's highway." Poppa's lesson, "A river leads to someplace beyond, but like any path, it's not without peril. Reward must be greater than the risk." I conjure an island. If I'm alone, I'd be without fear. Lost in mourning life's darkness, I want to swim away and find peace in its darkness, but Yitzhak would argue — "drown for no purpose."

I'm pulled from escape by Yitzhak. Determined to bring me to the revolution, and we follow the procession of sheep crammed between docks stacked with crates to one side and drawn into the brick fortress. Worries are lost to the clattering of wagon wheels and hooves striking against cobblestone.

I wave to Josef, his wife, and daughters, but Yitzhak has poisoned his trust by preaching to a minion of those he believes are with him— six Polish Catholics and four unkosher Jews lean over a fire that sends up more smoke than heat. Yitzhak's eyes narrow. "We will be the beasts!" They bond with approving nods as an oath.

More than twenty Cossacks watch us closely, hands on triggers—never this many watching. Their stares give me cause to look behind.

I find Yitzhak shuffling through the gate. Send a glance toward the guards, but he gives their threat no regard. This is his battlefield. Today, he lights the spark. Nothing will stop him.

We work in shadows. Only those making molds and inspecting what we forge have the new candles lit from a wire. When I asked, "Why no windows to light our work?" I was told, "Broke the glass in madness."

By the time daylight shines between the cracks of boarded-up windows, I'm dripping in sweat and can only think of how to escape.

Fear fuels misery. Time isn't measured by labor but by fear. Josef watches me, but we don't speak. The bond is broken. Another man takes my place. I'm ordered to fill a cart until it is heavy with coal and feed those bins that are mine to tend. The Cossack watches with a hand on the trigger. His platform is raised high enough to see over the long rows of men and machines. If our pace is slow, he waves his saber, and if you make a false move, he aims his rifle.

Yitzhak taps the grinding wheel. My comrade's signal. He swore an oath to the prophet to draw blood. The Cossacks are also hungry to draw blood. A ruble reward for our murder. Posts are nailed to the beams. "Shoot to kill." We are warned, "The General doesn't want prisoners."

Yitzhak is trapped in the dream where he leads an army from the factory to the palace. Stirred on with cheers, given honor, respect. Leon and the disciples were as if Lenin himself giving praise, and so he made the boast at the tavern, "I will kill the first Cossack with the bayonet they had me sharpen, I'll take his rifle, pistols, and I'll kill a dozen. I will show the lambs that the beasts are made of flesh. They'll rise up. A thousand men as our army." He has no fear. His hate has no bounds. Yitzhak would only confess that he was an abandoned orphan, but he didn't need to say any more—a childhood as a feral cat battling rats. His scars run deep. "I'll break the lock," his face red with anger, "I'll cut the chain! Set us free to storm the palace."

He's the warrior I wanted to be. To live without fear. To die for a righteous cause, but all I see is death without heaven on either side.

The Cossack keeps one hand on the pistol and the other on his rifle. I imagine Yitzhak will get no further than where I feed this furnace. The Cossack's killing shot will be hidden under the thunder of the machines—the noise, smoke, and soot will hide our dying bodies. Even if I were brave enough, we might kill more, but I don't see glory. There will be no notice, just a few more sticks of kindling gone as smoke.

Yitzhak believes glory is measured in the bodies of the slain. "We will die as martyrs. From our sacrifice, all will rise up."

Most are Polish Catholic. They see life as purgatory, a test to earn entrance to heaven. Many are like Josef; they take pride in this fiery work, have faith in Jesus, that heaven is their eternal reward, heaven in death a more trusted dream than converting this hell into a heaven in life.

I feed one last load and bang my shovel against the oven. Josef knows I want to say goodbye—but my friend has turned his back on me. He speaks plainly. A Polish Catholic who harbored no hate for a Jew from Latvia. He told me, "Be thankful for life's blessings. Honor this labor as worthy, bond with family, friends, and give thanks to God."

Doubt must choose a side: revolution or surrender.

Yitzhak sneaks about to recruit. I see nods, bonding, he's found comrades, but against my warning, he came for Josef, "Beasts don't surrender."

Josef holds up his carving tool— "You'll spread more hate." Josef crossed himself. "Jesus would ask to keep faith in God's plan. You fight for the future you want tomorrow, but his plan is measured not in days, but in eternity. We have many lessons to learn."

His hair was wiped clean by the inferno, bald with no brows, no beard, skin etched by the heat. He grabbed me as a father about to give a scolding but folded his hands— "I won't pray for you, but for all who your misguided deed will punish."

Yitzhak argued against Josef… "You believe in a fool's dream," he laughed, and spoke in a peasant's Polish as to mock Josef, "Oh Jesus, make the beasts lie down as sheep."

There's a break for lunch. We were ordered to keep to our station. The boys handed out bread and water.

Yitzhak is defiant. Goes from one man to the next. "Today, we bring the battlefield to Warsaw. I will kill the first," he stares the recruits in the eye, grabs the bayonet he just sharpened, “They are made of flesh and easily killed. ” They want to believe him. Nods are exchanged. With the guards distracted by mugs of ale, more of the boys, the younger men, exchange the oath with a glance.

Under the cover of the smoke that hangs like a cloud, he goes row to row with the same message. Too many were witnesses to the strikers being shot.

I lower my shovel and face Josef. “You are right. Evil won’t end evil.”

CHAPTER THIRTY-TWO – Warsaw- Dec 4, 1905,

The factory's wheels and gears are turned by the power of the river to bring machines to life. A rifle shot wouldn't be heard above their roar. The fires keep the forge in a fog. The air is so thick it makes you weary just from breathing. It infects us with the sickness of coughs and nails pounding into our heads.

We're ordered back to work. Heads down to grind a blade sharp. Josef pours the molten iron into a mold, I'm needed to shovel more coal, and push the wheelbarrow past the row of ten grinding metal, Yitzhak shifted to the far end. I'm thinking the iron barrel can be our shield and the racks of knives our arsenal.

Yitzhak has his eye on the Cossack. He'll be coming by soon to poke and prod, but suddenly, a hundred soldiers spread like locusts swarming across the factory floor.

I look behind. Yitzhak is paralyzed.

They march down the aisles—rifle across their chest—a grim stare of superiority.

Yitzhak awakens to his mission. He pulls me by the arm. "Now!" But I pull away.

"None will join. Look around. None dares even to look up." I plead, "We'll go to the tavern and join Jakob. Our battlefield will be tonight; we will burn the palace."

The afternoon drags on. The soldiers march up and down the rows. The officers take the Cossack's throne. The Cossacks want to prove they're the cruelest beasts and drag the most cowardly to torture with threats at gunpoint and knives to their throat. It's the screams, begging, crying, that bring them to rapture. The soldiers hold us prisoner. An hour beyond sunset, our day over, and I keep Yitzhak at bay with the dream of blowing up the Czar's palace and battling the palace guard.

The boys bring out baskets of bread and sausage, along with a barrel of ale. The beasts are distracted by the feast and flaunt their reward as if to taunt us into battle. The General's victory is easily won—bullets versus knives.

"We need to go now." Yitzhak pulls me to the shadows at the far end of our row. He shifts about, anxious, clenching the knife, "Or we make our stand here. Now!"

I draw close, and peddle a better trade— "Will a soldier's death cause these men to rise up?" Smoke and thunder hide our argument. The proletariat hides in labor. Soldiers celebrating their authority.

"They knew about the plan."

Yitzhak points an accusing glance at Josef. "Did he tell? Only a few hours until Jakob's army marches on the palace." He's ready to explode.

"We die here, but not before we light the flame."

I need a path to escape. "This is their battlefield. Tonight, it's ours."

There are fifty rows, ten deep. One end is the pile of coal and rows of iron bars, crates of supplies, all brought up by the large elevator near the warehouse. A heavy iron door separates the factory from the storeroom where they keep the knives and rifle barrels.

The warehouse door is usually under guard, but the patrols have left it open. The officers are inspecting the day's production. Racks are lined up at the front of each row.

He stabs his knife into the timber beam, twisting it until he spends his hate. He can't look at me. He knows he'll be killed the moment a soldier sees him. There are too many. They're everywhere—rifles drawn—watching. They'd earn honor and a ruble reward for each protester killed.

"Where is the glory in being shot if no one speaks of it?"

He stares at the guards and then turns to study the doorways. The heavy metal door to the warehouse is unchained. "You're right." Yitzhak nods toward the warehouse. "If we make it to the warehouse, I've heard it leads to the roof. I've seen the ladders."

The soldiers take their position beside the towers. The officers have their eyes on the prize of gun barrels, bayonets, bullet casings, and canteen shells. We have an opening. Their backs are turned from the warehouse door. We can sneak along the back wall, hide behind crates, and race a few paces to sneak into the warehouse. Only the shadow of a man can be seen through the smoke.

Time for me to decide. To stay is to betray Yitzhak, my brother. Traitor or patriot. Prisoner, or revolutionary. Vengeance or submission. Mr. Dayan told me that one day I'd have to pick a side. It's the memory of Lina, and the terror we brought to Riga that gives me a clue. To be shot while escaping is better than taking a life. I don't think I could kill. I don't want to light the fire. I don't want to start a revolution. I want to teach.

We race behind the crates as the officers and soldiers keep watch over the treasure. We sneak to within a few feet of the door, wait for our moment, and race under the cover of hell's inferno into the cold darkness of the warehouse—so dark as to be blind. We're not seen. We've escaped.

The warehouse is pitch black. Nowhere in the factory can a torch be lit for fear of fire. The new electric lights are turned on only when loading or unloading the treasures. Too many fail with sparks.

We're blind men finding our way by pressing a hand against the brick wall. To view the fortress from the outside suggests the warehouse must go on for a hundred paces.

I hear their claws scratching against the floor before my toes are stabbed by their sharp teeth. The rat gnaws at the hole in my boot. My hunger was so painful that I would squash and eat him. I give his courage honor, as I feel more the coward. I kick off the brave rat who shows no fear of a giant, and the rest scatter.

The wall suddenly ends, and we're left to grope, waving our hands in the air, stumbling in the dark. Yitzhak bumps against a shelf, there's the sharp sound of metal hitting the wood floor, and my heart stops. I hold my breath, but there's no storm coming, no shots fired, only the distant rumble of machines. I had hoped by now they'd know we were missing. I imagine the bullet hitting my heart or head, and the pain would only last an instant.

Yitzhak reaches down and picks up what fell. Suddenly, the lights came on. There's the echo of the officer giving orders, not the alert of escape.

Yitzhak tears a piece of cloth from his tunic, wraps it around the sharp metal. The crew on the floor below installs the wood handles. He hands it to me. I'm horrified to imagine plunging the blade into flesh.

We pass through shadows that are shelves, bang into a brick wall, but then the air turns cool. I can breathe. Fresh air gives me strength. A few more feet and there are streams of light. Come close enough to realize it's a board nailed to where there was a window.

Yitzhak pries it off. The middle bar was chiseled off. Did the thief break in or escape through the broken window? Was the bar cut during the strike to get in and steal the treasure or to cause trouble?

The wind blows hard against my sweat. Sunset paints the sky. We crawl onto the ledge. I look down at a ravine cut deep enough to be a moat. Yitzhak doesn't wait. He crawls onto the roof and uses the knife to stab the ice to keep from sliding off. Kicks away a foot of snow. Needs to work hard to keep from falling, slips, but at the edge of the roof is a bar from the top of a ladder.

The cold bites into tired bones. There is little left of my coat, just some patches of squirrel and rabbit barely stitched to what is left of the cloth, but between the sweat of escape or fear, cold is a tonic.

Let him go? But to surrender would mean torture before execution. I step onto the slippery roof, lie on my stomach, and, following Yitzhak's lesson, I stab the ice. After a few jabs, the blade cuts through the cloth, can't keep my grip, let go—and as I slide down the slate roof, I imagine the distance of the fall is my path to death, but then worry that it would be worse to be a cripple. My boots build a wall of snow that slows me down just as my legs dangle over the side. Yitzhak reached out and grabbed my hand.

I look down. Thirty feet? A mound of snow. A broken leg was more likely. My hands are frozen, losing my grip.

Yitzhak never takes thanks. Doesn't wait. Disappears over the side to climb down the ladder. It bangs against the brick, another hope of being found and shot, but at this distance, would the bullet kill me or wound me?

I grab the metal rung. Bare fingers burn against ice. I fear to quit as much as go on, but I hear Poppa and Gramps— "You must survive because the future has many paths and it's unknown which one fate has in store." They'd say, "There will be time in heaven for rest." I climbed down and nodded to Yitzhak. "Luck is on our side."

I breathe deep and listen to the pounding of iron being stamped and ground into weapons. They must have learned about Lenin's call for today as another spark for revolution. Why else were a hundred soldiers suddenly guarding us? We were prisoners kept from battle. To Lenin, we're kindling. He ordered our execution. The Czar said no. There's no siren or frenzy of soldiers running about. Our escape went unnoticed or given little regard. Two missing from a thousand.

Yitzhak points across the courtyard to where wagons load and unload. In anger more than defeat, he asks, "Who told them?"

"All have heard." A poor secret. "There were too many who knew."

He snorts, stands to leave, and shakes off the cold. "We need to move. Still time to join Jakob." He points to the guards stationed in the towers overlooking the courtyard. We hid under the shadow of the tall brick wall as tall as two of me. It circles the factory. “Max, bend over.” He climbs onto my back, and before he crushes me into the snow, he grabs the top of the wall. Calls down, “Grab my leg.” And lifts us over the wall. I then climb down his back as he hangs from the wall on the other side.

The road is barren. All were kept in the prisons. We avoid the checkpoints and patrols by keeping to the alleys, climbing across roofs, and making our way back to Jakob’s, but before we turn the corner to Aleksandrovsk Boulevard, I ask, “Is he going to be here?” but Yitzhak doesn’t answer. I can’t wait, and ask again—“Lenin is here?”

He grabs my arm and pulls me down a path disguised by trash, lifts aside a stack of empty crates to expose the secret passage into the tavern, and his spirit ignites from the cheers and boasts pouring out, but before he drags me inside, Yitzhak turns to me with a grin, “No.”

“What?”

“He isn't coming.”

“Not coming? You knew?” Angered by the betrayal, “He needs to be here—who will lead us?”

The thunder of revolution echoes out of the hole, but I don’t want to go in. I ask again, “Why didn't you tell me? He must be here!”

“The revolution is to be everywhere. Lenin will be everywhere tonight. Jakob will lead the attack.”

We entered the storm. The comrades are feverish. Jakob is standing on the pulpit of the bar. “Our time!” Holds the decorative steins in each hand. Drinks from both and then smashes them together to take command. Shards flying. Lenin’s imposter. He cries out— “We’re the wolves! The Czar our lamb!” the boast in a peasant's Polish.

Jakob does not honor the Jews. There’s no oath made in Yiddish. An ugly man who drinks half of what he serves. Spares a mug only to recruit. His revolution is revenge. Told by the boy that he was being forced to turn over his tavern to the Russians.

CHAPTER THIRTY-THREE –Dec. 5, 1905

The mob leaves no room to move. Drawn by free ale, bread, and tonic so hot as to burn your soul, the hundred or more comrades are here for revenge. Blaming the czar for any misery. Cries of "Liberation." All are drunk in rapture, wanting to take the oath, "Liberty or death. Not a slave!"

Courageous patriots or sacrificial fools? I think of Lina and struggle to defend my doubts as nothing more than cowardliness.

Leon takes to the pulpit and claps two tin mugs to hold court. He opens an envelope. Proudly reads the letter— "Comrade Lenin is everywhere. He calls on his comrades to march on the palace." Waits for the cheers to quiet, "We will wake the Czar by burning it down!"

The wolf swaggers across Jakob's bar, the board wobbling on emptied barrels. He commits the cardinal sin and grabs a bottle from the shelf—tosses it to his pack, then another, and another—until Jakob fires a shot. The bullet blows another hole in the thatch roof, patches of straw and boards that do little but block the sun and stars. He gives the wolf a warning by aiming his pistol at the wolf's heart—and retakes the throne by stomping across the board, face to face— "Who are you?"

"Stanislav!" Most have heard his name in whispers and tales of terror. The wolves hold up the stolen bottles and take long swigs, a sign of honor.

Jakob grabs the bottle. Waves his pistol— "Comrade?"

"Polish liberation army."

"Comrade?"

"If being comrade free me from the yoke of the Russian swine, then we are comrades."

Jakob hands Stanislav the bottle, takes one for himself, "To the Revolution!"

The wolf notices Yitzhak. He's pushed his way to be just below the wolf. His temper is spiked. "Comrades?" The oath means more to Yitzhak than having an ally on the battlefield. "A brotherhood." Yitzhak jumps onto the table to face down the Wolf. "We are not Jew or Catholic, not Pole or Russian, not serf or bourgeoisie—we are comrades!" Yitzhak raises his fist, but there are few cheers.

Stanislav flips his wolf's mask back. The scar runs like a red river from his neck to his ear. "I'm a Pole, a Warsaw Pole. I am here to kill Russians. And when I've burned the city, it will be for Poland, not for a Jew." The wolf puts his hate to vote, "Jews are the fox disguised as sheep! Little rats who have their teeth and claws tearing at our pockets."

I count a dozen Jews if I can trust their costume of a tattered black suit. I would preach the lesson if I had the courage, "A Jew could be a Marxist, but by half. There is no God as a fatherly master. When converted to communism, you no longer fear God's vengeance in death. The same belief that if the Czar is gone, they'll be free. Bred in punishment, revenge could be their idea of heaven, but not necessarily as believers in a united brotherhood.

The beasts will replace the beasts.

Yitzhak throws the wolf from this pulpit as if a sack of grain. "Know this—We are not Jew or Gentile. Not Polish, Litvak, German, or Russian, we are bonded as brothers. We are the proletariat. We have earned the right to revolution by our sweat. This is a revolution to end the poverty of being poor and a fair share for laboring as a slave!"

Their oath is only for want of more ale. They are about to attack the line of bottles on the shelf. Jakob fires another shot. Takes a bottle, stuffs a cloth rag inside, "They are the bombs that will set fire to the palace." Jakob marches across the long table, mocking the high step of a palace guard. He yells loud enough to be heard all the way to the palace—"Burn the Czar!" They cheer his hate.

I don't take shelter under the booth. The professors' stares test my loyalty. I'm pressed against the wall, surrounded by mindless beasts. I study the man beside me, whose skin is as smooth as a woman's. She's disguised as a worker in overalls and hides her hair under a miner's cap. She's standing beside another girl, maybe my age of seventeen, also wearing a similar disguise. I think of how Lenin respected Lina, how women, especially young girls, are the most abused of slaves. Nothing to do with the Czar, who is father to four princesses whom he dotes on, and his German wife, who is said to be the master's master. Poppa said that treating girls as less than men is a sign that the boy or man needs to believe they are a warrior. I whisper to the imposter—" The Prophet believes a woman deserves the same liberties as a man." But as I look around, I know that most of these men would beat a wife or daughter for wearing a man's disguise, let alone for a woman showing the courage of manhood by taking up the Cause.

Stanislav shouts out, "I will take ten of their soldiers before they take me." I hear Polish, Yiddish, Russian, Litvak, but misery and hate are easily understood by any language.

A beggar of a man pushes me aside. He wears the heavy wool uniform of a Russian soldier, torn and tattered by battle or time. The old man calls out in Polish as a curse—" The Czar is the bastard son of a Prussian whore. I will be the first to slit his throat."

Jakob repeats—" We are the beasts!".

I don't know if there's a Josef among them. I don't hear talk about pride in the labor of a trade, a passion, faith in the hammer, the sickle, the chisel, and the axe. I don't hear anyone arguing about this sacrifice before feeding their family. The Czar is to blame. They want revenge, not the bond of fatherhood.

The wolf throws off the cloak, climbs back onto the table, takes Jakob's bottle, puts vodka on the rag— "We will burn his kingdom."

My loyalty has taken me to the edge, but all I hear is the echo of Gramps and Poppa— "Faith in fables steals a man from truth. Beasts roam everywhere." Poppa wouldn't abide by this revolution. He would say, "*Be your master*." His manifesto, "*Choose your path*."

Gramps would call Lenin an ungodly dreamer. "He asks to trade your life for this fable of brotherhood." He'd laugh at the promise of respect between Goyim and Jew, master, and serf. He'd laugh, "That we could ever share equally." He'd say, "This dream of brotherhood is a story I cannot believe. Greed is tyranny. How does a worker win that battle?"

Jakob takes a well-aimed shot at the portrait of the czar—the hole piercing the gold medal over Czar Nicholas's heart.

The Poles argue and bond with the Ukrainians.

The Germans were here before the Russians and want to defend or win back Poland and Lithuania—neighbors against neighbors.

Lenin is a ghost casting its spell of a nightmare, everywhere. He'll be the General who looks down on the battlefield from a perch.

I searched for Leon and his three professors, whose pulpit was the corner booth. Are they joining these warriors to scorch the earth, or are they standing behind these pawns waiting to take the master's throne?

Hiram told me why Jakob offered free drinks and why he welcomes revolution. "The Cossacks came and demanded ransom. This is for revenge." He told me that a week ago, "The Cossacks threatened him— 'You own nothing. 'This is the Czar's tavern; you'll fill our coffers."

Jakob is the goniff of a thief who sells dreams that will never be. He had learned the peddler's art, to make lies truth by preaching in certainty.

The warning was too late, only one makes it through the door to cry out— "They're coming!" Jakob takes another shot at the portrait hanging on the wall, but a louder blast comes from outside.

The front wall explodes—splinters as daggers—smoke, the cannonball ripping across the room, rows of comrades torn aside.

Jakob jumps from the table— cries out, 'Death to the Czar!" Wounded but under the spell of rapture, they trample over fallen bodies, fire their pistols, rifles, throw daggers, spit curses, but at shadows.

Jakob and Yitzhak rally behind a shield of comrades, drunk and fevered with revenge. The mob is pushed from behind, row after row, an end to their misery, a mercy, not a sacrifice, to face the firing squad. Their flint shooting sparks that light the kindling for Lenin's bonfire.

Jakob holds two bottles. Yitzhak holds a torch to the cloth that lights the fuse. Jakob blindly throws the torch into the smoke. Yitzhak shoots at ghosts of the Czar.

I watched from the shadows of a barn burning in embers. The thatch roof was the tip of a torch. I didn't need to watch Yitzhak being shot. He found his dream.

I hide by the hole that is no longer a secret passage but a burning wall—the last of the kindling. The walls and thatch are embers drifting as fireflies in the night sky. Am I the traitor?

Aleksandrovsk Boulevard is no longer a peddler's market, but the nightmare of my childhood. As Josef feared and as I feared, the fire spreads. There will be no mercy for the innocents. No bystanders in war. Explosions and gunshots ring out.

I crawl into an alley that is burning rubble. But in the shadows of the fire's orange glow, the smoke as a golden cloud, I see the ragged brown suits, and the professor's black glasses looking back, his stare reflecting in the blaze.

I want to believe they share my doubt and believe this battle is not going to win the war. Leon wanted to preach as Christ. He argued with Lenin that teaching brotherhood is the only way to convert righteous souls to comrades. He worried that Lenin's cruelty would burn a teacher's hope for peace.

The fire spreads in all directions. They turn onto Tretolovsky, I try to follow, but the prophets disappear among the crowd and smoke.

I see defeat in the expression of frantic mothers clutching their babies, the elders and children helpless to find escape. Homes, stores, carts, and treasures more kindling for Lenin's revolution. But then think of Washington. America. The French. Revolution earns freedom.

Is Jakob a hero? Is he King David giving battle against Goliath. Will Yitzhak, Lina, and Jakob be honored with monuments?

But, as the innocents fall as sheep to the slaughter stirred by patriots and wolves against beasts, homes that gave a measure of shelter now ash—where the streets were villages of neighbors sharing the celebration of births, marriages, and mourning—now a cemetery. A life under a yoke—but it was a life with blessings as well. We are the mules who plow the fields, beavers who build dams, birds that make a nest," but isn't that the way? We are the Mothers, Fathers, Grandparents, families wanting to raise the next generation to know better— Josef's who take pride and earn the comforts. The revolution's toll is the ruin of the village where lives were filled—an open grave of innocents. The pious were killed in equal measure to the sinners. God seems to take no side.

I hid under a peddler's cart as the storm blew all around, but a dozen boys grabbed the cart. I crawl out, my cowardliness shamed by hateful stares. They rock the cart back and forth until tipping it over to make a blockade—the shield of cart and wagons trampled by warriors. The heroes are executed in a barrage of gunfire and combat with bayonets as swords.

Another gang of boys came racing down the road armed with clubs. Behind me is a lone soldier. He points his rifle at my chest. A moment as we exchange a measure of each other. He has the smooth skin of youth and blue eyes that seem confused. I grit my teeth, preparing to suffer the final pain of a bullet or knife, tearing me from life, and hope that death puts me out of this misery. I will die for no purpose without apology.

If I had a pistol in my hand, I wouldn't pull the trigger, but as he waits, he seems to struggle in his own debate; I'm surprised that he might feel the same. He turns away. Was I spared by someone sharing the same belief?

But the gang comes for him, and in self-defense, he fights as a warrior. Swings his rifle to return their blows, but there are too many. A boy no taller than my shoulder strikes a fatal blow with a pitchfork.

Lost in the chaos, I turn to find a path to escape, but before I can make a move, the gang is attacked. I'm caught in their battle. Look up at the horse's hooves, see his black boot, kicked by the stirrup, and the blow to my head sends me into the dream where Lenin is celebrating the bonfire. The Czar will commemorate the loyalty of his knights who defended the castle.

CHAPTER THIRTY-FOUR – 1905 -Winter

The fire spread from Jakob's tavern to homes, churches, and torched all in its path. Christian, Catholic, Jewish, secular, pagan, Polish, Latvian, German, or Russian, the flames of revolution exile orphans and families to their graves or a homeless path. All is lost. No matter whether the home was an alley, a shanty, or a palace, Lenin's battlefield leaves a cemetery of innocents.

I woke up to a nightmare, my mind lost in the fog of smoke and terror, choking on the stench of burnt flesh, but driven by an instinct to escape, I pulled my broken body and lost soul out from under two dead boys.

It's the blue sky of the morning after. Winter's cold shocked me to find my wits. My only thought is to flee Warsaw. I have nothing but a rag for a coat that offers no warmth.

Is it a sin to steal from the dead? I rummage through the soldier's pockets: flint, a pouch of bullets, and two rubles. The soldier's coat is spun with thick wool. I put it on. His knife is another prize. The musket is an old rifle, but still a prize. I pardon this as charity, not the spoils of war.

I can steal no more and follow a path beyond the edge of Warsaw to pass the last cottage that stands before the forest.

Hanging on the clothesline are the dresses of women who work at the mill and overalls showing the scars of fire, but before I can peer closer to see if it's Josef's, I'm startled by barking.

I ran across the road, only to look back, wanting to imagine it's Josef's home. Made with well-cut boards, framed windows, a home earned with sweat and kindness. Mold-making as a source of pride and not punishment. A wolf's howl keeps me moving. He boasted that his dogs were born from wolves.

The ice and snow are patches of slippery traps. At the crossroads, I face a decision of which direction to take—but there are few options. Berlin? Mrs. Dayan? I don't want to be a comrade. Without Yitzhak's prodding, still wobbly from the blow to my head, my thoughts lost to the nightmare of last night, I enter the sanctuary of the wilderness. By sunset, the branches sway as shadows of ghosts. I fell asleep as suddenly as death.

Blinded by the dark, I'm startled awake by the howls of wolves. Warned by David that a howl means the prey is theirs. A growl as a threat. A snarl to fight for who eats first.

The frozen ground makes it impossible to race away. I hold my breath. Had I given myself away? The howling comes from a distance that gives me time. Against a wolfpack, there'll be no place to hide. The rifle is old—a single-shot musket. I count six bullets in the pouch. I would get off one shot, maybe kill the leader, too long to reload, the pack won't retreat.

I pick up my pace and follow a creek. The ice is so thin it flakes off under the weight of my boots. I stumble over a log lying across the stream—but the branches are antlers. The Buck shakes and twitches. Blood is leaking from the bites on its side.

In mercy and hunger, I take the knife and finish what the wolves started—a mercy for a warrior who gave a good fight. The wolves are following the buck's scent. I have no time, but don't need to get far. They'll be satisfied with this bait. His sacrifice will buy me time to escape.

I stab a chunk of muscle from the loin, but my time is up.

The next few days are lost to wandering west toward the setting sun. Thirst is quenched by eating snow and ice from the creek. The loin is tough when raw, but stricken in fear of attracting strangers, I don't use the flint to start a fire.

It was five or six days when I came to a clearing of tall heather and found a path alongside a creek, followed it as it grew deeper and broader.

From the perch of a steep hill, there's the dark cloud of smoke. A decision: the wilderness as my test or risk the mercy of strangers.

I hid behind a thick branch of snow-covered pine to spy on a good-sized cabin of thick logs and a stone hearth. There's a fence holding fourteen pelts—more raccoon than rabbit, count two foxes, and four beaver. Good reason why I had no luck finding critters.

He's the size of Yitzhak. A tangle of wild dark hair hangs down to his shoulder. The scraggly beard has never seen a razor.

He spots me even. I'm surprised. The cover of the spruce's branches should have hidden me—a hunter with the vision of a hawk.

A whistle, and two more come from behind the cabin. Covered in fur, men as bears. He gives them notice that there's a stranger, and all three hold their axe high, call out, but stand still. The Viking is holding a jug, takes a long swig and hands it to the bear by his side.

"Lost." Better if Polish than Prussian? A risk that can go either way. What can I offer to make me worthy? I put down the rifle to pose no threat. I get closer, want to be one of them, and call out, "I'm a trapper. Was following tracks. I see you've found all the critters."

They pass around the jug while they study me. Can't hear their murmurings. My Russian coat? Do they think I'm a Russian soldier? What can I trade? They drink from the jug until it's empty. Water? I have only one skill, but they won't need fancy furniture.

I hear the bear call out, "Shnopps." They were drinking alcohol. I have another skill. It's a recipe worthy of a valued trade. My bubby's tonic.

"I make good vodka."

"You make vodka?" They're Polish. He comes closer.

I know their sort—trappers who will only trust those they know. I'm a stranger. You must prove your value and not be another mouth to bed and feed.

They study me in silence. He eyes my soldier's brown coat. "A Russian?"

"Polish." Need a good answer for the coat. I nod, "Warsaw," hoping to earn a measure of trust. "There was a battle. Took his coat."

They laugh in approval. The laughter brings out four more men of good size. None having ever shaved or cut their hair. They wear good beaver fur stitched over deerskin. The one with the tall hat of a red fox and a bear's snout to his cap acts as the leader.

Two women come from the cabin followed by a Bubby. She pokes me, "What have we here?" The old woman sizes me up. "A Jew from Warsaw," reading my nose, curled hair, and the child's pose of my small bones, "Escape?"

"Troubles. The Czar has no mercy."

There are groans, curses. They hold no love for Russians. There are boasts about how they've killed many. "Our land."

The other boy, closer to my age, steps close as well, and tells the fat woman with long white hair, "Says he knows to make vodka."

This brings her to study me closer. "What do you know?"

"I know how long to leave the mash, make a good yeast, turn a pot into a cooker, how long to cook, and I know what to keep, from what I boil off." Weak from hunger, thirst, and burdened by proving my value I beg, "Bread?"

The old woman's smile has few teeth but shows the caring of a Bubby. She leads me inside.

One large room of a log cottage with a worthy stone hearth. Told to sit at a table. The ten chairs are made with pride from antlers, deerskin, thick legs, carved back.

She ladles a bowl of soup from a pot boiling over a three-log fire.

It's no more than squirrel and rabbit but pickled in cabbage as I've never had. The big man fills a mug with their brew, and they watch me as if to test my skill. I take a sip, and it's a poor brew that holds fire, but give them thanks, "Pyszne," delicious.

Fed and weary, I'm taken by a boy my age to another cabin further into their patch of forest and shown a straw bed.

The next day, the Viking wakes me, pushing me through the forest to a spot hidden from view. Two young women with long braids are cutting potatoes, and a boy keeps the fire lit with a fan. An elder with a white beard down to his chest is stirring the kettle and hands the ladle to the Viking.

I'm put under the elder's watch for the rest of the day. He doesn't cook as Bubby, but I fear stirring his anger with advice.

Either they favor fire for drink, or the brewmaster doesn't know how hot, how long, or how to stir the pot, but they keep the pigskin pouch to their lips and swill this fiery potion as if water. I try to drink but can't handle its fire. Raised on good vodka, taught to take sips and avoid the spells of a drunk, and know how to measure just enough for comfort.

The next day, Karl takes me on a journey. We pass rows of cottages made of long logs, a large barn showing pride in the thin cut wood panels. This is more than a shtetl. It's a kingdom that spreads out beyond the homes I've seen. They keep some distance between each other. I count to a hundred cottages to larger cabins and think this is less than half of all who live here.

I'm invited into the cabin of the big man whom I met that first day. The large room is made smaller by his size, and a woman tending to a crying baby and the pecking of a toddler, but she's as tall as a good-sized man and manages all chores with laughter and cursing.

Proudly, the Viking introduces himself. I've earned his greeting.

"I'm Waleska," and points to a sack of potatoes. They waste no time having me prove my worth. "For the mash." Their Polish is their own, but I understand enough to get by.

I think to make the brew as Bubby taught me but decide it's safer to hold some of the recipe to keep from shining over the brewmaster's skill. After preparing the mash and leaving it to ferment, needing days to get to where I'm ready to cook, I question how I'll keep my value if I show them all my secrets. My path either way is as their slave or exiled to the wilderness.

They live as I grew up—family, chores, prayer, and tonic. Waleska is curious and pulls the elder brewmaster to watch.

I adjust the fire to where the heat is hotter than what would be to Bubby's liking, clean the mash. Had prepared the yeast, no barley to make the potion warm not hot, and there's no honey.

The day ends with the drippings from the spout and filling bottles.

Waleska has me take the first drink. It's not as Bubby would approve, but its heat warms and doesn't burn as bad as theirs. I nod.

Waleska swills a full ladle, and a smile forms.

I'm given the chore to make more.

My brew is poor, but to their liking. In return, I'm well fed, have a bed of straw on a perch off the dirt, and am warmed by a hearth. Except for the old brewmaster, I'm given nods of appreciation.

The men are gone most of the week, and the women tend to the children, cooking, and stitching cloth, fur, and hides—their clothes are well-made. The children are wild animals running about, causing trouble. The young girls laugh at me for my size. The older ones ignore me.

The men return in a foul mood. Vermin and deer also suffer in winter, only two boars give reason to feast. I'm led from the cabin. Not family. But hear them call to the spirits to give thanks. The echo of their prayer was made festive with fiddles.

The celebration demands many toasts, and the demand makes me a slave to the still. I'm impressed by their stock of flour, potatoes, milk, butter, and cheese. I haven't seen fields or livestock.

I overhear that we're three days in a quick pace to reach a capital city. Told half its people are German, half are Polish, who curse their countrymen for having lost their Polish soul.

Winter passes with tempers renewed by the first day of warmth that sparks the flowers to show themselves. I had made hundreds of bottles, but only the elders are privileged with a daily ration. The brewmaster watched me, learned my ways, and made it a point to turn everyone against me.

Waleska won't invite me into his cabin. "Our ancestors were prisoners of the Prussians, Swedes, Austrians, and my Polish grandfather was a Count shot by a Russian Captain who took his home. This is our ancestral land." Told with pride as a boast.

He explains their trouble. "We are between Warsaw and Berlin, but this kingdom is ancient Prussian. We are beavers caught between the wolves and bears." He speaks of both the Kaiser and Czar as equal enemies. "But the beaver will fight and draw blood until they quit."

He says nothing about my being a Jew. I'm not even thought of as a serf. I'm not welcome to their ceremonies. They suspect me for every ill. I must always take the first drink.

The elder brewmaster curses me, but fiddles with his recipe to copy my ways. They pay respect to Jesus but as a warrior who taught the 'true path.' There is not a week that goes by without celebration, funeral, birth, marriage, and songs as prayers in warding off fears. Punishment is doled out in deadly duels.

I want to ask for a reward beyond being fed and sheltered. I asked Karl if they sell what I make.

Karl told this to Waleska. He came for me, angry enough to smack me to the ground. He kicked my ass so hard I couldn't stand. "I trade only for a noble's favor," but in reverence, "For our General," a noble warrior.

Spring is welcomed with much celebration. The trees bud, the grass turns green, and the trappers bring back a bounty of deer.

I'm their mule. Waleska demands that I make this next batch special, promising me a great reward. By early summer, I'm put to work and fill a hundred pocket-sized bottles with the sweetness of a malt.

My reward is to explore beyond our village.

It's a day's hike to get beyond the hills that are at this forest's border. Karl follows the sun west, and by midday, we leave the woods to come to farmland that ends at the horizon. There's an army of hundreds planting seeds. The farmers are armed with sharp spades hitched to teams of two horses of such weight as to be giants. In the distance, there are large barns able to hold a hundred cows, pens of chickens and pigs, fenced fields holding herds of horses.

Karl tells me that further beyond the field is the master's palace. "He keeps a truce with the German Prussians by threat." My hosts, his warriors.

We sleep under the stars. Karl confesses his desire to marry Waleska's oldest daughter. He reveals to me that his wife died with their baby. Waleska's daughter is not much older than a child, but he tells me that she is ready to be married. He's worried because he must earn Waleska's respect to be his son by a contest to be held tomorrow.

We return the next morning to find hundreds gathering in celebration. The men assemble in lines. Some compete with spears, more with arrows. The test is to come as close to killing your opponent until you earn their surrender. They boast of taking on the Kaiser and Czar, but I foolishly ask Waleska, "What good is a sword, arrow, or spear against a rifle?"

He shakes his head and smiles, "We have rifles," and shows me. It's a fine rifle with a cartridge of bullets that he loads with a click into the barrel. "Good only for when your enemy is not on you."

He looks about the tops of the spruce and lifts the rifle to his chin— "I will kill the first with this rifle." He waits for the bird to show itself. The Blackbird swoops from the sky to a tree, an impossible target at fifty paces, and he fires one shot—the bird twitches before falling from the sky.

"The second is with a pistol." Grabs his pistol and in one motion kills a squirrel racing for its life up a nearby tree.

He draws his sword and takes on Karl in a duel. His finely crafted sword bangs hard against Karl's lesser iron, and with knives firmly in grip, lunges—only stopping a hair short of cutting into the boy's leather vest.

Waleska steps back. Poses as the victor. "All the rest will die by sword, then knife. They will get no closer unless my better," laughs, "and will have to kill me twice for I'll not go down from a knife's cut," to which he lifts his tunic to show branches of scars.

The warmth of summer is blessed with afternoon showers. The fields grow high, thick with grain, corn, and vegetables, bramble with sweet and ripe berries, and my vodka now known to all as a prize has me working into the night. I'm given the help of two boys, but always more potion in demand. I labor protected inside this kingdom of warriors, and no matter I'm treated as their serf, I haven't known hunger, comfort of a bed, good clothes, but this is not a home, not my people. I'm not welcome. Tolerated. The girls treat me as their slave, or as a curiosity to share their heartache over a warrior. Sleep comes as a good rest without nightmares, but I'm kept at a distance from the congregation.

I ask Waleska for a "A small reward." He hit me with the ladle, steps back to study me, and answers in anger. "I have let you live, work, eat, and rest, what more?"

If I escaped, where would I go? It would be better to stay here before dying as a warrior for the Cause. What purpose did Yitzhak's courage serve but to burn Warsaw and leave behind a graveyard of innocents. Waleska told me we're between Poland and Germany, just outside the German king's city of Poznan—the capital of the old Prussian kingdom of Posen. Prussia united by battle and favors with all of Germany. Berlin as the capital. Would Germans treat me any better than Poles or Russians? Mrs. Dayan would argue for Berlin. "Academics with enlightened beliefs."

These people are warriors who keep to themselves. They have no trust in outsiders—an orthodox congregation. My salvation is the potion. Their women are strong and as good as a man if put to a test of courage. I have my eye on a sweet girl named Sophie. She is only to my chin, treated poorly, timid, and such thoughts occupy a good part of my day, and make me restless.

It was a night of celebration with no regard given to me for brewing my finest potion yet. I keep to my bed in Karl's cottage as ordered, but as their revelry grows louder, I creep closer, hide behind Waleska's cottage, and hear talk of their General and the Count.

Karl told me, "The Count rules us all. He holds a village of your people to do his labor. This is the first I hear mention of Jews. I'm told, "If they don't earn their way, they are left to die of hunger."

CHAPTER THIRTY-FIVE – Polish King – 1906

I'm pushed to the back of a wagon, wedged between crates holding a hundred bottles of my best tonic. Waleska leads a procession of a dozen wagons loaded with corn, grain, and livestock. The wheels carve deep ruts in roads softened by a summer blessed with its healing rain. Our procession of wagons are led by ten warriors who follow in the same direction as when Karl took me to see the farm with its endless fields, and discover that beyond the barns, barracks, and gardens there's a castle.

Four horsemen rode out to greet us. The well-tailored red uniform is crowned with a polished silver helmet plumed with feathers.

Cavalry, cannons protect the castle, and a hundred soldiers. Another army armed with pitchforks--piles straw on haystacks.

Our six wagons pass near the palace but keep going until we're led down a tree-lined road to a barn large enough to hold fifty cows.

He rushes from the house as if under attack. His uniform is a black suit with a long-tailed jacket, and a stiff white shirt whose collar chokes on a thick neck. I climb down only to be smacked by his cane, ordered to unload a crate, and poked into a kitchen of busy bees.

I'm pushed into a corner and drink in the tempting smell of a feast as I've never imagined. Four chefs shovel generous helpings from giant kettles cooked over a bonfire inside a hearth the size of a wagon. Women load the bounty onto silver plates and bowls, then place them on platters held by six men in long coats made of a cloth that shines like a blue sky.

The women are angels descended from clouds—white dresses spun from a spider web of lace, a vision of fairies with porcelain skin, red lips, and golden manes braided into tails that hang down slender backs.

Ignored, no offer of food or drink, a prisoner below even servants, I'm kept in the corner until late into the night. The chefs and fairies are gone, replaced by women washing stacks of plates, pots, and pans.

when the two regal guards grabbed the crate, I thought it was time for my execution. We pass grand rooms beyond grand rooms, a forever hall ending at wide double doors defended by giants of guards. They eye me with suspicion but open the massive door on command.

Waleska stands beside a bald gnome made smaller by a Czar's throne set behind a desk Mr. Dayan would be proud of. Waleska cursed the Czar and Kaiser with equal venom. Their loyalty is to this Polish king. An elderly man, round- faced with a grand mustache twirling ear to ear beneath a pudgy nose.

Ten guards stand like statues before ten windows twice their height. The domed ceiling is a sky of blue with puffy clouds, and in the light of God, there's the sorrowful skin and bones of Jesus comforted by angels. The walls are paintings of kings battling invaders of old. The chandeliers are a hundred gold branches that sprout into a thousand glass leaves.

Behind the throne is the king's map with six blue flags set between Berlin and Warsaw. His kingdom is somewhere between Russia's Poland, and the Poland of Prussian Germany.

The room casts a spell. I'm in a dream.

I think back to Gramps and Poppa telling me the history of Prussia and Poland as a never-ending cycle of battles among Germany, France, Austria, and Russia, since the time of the Romans.

Waleska comes beside me, takes the crate, opens it with his sword, holds up a bottle, nods to me, and announces— "The brewmaster."

He pulls the cork, pours a few drops into the gold goblet, nods to the king and takes a sip—waits a moment, smiles, and pours a full goblet for the king.

The king takes a sip, another smile, and with a wave, the guards pull me from the room, led through the kitchen, taken outside, and marched from the palace. A full moon lights stone a path that cuts through the gardens to reach the crest of a hill, and I look down on a long row of stables, three large barns, and two rows of barracks, with twenty doors each. I'm locked in a shack behind the barracks.

A sleepless night pondering my fate. At sunrise the guards take me from the shack to the back of the barracks where there's a congregation of over a hundred Orthodox wearing black pants, white shirts, cared for by an equal number of girls to women to elders, all in black frocks.

The grinding wheel uses a mule to turn the heavy stone crushing grain to flour. Dozens of women work the looms. A flock of children feed thread. The older girls pull each new row down to add another layer to a sheet. Six men butcher pigs, boys pluck chickens. Four ovens heat long rods held by men blowing glass into a bubble from long pipes. I knew this trick of stretching the gooey ball into a bottle. As we pass by, I'm reminded of the hell of an oven's heat needed to transform sand to glass.

Thirty boys fill the bottles, and half as many girls cork them and load crates, while soldiers carry them through a guarded gate into a brick shelter. I catch a glimpse of a thousand bottles stacked on shelves, glistening in the sunlight.

I'm pushed through the gate and see four copper barrels hidden behind a tall fence. Steam pipes blow white smoke from boiling mash. "You will work here," the soldier tells me in Polish. He turns to an older man at the far end of the table. "He is to be a brewmaster."

There are sacks of grain and a wagon full of potatoes.

My fate was sealed the day I arrived at Waleska's and traded making vodka for food and shelter. I am to be a Josef crafting treasure for a master at the altar of fire.

The elder greets me in Hebrew. Our code to test kinship. "You make the golden vodka?" his smirk and the grunt of a laugh reveal a hint of jealousy.

"My Bubby's recipe."

"An expert!"

I don't know if I should feel embarrassed or proud.

He calls over a young man and woman.. "This is Joshua, and the girl is Sarah."

"Where are you from?"

"Riga."

"The Litvak has come a long way ."

Guards watch from every corner. I whisper, "I'll be shot if my vodka is not to their pleasure?"

"We are given a room and well fed, if there's enough." Joshua is a handsome man, a few years older, and tests me in Yiddish, "Treated no worse than the horses, but fed last. Work is sunrise to sunset. They let us keep the Sabbath."

Sarah hands me a thick slice of heavy brown bread smeared with butter and egg.

I'm given a taste of their brew. It's bitter but worry if I'm their better would it invite contempt, be replaced, resent my being the master? But the king is expecting what I brewed for Waleska. A trap. I have only one path, and confide, "More molasses to sweeten, and half more barley to cool the bite. Lower heat. Boil another day."

The two brewmasters listen with curiosity, smile, and as brethren their questions prove they already know most of Bubby's recipe, but for her secrets. A full day of teaching and learning ends at sunset with Joshua taking me to a room at the end of the barracks. I watch as all return to their rooms and discover that we're arranged by age, men separated from the women. Children share the middle rooms. The echo of babies' cries come from the far end, where mothers and daughters are rocking them to sleep.

Joshua opens the door to reveal a small room crowded by four bunk beds. Two boys face the back wall, bowing in prayer.

"Moritz," Joshua whispers, "The other is Philip." My roommates are curious enough to turn from prayer, show me a nod, and then turn their backs in a hurry to find escape in God.

Supper is a harvest feast set on long tables.

Their devotion shown by the meal being kosher, and Orthodox by keeping the women to their side, a long service of prayers as if a test against the temptation of a feast.

I'm a curiosity mostly eyed with suspicion. The young man sitting next to me has an intense stare under dark brows. "How'd you end up here?"

I debate what story? I need to learn more about their piety before I tell my story. The twenty boys and young men all staring with intent. "I got lost and was found by a village of Poles who serve this master."

"You from Warsaw?"

"Grew up in Riga. The last few years in Warsaw. I was apprenticing to make furniture, but the master left for Berlin, and I was to follow." The easier lie is to tell the truth.

"Warsaw? Were you there?" They heard? Were there? They lean closer. The one with a full beard asks, "We heard that many were killed." In a somber tone, "From what we know. Many killed."

I'm not surprised that word spread.

I ask Joshua how they came to learn of this. "The wagons come from everywhere for our vodka." Joshua pulls me close. "We heard that hundreds were killed. That Warsaw burned."

A moment to see if I was ready for confession. I want to hear more. "What do you know?"

"Hundreds of Russians were killed. More in St. Petersburg." I discovered that Lenin was everywhere. That another Yitzhak and Jakob lit a fire, but that Josef was right" The Czar's revenge was answered with a reign of terror. Pogroms spread as far as Minsk, Odessa, and Kiev; God knows how many were killed as punishment." The boys close their eyes in prayer. "Life has also been hard on all. Catholic Poles are only a hair's breadth above a Jew."

Their curiosity shows they know more than I suspected, "Do you know of Karl Marx," even softer, "Comrade Lenin?"

Joshua looks around for prying ears, and then tells me, "The Kaiser has taken to executions as a warning. Anyone caught with a newsletter or book about such things is arrested."

I think of Josef and his warning about the price of revolution. Joshua goes on to explain, "The feud between the Poles, Russians, Germans and Austrians, tests everyone's loyalty." Joshua is grim. "My brother works in the palace kitchen. There's great fear."

Winter comes, and our new chores are repairs and additions to the soldiers' barracks. I want to prove my value and show my skills in carpentry. The reward is to fix the windows and doors at the girls' barracks. There's one who returns my glance, and risks telling me her name with a smile, "Mindala." But their rule of separation keeps us apart.

Warmth is helped by the good wool coats and scarves our women make. Death comes at least once a week from fever, age, or as punishment for a sin as slight as cursing a guard. As if an act of favor, the General donated a small plot of land for burials.

The Kaiser's ambition is made public. "Wilhelm has declared that his ancestral land has been held for too long by Russian thieves."

I let it slip that I met Lenin, and even though I quickly added that I argued against his preaching for revolution, word spread and I'm put under suspicion. A sermon is given to warn that our loyalty must be shown as "lambs and mules."

I welcome this life of servitude. I have friends. A community of brethren whose piety is not mysticism or preaching fables of salvation, too busy with a day filled with labor. Making tonic is to my liking, but I'm shunned as the stranger who came from Warsaw with the smell of revolution. I thought to earn trust by confessing my doubts. But doubt is a poison to the certainty of their faith. They worried such thoughts could spread. Joshua was warned not to confide in me. The greater punishment was being shunned.

I posed as Orthodox, but my show of devotion was seen as a lie. I lacked fervor. I wanted to earn the trust of the only girl who returned my smile, but she has been warned that I'm not a "True Jew."

Winter is always about survival, so I'm grateful for the comfort of a bed, the warmth of the hearth, the hidden bottles of my Bubby's tonic, good bread with butter and eggs. Shabbos is celebrated with chicken. The outhouse is kept clean, and the girls wash out the lice with boiling.

Spring returns with its warmth, but winter's slow pace is left behind in a hurry. All but those I work with are put to the fields for planting.

Time is measured by the change in season. There's the sweat of summer, and the fire of winter's cold. Harvest is punishment needing double the labor, but the reward is feasts. I cook, taste the fermented potatoes, raise, and lower the flame, order the kettle to be removed, command the boys and girls to fill bottles, as if a master, but my authority is kept only to my corner.

My fourth year, about to turn twenty-two, and tested by the need for a woman. I want a marriage, family, and my desire for Mindala festers. I earned their trust and Joshua introduced me to the matchmaker who approved of my courting Mindala Kaufestky. She had rejected a number of suitors because she has little regard for devotion to Orthodox customs and shares my doubt, hangs on my stories.

Spring stirs talk of marriage. I press my affection, but before I steal a second kiss, Mindala confesses she wants to escape. "I'm nineteen and have seen enough to know I want to live as you had in your childhood. To have our own farm like your family."

CHAPTER THIRTY-SIX – NOV. 1910

Time loses all meaning when the labor is to your liking, few days of hunger, and the love of a girl who feels your passion.

It's the day of the festival, harvest collected, stored, pickled, and dried, but as the sun greets the day, we're awakened by explosions.

The frightening sound of bombs shake the ground. Thunder coming from the direction of the palace. Everyone rushes outside.

In the dim light of sunrise they swarm as locusts. A cavalry of a thousand charge down the regal path, across the fields, tear through the gardens, firing at all who come from the palace. Cannons fire on the King's army. The barracks blown to splinters. The soldiers descend from the horizon as a storm. A cavalry of Huns appear from behind a smoky curtain and exploding dirt. Their attack unleashed on the Count's half-dressed soldiers who race from the barracks still standing.

They raise swords, fire back, but caught by surprise, the Count's few hundred soldiers are quickly overwhelmed by this red suited cavalry of a thousand.

The King and a palace guard of six knights on fast horses race from the palace, but their escape was anticipated by the invaders' fifty horsemen who kill all but the king. They form a circle to hold him prisoner and show their disrespect by poking him with flags serving as spears. The king pleads for surrender, but they show no mercy and rip him from the horse with a whip that drags him to the good distance to the front of the palace where five nobles hold court from their throne of white stallions. The General is known by a gold helmet tipped with a spike. He raises a bloodied sword. The firing squad waits for his verdict.

The Priest is shoved beside the King, but the Catholic noble is not given time for a prayer before the General raises his sword.

Their execution is swift.

Shots ring out from inside the palace. A moment later, thirty servants are pushed, shoved toward the barns. Given shovels. Ordered to dig their graves.

They're unwilling to surrender, curse, raise their fists, want to die with honor, and attack with shovels, but shot before their hate is spent.

The soldiers herd our congregation as sheep, run their hands through our pockets, steal the rings and coins.

I hear Mr. Dayan curse our cowardliness. Would I earn his respect, be given honor, and hailed as a warrior comrade if shot giving battle?

The General goes down the line of servant women, nods toward the angels who are led back into the palace.

He trots a hundred paces from the palace to our barracks. Sets his study to our women. One by one he points his sword at a girl as young as a child to an aged woman who still shows temptation. The general gathers thanks from his officers who nod in appreciation. Those who fight back are tied by whips and loaded onto wagons, those who submit are taunted by the pack of wolves hungry in lust.

My heart is on fire. Mindala is one of the women who submits. I catch her glance. She's not a Lina. When I confessed my surrender to work at the forge and thought of assimilating, she gave me absolution. "If I'm ever taken prisoner, I'll cling to life and deny that submission is a sin. Each day to experience life in all its good and evil is our only real purpose, for I believe that death is the eternity of darkness." In telling her about Marx, she became a disciple. Easy to convert an atheist for they mock the mysticism of being held to God by a soul.

Joshua is the first to break from the line. He races toward the General. "Burn in hell!" Followed by half of our boys and men who find mercy in being executed before suffering the punishment of living a nightmare. Their courage is from having faith they'll find their loved ones in heaven.

Coming down the long path toward the palace are twenty wagons loaded with families who celebrate as they approach the palace, until witnessing the battlefield. The mothers try to shield their children from witnessing the price of their reward.

They're given greeting by the General who is their Lord. His command as gospel. Commandments written by nobles. Held by faith that they are no more than loyal citizens under another manner of threat.

The General gives them welcome with a wave of his sword. The mothers try to shield the babies and children as they shuffle into our barracks. The sons and fathers carry their belongings into their new home.

The General turns his attention to what remains of our congregation. No more than thirty men left. "Who is the brewmaster?"

Our elder, the brewmaster, Heschel, steps forward along with the two sons who are his apprentice. "I am."

"And who else?"

Trembling, he recites the kaddish. "Our reward is heaven, your punishment is eternity with Satan."

The General. "You will stay here and teach what you know. Produce and you live. But, I know it's a young man who is the better brewmaster."

I think it's better to stay here. "I make vodka."

CHAPTER THIRTY-SEVEN – Poznan --1910

I believe there's little value in the trade of shame for being shot, but my fate is not to stay here. I'm tied to a wagon loaded with twenty soldiers. The war was won. The army follows their General from the battlefield.

It's three days on the road. I'm surprised when the soldiers allow me to take a ration of bread, cheese and ale.

Poznan is as all cities, towering steeples of cathedrals, cobblestone roads, a river, homes, stores, carts, and the hive of bees making honey.

I can smell the brewery before I see a brick mill fueled by the wheels that are spun by a river to drive whatever machines are inside.

The soldiers lead me through long hallways sealed by iron bars as doors and windows. I'm strapped to a chair. Wait for hours before the door is opened. I conjure torture will extract the recipe and then execution.

The General finally enters. He twirls the corners of a black mustache. He takes a metal poker with some sort of drawing on its tip, and inserts it into the potbelly stove until it glows red. He turns to me with a smirk that speaks to his passion for inflicting pain. A smile as he presses it against my leg. Holds my eyes until it burns through my pants. The stench and smoke of wool just a moment before the punishment of pain close my eyes.

From hell, I hear him compliment my tonic. "Your vodka is very good." Bubby's blessing is my curse.

I believe I will live only for as long as I hold the secret. Inheritance rules my fate as it does for a prince. My cry holds in a scream as I stutter in the grip of Satan, "How may I serve you?"

"You speak German. Always the clever Jew."

He waves a crystal bottle, takes a sip. "It will be your privilege to be my brewmaster, will it not."

"I only hope not to disappoint."

"Yes, of course."

I look down to realize that it's an eagle holding a serpent etched into my thigh. I've been branded as if his cow, horse, mule.

The general's laugh haunts me as the door is opened and he leaves.

I'm untied and taken to the brewery. The Captain introduces me to a crew of four wearing gray overalls. An elder of some stature is honored by a white uniform. His thick white hair and beard are trimmed with style.

The brewery is no different than a forge or mill but with huge copper kettles and the pipes that leak the brew. I struggle in debate as to how to keep my secret. If I make the mash according to Bubby's recipe, they'll not need me. I think to keep the last ingredient of barley and the final minutes of cooking time and heat a secret, but fear I'll be tortured or shot if the potion isn't to the General's liking.

The five are waiting for the lesson. I need time to plan. It takes two weeks to ferment. I'll prepare the mash to her recipe in hope I'll find a path for revenge.

The day ends at sundown because a torch or spark from an electric light could ignite the fumes of alcohol. I'm taken down a hallway lit in shadows into a large open room lined with bunk beds. The room is divided by those in gray work overalls from those in blue. The top bunks are for the guards who watch us as hawks. My bed is a board, theirs is a mattress of soft feathers.

Locked in a brick-lined cell, sunrise is when the bugle blows.

I couldn't sleep. The pain served as punishment for being a coward and not taking the path of escape in death with honor. My heartache burns hotter than the brand—too many regrets. Patriot, traitor, coward, or under the spell of doubt, I confessed my sins to darkness.

Under guard, we're led to a kitchen with a large stove. There are five long tables, each with benches of equal length, always watched by the guards. We must wait in line. The thirty in gray are served first. I'm last to be served a ladle of mush and a slice of bread.

There is a pecking order to this flock. Those who wear gray have sausage, eggs, cheese, and a thick slice of bread.

I quickly realize that those who labor in gray overalls are the Kaiser's loyal Lutheran Germans. They cheer his promise to make Germany the wolf, yet they are also bound as a brotherhood. They share the same faith as a Josef, craftsmen who take pride in their labor.

The Poles, Jews, and peasants are given those tasks that require the foulest of routine. They grind the mash, lift heavy sacks of grain, peel potatoes, or, if deemed unworthy, send them to the basement to feed the ovens in the floor below. We are forbidden to have none of what we brew. If found drunk, it's a serious crime. Our day begins just after sunrise and ends at sundown. The gray knights take long breaks, and time is set aside during the day for these good Lutherans to train for war. We can see through the large windows as the knights take to the courtyard to train for battle. They are given a rifle that can fire six bullets in rapid succession. There are duels with wooden swords. They are soldiers. The brewery has barracks. It's a fortress. The loyalists are well-fed given the privilege of days off to visit their families.

For those nineteen of us in the blue overalls, our day is spent cleaning, doing laundry, grinding, pouring, feeding the ovens and stirring the mash. The elder brewmaster observes my preparations with skepticism yet makes notes. My only honor is to dip the ladle into the kettle for a tasting.

For the next two weeks, my mash is left to ferment. I'm taught by the only ambitious member of my crew, the math of cooking vast quantities.

I'm surprised how the elder brewmasters lack an understanding of heat and time. In the two weeks watching them make ale and vodka, it's obvious why their brew is different batch to batch: either it burns the throat or it's little more than water, casting a spell of drink. Never smooth or having a tempting flavor. The elder is Prussian. Stubborn, prideful, and wouldn't make a change unless under threat of death. But there is no threat. Each batch is celebrated as alchemy. It serves the purpose of alcohol. Getting drunk is second only to their faith in a Christ who champions crusades for conversion, and their Lord is the Kaiser.

We're sealed in a prison. I couldn't commit suicide for the guards being so close. I don't comment on their piss. I don't explain how to adjust the time of fermenting or the temperature of the heat. I'm only allowed to nod or shake my head.

Once my mash has fermented to my liking, I make a small batch. The brewmaster shows his disdain for how I clean the mash. Without betraying all my secrets, I spend two days under a slow boil instead of raising the heat as I was taught, but I'm possessed by the need to prove my recipe is superior and, for some reason, want to earn the general's respect. But when I taste the tonic and realize that even though I followed Bubby's recipe, it's not to her softness. I know that the ingredients make the difference—their potatoes, barley, sugar, and molasses. And then there's the water. It's the river water. Even though it passes through a sand filter and is then boiled, the river is not as pure as rainwater skimmed and filtered through cloth. I fill a small bottle and steady myself. It's not Bubby's but its heat stirs the comfort of a healing potion.

I waited two long days for the verdict. The Captain took a sip, but his stare had the expression of surprise, not flattery.

On the third day, the Captain called me to his office. "Baron Von Brandenburg wants a thousand bottles by the end of the month."

I had learned that the General is a Baron under the thumb of a Count who rules Poznan under the thumb of the Kaiser. But it's not a surprise that I'm kept on. The Baron must know that his elder brewmaster is useless. I was informed that Dietrich Bismarck is a nephew of the Chancellor, and since the Count controls the brewing and distribution of all alcohol sold in the province of Posen, there was no need to do better than serve a potion that got the customer drunk.

I'm kept under watch while the grays take notes and study my methods, but my secrets are kept hidden by being blind to the craft. They have no mind's eye for how I chose the better grain, better potatoes, or the magic of preparing yeast. Many refuse to drink my potion as if sacrilege.

My reward includes sausage and a soft mattress.

The Baron holds me under a tight leash. My hate and want for revenge is kept to a simmer. Over the next year, routine slowly filters to anger, and by the end of my second year, a routine of an easy day where my helpers do the tedious chores of stirring, feeding the fire, filtering water, and peeling potatoes fuels a healing with pride, power, and respect, even if despised. My rebirth sands the rough edge of hate to anger, and by the third year, pride and authority filter nightmares to distant memories as fading echoes are lost to the privilege of a well-fed routine of my making.

CHAPTER THIRTY-EIGHT - Brewery – 1913

News of the Kaiser building an armada to rival his grandmother's British fleet finds its way into our prison by the boast of the grays. Learn that the Germans have an army of a million men wanting to prove that Germany should rule the world. The summer of 1913 brings the Poles to heel, Prussians to patriotism, and a spirit of all Germany united in tribal bonding that has the proletariat silenced by putting hard to work building a war machine under the watchful eyes of farmers and laborers given authority as police, soldiers, and nobles finding pride as Officers.

I'm given a helper who is not a gray but wears a blue uniform. The grays had built such resentment for a small Jew who rules the brewery that the Captain fears for my safety. At least one attempt a month is made on my life by a gray. I was given my own room, my own schedule, such is the respect I've earned for making the Baron a fortune. Others have tried to copy my ways, but they don't understand that filtering water, and knowing the better ingredients is the key.

Ludwig is a weak man who I suspect is Jewish because of dark hair, eyes, a fuller lip, a broader nose, and his care in crafting a dutiful temper. After a month of following my instructions and watching my back, he finally whispers, "Marxist?" He tells me in a whisper, "I was a Jew, but now a socialist. My being shunned earned Ludwig's trust. He tells me that he has three comrades wanting escape or revenge. He admits to being imprisoned for peddling, but it was his wife and son being cast out that is at the core of his want for revenge.

His temper ignites memories that I've kept dormant under privileges that filter my nightmares.

Ludwig is a proud Marxist. He boasts of being a member of a bund in Berlin. A peasants tavern ruled by a Jakob who also recruited thieves and peddlers. Bonded not by Marx, but finding profit in the black market of alcohol, gambling, prostitution, and whatever sin or treasure that earned funds for their brand of revolution.

He triggers hurtful memories. My doubt about the value of revolution remains unchanged. I am Leon. A preacher, but my want for revenge against the Baron is fed by the brutality of his war against the Polish king.

It's March and spring weather thaws tempers. Four months of the brewery as an icebox keeps everyone thankful for its warmth, daily ration, and shelter. Always under watch. Even in sleep, but with Ludwig at my side I'm reminded of those nightmares I wanted to forget.

Ludwig is from Berlin. He tells me how he left years ago thinking that Poznan would have less threats. He goes on to tell me, "Berlin is where Germans show their kingdom as greater than heaven. A city so grand with wealth, you think you're invisible." Ludwig closes his eyes to a squint. Squeezed shut to suffer a painful memory. Forces a smile as he stares into my thoughts for acceptance. "But it can be very small if you step on another's trade. Like Poznan, if the master wants you to be found, they find you." I knew how the innocents of his family suffered for his desperation to earn. The father, a husband's pride spent in providing.

It's Easter and the guards are sleeping off the drunk earned by not being allowed to celebrate. Half the grays are home with family. Ludwig pulls my arm, "Come with me." We have to feel our way in the dark to reach the toilets. A wooden bench cut with a dozen holes to sit or stand over, water taken and given from the same river that fuels our brew. Only the boiling keeps the ale and vodka from spreading poison.

We are all made to shave and cut our hair, but the barbers hold the blades. We must take a shower every third day. The cold river water sprayed on with hoses. The Germans hold to rules and discipline, and keep great stock in cleanliness, more mindful of rats, lice and vermin spoiling their brew.

Ludwig takes me past the showers to a small room. I recognize the three other men, but we've never spoken, only exchange the knowing nod of a fellow prisoner. I'm introduced to Abraham. A young man, maybe my age, my size, but his stare demands your attention. We converse in Polish, but he knows Yiddish.

Ludwig introduces me to Michel. The pipes and a pump make such noise that our talk needs to be near an ear. Michel is tall, as thin as a beanpole, a ghoulish skeleton with sunken eyes and pocked skin. He talks of nothing but revenge. The Prussians stole his father's farm.

Gorgy is thick boned and shorter than me but strong enough to lift barrels all day. He wants revenge for losing his wife to a noble who imprisoned him to have his way with her.

I confess my tale of that night in Warsaw. I tell most of it but don't admit to fleeing the front-line. When they hear how Jakob and Yitzhak sparked the bonfire, they become feverish. “We must do the same.” I realize that I’ve unwittingly lured them into the darkness as a messiah.

“To strike is to be shot.” Michel takes my tale of Jakob as his own. “We should burn this prison down.” I hadn’t thought it through, but my story stirred them to revolution.

Ludwig agrees, “I want to believe that in death my nightmare will end.”

Abraham’s hate gives him courage. “I am ready to die tomorrow if we can succeed, but how?”

Michel is under the spell, pacing, plotting, “Steal the rifles—take an axe to the tanks,” he hits the brick wall—a revelation— “We will burn it down.” He pulls us close. “The bomb is the still—the gunpowder is what we brew, all we need is to light the fuse.”

“When?” Ludwig steps in Michel’s way.

“Soon.”

“Tomorrow!” Gorgy takes hold of Ludwig. “Why wait. What is there to live for.”

“What is your plan?” Abraham is ready to light the torch.

I suffer in the memory of the carnage of innocents. I think of all who might perish. The gray uniformed Poznan Germans are truthful, hard-working men who preach their gospel and live by its rules. The brewery is their craft and trade—Christ their redeemer. The Kaiser their God.

Ludwig would have been by Yitzhak’s side. He believes his miserable life of knowing his wife and children could be dead, or at best suffering for his being arrested. His purpose is revenge.

I imagine the explosion. Blowing up the brewery will bring untold punishment to the innocent. An act of such terrorism will excite the beasts. The Baron will build another. The Kaiser gains another excuse to execute all he believes stand in his way.

Michel votes, “To die as a warrior.”

I want to confess my doubt about the value of this trade, but in my confusion, my hate for the Baron, I become feverish. Too many memories: Mindala, Lina, my family. Revenge poisons my heart.

Abraham preaches—“The Baron will feel our pain. I know a way. They’ve let a fox into the hen house.” He conjures the plan. “I’m not suspected. They have me tending the furnace.”

We hear someone come into the bathroom. Michel looks out the door and then returns to pull us into his plan. “End of day, as everyone leaves, just as I'm to smother the flames there will only be the pious Prussian who is always by my side, and two guards who will have finished a second bottle by then."

Ludwig is in fever. "The room where we ferment the grain sits in giant vats. The fumes are vented by pipe. It's beside the room where the large kettles distill the alcohol. A spark could set off this bomb."

Michel works in a prison cell of a room. He keeps the furnace under his watch. The furnace is below the vats, and the vapor of alcohol is sent through pipes spanning the factory above.

Abraham has his own plan. "The vapors rise from the vats. I'll break the pipe."

Michel's plan, "A torch to the fumes."

Ludwig, "The shovel could puncture the tank that holds a pond of raw alcohol, but I need flint to set that ablaze." He looks to us. "We do all three?"

They look to me. "I'll watch for any soldiers who might be coming and use a pipe to knock them out and steal a rifle."

Ludwig presses the plan. "If the two Prussian give you trouble, It could distract them long enough for Michel to bring a torch from the furnace."

We sneak past the sleeping guards and wait.

Go about the day exchanging nods to confirm the plan.

Sunset is the moment to strike.

I take a last look. Without prayer or cry, Abraham, Gorgy, stand behind Ludwig as he pulls a pipe from the vat to release the dangerous fumes.

The guards hear the break, rush to see, and panic at the sight of the broken pipe and the rising cloud of raw alcohol. Gorgy and Abraham fight off the guards with the broken pipe.

Abraham is pushed to the floor and shot.

Gorgy is strong enough to defend himself.

I retreat as a coward or for suffering the guilt of once again unleashing a nightmare. I race up the stairs to the warehouse and hear the echoes of Jakob, Yitzhak, and Mr. Dayan telling me to go back down and die for purpose. I am not of their faith. No faith in revolution. I am either a coward, agnostic to no faith in anything, or I only believe that Jesus can spread the miracle of brotherhood to save us.

I sneak like a rat between the bottles and crates to find my way to the dock and knowing there are only moments left before the bomb goes off, I hide between the rows of heavy wood barrels. The courtyard is crowded with wagons that travel far beyond Poznan to all of Posen, and perhaps beyond to deliver the potions.

I conjure the vision of Ludwig igniting the broken pipe—the bullet as the flint and spark. I imagine Michel lighting a torch from the furnace's embers. He'll stand proud as his torch ignites the sinking vapors from below.

The guards are on alert by the sound of burst pipes, and with the blast of gunshots, they race as heroes into battle, but they are too late, the explosion is ten times the thunder of Russian cannons. I've rekindled Warsaw.

I crawl to hide between crates and barrels that shield me from the scorching heat of fireballs racing past. The horses jolt from the dock into the courtyard to outrace the flames. The barrels begin to smoke, and I crouch deeper into the corner.

The explosion will be heard as far away as the palace.

The fire leaps the length of the building as the flames race up the road as fast as a horse at gallop. The rats are first out, guards next, followed by prisoners howling from behind the bars, unable to escape, their gray and blue wool uniforms set on fire.

Chunks of brick and beams tear at the crates and barrels. The two drivers are blown from their perch. The wagon breaks, the horses torn apart—shrapnel is flying in all directions. I'm saved by a shattered half barrel, held as a shield against flying brick, shards of wood, and glass.

As sudden as the war began, the lightning and thunder fade, but the carnage leaves behind a funeral pyre that rages on, and any path out is hidden in smoke. My choice is to die crouched in a corner or chance escape. I hold the half of a barrel, and race between burning bodies, a battlefield littered with Poles, Germans, Prussians, Lutherans, Catholics, Jews—no one is spared.

If I were of faith, I'd believe I'm Satan's disciple.

I find my path through the gate and amidst the chaos I'm invisible. I'm about to turn onto the River Road when a regiment of soldiers are marching toward the battlefield as if in parade. They show their dedication with the high-kick to their step—all as one. No longer a man seeing life through his own eyes—but studs on the shield—their life given to the cause of protecting a merciless master.

The General holds up his hand—but there's no army to fight, just a burning battlefield. The army is no match for four terrorists.

As though a dam burst—they pour out from the surrounding factories and mills. A wave of workers race past the guards who shoot at a blur, fleeing what they believe is war.

I am swept inside the wave, my escape hidden inside a flood of workers streaming down the road until the wave breaks apart. The side streets and roads each take a share from the river of humanity. I'm pulled by those who share my fear. Race blindly for escape.

CHAPTER THIRTY-NINE –Berlin –1913-14 –

I can't bear to witness the punishment of innocents. I flee as a cripple on tired legs. Lost in a daze, confused, suffering that familiar heartache of guilt. I take no notice of the soldiers, wagons, and a parade of other lost souls in flight from war. It's only as I reach the edge of the city and come to the crossroads of paths leading in all directions.

To the south is the unknown prejudice of the Slavs. North is back to Vilna, perhaps Riga. The sign shows a well-traveled path to Berlin. A spike of want courses from my heart to my mind. To find Mrs. Dayan. Only she can absolve my doubts. She'd blame the spell of sympathy in a world of cruelty.

The road is held by the migration of other lost souls, merchants, soldiers, wagons, carts, and trucks, all cast in the spell of fear. I keep to the bramble. There'll be no mercy from any path.

Farms stretch forever to the sunset, barren, harvested, picked over, the grain in hiding, the livestock in a barn, and the farmers keep a musket by their side. My prison blue uniform smells of smoke. There's not a ruble in the pocket, nor a knife, nor a warm coat to shield me from winter's cold, only my boots, but I shiver more from memories than the chill.

The forest borders the farms that border the road, and by the fourth day of wandering, with little sleep, I would pass out until drawn from my nightmare by the pain of hunger.

I don't know how long it's been when I smell smoke, but I have no mind to decide if a warning or a welcome, so it's in the fever of madness that I stumble upon a band of men huddled over a fire.

Three are wearing the familiar blue uniform of a factory worker, and two are in the uniform of a Polish soldier. They're passing around a pot, using fingers to scoop out the meal. I risk giving up the freedom of solitude, uncertain of their intent. I reveal myself. One of the young men in the blue uniform holds up the pot, nods, "Come, join us."

I grab a handful and gratefully wolf down the warmth of mush.

He asks, "You are also running from Poznan?"

Unable to conjure a story, I confess, "The brewery."

"We were at the forge when your brewery blew. What happened?"

But my wits return at the thought of confessing my involvement. "Lucky to be some distance. I was loading a wagon."

"Lucky boy."

"Where are you heading?"

"The Poles will turn against the Germans. Poznan will be their battleground. I think it's better to go to Berlin. So many people, it'll be easier not to be noticed."

The two soldiers are armed with pistols and a rifle slung over their back. They each scoop up a handful of the mush, neither showing a hint of threat, and tell us in Polish that they're going to return to Poznan and join the battle.

"Poznan is no better than Berlin for the likes of us. Not our war."

The three are a mixed breed. The host is smart, engaging, the other two are wary, quiet, but they're Jews by speaking Yiddish. The tall one acts as if their leader and explains that they were prisoners at the forge. "We made their barrels for the Kaiser's rifles and cannons."

Daniel, Matthew, and Samuel have the nose, lips, and curly hair of Jews. The tall one boasts that they are Marxists. "We should find willing comrades in Berlin. Poznan Jews only care about the next meal."

I decided it's better to pose as a comrade and have companions willing to share their food for the journey to Berlin. But I've lost faith in trusting Marxists. My only dream is to find Mrs. Dayan and escape to some distant paradise.

They collect their treasures in a sack, the pot, knives, some clothes, and we thread our way through the maze of the forest, always heading west to Berlin. Matthew tells me of his plan to find a bund. He poses as a devout Marxist, but has little knowledge of Lenin, other than some imagined dreams of a prophet leading us to liberty.

The road is crowded with soldiers, so we stay to the bramble, and after three days at a good pace through flat farmland, villages grow more churches, taverns, inns, general stores, dirt to cobblestone, we're close to Berlin.

The mountain that is Berlin is twice that of Warsaw and more of a city than Poznan. The towers are grander, owing to German pride.

Matthew leads the way around the edge of the city. He shows no shame for asking for a handout from the peddlers, but none offer up free meals. Seeing the sacks, their hands are out for a trade.

Daniel has no want for a beggar's charity. "Easier to steal," as he grabs a potato.

Samuel acts humble and gracious but is suspicious of everyone.

As sunset approaches, we find ourselves in front of what I believe is a Christian cathedral, but as we get closer, I see the star—realize it's a synagogue. The grandest I've ever seen.

The congregation of men show their pride with handsome fedoras, pressed white shirts, and black suits. Bonded in conformity, they form a line of hundreds. The women enter through the side entrance in well-tailored dresses, herding their flock of playful children.

Matthew whispers, "Certain to be given charity by these rich Jews."

We wait until the man who could pass as a noble, tall, handsome, thick hair, blue eyes that penetrate to my soul, the greeter dressed in the black robe of a Rabbi, the gatekeeper who is about to close the door, when Matthew approaches with boyish charm and pleads for help by confessing to our plight. "Escaped from Poznan. We'd be most thankful food and shelter in trade for doing chores."

The Orthodox congregation doesn't shine a light on piety with payot, tallis, or shtriemel, but the fedora and bowler hats of the prosperous. The gatekeeper forms a smile, and with a nod of acceptance for our smell, dirt, and poverty, leads us to a pew in the back of the synagogue. The last five rows are noticeable as that section of the congregation wears the tattered cloth of peasants. "Time for prayer. After Services, we'll see what we can do."

I stare up at a tall ceiling, perhaps fifty feet high, held by columns as art carved from wood and brass. My soul suffers in the silence of this imposing synagogue. Heartache poisoned by guilt. A heretic asking for charity. I'm overwhelmed by the grandeur of an altar you'd find in a church, but the tone of prayer, the mood of the congregation is not the fervor of the Hasidics. The mezzanine of women scolding and soothing babies and children is not frowned on but embraced as the noise of family. I'm filled with wonder and questions.

The gatekeeper sits on a throne behind the pulpit. The Rabbi steps to the podium, holds up his arms, and even though I'm forty pews removed, there's no doubt that the Rabbi is the gatekeeper's father.

The two-hour Service ends with the congregation calling to heaven "Amen," and then there's another hour of mingling. The women pass around platters of cookies that they've used to bribe the children to behave.

The peasants pay their respects and politely bow in gratitude for charity.

As instructed by the gatekeeper, we remain seated in the last pew. Stares of curiosity, tinged by disapproval for our haggard appearance, take note of our presence.

After the pews are empty, we're led by a young man past the pulpit to a door behind the altar. A long hall ends at an office made regal by walls lined with books and behind glass doors, artifacts: menorahs, mezuzahs, and a series of Bibles bound in leather that show their age as if to be biblical.

The gatekeeper's elder Rabbi greets us from behind his desk by lowering his glasses and waving his hand. "Poznan?"

Matthew tells our story, "The brewery blew up, and we fled."

"Was this a Marxist? Do you know?"

How much to share? Too soon. None of us gives an answer.

"The Kaiser has blamed this on Marxist anarchists. He's called for 'True Germans' to rid the empire of unruly dissenters. The Rabbi is solemn. "We pay the price. The Kaiser has a temper for Jews."

Josef must be moaning in lament. The sin of burning down the house of our host. Mr. Dayan would raise his fist, "Gratitude should be paid for a ration of bread and water in trade for long hours of grueling labor."

My comrades do not share my guilt. Our journey had all three extolling the virtues of the revolution, but all I hear is the plotting of thieves. I told them nothing of my truth and lied with a pledge.

The Rabbi says with pride, "This is the finest Synagogue in all of Europe. Ten years ago, we had the blessing of the Kaiser; today, who knows?" He gives his verdict: "Feed them, show them to a bed. I'll see if there's work." His manner is that of a father who is disappointed by his children.

We're led by a young man who takes this chore on as if punishment. We're led down another hallway that leads us outside the temple to a large courtyard surrounded by three buildings.

Ordered to strip, "You're infested." We take off our clothes save for the *longjohns* and hosed down. In the dark, long past sunset, and ordered to take off the underwear, given a towel and told to scrub off lice. Our clothes are put in a sack, and he pulls out a fresh pair of pants and a shirt from another sack.

We follow him up five flights to an attic with a sloped ceiling so low we need to crouch, make our way past a row of beds, the long room with a leaky roof is shelter for the multitude of lost souls in need of charity.

The young man shows his suspicions while explaining the rules. “You will come down to the first floor at sunrise. Hands out biscuits taken from a box at the end of the hall. Stay here if not doing chores.” His expression is most serious, “If it’s found out that you are from Poznan, and we took you in, it will not go well for us.” He goes on to explain, “We are Berliners. The anarchists have betrayed the German people’s trust.”

I crawl onto the board that is a bed, and poisoned by nightmares, the coughing, snoring, and moaning, and savor each bite of the biscuit.

At sunrise, there’s the call for a breakfast of boiled eggs and matzah. Mops, brooms, and rags are handed out. We’re led through the courtyard. Put to work scrubbing a hospital that has twenty beds on either side of a large room. The sick cough, moan, and bleed. Cared for by nurses and doctors wearing stained white smocks.

A short break and another ration of eggs and matzah. That afternoon, we mop the floors of a school with four floors. Each floor has rows of classrooms. The top floor for the boys, and the floor below, to my surprise, is for the girls.

Benjamin, our boss, guide, and guard, informs us, “A thousand students attend this Yeshiva,” boasted with reverence. “Taught to be a doctor, lawyer, scientist, and engineer.”

I want to ask why they bother to teach a profession that has little chance of finding a job. There are strict quotas of one Jew to ten Gentiles for any profession with a title. I think it would be better to know the value of trade, or at least how to weld pipes and bring the wires inside to transform gas lamps and wires into rooms to be lit by electricity. I want to learn how to make motors that do the work of a horse.

Daniel and Samuel have no patience for chores. They leave without a word. Not thankful, angered by charity.

Matthew is the sort of peddler my Gramps and Poppa warned me of—a dreamer trading false promises. He pretends to work but spends his time shmoozing with whoever will listen. In search of opportunity with the charm of a showman. But there is not fool among us.

A teacher catches him stealing his pack of cigarettes. “You’re to leave now.” A small bald man who could be swatted away by Matthew, but has the courage of a lion.

“What for?” Acting innocent.

The teacher notices. “Those are mine. I would’ve given you one, but not to ask is the sign of a thief. We gave you charity and this is how you repay? Please, leave.”

“I was going to leave anyway.” Matthew crushes the pack in a fist and struts down the hallway. Our guard, Benjamin, apologizes to the teacher, blames needing to use the toilet, and rushes ahead to make certain the thief leaves before stealing something else.

I expect to be exiled for being a comrade and rush after Benjamin. We watch from the courtyard as Matthew leaves, and I plead my case with more lies mixed with truth. “We met on the road. They were fleeing Poznan. Strangers who led me to believe they were Jews with good souls. I want to prove my worth. I’m skilled in carpentry. Can make desks, chairs,” beg, “please give me a chance. I want to earn your trust.”

This temple is a palace. The windows are magnificent paintings of God, Moses, the Ten Commandments, and Solomon’s Temple. The columns and walls are the wood carvings of artists, but then I think of my father. He’d say such a show of wealth is the sin of hubris and conceit. But as the Rabbi explained in his sermon, “We made this investment as a show of respect for the Kaiser. The privilege of being a Berliner. A pledge to be good citizens. I realized that these German Jews take pride as Berliners.

I explain in Hebrew, and then demonstrate my command of German, Polish, Yiddish, and Russian. “I will gladly do anything to stay here.” I want to prove my worth.” They are not Hasidim who demand singular devotion, but they speak with an open mind.

The Rabbi who greeted us, the son of the Rabbi, Rabbi Finkelstein, hears my plea. I boast of my skills. He asks me about my roots.

There’s the truth of peddling, carpentry, but the truth blurs to my doubts, not a lie, “Not a comrade.” I didn’t light the fuse.

“A Litvak.” Rabbi Finkelstein leads me down the hall and opens the door to a bare room. Prove your skill. Give me a wall of bookshelves worthy of books.”

“And a desk and chair?”

He laughs. “Ambition comes after earning trust with proof.”

The chore reminds me of the passion I felt when crafting wood.

I trim the borders with scrolls and carvings of swirls. He's impressed. I'm given the privilege to work in the Synagogue. "Repair the pews."

I work my way toward the front. It is my third day of making repairs when I'm stopped by an elderly couple who arrive early each day and spend their mornings reading the bible, always in the front row, even though there's no service. The old man struggles with a curved back. They watched me for the three days without a word, but as I worked my way to the front row, he turned around and asked, "Can you fix it so that I can sit without punishment?"

Uncertain if he's boasting about doing penance, I reply with good intent, "I can make you a cushion."

The old man shakes his head, lifts his aged bones with a cane, and walks behind the pulpit toward the Rabbi's office.

A few moments later, Benjamin comes out in a fever and stops me from repairing the pew, "Come with me."

Ten well-dressed men are sitting at a long table. The room is a library lined with hundreds of important books. The elder is given the comfort and honor of sitting in the cushioned leather chair that surrounds the long table.

The Rabbi studies me with a harsh stare, "What is this about a cushion for a pew?" His tone is scolding, "Such a thing!" The nine other men in regal black suits shake their heads. "The pews are hardwood for good reason. A synagogue is not a parlor!"

The Rabbi's son, who I think is too handsome, would pass as a Gentile, but for a dark beard, thick brows, thick curly hair, interrupts—"Where is it written that a pew cannot have a cushion?"

There is no answer.

The Rabbi turns to me. "Why did you make such an offer?"

The elder saves me. "I asked. Eighty years I've sat in a pew without suffering, but lately I suffer to the point of thinking I can no longer consider this my home. My father suffered from a bad back, and my mother made cushions for him. Cloth stuffed with the down of feathers. His Rabbi also argued against, and so my father suffered in silence, except to me. I had to hear his complaint at least ten times a day. He left you a generous sum in his Will. A donation I honored fourteen years ago when you showed me the drawing for this Synagogue. I suffer in silence, but my wife and I are at our end. This young man thought to ask if I'd like a cushion." The elder struggles to stand. "His intention is kindness," and he turns to give me a wink with a nod.

I imagine I'll be exiled. I make a plea, "How can I make this right?"

Rabbi Finkelstein's son stands up for me. "A lesson for all of us to ponder. A good question. To give comfort in regard to our elders."

In the days that follow, I'm given chore after chore. His office was where I built the bookshelves. I'm given good walnut. "Make a desk so that I will look across to my students, mentors, and devils."

He'd stop by each day as the desk was taking shape. My devotion to each detail would need a month, but I work from dawn to dusk without rest. My only break is when he comes to bring me an egg, a biscuit, a cookie, and asks about my life.

I navigate around lies and win his admiration when I read a passage from Spinoza and boast that I could translate the Hebrew to Litvak, Polish, Russian, and, of course, into Yiddish.

Daily acts of terror by the Marxists put the community on watch. The socialists don't retreat. Protests, theft, murder, and strikes. Word comes of pogroms against Jews spreading from Odessa to St. Petersburg. The Kaiser promises to rid Berlin of anarchists. Every day, there's another front page story of a Marxist arrested, exiled, or imprisoned.

Two weeks later, I rush to find Rabbi Finkelstein. I pull him to the office, and in a presentation filled with pride, I take off the blanket that hid the scrolls I painstakingly carved along the fringe.

He rewards me with a broad smile. "Max, your carpentry is worthy of a guild's craftsman. You have earned a true reward. I have found you a benefactor who offers lodging and salary in exchange for your skill."

It is then I discover that the old man who liked the idea of a cushion, was Moses Weinstein, and his son saw my handiwork. Was also grateful his father and Mother were honored with a cushion. After much fuss, the debate was settled. I stitched the cushion with a generous pile of wool, stuffing it inside the embroidered cloth furnished by his magnificent store's seamstresses. The Rabbi explains, "There was great debate. It took Solomon to settle the question of whether suffering is necessary show of piety." Rabbi Finkelstein tells me that I'm very fortunate. "The Weinsteins are defying the Marxists and showing their loyalty to the Kaiser by building another of their fine stores." I'm handed a fine black suit, white shirt, and new shoes. "The suit is your new uniform."

I forget my place and give Rabbi Finkelstein a hug. “A true mensch,” said in tears. “I’ll be forever grateful for giving me hope. When I arrived, I was in such despair that I longed for death.” I want to confess my involvement in Warsaw and Poznan, but he sees into my soul without my need to confess. “I’m not a priest. Absolution is by deed, not confession.” He pulls away with a smile. “You have told me of your doubt with faith. Faith cannot be taught. It is learned, earned, or blind. But for the doubter, there’s a search needed to find their truth. You’ll know that you’ve found faith when you find peace.”

My friend and scholarly teacher took me the next day from the Synagogue to my job. I’m wearing my new suit, and from the Synagogue I’m led a mile to turn down Berlin’s most prestigious boulevard. The wide road was crowded with wagons delivering all manner of goods. Soldiers everywhere. The Berliners are well-dressed and respectful, but their eyes scan for trouble. Beautifully decorated stores, and the tallest, the most magnificent, belongs to the Weinstein’s. It’s the crown of their empire. But we keep going. The Rabbi fills me in on the history of Berlin as a Jew’s paradise until recently.

Another mile before we turn at the river toward the Jewish ghetto. It’s a construction site at the central square. Scaffolds reach four tall floors high. As we get closer and are about to walk under the wall of scaffolding, I study the mason’s skill with admiration. The trim and molding do not leave a patch without a proud artisan’s touch.

Rabbi Finkelstein pulls me inside. “To serve such a family is a privilege. This is a great honor.” He goes on to explain, “Everyone in Berlin knows the Weinstein’s. They have three stores, and this is the fourth. They sell everything from clothes to pots and pans, dishes, silverware, and even furniture.”

I wonder but am embarrassed to ask—*what trade would a Jew have made to have been given the Kaiser’s blessing to be allowed to own such a thing?*

It is nearing sunset by the time I enter a room with half the wall missing. There’s the noise of hammer, chisel, and saw. The room is hidden in a cloud of dust. The bustle stirred in battle by an army of workers. I lose count at thirty. Captivated to watch the mason swiping brick with mortar as if buttering bread. Five men are on their knees nailing wood planks of oak or possibly chestnut, too much sawdust to know.

We go down a long hallway toward the back of the store, passing bare rooms, and the Rabbi knocks on beautifully finished double doors, waits for permission, and someone calls out as if annoyed, "Come in!"

It's a king's office. I recognize the man standing behind a cluttered workbench from the Synagogue. His boyish face is cleanly shaven. The top of his head is bald, with neatly trimmed sides. He's portly, not a big man, and wears no tie or coat. His fancy white shirt is stained with paint, and the sleeves are rolled up.

It's as if we've broken a trance. He stops writing in a notebook. He looks out the window to realize it's dark. "Didn't know the day was over." In a hurry, he puts on his jacket and leads us out of the office at a brisk pace, back to the hall, and out the back door to a large open courtyard.

Rabbi Finkelstein bids us farewell. "I'm going to give tonight's service at Rabbi Horowitz's synagogue."

We're in the Jews' ghetto. A village inside the city.

"Tell me about yourself," the king asks as he steps into the backseat of a fine black motorcoach. I'm too excited by my first ride in such a thing to answer directly, but as we turn onto the road, he presses me. "Don't worry, we all have secrets."

I foster sympathy when I speak of my family's misery, but don't admit what happened in Pozna, or Warsaw, always in fear of being thought of as a Marxist. No longer a lie. I'd chosen sides. But I know that I'd be found guilty if judged by the evidence of my past.

He told me all about his plans for the store. "I've seen your skill and you show you have a gift. And to do this for the synagogue as a donation shows your character—a skilled carpenter to make a trade of skill without asking for payment. And my parents thank you for the cushions. I plan to put your talent to work. We're building such a store at the low end, and we want to make it a new beginning. Quality for the poor at a fair price. We have mills and a thousand needing jobs."

We speak in Yiddish as if to bond. "My Gramps would say the power of the rich is to trade today's profit for a distant tomorrow." Mr. Weinstein taps the seat next to him. I sat beside him—the honor of looking forward.

We cross the guarded bridge with salutes from the soldiers and enter a paradise without ditches and holes. The smooth stone road runs straight and true for a distance. In between patches of forest, gardens, and ponds are rich men's homes. Plastered masonry decorated with shutters and slate roofs. The wide boulevard doesn't have the bustle of traffic. This is a noble's neighborhood.

A moment later, we turn off the boulevard and ride through a lovely park. I tell Mr. Weinstein, "Is this heaven?" He laughs and goes on about his plans for the store. "You will build cabinets. We need to display dishes, pans, clothes, and shoes…" but not stopping as we pull in front of the palace, still adding details as to size and shape.

A white palace with pillars holding up a grand entrance. Only a few miles from the store, but it's as if another world. I would have been intimidated to sit beside a man who is as rich as a Count, but he treats me as if I'm his equal. Wants my opinion. Respect.

Joshua Weinstein speaks in German, but to make a point he pulls from Yiddish. "I'm the youngest child of Mr. Moses Weinstein's four sons," and tells me he just turned forty, and with pride, "A father to five, three boys, two girls, ages five to twelve."

I tell him, "Such blessings, but I'm the son of a peddler. This was earned."

He holds me in a stare that suggests a bond. "My mother didn't allow for a child's behavior. My children are soldiers under strict rules. My wife's family are Bavarian." His tone is not of pride but confided in surrender. The Prussians and Germans are on two sides of a thousand-year-old civil war.

Mr. Weinstein introduces me to a young man in white overalls, holding a lantern. He comes to open the carriage door. "Max this is Harold; he'll take you to your quarters."

I follow the young man along a path flanked by hedges, but I look back and spy, between the trimmed shrubs, a formal dining room. Five well-dressed children are sitting properly at a long table, served by two young girls in bonnets. The platters of food come and go.

I spy Joshua Weinstein coming into the dining room, but there's no fanfare of greeting. He sits opposite the strong-willed wife. The woman sits as a true queen. She's a full-sized woman wrapped in a white dress, and sitting tall between the children. The Prussian grandmother who commands a strict upbringing.

I'm led past a long cabin, and Harold explains, "This is for those who work inside. Our beds are above the stables." He opens the barn door and points to five stalls. The horses poke their heads out to see the new serf.

"I was hired to be a carpenter."

“I am a tailor, but today I’m busy with planting and tending the garden. We are in service to the Weinsteins,” said with pride, “and your chores will be whatever needs to be done.”

“When do we eat?”

Harold opens a cabinet stocked with bread, cheese and jars of jam, and pickled vegetables. “All for us?” he nods, laughs, and walks off.

I take a small portion, not knowing what I’m allowed.

Harold returns a few minutes later with two other young men and introduces me to our roommates. They are as short and thin as me. Both are soaked in sweat. They show no shame as they strip naked and hose off the mud and muck, the other working the pump.

I’m taken through the barn and up a ladder to a hayloft. Shown my bed with a cushioned mattress on a wood frame. “Take this one.”

I sit on soft cloths filled with feathers and want to cry in joy. The Rabbi's generosity didn’t include moving me from the attic to the good rooms on the lower floors.

We talk as we eat, and I learn more about this blessed family.

The Weinsteins have many stores. Their first store was built over a hundred years ago. Their dynasty was inherited from a great-grandfather. The first store was in a kingdom called Potsdam. Their family was Prussian. It is said that the grandfather was on the King’s council.”

I share stories of a past that is less of who I’ve been.

The next morning, I’m handed blue overalls and a cloth shirt. “Today, you get your wish. We’re going to work at the new store.”

A motor wagon is waiting for us. I share the long bench seat with the four young men who share the loft.

We leave the estate by a different road from the one we came in. A rough ride through a small forest to its end at the river, where we cross a wooden bridge back to the Jew’s side and follow the river road until we’re finally dropped off at the store.

I step through the mess of construction and the traffic of workers. Guided by Harold, we enter a small entry room ruled by a dapper man dressed in a blue suit.

“You are Max, I take it,” and hands me a heavy hammer. “The walls are to all come down.” He laughs and tells me by way of a proverb, “To be a carpenter takes patience and skill, but before we challenge you, you’ll take down this wall.”

The boss is a well-tailored middle-aged man who flaunts his German with a noble's temper. He gives off more fright than a Cossack, even though he wears a schoolteacher's spectacles. "I am, Herr Holzstein," and makes it known he is my master. "This will be the front of the store," he points to the walls of the narrow hall, He lingers with a cold stare, "It must be perfect." He boasts, "All of Berlin will cross the river to shop here."

I rejoice in the good fortune of such labor.

In a dream where the days pass without fear, misery, hunger, or suffering, my only worry now is that I'll awaken to my nightmare.

That night I found out that our hot meal of noodles, cabbage, and chicken was because Ingrid is sweet on the boy. She's Lutheran, converted to Jew, with golden hair, and the face of an angel. More a woman than a girl, Ingrid is a cook, but as with all of the Weinstein employees, we're shuffled about. She's also a maid, server, and nanny.

I ask Harold if marriage is a possibility. He's Jewish. He won't confess that he's in love, but for Ingrid, it must be love. She brings him leftovers of tender meat and sinful desserts.

Harold, along with my other roommates, also found their way here from the synagogue. They proved their worth to the Rabbi before this honor was bestowed.

We are expected to attend Services. Friday night and Saturday morning, we detour and take the wagon to the Synagogue. But on the holidays, the Weinsteins lead the procession of favored staff driven in horse-drawn wagons and the family in motorcoaches.

Mr. Joshua Weinstein puts on none of the airs of nobility and is the hardest worker in the store. He's everywhere doing everything. Takes personal charge of everyone's task. "I want more cabinets,' points to a wall of shelves, "Take those down, and make cupboards with glass doors we can lock." He asks me to stretch my talent.

Given fine tools and wide boards, I work alongside five other carpenters. Needed to earn their regard as a worthy craftsman.

By Yom Kippur, we thought we had made great progress, but Mr. Moses Weinstein showed the other side of a humble temper. An impatient tyrant, the wise owl sees the trade through a customer's eyes. An early riser, he paces about, studies our work as if searching for a lost coin, and calls out to dutiful son, Joshua, "Faster. Hannukah won't wait.

CHAPTER FORTY- Lenin -1914

I hurry to chisel notches and split the wood, struggle to work faster, but speed is an enemy to craftsmanship; it only makes things worse.

Herr Holzstein calls for me. I follow in fear that I'm about to be fired, and expect the worst, but as we cross through the front of the store, I see a ghost wearing the disguise of age, scars of battle across hollowed out cheeks, the curls of dark hair dusted with streaks of white, standing tall, pride shows the certainty of my master.

Mr. Dayan drops the familiar prized toolbox. Doesn't need to see through my disguise of age. He fixes his gaze on me with that knowing smile. The one that steals my devotion. "Max!"

"What is this about?" Herr Holzstein interrupts our reunion. The master has no patience.

Mr. Dayan waves him away as if to declare he'll have no master. "We need a moment." I'm in shock. I struggle to adjust to this fateful reunion. He studies my hutch, picks up his fine carving tool, files it as sharp as a razor, then hands it to me. "Study the grain as I taught you. Let the wood show its paths."

I am lost between the nightmare and this dream. Another life.

He stops before quitting time. A protest. "That's enough of our labor for what they're paying." He refuses to listen to my protest. Pulls me into the crisp night air—winter making itself known. We stood outside the entrance. I want to go back inside and finish the job, but Mr. Dayan stares hard enough into my eyes to give me worry. "Mrs. Dayan won't forgive me if I don't bring you home."

I want to tell him that I'm the enemy, the proletariat who is loyal to his master, devoted to a Rabbi, and found faith in craftsmanship. A lie would be to pledge my life to lighting the fuse. "Maybe tomorrow night." I see the wagon waiting. I don't know what to do. "I have to take the wagon." And join Harold and the others. Yell back, "I'd really like to see Mrs. Dayan."

Shakes his head, gruff, "Tomorrow then."

All that night, I spin in circles. Torn by wanting to see her and fearing a reunion. I thought Berlin was endless. I'd be invisible from my past.

The next day, I want to impress him with my skills, but all Mr. Dayan wants to hear is how I ended up in Berlin. "And to gain employment with the Weinsteins, such an honor." A mocking tone to return me to thirteen.

His second day, and his temper has already put him under suspicion by Herr Holzstein. I use the excuse of needing to finish the cabinet door to be the last to leave, for not wanting to be seen leaving with Mr. Dayan.

He keeps to a slow pace, as if searching for direction. We wander deeper into the poorest of neighborhoods. A village of such despair that it can only be inhabited by thieves, beggars, orphans, and sorrows.

He presses me to repeat the story of Jakob's tavern. He knew Yitzhak was there, but he didn't let on that he knew I was there as well. That was until I told him about Lina and how Yitzhak fought off the police. He would have known. I tell him this truth to blur the lie of my retreat. "Yitzhak led the charge," and with the certainty of a good peddler, "I was knocked back from the blast. Saved by being given up for dead. Passed over by the soldiers." I want to escape, but I'm lured into his web with thoughts of seeing Mrs. Dayan.

Mr. Dayan grins with pride at my false confession. "Comrade."

"I was sixteen when you left. I'm about to turn twenty-six."

"I learned of Yitzhak's fate from Lenin himself," and smiles with pride. "All know of that night. From Warsaw to St. Petersburg. The fifth of December 1905, the sparks that lit the kindling." He stops. Takes me by my shoulders. "That spark has become a flame."

"Lenin knows about Yitzhak?"

"He told me he met you and Yitzhak. You took the oath," said with pride. "He praised your dedication to the Cause."

What does he know? Lenin? I dare to probe, "They came to your home in search of him." I'm unable to hide my accusation.

"We're kindling for the flames of revolution."

He draws me along a narrow road. The dirt is littered with foulness. I can see through the cracks and holes of shanties, bare rooms crowded with elders to children, smoke from a stove if so fortunate, more blessed if cooking potatoes or mush, noodles, or bread—the hunters needing a good day in theft or begging. The crying, laughing, but it's the music from someone whose skill makes the strings of a violin weep or sing, everyone trying to find a way to survive in this city's wilderness of harsh paths.

He turns to enter a shack that creaks and shudders from its poverty. I enter an almost bare room where she is stirring a pot on a one-log stove. It takes me more than a moment to recognize Mrs. Dayan. Her light-colored hair is now dark, her wide eyes somehow smaller, and her smooth skin is pale and creased with lines. She looks at me as if she's awakening, and without regard to custom, I rush to her side, wanting so badly to give this misfortune comfort that I forget myself and take her in a hug.

Mrs. Dayan is hardened. She pulls away to collect herself, "Max!"

We celebrate with a toast of decent vodka, and she sets a bowl with a boiled potato and bread. The room is that of a prisoner. The mattress is made of burlap sacks. There's a small table and four chairs any fool could make. The wood stove gives off only enough heat to make you want to draw close. Mr. Dayan makes the toast, "To Max, a true comrade," and I fake a sip. I can't give honor to the lie. Mr. Dayan drinks all that is left in one swig and prods me to repeat the story of Jakob's tavern.

"Attack was sudden, no warning. Yitzhak led the charge. I was in back at the corner booth where I was listening to four scholars argue for revolution, when the walls came down. Yitzhak was lost to a firing squad. I awoke from death and ran."

A drunk Mr. Dayan applauds and lifts me as a salute of honor. "To have been a part of such a thing," I earn his regard for the price of being witness to that horror. I would argue for sympathy—sorrow for all the misery it caused. I know not to confess to being a prisoner of the Baron at the brewery.

"They will be honored as martyrs. Your story must be told."

I see nothing of the Mrs. Dayan I knew. She sits in silence. This is not the spirited woman who would raise a fist in salute.

"It's late. I should go."

"No, no. Our meeting was no accident. I heard you were working at Weinsteins." He said the name as if speaking of the czar. "You will come with me to meet our friends."

I don't ask why Mrs. Dayan is a ghost, or why they have only a few clothes, no possessions, none of their treasures, or why their home is no more than a prison cell. He says that they've been traveling for the past ten years and only recently returned to Berlin.

I study her eyes for a clue, but as we hug to say goodbye, she whispers, "You must not be a stranger." There's a trace of the woman I remember. Her invitation pulls at my heart.

He leads me through narrow alleys that reek of foulness, rats ignore our intrusion, bodies of dead or sleeping don't stir, he looks each way as if suspecting a thief, and at each corner, he shifts direction. I rush after him as he makes a quick sprint to the next row of shacks. Looks both ways and pulls me down a short flight of stairs. He knocks four times on a heavy wooden door, then two, waits, then three.

Wary eyes peek through a slot. The big man hugs Mr. Dayan, they exchange a knowing nod, "This is Max," and with a moment of study, he leads us into a dungeon chiseled from stone. The room is dimly lit, clouded by a familiar scent of smoke that sparks a memory that haunts me whenever my thoughts turn to that night. I'm pushed through the fog and he steps out from the shadow, "Comrade." Lenin wears the disguise of a fake beard and thick curly hair, but it's the gray eyes that give him away.

The table is cluttered with bottles, cigarettes, pipes, and pistols. Lenin pours Mr. Dayan a drink and holds up his mug, "To my general." He turns to me, "To our Comrade, Max." And with the toast done, the four scholars return to argue with such passion that I'm worried there'll be blood.

"Switzerland before Petersburg. Not time yet," Lenin ends the argument by putting his hand on my shoulder.

Leon offers me a bottle, "Max was with Yitzhak at Jakob's."

Lenin gives me a stare, "So many years ago, yet that flame still burns. How did you happen to end up here in Berlin?" He takes off his beard and wig, "My closest comrades." Mr. Dayan clinks his bottle to mine, then Lenin and Leon. "Max, tell them about the brewery that blew up in Poznan?"

Leon takes a puff off his pipe, "The bomb was lit by comrades? Heard talk of a young brewmaster who preached of our Cause." That stare, what does he know? How? "You make good vodka. I remember it well."

They know. "I was there. It was no accident."

Lenin smiles. "So modest. A true comrade." I'm given a hug from Lenin himself.

The other two rise from the table to toast me as a hero. "I'm Leopold," the bookish one introduces himself.

Lenin takes a long swig, "Please give us the names of those who did this brave deed."

"We were prisoners. Four comrades." A broad smile and another toast. "Michel, family man, caught trading vodka. He lit the flame. The vats of alcohol were the bomb. Gorgy, the warrior, our Yitzhak, he fought off the guards."

Lenin raises his bottle. "To the revolution—we salute you."

Leopold takes my hand in a firm shake, "True comrades."

Lenin reaches under the table and pulls out another bottle. Another full pour. Raises his glass, "To the martyrs on whose sacrifices the revolution burns its path to the thrones."

Leon's been quiet. Still smokes his pipe as if breathing. A knowing grin. Shows keen intent as he studies me. I'm unable to speak. I think confession? but then think of lies. My fear and doubt suffer the misery of a heretic comrade.

His ally, the professor who spoke on behalf of anarchy, Julius, shakes his head. 'How did you escape such an explosion?"

A well-rehearsed lie. "I was pulled to the warehouse by a guard. Ordered to load a wagon."

Lenin defends me for his own reasons. "Of course, this was the work of comrades," a boast with pride. "And of course they spun this an accident. Sabotage is what they fear most."

Leon sits back on the couch. Leopold joins him. Julius pokes me before he pushes them closer to sit beside them. "How did you happen to be at the brewery?" Julius isn't asking, he's accusing me of a lie. It's his manner. I remember, but when with such comrades as Mr. Dayan, who would shoot me for doubt, I kept to my lie as a heroic comrade. "I left Warsaw after that night and wanted to find Mr. Dayan in Berlin. I was lost in a wilderness outside of Poznan and was taken in by a Polish army of sorts. They were attacked by a noble from Poznan. Baron Brandenburg oversees the brewery in Poznan as Count Mizenkampf's general. An army of over a thousand. They killed hundreds of these Polish soldiers. Shot their Count, general, or king, I don't know his title, but without hesitation. Servants killed. I was with a hundred Jews. We were set free after we dug the graves. He had no use for us. A hundred Prussian families were brought in to run the estate."

"The Baron?" Leopold puts down his glass.

"Yes, Baron Brandenburg. He knew I was the brewmaster and took me prisoner. Taken to the brewery in Poznan.

"You were the brewmaster." Leopold has the character of a lawyer.

"My bubby's recipe." I think of how Poppa taught me to mix a teaspoon of fable with a cup of truth. "The Baron had tasted my vodka."

Lenin and Leopold applaud me, but Julius and Leon show a different side. Julius asks, "So how did it come that these comrades blew up the brewery—what was your part in this?"

"Michel, Gorgy, and Ludwig were already comrades when I told them about what happened in Warsaw. They wanted to be Yitzhak." I take a long drink. Julius tests me. He smells my doubt. I need to hide my loyalty to Mr. Weinstein. "To blow up a brewery only took a match."

Lenin and Leopold want to boast of this terror as the work of comrades.

Mr. Dayan puts his hand on my shoulder. "You know his story. Max was with Yitzhak when he killed the four agents on your trail."

"Yitzhak!" Lenin toasts, "A great man."

Only Lenin and Leopold give honor.

Julius, Leopold, and Leon were the prophet's messiahs who stirred the crowd, always in Jakob's ear. Leon's hair is grayer, beard thicker, not trimmed. Still, the professor with thick black glasses smokes a pipe with the stink of his importance. I'm the boy who ran behind them. Lenin is czar. Julius, Leon, and Leopold are the council. Yitzhak and Jakob were the sacrificial warriors. Lenin is the general who looks out from a perch above the battle and commands his pawns to die as martyrs. The anarchist wins in defeat or victory as long as the pot is stirred.

A knowing stare from Leopold. "I toast to Max. Flint for sparks."

Leon pounds his mug against the table. "Blowing up factories and mills won't unite workers. It makes us look like the worst sort of evil." His tone is solemn, harsh, and pointed at Lenin.

Julius stands beside Leon. "War is coming. Soldiers will return from battle with no temper to be slaves in a factory. That's when the revolution will be won."

Lenin stares down Julius. "They'll go on strike! Protest! Be led by you as a preacher? You think a strike will make the Czar and Kaiser cower! The nobles and bourgeoisie need to fear revolution."

Leon takes off his glasses. Steals a moment for thought. Wipes them on the edge of a torn sweater, puts his glasses back on, and moves closer to Lenin. Neither shrinks from the other's stare. "Whether we kill one wolf or a thousand, the Czar and Kaiser will call us murderers."

Julius turns to Leopold, then confronts Lenin: "This war will leave everything in ruins. And then we add to the misery. How much destruction and sacrificial lambs will it take to convince the czar?"

Leopold sides with Lenin. "As many as it takes. We will rise from the ashes as an army bred by battle, not prayer."

Lenin stares Julius and Leon down. “Washington won by raining terror. We need warriors like Yitzhak, Jakob, Dayan, but they need to wage this war on battlefields of our choosing.”

“Or we can win hearts and souls as Moses and Jesus,” Julius speaks as a teacher. “Not a warrior.”

“Tell that to Mohammad or King David.” Leopold wears the pose of a scholar. “They knew that preaching only would take them so far. In the end, they knew they had to go to war against those whose loyalty is held by faith that their king is god.”

“We must be the fox, thieves, assassins,” with a nod to Lenin, “our battlefield. Burn the palace. Prove to the people that the czar and Kaiser are mortal.” Mr. Dayan breaks his silence.

“My warrior.” Lenin scratches his goatee as if wanting Mr. Dayan to take Leon and Julius by the throat. “To preach for a thousand years to turn pagans to Christ. “Would the French have been better off with Jesus than Napoleon? Washington surrenders because liberty costs lives. Lincoln retreats because ending slavery is not worthy of a great sacrifice. War is the only way to make the blind see the light. The nobles' and masters' greed is a curse. Revolution is what it takes to break their spell.”

Lenin turns to Leon and Julius, “Hymns and prayers will bring beasts to their knees. A revolution won with debate and speeches. Bring them to their knees with strikes and protest.” He snorts in the cruelest growl of threat. Throws his glass against the cave wall. “We must face the wolf as a wolf. Cut off the heads of the snakes!”

“Kaiser and the Czar send all to war without a tear shed for the million boys they put to death.” Leopold softens his tone to that of a professor. “To defend their throne and build a grander palace.”

Lenin turns to Leon with the same certainty. “The Germans are warriors. They see Marx as a dreamer. The Kaiser speaks to their faith in war.” He snorts, “Only a general can lead them to the Promised Land.” Lenin puts his hand on Leon’s shoulder. “You have your place. They need to be taught with sermons. The proletariat are born sheep, mules, and serfs. They believe change is hopeless because their priests and rabbis preach to the reward of heaven as somewhere in death, not the truth that life is heaven and only man can forge our world into heaven.” Lenin casts his spell. “Russians are raised to believe they’re the czar’s children.” He leans on Mr. Dayan, nods to me, “Our warriors will clear the path.”

Leon interrupts, “By burning the cities? That closes minds. They need teachers to open their minds. A nightmare sends you into hiding. Marx does not teach terror, but enlightenment."

Leopold is furious, "You are a fool."

Leon is agitated. "I am a comrade. The truest comrade. I take great risks. My life will surely end as a martyr, of this I'm certain. You will turn the bourgeoisie against us." He turns to me. "Your comrades blew up a brewery—but did this bring Poznan's proletariat to rise up? No! Did this bring Poznan's nobles to fear and cower in handing their mills and factories to the workers? No! Bombs will not convert. Fear will not convert! Poznan is a prison. If we're all workers, who'll be the creators? Children need a father who teaches by example with truth and patience, not to beat the child into submission with a whip."

Mr. Dayan makes his stand. "I'm with Comrade Lenin. I will light the bonfire and set fire to the nobles' kingdom, because only its ashes can we build a heaven."

Leopold takes Mr. Dayan's hand and raises it, "Our Washington."

Leon shakes his head in surrender. "Blood will transform poor soil to fertile fields and brotherhood will turn rock to iron."

Lenin pushes him aside. "America had to fight twice. A war to free their bodies from tyranny with rebellion, and then a bloodier war to save their soul from the sin of slavery."

"Only for the freed slaves to become prisoners of bigotry. Bodies surely bloodied, but the souls of those who believe they are the masters did not surrender," Lenin takes a swig, "The master must pay the price. They take a hundred rubles and dole out crumbs to the worker."

Julius and Leon put on their coats. "All you'll leave are ashes and hate." The door slams shut.

CHAPTER FORTY-ONE - Berlin – Winter- 1914

Lenin pours another drink. Leopold raises his glass, "To comrades Julius and Leon. They are as Bismarck, peace at any price, and will be our Jefferson and Franklin to write a constitution, but we need warriors."

Lenin raises his glass to Mr. Dayan but then turns to me with a stare demanding my allegiance. "Everywhere will be a battlefield."

Mr. Dayan grabs my arm, goes on and on about how Leon and Julius were foolish to think a preacher could win freedom. I was a carpenter reborn, proud and at peace. I'm blinded by a bright sun an hour above sunrise. The roads and boulevards are crowded. The guard holds the door open with a greeting.

Mr. Joshua is staring at our cabinet. He's in a foul mood. "You are late. Worse, you have done as you wished." He points to a table of dishes and silverware. "Where shall I put all this?" My stomach turns.

Mr. Dayan argues, "An extra foot of depth will crowd the room."

"I need to show all my dishes! Not just teacups and saucers!" His temper boiled by a peddler's need for profit, and still in the fever of Lenin's preaching, Mr. Joshua pulls Mr. Dayan's trigger. He wants my pledge, but my nightmare has awakened, and I face a day haunted by visions of Jakob.

"How many of your rich man's dishes does a princess need to think herself a queen!" Mr. Dayan rips off the glass door in an explosion of splinters that brings everyone to see what's going on. Mr. Dayan looks at me. I'm caught in a trap, but Leon has my faith, not Lenin.

A crowd forms. Mr. Weinstein's two guards pull their pistols. Mr. Dayan is cornered, gives me a cold stare and pushes me away as he kicks open the door, yelling back— "The day of reckoning is coming."

I distance myself with a pledge of loyalty to Mr. Joshua and share in the outpouring of anger toward Mr. Dayan, "A Marxist devil." My record gives testimony to not being of his kind.

I work long into the night to rebuild the cabinet to Mr. Weinstein's desire. Exhausted, I leave the store, need a tavern, but as I turn the corner, I'm grabbed in a harsh grip, but I didn't need to look to know. I wasn't surprised. I was dreading this moment. I thought of sleeping in the store under the guard's watch, but I was worried that he'd attack.

"You take the rich man's side!" Mr. Dayan drags me into the alley. "This is war. He's the enemy."

"The Weinstein's are good people."

"Good people!" He frightens me. "He's a pig who thinks himself our master. Doles out a crumb while he takes the loaf."

It would be useless to explain that without the rich, there'd be no store. My decision is made. To pose as a comrade is a path to hell. "He's the hardest worker in the store. If not for his generosity, too many of the Jews in Berlin would be out of work. Their charity saved my life."

"As their serfs!" He shakes me, "You've always been a coward. I excused this as a frightened child." He lets go. Takes a deep breath. Studies me. "Have I taught you nothing?" Said as a plea, not in anger. "You're a serf doing a master's bidding."

"Not his bidding. Not a serf. The pride of the craftsman you trained me to be. The passion you gave me. You and Mrs. Dayan taught me everything. I owe you both my life, but I have seen the price of revolution, and it's not a trade with any value but death."

"Know this," his face red, trembling in anger, his scars as a badge of honor—"Lambs are livestock for the wolves. They'll feast until killed."

"The Cause is right. I know all too well the cost of tyranny. They murdered my family. The Cossacks cursed my life to nightmares. Would it have been better if I had died beside Yitzhak?" I can't help but confess—"Trotsky and Leopold fled from Jakob's barn. I followed."

He lowers his eyes from the stare of hating me.

"I loved Lina. She was raped but fought back. A warrior as you'd wish me to be, but she died because we were with Lenin the night before. He was being followed. Yet Lenin thinks of her sacrifice as kindling. Warsaw burned. More women and children as kindling for Lenin's revolution. Poznan burned. More kindling. What has this terror proven but to stir the beasts and divide us further by hate!"

He softens. Eyes closed, let out a tired moan. "I know," he whispered in finding his way to our past. "I know the price you've paid." He takes a deep breath. Grips my arm. "When the time comes, you will have to choose between a meaningless death as a lamb, or to kill for purpose. I only ask that you die as a comrade. What else is worthy?"

Mr. Dayan walked away. I wanted to believe that he set me free, but I found faith in Leon and Leopold. I'd be a teacher if the time comes.

I entered the nearest tavern and drank the piss of vodka for the first time in a long time, but the poison only drove me deeper into the nightmare.

I went to work in sickness, not from the poison of drink, but in fear of knowing what's to come.

Mr. Joshua thanked me for rebuilding the hutch, and as a reward, he gave me the honor of assisting the well-known artist. "You'll make the frame for what will be a prized entrance."

The master of stained-glass is the age of gramps, and over the next four days, the nightmare is distracted by learning the craft of cutting different colors of glass to make a puzzle of broken glass of various shapes and sizes into a painting. He wraps the shards with strips of solder, takes a hot iron to seal the glass inside the lead frame, creating a masterpiece of flowers and birds.

It is half done, still on the table, when Mr. Moses comes to inspect his investment. He takes a moment, looks at the expanse of entry, and then back at the painting. A frown. "What is this? All this color? How will my customers see into the store when the door is closed?"

The artist is calm. There's a smile, "I'm experienced in suffering for the opinion of my clients and the public." He bows, "But the door is to stir their imaginings to wonder what lies behind. They'll want to come back and see what's inside the pretty box."

Mr. Moses takes a moment. Picks up a plate of clear glass. With a rare smile, he asks Herr Fredrich, "A window enough for a peek."

The store is a sanctuary from the rumors of war. Days turn to weeks, and the store is finally finished to Mr. Moses's vision. Like all the workers, I'm thinking this is the end of the path. No more carpentry, no more furniture to craft. But held in such regard, I'm kept on to help the plumbers and electricians.

But the plumbers and electricians were not teachers. They don't ask for an apprentice, and I suffer to learn the difference between a wire that is connected to fire and almost killed in the grip of electricity—a similar lesson sealing a copper pipe by melting lead. I earn new scars for the dripping, but suffering has always been the teacher's stick. Pain is what makes a lesson unforgettable.

Mr. Joshua leads his brothers and father around the store. My dedication is on display, and he flatters me in front of his family. "You have proven yourself invaluable. The favor of the Kaiser and the good people of Berlin blesses us." He pulls me aside, in a whisper, "If there's war, as long as we're able, there will be a job for you." His loyalty and sentiment are the glue that repairs the cracks left behind by Mr. Dayan.

Later that day, in the quiet of his office, I finally asked for the reward I had dreamed of the first time he had me repair a wall smashed by tenants. "I know that besides your stores, your family owns apartment buildings. Perhaps I can make renovations and repairs."

"Max, you delight me." He puts down his notebook. Without another word, he puts on his jacket, "Follow me."

He keeps to a brisk pace as we cross through the poverty of the Jewish ghetto. The Weinsteins are known to all. He politely tips his hat to his congregation. A moment later, we came to a large brick building.

He needs a moment to find the right key on a chain of keys, and as he continues to search, Mr. Joshua tells me—"You're right. I need your help keeping my buildings in repair." He unlocks the door.

I look up at five flights to a ceiling stained brown by leaks and cracked walls. "As soon as an apartment opens, you'll move in. Shouldn't be long. Someone is always moving out." He reads my mind. "No rent. The exchange of a room for your labor is to my side of the ledger."

The next day, I returned with my toolbox to repair the skylight. I climb a ladder and enter an attic made useless by a steeply pitched slope, cracks wide enough to see across the river, and a view of the palace, conjuring a new dream of creating a fantastic apartment by adding dormers and a new roof.

I wanted to extend the plumbing to the top floor, turning the unusable attic into a home worthy of the investment. Mr. Joshua is thrilled and willing to supply all I need.

I introduce myself to the tenants to explain that I'll be adding a bathroom to each floor.

My days are spent welding pipes to reach from the basement to the attic. My nights are spent finishing the roof. A month later, winter fast approaching, in celebration, having held Mr. Joshua to wait until I was done, and when he looked out through the windows, I cobbled together from the glass leftover from remodeling the stores, he was mesmerized. "This is only the beginning. You have earned my partnership." I feel a kinship as we gaze at the starry lights of a new Berlin transformed by electricity. I'm rewarded with forty gold marks, but more importantly, I have a partner.

But this sudden luxury of living on my own surprised me. I was lonely. I just turned twenty-six and feel the loss of never having had the experience of being with a woman. I walk the streets where such things are for sale. I'm easy prey, seduced by a woman's lure, a temptation that could trap a fox.

I pay her with the lesser valued five Paper Marks, the same price as a bottle of good ale and a meal of noodles at the tavern. The Kaiser's new paper Marks are trading for a third of the Gold Mark, and even less for the more precious gold coin, as everything was costing more.

The joy was a moment that needed coaching. Her bait hooks me. In a hurry to return the next night. The sweetness of a prostitute comes at a high price. The garishly costumed Jewess is a few years older, feeds a large belly with the expected tip of pastry, and likes to smother me in her bosom. A moment after our second brief union, the reward is short-lived. She pouts with despair about her expenses. "My landlord would appreciate payment in Gold Marks."

Under the spell of lust, I propose marriage.

She pinches my cheek. "Such a foolish boy."

I spent a total of twenty Gold Marks—almost half my savings. An amount equal to eight weeks of generous earnings. I asked her to move in with me, but she laughed to say I couldn't afford her. I made the mistake of boasting that I work for the Weinsteins. She knew everything in the store. Called herself Missy, and Missy has an eye for finer clothes, jewelry, and an addiction to expensive cosmetics.

On the fifth night, my addiction dug a hole in my stomach. I needed her heart as well. I brought a gift of perfume, but arrived early, only to find her in the arms of a soldier. I felt like such a fool for heartache in falling in love with a whore. Poppa warned me of lust as temptation, a chocolate cookie confused with love, another lesson learned the hard way.

I finish off a third mug of ale that poisons me with nightmares. I'm lured by a goniff into a game of cards and lose ten Paper Marks. The intoxication of gambling is equal measure to ale and flesh.

I sought advice from Rabbi Finkelstein. "I took a bite of Eve's apple, then I tried to erase the sin with ale, only to fall into a trap of gambling. Temptations are not only the punishment of losing hard-earned money, but they cast a spell of cravings beyond hunger. The cravings are fed, but the stomach remains empty, and without end."

"It's a nice day, let's take a walk."

Spring is shedding winter: green leaves, budding flowers, and a soothing, warm breeze. The parade of romance and picnics made the hauntings of murder, war, and revolution seem faraway.

The Rabbi takes off his disguise of holiness and smiles that knowing smile of a father. "King David showed this craving to be evil. He committed the worst of sins by sending Bathsheba's husband to war. His craving was to have the beauty for himself. Sending Uriah to war was the same as murder, but we are all lured by the temptations of sin, and this is why so much is said in the Bible about its punishments. The spell of temptation is a harsh test by God. We are children learning about life. Taught through punishment and reward. Loneliness, idle hands, free will, doubt, curiosity, all these sinful stirrings are tests to find our path."

He stares off to the river. "I fear that all too soon survival will be our only concern." The current is swift, there's no wind, and the iron ships of the Kaiser's navy patrol the waters.

"Too many are blind to receive this gift."

Lenin, Leon, and Mr. Dayan haunt my thoughts. A revolution is coming. The battlefield will be everywhere. I'm as confused about what we'll be fighting for as the philosophers, warriors, and kings who preach with certainty that they know best.

The next day, Joshua wants me to build a second cabinet to double the display of cuff links, wedding rings, necklaces, and fancy men's watches. The fear of war is fueling commerce as never before. The future value of paper money is unknown. Gold, diamonds, and clothing will be easier to trade, use as bribes, and wear or hide when in a hurry to escape. The panic brought in so many wanting possessions over Paper Marks.

The entrance to the flagship store is blocked by a long line of girls to women interviewing for a sales position. Mr. Josiah Weinstein, eldest of the four brothers, and handsome in the way women favor: tall, blue eyes, intense, thick hair, is the crown prince, wields his power with Gold coins.

He asks one hopeful applicant after another, four direct questions: "Name? Where have you worked? Why did you leave? What are your skills?" Instead of cutting, sanding, and finishing the new chair for his office, I listen in, as I do.

From a long line of candidates, the curvy, tall woman with curled blonde hair fusses too much, dressed as if a customer, layers of pink lace wrapped around a flowery white dress, catches all eyes.

I pretend to carve the arms of the chair but listen in as "Greta Morganthal" answers Mr. Weinstein's four questions. "I was working for my father. We made wedding rings and fine jewelry, but he recently stopped making jewelry to make badges, pins, and medals for soldiers. I'm not going to sit at home and care for my brothers' and sisters' babies."

Mr. Josiah smiles, "I believe he's made a mistake. Anyone with cash is buying gold and silver. Do you know how to value jewelry?"

She nods at the assortment of necklaces, rings, watches, and earrings on his desk. Greta takes out a magnifier from her purse and gives a value to each item. He sits back in his chair. "Well done."

He notices my listening in, but with a smile, calls me over. "Max! I need you to build a display. You'll work with Miss Morganthal." Looks to Greta, "We'll price them as you have so rightly calculated. But tomorrow and thereafter, you'll have your eyes on the market. Value is moving fast."

I spend the afternoon under her spell as she dictates the cabinet's design. I summoned the courage as we left for the day, with an invitation to join me for dinner.

Her laugh suggests I'll never find a wife of her breed.

I turn to go home—but not halfway up the street, just beyond the crowds milling about, I'm taken by surprise—sent into shock—Mrs. Dayan takes my hand and pulls me to the alley. "He's gone. Come with me."

I follow her without another word, but not to where we met, but to another neighborhood of thieves and beggars. Her dress is layers of tattered cloth, a wool shawl, and a man's boots. The fourth-floor room has no stove, not even a sink. There are four stools, a small square table, and three sacks of flour she's made into a bed with a blanket and pillow.

"Mr. Dayan is gone," and begins to cry. The visit is not about her missing me but about consoling her worry. "Maybe Poznan, Frankfurt? Perhaps Warsaw."

I struggle to keep my wits and struggle to hold back my passion. I ask her to stay with me at my apartment, but she shakes her head. "He'll want to know where I am." She pours out her sorrow about the price of revolution.

I confess my cowardliness. She gives me absolution, "I wish he were more like Leon, a teacher of Marx"—panics—"But you must never tell him I said that."

"Don't leave. Begs me to sleep on the sacks of flour. Her only smile, "He thought better to have flour as a bed than wool or cloth you can't bake into bread."

I hide my passion in friendship as it soothes our loneliness. Read Mark Twain to learn English. The novel brings a laugh as easily as it makes us cry.

I returned the next night, and the next. She wouldn't speak again of her husband's belief in terror over preaching. Blames the Czar and Kaiser. I don't argue. It's enough to fight my desire not to take hold of her as a wife.

On the eleventh day, I go to the apartment, but without a word, no warning, no note, she's gone.

The revolution finds new recruits—homeless, hungry, full of hate for whatever reason: poverty, loneliness, sin, punishment of cravings, jealousy of temptations, Lenin's newsletters call on workers to fight back with more than a strike. Thieves and murderers are told to burn or steal the fabric of society with bombings and attacks.

The terror is met in kind by the Kaiser and Czar. The revolution spreads from Moscow to Berlin. They ignite a pogrom of persecution toward immigrants, the universities, factories, and Jewish publishers. Strict rules and curfews are mandated. Checkpoints and raids put a grip on when and where we can go. The bridges are the gatehouse.

Unions are tolerated only if negotiations are in the Kaiser's favor. Jew or gentile, noble, bourgeoisie, proletariat, or farmer, all are called on to grow commerce and build an unstoppable military. Fear makes the only hope for security, tyranny.

A Jew's cost in doing business is doubled by paying bribes.

CHAPTER FORTY-TWO – Berlin - 1914

Mr. Joshua can't make up his mind. He's a changed man. No longer the calm in the storm, our humble boss has become an anxious tyrant. Under the sickness of fear, even the wealth of the Weinsteins can't provide a protective shield.

War invites Draconian rules. All of Berlin is in fever. Kaiser Wilhelm wants revenge against the Serbians for the assassination of Austria's Archduke Ferdinand, who was about to take the throne of a most important ally. The Austrians are needed to split the Russian army.

"Shelves? Maybe pegs." Mr. Joshua is unable to focus. His soft temper was taken by the fever of a world gone mad. "Pegs. We'll put the worker's cap on the bottom, the bowlers in the middle, and of course the top hats on top," and like a foolish child, he sorts among the pile of hats scattered on the floor—confused, he sighs, "Perhaps the fur in the middle." Rumors of the Weinsteins' fleeing are addressed every morning with another pledge from Moses, demanding his people stand by the Kaiser. "We are Germans. Proud Berliners."

I grab a strip of oak and brush a dark stain on it—then ask Mr. Joshua, trying to hide my frustration, "Do you prefer a darker color?"

A bomb goes off. The large front window shatters—an explosion of glass—a hailstorm—shards ripping the silk dresses off a dozen mannequins—the window display as bombs bursting on a battlefield.

He's wearing a policeman's uniform: a blue coat, badge, brass buttons, and an officer's black helmet topped with a spike. He leaps through the shattered window, stomps over broken glass, steps on the two bodies, kicks the screaming woman, kneeling beside a young girl's white dress covered in blood, threatens the men about to attack, and smashes a glass display with his rifle.

In shock, paralyzed, taking cover. I peek from behind a rack of coats.

The policeman aims his rifle at our two guards. They're too late to fire off a shot. Screams, panic. Glass and wood fly about the room. Blood stains the wood floor.

The next policeman purposely breaks the stained-glass doors. Racing into the store, without hesitation, shooting at the Weinsteins' onrushing sentries. Get to fire off a shot before they drop to the floor.

Mr. Joshua and I are not ten feet from the battlefield—hidden by a rack of hats, crouched down, no path for escape. Forced to retreat by violent explosions deeper into the side room. I crawl toward a rear doorway that separates us from where Greta has her displays. He threatens her to fill his sack with the valuable men's watches. He has his back to me. Greta is holding up her hands in surrender. I finally find the courage, a cause to die for; she gives meaning to my sacrifice, but before I leap from the doorway, he smashes the glass cabinet and orders her to fill his sack with the jewelry.

I want to be a warrior. I want to kill the beast, but as I'm about to attack, I'm pushed back by splinters and glass flying at me like knives. A fourth masked policeman walks in, slowly, studying the battlefield.

Three of the men hiding behind the displays come for him, armed only with canes and fists.

In rapid fire, he kills the knights and empties the clip into the crowd of well-dressed women and men. Greta tries to run away, but without mercy, the beast reloads and executes her and the customers trying to flee.

No one to save, I'm in retreat, and crawl beside Joshua. The rack of hats suddenly gets thrown aside. Behind the policeman's disguise and a mask, I know the dark eyes, the scar on the forehead, but before I cry out in a plea for mercy, he kicks my chest, "The rich man's comrade," purposely aims his pistol at Joshua. "Beg for your life as you have made your slaves beg."

He holds his hands in prayer, "I fear no evil for thou art with me."

The dark eyes hold me in his grip. "We are all soldiers, and today, this is the battlefield of my choosing."

We're locked in each other's stare. "I beg! Preach, not terror!"

He spins the pistol around, "A day of reckoning. You made your choice." He shoots Mr. Joshua and then hits me with such force that I escape to the peace of darkness.

The grand store of dreams created by the Weinsteins was kindling for Lenin's bonfire. I didn't see the three beasts that were his shield. Three more Yitzhaks were shot down, leaving the front of the store, martyrs ready to die for Lenin's purpose. The Kaiser's army was too late. Their armada is useless to defend a battlefield of terror. I didn't see him escape over the many bodies of innocents. I didn't see him tear off the policeman's coat or hide among the crowd in the second disguise of a bourgeois suit. I was suffering in my familiar nightmare.

CHAPTER FORTY-THREE - Conscription - 1914

The nightmare is interrupted by moans and groans from somewhere close, someplace worse than my nightmare, worse than my pain when realizing this isn't a nightmare, but the greater nightmare of the victim's pain. I suffer in shame, frustration, anger, and guilt.

I look over. He has bandages wrapped around chest. He's reading a newspaper. I see the bold headline, "Massacre at Weinsteins." Under the headline, "Marxists, anarchists, executed."

The nurse pulls it away, "You need to rest."

I ask her, "How long have I been out?"

"Since yesterday."

"How many died?"

She comes close enough to whisper, "Ten."

The pain of heartache.

"Max, is it?"

She comes close, a smile for comfort, takes my hand, "It's hateful."

I dare to ask what I already know, "Mr. Weinstein." More pain,"The girl, Greta—Greta Morganthal?" She nods.

"Who did this?" To cover my guilt. "Marxists?"

"They don't know yet. The three were shot."

"Three?"

The man beside me is a favored customer, Mr. Krazinsky. "Thieves pure and simple! They ran out holding filled sacks.

Two men wearing long blue coats with badges on their helmets are beside Mr. Krazinsky's bed. But then I realized that two others, wearing black leather coats, were at the foot of my bed. They come closer, lean in to study me. Close enough to see my reflection in his wire-rimmed glasses. I have a blood-stained bandage wrapped around my head.

In German, "How many were there?"

I'm haunted by knowing. What would the truth earn but more questions that I don't want to answer. He's gone. I had chosen sides. What warning could I have given that we didn't already know? Lenin's war was everywhere.

"I saw three, could have been four."

He nods. "Four?"

"Did you hear them speak? Was it in German or Polish? Yiddish?"

"All I heard was shooting."

"Did you see who shot Mr. Weinstein?"

"He was wearing a mask."

"Lucky you weren't shot." Suspicion? "You recognize any of these men?" He shows me three well-drawn pictures of the dead men.

One looks familiar, Balkius? I answer, "No."

In frustration, they move to the next bed.

Mr. Kravinsky is in great pain but needs to tell the inquisitors, "There were four. One ran out the back as the other three ran out the front."

I listen in.

He shows him the pictures. "Do you know these men?"

He studies with some effort. "No." But then reminds him he saw four, "There was one who had a scar on his forehead."

The scar. Anger more than pain. I lean over to grab the newspaper. The story reports that there were four. The one who got away was not yet identified.

I wait for the nurses, doctors, and police to move down the long row of patients. I'm in a white gown, naked underneath, but I need to leave. Guilt or thinking I can escape this nightmare, I slide off the bed only to be attacked by nails pounding my head, each step, a struggle.

I peek around the doorway. The hallway is a mob of nurses and doctors busily tending to the sick. We're in Rabbi Finkelstein's complex of synagogue, school, shelter, and hospital. Everyone is too focused on repairing flesh to give notice of my escape.

I sneak into a room lined with shelves of pants, gowns, and shirts, and steal a pair of a doctor's white pants and a white shirt. The front entrance to the hospital is blocked by a crowd, somber in prayer.

The congregation was all of the Berlin Jews and those Gentiles who held respect and regard for the Weinsteins, and the friends and family of all who died for being in association.

Lenin's revolution had lit its bonfire. I could argue against terror, but Lenin was right when he said it would cast a greater spell than preaching.

Mr. Moses Weinstein is at once a madman who wants the past erased and a frightened old man, fragile, weak, crippled, who stumbles about the store, stuttering incoherent orders. A wounded king possessed by demons, also unable to escape the nightmares.

I do my best to sweep up the glass, wood, and mop up the blood. I'm too tired to cry, too busy to see their ghosts. I take out my suffering by repairing the store, pounding nails, and sawing wood.

The newspapers revealed the identity of the three who were killed in front of the store. It was Balkius. He was last seen leading the strike at the iron forge where eight of the strikers were shot. The Kaiser was quoted as saying, "Not a moment of production was lost," as if to boast of his power.

Soldiers took the place of the striking workers. They shovel coal and pour ore into the buckets.

My path from apartment to store is no longer welcomed by smiles and "Hellos," but met with a somber routine of lamenting events. The Kaiser uses fear and anger to preach for war.

Lenin fights back with a call to arms, posted as warnings and missives nailed to poles. More walls are painted by invisible comrades with hateful slogans against the czar and the rich. Lenin's declaration of revolution can't be torn down by the army fast enough. His thieves are everywhere. His ghost swirls about London, Paris, Vienna, Saint Petersburg, and Berlin. He's an invisible czar who preaches for revolution with the spirit of a pope, god, or Moses.

The Kaiser fires back. His army practices warfare against Lenin's thieves, thugs, and murderers. Anyone under suspicion for not volunteering or proving their loyalty with deed, bribes, or taxes is either shot or sent to war. Prison was reserved for those who were favored.

Lenin's ghost also haunts Czar Nicholas II. Russia is a poisoned well. The Bolsheviks join with the Mensheviks to silence the Czar's ruling loyalists. News is filtered through propaganda by both sides. Newspapers and broadsides only speak of the French and Russians preparing for war against Germany.

The Kaiser funds his ambitions by printing more Paper Marks. The gold coins are ten times their value. The price of bread, cheese, vodka, and milk cost ten Paper Marks to one gold sovereign. War lifts the spirit of a Germany unified by the purpose of eliminating the threat from France, Belgium, and Russia.

I'm in the crush of a crowd lined along the palace bridge. The Kaiser's speech is blasted from giant cones. He declares war on France.

The newspapers post pictures of his mighty fleet of battleships. There are pictures of a new kind of boat that can dive underwater and fire a cannon—a U-boat.

Conscription has all men looking over their shoulder. Patriots and prisoners are doing hard labor in mines, factories, and farms. War needs bullets and bread. The nobles are anointed Officers with the power of god. They raise their swords to battle. If you retreat, you're shot.

I saved twenty-five of the valued Gold Marks, thanks to Mr. Joshua's generosity, and an end to whores and gambling, but there's no steamer to London, or train to Paris, the border is sealed. There is nowhere to escape.

Only two months since I walked the streets with the pride of work and the friendship of neighbors. You could board a train or ship for five Gold Marks. Lenin's terror fed tyranny. Both sides of the river are put under a strict curfew. Everyone checked.

To hide is to starve if no Gentile helps. All Jews are under suspicion as Marxists, owing to the Rabbis' calling for peace. Escape would mean a risky journey through the battlefield wilderness of Bavaria. Mr. Moses is at death's door, and his sons take up his preaching, "This will pass."

I need to hide my savings before it's stolen. I'm in the basement chiseling out a brick, still in hope this will pass and that one day I'll retrieve the coins, but for what dream other than working for a Weinstein?

I hear the howl, there's a gunshot, more screams, and there's no escape. I'm trapped. I think this is the moment where Gramps is saying, "Pay a bribe, pay the ransom." A moment of pride that I don't need the inheritance from my boot. I'm defenseless, caught with the treasure in my hand. The soldiers laugh when I ask to trade the coins for freedom. They take the coins and drag me outside.

I join my neighbors, boys to elders, loaded at gunpoint, twenty to a horse-drawn wagon. We cross the bridge and leave Berlin to join an endless line of thousands. Hours later, it's my turn to be interviewed. I'm pushed into the tent to give testimony to the fancy uniformed Captain Meister. "Your craft?"

Having spied on the others before me, my fate is either: Battlefield, mine, factory, and for those with a skill, kitchen, transport, or servitude to the army, but then I hear the word, "Kiel," and the proud Berliner behind me boasts—That's where they're building the Dreadnaughts.

I think of what skill could save me from the front lines. I tell Captain Meister— "Carpenter," but he dismisses that as a peasant's skill. "Electrician, connect wires, know motors, weld pipe for plumbing."

Captain Meister nods to his guards, "Shot if lying. Kiel."

CHAPTER FORTY-FOUR – Dreadnaught

An officer sits beside the driver on a cushioned bench inside the motorcoach that hauls this wagon's heavy load. I'm pressed between four wolves and four lambs, along with two large crates of chickens and two barrels of oil. Two soldiers look down on us from the crates, their grip on their rifles firm. We're soaked in the dust and poison of the smoke from these foul and noisy motors, as we follow a long line of wagons loaded with cargo and recruits, the procession well-guarded by a cavalry. They said it'll take a week or two to reach the seaport, but after three days of this ride in hell, squeezed against the four wolves who do nothing but curse us Jews and praise their Kaiser for purifying Germany, I was ready to take my chances and make a run for it the first chance I get, but the journey is given a measure of comfort from the three other Jews who share what we know in the code of Hebrew.

Professor Solomon Bergman knew all about the Kaiser's plans. "We're being taken to Kiel to build battleships or these boats that can go underwater, called U-boats." He confides, "You must have a skill. I know radios." The nebbish sitting on my other side boasts how he knows electricity and instruments and gives thanks, "At least we're not being taken to the quarry, or god forbid, the army."

Berlin to the coastal harbor of Kiel was nine painful days on roads softened by October rains, digging up ruts and holes, but regardless, it's a long day being shaken and breathing poison and dust, we only get two eggs and a slice of bread, so there's little to vomit up.

We arrived at a harbor that's a factory of massive iron tubs lit by sparks and the thunder of hammers as they seal panels to the iron shells of three enormous ships, each in a lesser state. Two appear as a giant's bathtub, but the one closest is made known as a dreadnaught by a fort on top of another fort, each with three cannons the size of a telegraph pole.

We're ordered to follow an officer whose white uniform bears the dangers of our labor: torn holes, burn marks, and rust-colored stains. He leads a parade of dozens who have been assigned to this ship, and down one ladder after another, until we're inside a storm of smoke, thunder, and lightning. A hundred men are perched on scaffolds, welding sparks flying as bolts seal the large panels of thick iron, lowered into place by cranes.

A younger officer, without a jacket but wearing only a shirt, has me and four others follow him across narrow iron beams to make our way across a ship that is like a mountain, forest, and field, a trick to keep my balance. "This is where you sleep."

A long row of hammocks. The officer points to the buckets. He issues the law, "When the bucket's stench is too great, throw it over the side."

Weeks pass. I'm driven to madness from exhaustion as we're pushed to race through our chores. I climb ladders, bolt in clips, and run wires throughout a ship that seems without end.

My hammock is one of a hundred strung in a room the size of a train car. The noise of men climbing ladders is a constant clanking with a new chorus of propellers pushing this massive iron monster. The vibration rumbles throughout the ship. Always the slamming of heavy iron doors. So many chasing about the ship that everyone has a finger, hand, arm, leg, or foot in a bandage. Life and limb as casualties of war. The hallways are too narrow, bang into pipes, slip on wet stairs and ladders, and get cut by the sharp edges of a ship made of iron.

Another month, another floor. There's little thought of anything but making it to another day.

The heat of summer, the chill of fall, and a year passes to suffer the enemy of winter once again, kept from frostbite by barrels of oil set on fire, no matter that its smoke fouls the air, but better than the stench of bowels that sickens.

There is little trust among the men. The Officers wear white, seamen in blue. Prisoners known by brown overalls. The curse of Jews as cowards. We're shunned. Punished by the labor of crueler chores and shamed to wear a yellow uniform.

I'm tasked to prove my worth when the crane lowers the locomotive-sized engine to the bottom of the ship. My job is to thread a mile of wires through pipes that I've bolted to the wall. Having laid a mile of pipe and threaded two miles of wire to get from the engine to the Captain's perch. My reward is that the wires end at the captain's perch. And while Professor Solomon attaches the wires to the instruments, I get to breathe fresh air and look out on the Sea and think of that adventure of digging up amber with my father.

In January, we celebrate the reward of heat and electricity. The massive boilers give life to the engine, and the engine brings life to the magical batteries that somehow store electricity to power the lights, provide heat, turn on the instruments, and bring the ship to life.

By April, the dreadnaught was ready to take out to sea. There's a celebration with bands and a parade. The Kaiser himself is here to christen the ship. I hear the echo of his speech. "We are the Huns, warriors, we take no prisoners, the world will bow at our feet."

The next day, I'm no longer needed as an electrician and sent to shovel coal. From the bowels of the ship, we are made deaf and blind by the shuddering of the engines, the propellers set free, attacked by a cloud of smoke billowing out from the furnace. The officer writes on his clipboard that the smokestacks are either clogged or improperly connected.

Covered in sweat, soot, dizzy in thirst, no longer able to lift the shovel, I'm saved from entering the furnace by the echo of Poppa's plea to hold onto hope that on the *other side of today is a new path tomorrow*.

My angels keep me from joining a long list of those who surrender.

I'm kicked awake from the nightmare by the Petty Officer who orders me to report to "Lieutenant Schmeur" — needing directions: "Room 182, just aft of the mess hall."

I make my way through a maze that takes me into the forbidden areas where we store bombs and bullets. The Lieutenant's room is made even smaller by boxes and piles of paper. The walls are shelves lined with books. He studies a file, then hands it to the next in line, who files it in a particular box.

I stand at attention. The lieutenant finally looks up when his assistant asks what I want. "I'm Seaman Max Gutlian. Ordered to see Lieutenant Schmeur."

The lieutenant searches the stack, pulls up a sheet, and reads the report as though I'm not here. But then he looks up. "A Jew!" Surprised, "You installed the wires?"

"Yes, sir." Shaking. What's this about?

"It says you are a Berliner." He studies me, "You are German?"

His question puts me in a panic. I had told the arresting officer that I was German, believing it would buy me a measure of trust. "Yes."

"You were raised where?"

"Berlin." Berliners are recognized as a superior breed.

He squints. The monocle is pressed to his eye. Needs to see into me. "Yes, I see. A Berliner. I, too, am a Berliner."

"The Kaiser's capital for a great German empire." Not knowing his prejudice, I don't mention the Weinsteins. Flattery is my only trade.

He looks down at the paper. "You are a Jew, yet you have given no grievance."

"I think of myself as a loyal German." A truth for what the Weinsteins would ask of me. I study his expression; he gives no clue, but I know that if you don't take the pledge, you're shot as a traitor.

"Are you not more loyal to Jews—to the socialists?"

A pledge of loyalty or a traitor. "My faith is with the Kaiser."

"You're Christian?"

I nod, "I believe that Jesus is the Messiah." I don't turn away. A trade needs certainty. "You're to report to the Petty Officer," he signs the paper and hands it to me. "You are being transferred."

"To where?"

He stares at me as if I've sinned to even ask. "You will take this to the Petty Officer. He'll take you to your assignment."

CHAPTER FORTY-FIVE – U-boat - June 1915

The harbor is a beehive of crates being unloaded onto the four battleships. I'm led by the two guards out from the fortress, across a bridge, and onto firm ground, where we make our way along a field strewn with machine parts that stretches a hundred paces to towers at each corner of brick walls topped with barbed wire. Ahead are two large buildings. I'm pushed past in a hurry. There are warnings posted on large signs— "Trespassers will be shot." The windows are barred and boarded, a cluster of officers milling in front.

We're stopped at a checkpoint secured by an iron gate welded with rows of spikes. The two guards study my papers and give me such a look of surprise that they question my guards about letting a Jew in before they unlock the gate.

I finally discovered what they were hiding behind a high wooden fence that separated our battleships from these rows of bullet-shaped black boats.

I count sixteen of these floating bullets under construction before they are presented to the captain, holding court before a crew of twenty in blue overalls, five in orange, and three officers in white suits and black-rimmed caps.

The boat is made of magic from a conjured fable. We heard rumors about boats that can swim underwater and fire strange bombs.

The captain is annoyed by my intrusion. He's a sturdy man with a trimmed beard and hair that is the color of the sun. The Captain's authority is noted on the cap of a black beak with gold trim. The two junior officers don't have the fancy braids.

He reads my papers in a hurry and abruptly dismisses the two guards with a salute. "You will finish your assigned duties in ten days. Each day past ten days, and your favored rations will go to bread and water."

And went down the list of our assignments: weld pipes, mount the hatches, connect the engine to the propeller—and that's when he studies me. "You are a Jew? Yes."

"In birth only."

"Converted?"

I look down. "Baptized."

"I am now your god." He uses the tip of his finger to lift my chin. "You are scared to look god in the eye?" He laughs as if he knows the lie of a heretic. "Do your job and prove me wrong."

He is not much older, perhaps thirty. God's eyes have no color save for the lightest blue that fix your attention—a Viking, but not a beast. A scholar with a warrior's soul. It's the spirit of certainty that brings courage and what is needed to make a man a master of such a magical sword.

He turns to the elder. "You will use this—Jew—as your helper." He tugs at my overalls. I'm wearing the yellow overalls. "Give him orange overalls and proper shoes." I look down to see that their shoes are made of white cloth with a rubber sole.

The captain walks the line of his crew. "This boat has a diesel engine," said with pride, "To be a submariner is a great honor. It's two hundred feet long and carries ten torpedoes. Each bullet is precious."

Fritz leads me across the gangplank, and we climb down a ladder into the coffin of a narrow tunnel cluttered with pipes, wire, tubes. I need to watch my head. The width is to go side to side, with three good paces. We climb over the obstacles and make our way to the front. There's a stack of four large bullets longer than a man, and with a propeller and fins at its tail, each on a bed that leads to a hatch door. Beneath the bombs are four hammocks strung to a clip.

Fritz has the scars of an electrician, with those red lines burned as a brand. He doesn't look at me, has yet to say a word, and just hands me an orange suit of light cloth. Of course, it's too big, but I use the belt from my uniform to pull it tight to my waist. He then hands me the white shoes. More like a sock, but with a sturdy sole of rubber.

It comes as a surprise when he opens a hatch in the floor and climbs down a short ladder. He pulls the wire from a spool and orders me to push it through the pipe. When he points above my head, he says, "Then go back up and pull it to the end of the boat through the blue pipe marked wire."

I do as he asks and breathe easier once I've climbed back up the ladder. I know the routine and see why I was transferred. It's a trick to thread a harder wire through the pipe, then tie the thin electric wire to pull it back through, an inch at a time.

As I work the wire toward the middle of the boat, the three officers huddle around the pipe. This is the captain's perch. He shoots me a harsh glare as he orders his officers to lift the pole in the middle of the room. "This is our eyes, a binocular, our line of sight, a periscope." He swivels the pole and has the officers take a look.

The Captain grabs me, "Do your job. Go!"

I need to climb over pipes to pull the wire, but he pushes me out of his way to pull aside a curtain that hides a small room with a bunk and a desk. The other side has four hammocks, a storage locker, and a small desk.

I bend, breathe a new sort of foul air, soaked in minutes from the coffin's heat, but suffer more for being in such a cramped space. At least the dreadnaught had room enough not to have to wrestle each crew member to get past.

Our reward is dinner on deck. I'm shocked when the Captain waves me toward a sailor manning a cart and filling my tin with a feast of steak and potatoes, but the stench of the harbor spoils the meal.

We're a village. The next U-boat is beside us. The officers trade boasts and dares.

Fritz notices my fever of surrender and pulls me from my dream of swimming off, "We have a mission." And then he orders me to go below. "We'll have the cabin to ourselves to finish attaching the first wire to my damn batteries. But it won't do any good. Tomorrow we'll need to find the loose threads."

I felt a strange kinship to Fritz, but his temper would suggest otherwise. He orders me around like a mule.

Sleep is the same as on the dreadnaught. A cocoon of rope with your neighbors above and below, all bound in the hammocks, a night of grunts, groans, and the familiar sounds of men who have lost all awareness of shame. I ask Fritz, who has the top hammock, if I can sleep on deck. He calls me a fool, "No." And given the rule about the blue suits, gray suits, orange, and white in a pecking order of such privilege. "You're a prisoner." But he said it as if he weren't a member of the crew, either.

The one toilet is for the officers. We use the bucket. Fresh water is for drinking and to wet a cloth at the end of the day. A roll of rough paper is to wipe off our bowels, but there's no way to wipe away the truth that we're floating in a sewer.

This chore is another test that fuels me with its challenge. Whether it's welding pipes or connecting wire, I know the difference between doing the job right or setting us up for failure. The captain keeps his eye on me, and when he's distracted, the officers watch our progress with great interest. I'm only allowed on deck for the two meals.

Ten days' done, it's the day of the Captain's deadline, Fritz hasn't gotten the batteries to work, the copper wires, and layers of tin, zinc, and nickel have a mind of their own. They work for a short time but then quit.

While the Captain tears into Fritz, I hear Mr. Dayan ordering me to blow up the boat. It's Satan's weapon. Invisible and deadly. I imagine hitting the torpedo with the tools they let me have, pliers and my guide wire, but where? The tip? No guns on board. Is this my purpose?

It's the end of May. The boat is an oven. The captain has made it clear to Fritz that this is his last chance to get the batteries working before he's replaced.

I'm put on notice until the Captain tests my wiring by having his officer touch one end with the small battery they use to light his perch, and then put a bulb on the other. It lights up.

He then has me go to the engines and connect the wire to a terminal.

The shock is beyond fire, beyond cold; it's as if my entire body is boiling or frozen in alternating bursts.

The batteries are working.

The next day, our crew is let off, and a new crew in blue uniforms takes their stations, and the Captain has his eyes pressed to the periscope's mask, turning knobs, swiveling. The dozen blue uniformed seamen are watching valves, turning the steering wheels, shifting levers, and with each command, the boat twists, turns, lurches, vibrates—more noise of valves and motor, and with Fritzy's hand raised, suddenly, there's the sound of fans and the air loses its stench.

I can breathe, but then drops spring leaks from the hull, soaking my short hair, dripping on my face, and I yell out, "We're sinking."

The crew turns, the captain and lieutenant lean into the room, and I point to the dripping. The lieutenant laughs. "This is how we know where to patch." The captain looks at me with fire, but suddenly the lights flicker; the fan goes quiet, fumes fill the cabin, sparks shoot up from the batteries.

We're towed back to the dock, and everyone is ordered onto the deck. The captain grabs Fritz by the arm, shakes him, cursing.

Fritz spits in the Captain's face— "Death to the Kaiser," grabs a heavy chain, and jumps overboard. We lose sight of him as he dives under the boat. His body floats to the surface a few minutes later.

I'm questioned by the captain and repeat my pledge of loyalty, but I believe my fate is tied to Fritzy.

Under the suspicious eye of the Captain and crew, the two guards grab my arms and pull me from the U-boat. I'm pushed along the dock. Draw stares from the hundreds of mariners. The Captain speaks on my behalf. "The wires were correct," but I'm condemned as Fritzy's comrade.

Fritz hid behind a mask of loyalty, waiting for his moment, wanting to die for a purpose. Lenin would be proud. I was an unwitting apprentice, dutifully following the orders of my master. I had no clue.

In shock and confusion, I'm given a soldier's uniform and led to a wagon, chained to the rail, joined by six others who tell me our fate—to be executed by the firing squad on the battlefield.

CHAPTER FORTY-SIX – War – 1915

Our wagon joins a line of three other wagons pulled by mules and horses. At the front of the parade are two Motorwagen with officers in the back seat. To the rear, a wagon of dutiful soldiers stands guard, rifles raised.

It takes a moment to recognize the skeleton. "Zeitl?" I whisper in hope of finding an ally." I know the boy chained next to me from the Dreadnaught.

His eyes shift about, body twitching, I don't exist. He contorts in uncontrollable spasms, driven to madness, a loud curse to the Kaiser.

The wagon stops. Two soldiers jump from the rear wagon, come close, shoot him, unchain him, and throw the body on the side of the road.

"A madman." My loyalty is shown with a salute. No matter how much I want to be shot and end this nightmare, I either lack the courage or my parents' lessons on survival keep me alive with hope.

Three long days of travel are further slowed by long lines at the checkpoints. We're heading southeast from Kiel, and that means we're going into Poland.

Worn by miles measured in days, we arrive at a city made of tents. A sprawling field covered with ants dressed as soldiers. A hundred to a marching square, too many to count, all marching in a straight line until turned around to do it again.

We're ordered to strip off our brown, orange, and blue uniforms and given a grey uniform. I'm fitted with a cap, boots, two belts with pockets for a canteen and two tins of rations, and bands of straps to hold bullets, and ordered by a sergeant to march onto the field. We're handed a rifle that is no more than an iron barrel fitted into a wooden block, the only weapon being a bayonet that Josef might have forged.

We spent the next ten days pretending to shoot. Bullets are too precious to waste on training. The bayonet is given practice as we plunge the blade deep into the straw dummies wearing brown Russian uniforms.

On the eleventh day, we leave the camp and, led by a parade of cavalry with flags, followed by officers in fancy motorcoaches, we head east toward Poznan. A road I'm familiar with. I'm surrounded by pious

Germans who have faith in the glory of battle. My regiment is four across and twenty-five rows long. The true Huns were given belts laden with clips of bullets and the new Mauser rifle, which can fire five bullets; a marksman can hit a bullseye from a hundred paces. My rifle is a pole with a bayonet. The yellow badge on my sleeve means I'm not trusted.

But I'm better equipped for the wilderness than I've ever been. Given a backpack, mess kit, flint, an extra pair of long johns, powder for lice, extra pair of good wool socks, a canteen, a shovel, and the leather boots with metal tips on the soles and a burlap strap buttoned almost to my knee. The helmet is a bowl forged from iron. I hear Yitzhak, "You are going to die for the Kaiser!"

The regiment extends as far as I can see, no end either up or down the road. It won't be but another day before we reach Poznan. Rumor has it that we're to reinforce the front line against a stubborn Russian defense. That would be the armada of Russian soldiers that were holding Riga to Warsaw prisoner. I overheard that the Germans won this battle, but since last year, they've only been able to keep the line. Both sides dug in. The tunnels and trenches are a mole's fortress that stretches from here to Hungary.

We pass fields with the grain and corn that are better than half-grown. The summer has been kind, with a fair amount of rain. The battle is meant to secure the harvest.

With Poznan in sight, our procession is ordered to a halt. Our Lieutenant returns. He barks out the order: "Gather cows, pigs, and grain. We're to load as many chickens as can fit in the wagons."

There's no sign of the farmers, but just as my squad of thirty strong Germans races about to round up the pigs and cows, there's a shot. The soldier who was not ten paces from me is the first to fall. Blood stains his chest. Another shot. Another soldier screams as he clings to the dirt.

We follow the echo of the gunshot to a patch of trees that border the farm. Another round of shots is fired. Waleska and his people will kill Russians or Germans. The Baron's battle only took out the palace guards. I wondered what became of Waleska and his kingdom. His warriors won't march onto a field in a line but as snipers picking us off one by one.

Our regiment scatters. I hid behind an apple tree. Most duck down in the tall stalks of corn. But retreating isn't an option. I'm ordered to stand as a target. Three more are shot before the shooter's perch is spotted at the top of tall pine where the forest borders the farm. The Lieutenant fires the shot with a well-aimed mouser, but only the crows scatter.

The sniper takes out two more before we surrender the farm. The eight dead and three wounded are left behind.

I would argue the Kaiser was foolish to start a war in the heat of summer. A much greater prize to have waited until October, when the bounty of a good harvest could feed his army for months. Our raid stole only four cows, a dozen chickens, and six goats. The corn wasn't ready.

The next day, we are ordered to plunder another farm. Once again, we're under a fierce attack by a Polish marksman—an invisible ghostly sniper. Lose four in trade for two cows and seven goats.

Our lieutenant is about my age. He assumes the role of elder by virtue of noble birth. Tall, strong, handsome, the custom of heritage earns a noble's son the honor of leading the charge. Lieutenant Niederhofer is a proud Berliner. He is the warrior I wished to be. A Yitzhak, but Regal. His faith is also in the mission. Death is a portal to some grander heaven. He speaks excitedly of marching into war as if we're marching in a parade.

The generals' fancy motorcoaches are protected by a regiment of cavalry to their front and a regiment of thousands in rows two across following from behind. Their shield includes lesser officers rewarded with the black stallions. As we approach Poznan, the General takes the lead at the front of the parade, flanked by flags held high.

The most loyal warriors are given the honor of following the General's parade over the bridge to the German side of the river. His battleship of an army pulling into home port.

My return to Poznan poisons me with guilt. We don't cross the bridge. I'm punished to march past a new brewery most likely built with the brick Michel blew apart. The black cloud of its furnaces rises from the smokestack. There's the smell of grain and potatoes boiling into ale and vodka.

Our battalion turns onto Petrovsky Boulevard. My heart sinks as we enter the Jewish Quarter. The Captain stands on a wagon, holds a cone-shaped speaker, we're in front of the B'nai Torah Synagogue where thousands of Jews crowd the square in silence, no weapons, no protest, no threats, but surrender in hope of being spared.

The pious believe they have God's shield. The merchants think they have the sword of commerce. Most believe they are vital to serving the masters' needs and wants.

The Captain is clad in a white uniform decorated with medals and braids. The spiked silver helmet shines under a sunny summer day. He declares our intent. "We are here to gather provisions."

My lieutenant forms our regiment into three groups of thirty. He holds up his right hand. "You will gather everything of value."

The crowd is in shock. Cries of betrayal. Their loyalty carried no favor. They scatter in a hopeless attempt to defend home, property, and for those who don't surrender, there's execution.

The sergeant orders the pillaging to begin.

I have no bullets. Jews and Poles have an ancient one-shot rifle with a bayonet. I'm once again the coward who justifies doing nothing with the excuse of being helpless to stop the beasts. Even if I had a soldier's rifle with six bullets in the clip, would I shoot the sergeant? The lieutenant? I would be shot, of course. Would my sacrifice inspire the unarmed shopkeepers to take on armed soldiers? If they did, wouldn't it only be their execution? We'd all die for a worthless trade. Unarmed against the armed. Lambs against wolves. Not the battlefield of our choice. Mr. Dayan is laughing at me. He's telling me to preach for peace.

The beasts bring the plunder to the wagons. I watch, as if taking the bullet myself, as Nathan Braunstein is shot for putting up a struggle.

The sergeant stands above me, pistol at the ready, and my choice is death or to load the sacks of salt, bread, sugar, and bags of flour.

Tears don't stop the plunder. The Kaiser and Czar ordain thieves and murderers. The sausage maker and the baker are forced to cook until nothing remains.

We can't hear the loud cries echo from the Pole's village. They are dealt no less of a trade. Waleska won't fight on this battlefield.

Our tents fill the Square. The officers took over the temple as if it were an Inn.

CHAPTER FORTY-SEVEN - Soldier — 1915

We leave Poznan two days after all the shelves are bare. I hear rumors we're to reinforce our victorious troops. The officers spread the rumor that the Russians are ready to surrender.

Confidence had been instilled from last summer's battle near Tannenberg. The first major battle of the war, against the Russians on the Eastern Front, was declared by General Hindenburg to be a great victory for Germany. A hundred thousand Russian bodies measured against tens of thousands of Germans.

We're two days' march heading toward Poland from Prussian Poznan when the first explosion brings all to alert but not allowed to move. The officers holding up the hand to signal all to stand at attention.

The battle rings as an echo of thunder coming from some immeasurable distance, but then another bolt of thunder, another even closer, and then the earth erupts.

The Russians had taken heavy losses last year, but an endless supply of fresh bodies, bullets, cannons, and their cavalry keep coming.

This summer, Tannenberg is a battlefield of the Russians' choice. Their cannons fire from the protection of the forest blowing apart flat farmland. Suddenly, as if gophers emerging from holes, a swarm of vermin rises up from the cover of picked stalks of the cornfields. The Russian cavalry appears from the forest as locusts.

Our army is exposed. The peaceful road was a path to execution.

The lieutenant is beside me, stares at the box of ammo, and orders me to hand out the precious bullets and clips.

I don't move. I have no will. He yells at me again, this time with his pistol to my head— "Traitor or patriot?" and pushes me toward the box of ammo.

The Lieutenant orders the fodder of cowards to the front as a shield for his Prussian warriors. Their rifles pointed at the pawns' backs.

The Russian attack slows as bullets and cannon balls are spent. Silence. A moment's break to reload.

The German charge toward the field. But the silence wasn't to reload, but to retreat and leave the field as bait. A vicious round of cannon fire tears into the charging Germans. Thunder and lightning. Gunfire aimed by men blinded by the spell of war. Souls turn to beasts. No mercy by either side. All lines broken, platoons scattered, the battalions wage their own war.

A nearby explosion digs a hole. Three other cowards jump in, and before I crawl into the grave to join them, a second bolt hits the hole.

I hear his war cry. Look behind. The Lieutenant races past in a hurry to earn honor. My cowardliness is not given a glance—the warriors are infected by a rabid fever.

Tens of Russians are within reach of the Lieutenant's attack as he unloads his pistol. Two go down, but more keep coming. He swings his sword high, fends off a bayonet with an arching swipe. With a swift motion he slices off the young soldier's hand. In rapture, the Lieutenant won't retreat.

I watch from my grave of a ditch as an equally fevered Russian officer disregards sword play and shoots the lieutenant. He drops to his knees, but driven by hate as blood, his pistol in his left hand, he proves the dishonor by shooting back at the officer, but had emptied the clip, and the officer finishes the execution.

The gods look down on this hell from the comfort of tents set high on a perch at the top of the hill. The generals and their palace guard will not see the tip of a blade. They order death from far above the battlefield.

I pose as dead in a field littered with death. The earth trembles. The storm rages on. In haste to kill and die, none take notice or disturb my death.

The day's battle ends when the battlefield is in the dim shadows of a moonless night. I lift off the arms and legs that hid my cowardliness, crawl out of my grave, but need great care to avoid falling over bodies.

I follow a long ditch that leads away from the thunder of battle and settle into the muck of a brook. No rest for the cries, stray battles, shots fired at random and all too soon the sunrise awakens the battlefield with a thousand cavalry and more cannon fire as the generals are still hungry.

Days turn to nights and nights back to a day. The turn of a day measured by war is made endless. The battle stays close enough to keep me hugging the muck. Thirst, hunger, and suffering as punishment for my cowardliness.

Under the shadows of a starless night, I strip off a uniform infested with lice and use handfuls of muck to scrub off the pox of the vermin. I'm trapped in a prison of despair to think the better escape is death, but from a nearby heaven I hear Poppa, no Mamma, Bubby? Gramps? Their spirit whispers to remind me of their most solemn lesson.

"Death is not your choice. Until your time is taken, savor the gift of another day, for no matter its suffering, there's always hope for tomorrow to be the day where you're rewarded with life's many gifts."

They give me the strength to press on. Naked and afraid, I scan the bodies of men and horses without a soul stirring. I have my pick of uniform, weapons, bullets, canteen, and rations. I grab a tin and eat the salted fish. I drink sweet water from a canteen. I find a boy my size wearing a Russian uniform, shot in the head, no holes or blood stains. The boots fit; put on his jacket and pants. Push away the guilt —the boy is dead —but I'm a thief as I steal the three rubles in his pocket.

I crawl towards the forest, the war behind me, and question my choice of a Russian uniform. Who won the battle?

I see a light flicker in the distance. Hide in the tall grass. Shadows are picking through the pockets and stealing prized weapons and tins of rations. Are they also deserters turned grave robbers? They fill a wagon and return to plunder.

I'm hiding beside a dead German lieutenant. Think of changing back to German? But what Jew was ever an officer?

Warsaw, Vilna, or Riga? Wilderness or village same danger of wolves and beasts. South to the Slavs. No mercy for any but their own. North is the kingdom of hateful Prussians—generations of nobles born to defend their kingdoms.

But if I reach the sea and go north to Lithuania along the Baltic, would that be far from the war?

I set my direction. I'm surrounded by Russian soldiers scavenging the battlefield and need to hurry before I'm shot simply for being seen. I search to find the better mouser rifle but struggle to pry it from death's grip. I unbuckle his leather belt, grab three clips, but only find two tins of rations. Tins kept on the supply wagons, not to be wasted on a battlefield. The greater reward is the rifle and bullets.

Sunrise. They're close, but busy picking pockets, not twenty paces, the same distance as the cover of bramble and trees. I hear cursing. They're not Russians but Polish. I wait until they've gone far enough away to not see me race into the forest and run until dark before I collapse into sleep.

My nightmare is disturbed by the sound of a mob. I crawl close enough to see they're not soldiers, but in tunics, must be Prussian hunters. In the distance, cast in moonlight, is a castle of some regard.

Their stories are told in German. Boasting of a victory for Germany. Twenty lanterns hang along a great barn and stables. I count over a hundred men and as many cattle and horses behind a rich man's white fence.

I use the cover of the night and order my tired legs to flee in the other direction.

I finish the two tins of fish ration, but hunger is not a worry. I find berries, nuts, mushrooms, chestnuts, thistle, and dandelion. Drink fresh water from running streams.

I follow a path under the cover of trees and shrubs. I navigate between villages and farms until after so many days, I've lost count, and don't know where I am until I come to a barn that gives me my location. It's a round sign of red, green, and blue with the Russian cross of three bars, and this tells me I've left Prussia and must be in Lithuania.

The Lithuanians have been under the fists of their neighbors since before the Vikings. Invasions by the Swedes, Prussians, Poles, and Russians have hardened its people and bred a strong breed of warriors. I can't know if they'd have charity for an atheist Jew. Hanging on a clothesline are tunics and pants of a native. I have a choice. Would I be better off as a lost soldier or Lithuanian peasant?

Three grown boys and the father come out of the barn. They yell to one another in German. It's not worth the risk to show myself. I've been wandering for weeks, living off the land, and freedom brings me to peace.

It is late in the day, shadows make it hard to know what I'm looking at, but there's some large animal propped beside the tree trunk. I look around. Only the crows try to scare me off. I sneak closer.

It's an old man leaning against the tree, white as a ghost, died recently, not been eaten. Sunset shines a flicker of light through the branches—Scars on his skin! Pox! I back away slowly so as not to disturb the sickness, but stumble when I step on something round—look down, and then up, he died under an apple tree.

The first bite is as good as cake and a feast. But as I rest, I can see the hoof marks of boar, deer, paws of a bear, and further ahead, the deeper paw prints of wolves. I take hold of my rifle. I'm prey?

This is the Garden of Eden I had hoped for. A worthy place to make a home. I'd set traps of deep holes covered with weak twigs and shrubs. The tree is bait. But as I dig a hole with my knife and am about to collect branches, I hear gunshots.

Hide, wait. It's not long before the hunters fire again—coming closer. An orchard is a well-known lure.

It pains me to leave this Eden, but stuff two apples in my jacket and race between trees to continue north.

Two more nights, and I can taste the sea. The air is scented by salt. I hurry my pace. I've come to the end of land. I've reached the endless sea. If I follow the Baltic, it'll take me from Lithuania to Latvia. I could continue past Riga and reach Estonia, further and I'd be in St. Petersburg, and then to Finland, and if I'm lucky, I could reach Sweden.

I continue north on a path of all sand. I think of digging for treasure in the dunes. To trade amber for gold at that trader's home in Riga.

Settle here? The life of a fisherman?

Need a river, pond, brook, seawater is poison, but the cool sea air flavors my breathing with its tonic. I take off my boots, belt, and leave the rifle, knife, and cap on the rocks, strip off the uniform of britches. Naked, I plunge into the cold water. I feel reborn.

A good night's sleep and wake to realize this path is an endless stretch of beach. I turn back to find a sandbar taking me to a stretch of trees. By late in the afternoon, thirst hurting my throat, I came to a river flowing from the forest into the sea. Fresh water, fish, and I look to heaven and wonder if God is on my shoulder. I say a blessing to give thanks as my faith is taken by his bait.

No need for a pole or bait, the river is but a stream as it gets closer to the sea, and I'm able to push the fish to the bank. I think of making a fire, but in the distance are lights from lanterns, candles, and fire. Can't trust greeting a stranger in this Russian uniform.

I clean off the bones and skin and eat the sweet meat that needs no cooking and celebrate the feast with more prayers and blessings.

CHAPTER FORTY-EIGHT – Latvia - 1915

I wake to three men wearing the familiar tunic of a Livonian—the Livonians were the most ancient of native tribes and their craftsmanship with needle and thread is remarkable. Scrolls of red thread trim the edges of the white shirt. They're standing over me, having kicked me awake.

"Russian?" The elder asks where the rest of my regiment is in Russian.

"I'm the scout. My squad is a day behind."

They ride off on fast horses as if my answer was what they were hoping for.

My dream of building a cabin and making this home is a dream. Nowhere is safe. Nowhere is a wilderness not guarded by a fisherman, farmer, hunter, a noble, a sheriff, or a landowner.

I stumble through another day of dodging branches, roots, critters, and miss the sand dunes, and calming sea, but it's a cool, dry day that eases the journey. The forest is as I remember from home, a wilderness so endless, without village, farm, and only deer and birds to keep me company.

Another day, begin to think there's no escape, when, as if a wish granted by God, I notice movement, peer through a wall of thick branches to spy a herd of cows, sheep, and as many goats, not roaming free, but held inside a fence that would have used all the branches of three or four tall pines to stretch across a sizeable pasture.

It's a fine farm with a good-sized barn and a fine home. I sneak close enough to see a girl milking a cow, with her back to me. A knotted tail of dark brown hair sways as she grabs the bucket and leaves the barn.

Three boys are lazily feeding a pen of chickens and pigs. The youngest boy is a child, maybe four. The next oldest looks to be about seven, eight, maybe nine, the shoulders of someone older, but a boy's face. The eldest is maybe twelve, judging by the fact he's almost as tall as me, but yet to sprout a beard. Curly hair and a broad nose suggest they might be Jewish. The eldest tends to a family of pigs, ranging from young to fat. The younger brother spread grain for the chickens, the little brother is chasing after the chickens.

The girl stops. Studies the trees. It's as if she knows there's someone watching. Ten paces away. I can't get a good look at her through the thick, needled branches, but I can't help staring back at her piercing dark brown eyes.

She puts down the buckets. Her right hand lifts her long dress and grips a knife from a strap around her thigh. "Who's there!"

Speaking Latvian, "I'm alone. Not going to hurt you."

At the sight of a Russian soldier, the boys rush to her side and look at me like I'm a beast. I hold my arms up in surrender, the rifle strapped behind my back.

Her father is too busy driving a strong horse, turning over a good field, clearing it of the stalks left behind from harvested corn. He wears the embroidered white tunic and red cap of a southern Latvian. He's not a big man, but strong. His thin beard is lost in a long face colored by a farmer's day, a summer spent under the sun. His arms show the muscles of a mule to labor.

Beyond the field is a good-sized cabin. My father and grandfather would appreciate a solid home made with logs cut to the length of a man. The labor of lifting heavy logs reminds me of Poppa's drawing and my grandfather's lessons on the power of a pulley, and a full toolbox with a good axe, saw, hammer, but even if built by two strong men, this was months of hard labor. The logs are neatly stacked with a sharp point at each corner in the style of a fort. The long rows of skinned trunks are sealed with heavy packing of well-attended mortar. The stone chimney is tall. Good height windows and wrought iron-clad doors, you'd pay the carpenter his due of respect.

Working a loom on the front porch is a woman my mother's age—same dark brown hair, round face as her daughter, and shows serious intent in her work.

Feeding the loom is a tall girl, not like the others. She has hair the color of wheat and is taller than even her father.

The sight of this family and farm fills me with longing. I want to show myself, but I worry about approaching with a rifle in a Russian uniform.

The girl turns. She senses me. Stares in my direction. The instinct of a fox. I duck back. Peek between the thinner branches, but her intuition is strong. She puts down the buckets, pulls a pistol from under her skirt, and calls out— "Who's there?" said in Latvian, but not friendly, the gun held firm.

"A friend," I answer in Latvian to help put her at ease, and with a longing to be found by this family and their fine farm, I surrender with arms raised. "Nobody to trouble you. Just passing through."

She comes closer. "Passing through! Where's your army?"

"I'm alone?" Not knowing if a deserter is a traitor or a patriot. Charm the lie, "Separated from my regiment during battle."

"You're a deserter." The girl has my bubby's gift.

Disarmed to surrender to her intuition, I take confession, honesty to earn trust— "Maybe a coward, but maybe I'm a schooled peddler who knows the value of a poor trade. My life for the Kaiser?"

She comes close—no fear—studies me. "Jew?"

"I am."

Her squint lightens to a smile.

Alarmed, her mother sees us coming and stops threading the loom. She looks behind me, searching—and asks in fear, "An army?" said in poor Russian.

"I'm alone," in Yiddish, then Latvian, hoping to put her at ease.

The girl tells her mother, "He's a Jew deserter," and goes to the porch. The boys follow close behind.

"Deserter?"

"Had no faith in their war."

"War?" The father makes himself known from behind the barn door. "Germans? How close?"

"It's been weeks to get here."

"Everyone, go inside." Possessed by curiosity. They're in no hurry.

He comes close. A grim stare. Asks in a whisper, "The Kaiser?"

"Wants Poland." Goes unsaid between us that the Kaiser is greedy for good farmland.

He shakes his head. "Wilhelm's ambition to be Goliath is cheered by a united Germany with Prussian generals hungry to prove their worth in battle."

I need to put my hands over my eyes to keep from seeing my tears, crying for the warmth of being with a family.

The father waves his boys back. The window watching from the window. Not knowing might be worse than telling them the truth. His hand on my shoulder. "Are you Russian?"

"No. Stole the uniform. Wasn't German either. I'm from Riga." I take a deep breath.

He hands me his flask. A sweet wine.

"Germans are heading toward Warsaw. Not sure who's winning?"

"The Russians stopped them?"

I shake my head. "Few left that cemetery alive."

We're interrupted by his boys.

"Go back in and we'll talk at supper."

After some protest by the eldest, he gives the boy a swat, "Go and help your mother. We need to feed this man."

He pulls me toward the barn. Wants to shield the boys. I give him the bad news. "The Kaiser has magical weapons—a rifle that shoots so many bullets so fast you'd think one man was a hundred." I show him the mouser. "Their cannons fire great distances. They have battleships with even greater cannons. They have boats that can go underwater and fire these man-sized bullets at ships, lurking about as if they're ghosts."

"This is madness."

"You're some distance. I've been traveling for weeks—maybe a month." I scan the horizon of this forest. Memories send me back to my grandfather's fables about how the forest is a fortress. He's shaken. Knows better. I feel the guilt of a messenger bringing bad news.

"You're from Riga." His Yiddish is flavored with Latvian.

"I'm from Riga. Born there. My brother is there. He has a clothing factory. I left the city to find peace." A smile, more of a smirk.

"As did my family."

He shakes his head. "You going to Riga?"

"Don't know where I'm going."

He takes my wrist— "I am Juska Balyarus."

"Max, Max Gutlian."

"Let's get you fed and cleaned up." He grips tighter, "But no more talk of this war other than to say it's in a foreign land."

The girls are stirring a soup that reminds me of home. The copper kettle is boiling inside a wide hearth. Their mother is rolling dough, the boys chase after each other, and I'm lost in memories of Bubby and Mamma by the hearth. I can just see Poppa and Gramps at the long table. This room is twice the size of our home. A long table surrounded by eight chairs still doesn't take up half the room. A sofa of oak, cushion, big enough for three, I guess a loveseat needs a chaperone. Still room enough for a rocking chair, and another hearth. A hall leads to more rooms.

He leads me through the kitchen, "Follow me." I'm led past three good-sized bedrooms, bunk beds for the boys, the two girls, each having their own bed, cloth stuffed, quilts for a blanket, and at the end of the hallway, he opens the door to a room with a tub and toilet. The kind with a box of water above. Shows me how it works. "Pull the chain and the water flushes down a pipe to a hole in the ground."

I'm in a heaven of this man's making. He cranks the pump—"Water comes from my well by pipe."

"This is a marvel."

"My grandfather learned this from the German who helped him build it. He left Vilna." Juska is as uncertain about God as I am. I suspect for the love of this farm, he feels like he's been delivered to heaven, only to be tested by Satan's Hell.

There's a mirror. I'm a beast with a scraggly beard and hair over my ears.

She comes into the room with a bucket, and the girl, matter-of-factly, introduces herself. "I'm Mae." She pours a bucket of hot water into a tub carved from the thick trunk of a chestnut. Puts fresh clothes on the table. Wants to take my uniform. I grab my knife. "What are thinking of doing with that thing. Let me get my scissor."

Mae cuts the long ends of my hair and beard, lingers beside me, I'm in the fires of heaven, she hands me a towel, "Now you're quite fetching." She lingers, likes to talk. "I've been to Riga."

I wait to unbutton my jacket. The young girl stares into me to where I need to look away. She studies me with curiosity and no sense of shame for being beside me in a bathroom—that was until her father returned and pulled her from the room. "Mae!"

I bathe in heaven. The tunic and pants must be from the eldest son because Juska's would be much larger.

The tall blonde is busy setting the table with food enough for a feast as the boys in circles around her, a game of dodging. "Etta," Juska calling for his wife. "Calm them down." Etta? A sign? Mrs. Dayan was Etta.

"You came from Poznan—where's that?" Mae is eager to ask questions. Her father is seated, her mother behind me.

"A month of walking all day through wilderness that tests all of your wits." I want to keep the talk away from the horror. "Warsaw, Berlin, Poznan, are as Riga but with larger cathedrals, palaces, and longer mazes of roads, more peddlers," I laugh from the healing, "more dumplings, pastries. Capital cities have a wide river with ships run by steam engines."

Mae shares my need for answers, "But what of this battle?"

I look to Juska for help.

"The fighting Max spoke of is far away. Warsaw has long had its own troubles. Poland has long been a battle between the Kaiser and Czar."

Elsa, the blond girl, interrupts, "I think there's always some fighting. I was blessed to be saved by this wonderful family." A Prussian accent that betrays any Latvian roots. Elsa tells me how she was left to make her own way a few years ago when all of her family died with the pox. "I was living at the nunnery and spared to live with this wonderful family."

Her gratitude holds God as witness.

Supper is a dream—noodles, beets, cabbage, corn, and chicken. I learn that while they're Jewish by heritage, their faith is in survival. There's no mention of prayer, being kosher, or having faith in God more than Juska professing, "Lord helps those who help themselves."

Mae can't get enough of hearing about my made-up adventures taken from kernels of truth and mixed with fairytales.

The eldest boy, Darius, thankfully interrupts when I get lost in thoughts burdened with heartache.

"Took that wolf with one shot." He'd been admiring my rifle, "Can Max and I go hunting. I sure would like to try this musket."

I put him off with the value of the trade, "Bullets are too dear."

I follow them to their room. The two youngest agree to share a bed and give me the bottom bunk, but I tell them, "I'm used to sleeping on the ground. Soft cushion might be too much spoiling."

The boys are curious about everything and think of me as a knight from a fable. They demand I tell a story. I tell them my grandfather's tale of the warrior boy who traps a dragon, but before I trap the dragon, we've all fallen asleep.

The boys wake me at sunrise just as the rooster screeches out the alarm. Mae greets me. "You'll help me with my chores. Milking is first."

I see my uniform hanging on a clothesline, as she leads me to the barn, still full of questions, "How old are you?"

"Twenty-seven. Getting old."

"My father says I'm much older than my seventeen years for raising my brothers." Her smile was casting that spell to think she'd be a prize for a wife.

I help Mae milk the cows. The eldest, Darius, is splitting logs and building a tall pile. The youngers are feeding the dozens of chickens.

Toward the end of the day, Juska tells the boys to get the shovels.

I'm asked to join and follow him some distance from the house. Juska starts pulling up shrubs, "Help me," and we clear a plot. "We'll need to dig deep. I want to store some grain in the ground."

Kerrin and Tobias shake their heads. "What's this for?"

Upset, "Had a good harvest. Don't need all of it in the barn."

I know what this is about. Going to hide food. I've infected their peace. After the hole is deep enough to be the same height as the eldest boy, Juska hands us boards to make it an underground shed.

On the way back to the house, Juska invites me to stay on. "You know how to butcher," I nod.

By the end of the week, I feel like one of the family. Mae has me under her spell. She needs to know everything. The spirit of a warrior. She reminds me of Lina. Her mother noticed and chaperones with her eyes on her daughter. Knows when to interrupt when Mae gets too affectionate.

I confessed a half-truth of my journey to Juska but made no mention of comrades.

He admits to having no loyalty to Russians or Germans, but adds, "I've been fortunate to be under the protection of isolation, a long days ride to the nearest neighbor, and he's a Russian who says he's a Count, and so owns all the land for miles. He likes his privacy as well. The Russians took all this land from a Prussian noble some time ago. He's more farmer, better as a sheepherder than cattle, but only noble when he needs a favor or tax. Says it's my share of his. Tax pays for the Sheriff.

Mae lures me to her room with the bait of seeing her collection of books. Proudly shows me that she knows how to read and write. "I try to teach my brothers, but except for Kerrin, they have no minds."

The first snow comes, it's mid-December, but the warmth flowing in from the Baltic melts the white blanket.

I settled into the comfort of a family's warmth with meals of delicious meat. It was a winter of joy I had only when a child. No thought of the outside world. Cocooned. Mae and I couldn't help but fall in love. The first kiss was magic. I discovered a depth of love that has the soulful loyalty I shared for my family. This is different than what I felt for Mrs. Dayan, perhaps because I had to protect my heart. Mae touches my heart in a way that leaves me in fear of being parted.

The first signs of spring as buds appear on the branches. Juska has me help him butcher a cow. He confesses as we saw and trim the meat, "I need to pay the tax to the Count. I'd take you, but that would draw suspicion."

"My family had the same burden. "We also paid dearly for our Count's protection.

"This meat and two sacks of flour should seal the trade."

He's gone for two nights, and when he returns, he's in a fearful state. "They're coming. We need to prepare." I think back to when I was ten. When I learned that you can't hide the truth of beasts.

Juska sets the plan. Tells me, "You'll take them to Riga. My brother will care for you."

He orders all of us out to the barn. "We'll bring Jeremiah the hides. He'll be expecting a thick bale of wool. Tell him I have five more."

He doesn't listen to his wife's plea to stay and opens the gate to pick which of his six horses and two mules to take. Turns to Darius, "Hitch the two mares to the wagon." He looks inside the barn. Tells me, "Take the two cows that aren't pregnant." Turns to the pen outside. "Mae, you and Elsa, help with the four young pigs. We'll leave five females and one male in the pen."

He crams ten chickens and a rooster into a crate.

The fenced pen has dozens of sheep and goats, but he only allows for ten females of each to be taken. "Need to leave enough to satisfy even the greediest of German Commanders."

We tie them to the back of the wagon along with the cows. Juska debates his plan. "Is this foolish?"

The wagon is loaded with the chickens and pigs, the cows, goats and sheep are tied to the back of the wagon and already fussing. Mae takes charge as is her way. "Leave them here and take our chances the Germans don't butcher the lot and take it all, or taken as bribes along the way, but if we can get them to Riga for Uncle Jeremiah, and the war comes to Latvia, food will be everything. He has a factory, not a farm. We need to convince the soldiers and thieves that you're under orders by someone really important to bring food to Riga." A moment of thought. "I can write a letter. I'll make it look official like that deed the Count gave you. It'll say Max is under orders."

Etta takes Juska into her arms, and after a long hug, she cries, begging her husband, "We should stay here. Why are you doing this?"

"The boys need you, and I need to stay. The Germans need farmers to feed them. Once I get that settled, I'll come get you."

"And then what?"

An unanswerable question. "Their war needs food. You'll be safe with Jeremiah. Riga is well fortified. The war won't get that far. Jeremiah will negotiate a deal with the Russians. He can make uniforms and coats for the soldiers. They need his factory."

To argue with Juska is to argue with a Yitzhak or Mr. Dayan.

Mae comes from the house. Hands me my uniform. "You'll go back to being a Russian soldier."

"I don't understand."

"You're a Russian soldier bringing supplies to feed Russian soldiers in Riga." Shows me the letter. She's an artist. Copied the Russian Seal. My family would love Mae.

The boys are held in that imprisoning spell of fear I know so well. They settle in the back, wedged beside the sacks of grain, pickled meat and vegetables, crates of wool, hides, crates of chickens, and pigs. Juska worries it's too much temptation. The cows, sheep, and goats are tied to the wagon. Has he put a target on their backs? King Solomon's choice?

Mae and Elsa fill sacks with clothes and supplies. Tobias his wooden horse, Kerrin his wood rifle.

Darius is a man of thirteen. He holds his rifle as a soldier. I slide mine under the bench and take the reins. Her mother sits between me and Mae. Etta's cautioned both of us about falling in love during such troubling times. Elsa sits in the back with the boys. The wagon is stacked high and we're a target, but there are no good options. I've seen what the soldiers do when they plunder a farm. None of us would be safe.

It's almost dark by the time we leave. Mae jumps off the wagon to lead the horses along a path through the forest. We travel through the night. Sleep wasn't possible. I join alongside Mae to guide the horses, my rifle over my shoulder, on guard against the dangers of the wilderness.

Not long after sunrise, we reach the main road that connects Vilna to Riga and discover to our shock that we're joined by a parade of a hundred families also fleeing north. Wagons crowd the road. There are waves and greetings by our fellow Latvians, and we take a measure of comfort in being a caravan of strangers bonded by heritage, fear, and sharing hope.

It's late afternoon when our wagon train is stopped. We're somewhere in the middle of the procession and I need to stand on the wagon to see that it's a checkpoint. The train moves slowly as ten Russian soldiers and a lieutenant collect their bribe.

Mae had me practice my story. She's as clever a peddler as I've ever seen. I was amazed at how well she forged a letter to sell the lie of my mission. She showed a remarkable skill in copying the Russian crest to make the paper look official. Her handwriting shamed mine.

I show the Officer the letter. I'm under orders from Colonel Torchinsky. He was the feared commandant who ruled Riga ten years ago, but at least the name of someone they might know, how would they know if he's still in charge? There are so many officers from so many different regiments. Latvians, like the Poles and Lithuanians, would distance themselves from their Russian lords. If we keep going north past Riga, the Estonians are hunters shooting at anyone trespassing on their land. Finland demands you have the skin of a Reindeer.

The Officer takes his time. "Colonel Torchinsky?" He doesn't care about holding up the exodus. His squad of ten are only interested in the bribe. "You tell Torchinsky that Lieutenant Marlov will guard the south as long as we have bullets." He studies our load, "We'll take two chickens and the pig, "We need to eat as well," then waves us through.

At the next checkpoint, we pay with four chickens. I argue we need male and female cows and pigs if we're to last more than a month.

Over the course of the three-day journey, we're lost in the flood of the exodus. With so much to steal, the hoard piling up alongside the checkpoints, more and more soldiers man the gates. It's thanks to Mae's letter and my act of certainty that saves half of what we brought.

We enter late in the day, amid the madness. It's a city turned fortress. Still a mile out, and rows of trenches are dug deep.

At the final checkpoint, I'm asked by the captain, "How far? How far are the Huns?"

"Three days to get here, and they were a few days behind." He eyes the livestock, but as I reach in my pocket for the letter, something tells me to stop. We're only a stone's throw from the Colonel. I pay the tax with two rubles from a pouch that began with thirty-two, and was now twenty-two.

The Captain sits atop a stockpile of livestock and grain. 'War tariff," as he calls it. He also takes a pig. One left. But we still have the two precious cows, two sheep, four goats, and two of the three sacks of grain. The horses eyed more than the livestock. That cost four extra rubles.

I purposely drive through my old neighborhood—the roads crowded with wagons—and become lost in memories. Ten years. So much has changed. Three large brick factories and two mills. I knew those farmers. More farms now long rows of shanties. I think of Mrs. Dayan, my family, but Mae pulls me from dreams.

We turn a corner, not surprised that the temple still stands, and when Mae tells me to turn right. I look down at a row of brick factories, warehouses, the junkyards of anything worth scavenging, and think I know the factory. Mae calls out first, "Uncle Jeremiah!"

He shakes his head, waves, and comes at once to greet his sister-in-law with a hug. "I hoped to see you." Looks around, and Etta answers his confusion, "Juska stayed at the farm. We'll head back as soon as things settle down."

Mr. Jeremiah Balyarus rolls his eyes but shrugs off the news, then turns to welcome his family with hugs and pats on the head. He has gray hair, is shaven, dressed in a black suit, and wears a merchant's bowler. He nods to the two men helping load a wagon with winter coats. They tip their caps to us and drive off.

It's a large building, about the size of four or five homes if put together. Mr. Jeremiah Balyarus lacks his brother's muscle. Pale and thin, but with the same warmth of a smile from the eyes.

He studies me. But before I can introduce myself, Mae takes over—"This is Max. He saved us."

I'm embarrassed as Mae tells the story of how I saved them. She pulls him to celebrate all that we brought. "Max saved us from having to give it all by saying it was for this Colonel Torchinsky," and she has me show him the letter. "I wrote it."

He laughs. "How did you know the Colonel is still our master?"

I explain, "I left Riga ten years ago and imagined the Colonel would never give up his throne."

Jeremiah is in rapture from the bounty of cows, goats, chickens—"Worth their weight in gold," and leads with a wave of his hand to go inside a large room that is brightly lit by many windows. He notices my curiosity, "Good light is most important for our work," and proudly introduces us to a room full of young girls to elder women spinning the rolls of thread into coats. The sewing machines hum as they crank the wheel, their tables buried under cloth. Two men of my father's age load and unload heavy bolts from the row of shelves. Three boys keep busy loading thread. The floor is covered with boxes.

Jeremiah holds up a Russian soldier's brown coat. "We have an order from Torchinsky for as many coats as we can make," clasps his hands in prayer to heaven," but that we'll be paid?"

I feel the thickness of his coat and smile.

"You must be weary from such a journey. Please follow me," and Jeremiah leads us up a long flight of stairs to the second floor, and down a long hallway that has many small rooms with beds, a stove, a bucket of coal, and at the end, a larger room with a pump, sink, and a flushing toilet with the same box and chain as his brother has. Each room has four beds on a bunk bed frame. A chest with drawers, and each with a lantern, separates the beds. There are dresses, underwear, pants, carvings, and trinkets scattered about on pegs.

"You boys will share this room with the two boys who work for me." He goes to the next room. He tells Mae and Elsa, "You will share this room with two of my favorite girls—Pieta, and Marta."

Etta Balyarus is shown to a small corner room with a single bed.

Jeremiah Balyarus pulls me away. "Work to do." I follow him back to the wagon. He introduces me to Isaac, a young man with kind intent. Holds his arms out wide as we inspect the goats, sheep, cows, and chickens—"Traded the pigs for passage." The hides and wool almost bring him to tears, laughing, dancing, and then a prayer. "How you managed to make it here," choked up, "Is a miracle." He has Issac take the reins. We unload the crates into a wide shed.

Mr. Balyarus pulls me aside. "You said you're from here."

"I grew up on a farm three days from Riga." I think I can trust Jeremiah as I do his brother, but to tell my story would give him too much cause to worry about trust. "Lost my family to sickness and such, but it's good to be home."

He nods, "You did a mitzvah bringing this. A soldier?"

He understands my sentiment. "No. I wouldn't kill or die for the Kaiser or Czar. The Germans will make us German, and the Russians will make us Russian. We have no side but our own."

Jeremiah studies me. "This Lenin? His dream of brotherhood, I don't understand." Suddenly, a hug, "My brother and I owe you a debt for keeping my family safe. What are your plans?"

"Who knows? Where is there to escape?"

CHAPTER FORTY-NINE - Riga –1915 –

Two weeks after we arrived, Juska surprised his brother by coming in the middle of the night, sneaking into the factory, putting his hand to Jeremiah's mouth, scaring him from sleep—"Shhhh."

"Juska! How? What's happening?"

"The Germans had taken the farm but left after taking most of the livestock. What I hid in the forest will need to survive on their own. I followed a trail of my own making and spied a mile-long line of Russian troops. They've pushed the war back to Vilna. Can't know when I'll have another chance, because now our farm is known by both Germans and Russians."

The brothers shed their fears before falling asleep, only to be awakened by Etta smothering her husband with kisses. She doesn't let him go until Darius and Tobias discover their father, and it's their turn to smother him.

Over a breakfast of bread and eggs, Jeremiah thanks his brother, "Your cows and goats are a mitzvah. The wool, hides, you saved me again."

Juska tells us of his journey, "Nowhere is safe. Russian, German, thieves, there's no regard for mercy. The soldiers took everything I didn't hide. A built Noah's Ark. Hid a male and two females of each. Cut up the cows, drying the meat as we speak." Proud, but needs to console his heartache. "Need to go right back."

Etta is pleading, holding him, "You must stay."

"I can't stay. I can't protect you. They know about our farm. They'll be watching. You're safer here."

Juska waits for the night. Says his goodbyes. The boys don't let go, but Etta takes hold of Kerrin and Josiah.

Juska pulls his eldest son aside. "You're a man. If caught, they'll put you in a uniform. You must stay by your mother's side—your brothers need you—you must be brave."

"We will be brave soldiers."

Before the war, Riga had many Jewish newspapers, but the Socialists called on the Latvians to fight for their independence. To keep from preaching, the Colonel sent out the secret police, one by one, the Cheka beasts forced the printers to destroy their press. Those who hid were shot. A test of loyalty makes everyone fearful.

"Ira Mendelsohn knew they were coming, and printed his last edition, took apart the press, buried the rollers, the wheel, the gears, the bed, and hid the precious alphabets of engraved type."

Professor Mendelsohn was a learned scholar who taught philosophy at the Yeshiva in Vilna and had received word from his brother via telegraph—the operator was a secret Marxist— "German U-boats own the seas. America neutral. Paris hides behind a border of trenches. Poland, Ukraine, and Lithuania have fallen to the Germans. Our prayers."

The Colonel kept three thousand of his best soldiers in Riga, not to defend the city or stop the Germans, but to steal all he could. His threat was made known with daily executions. A network of nobles and merchant bourgeoisies paid him a hefty ransom, and he acted as a spy; most have fled. The Colonel is right to be in fear. "The Latvians are an army of twenty thousand, armed with pistols, rifles, and swords," whispers to the men, with a sigh, "but there'll be no victory." We do not have cannons or machine guns. Worse, we are not united in our beliefs. Some are Marxists as if freedom can be won—a dream of independence."

After reading Mendelsohn's report, Jeremiah confided, "I think we will all be Germans before their war is over. They have better weapons."

The Colonel's raids are random. His soldiers plunder the rich first, and as Jeremiah's factory is among a village of the poorest shacks, our turn is given more time, but word reaches us that they're coming soon, and so we work through the night to make our preparations.

The Gentile who sells our coats to the Colonel and lately, the Latvian soldiers, is a mensch, has great affection and respect for Jeremiah. He whispered what he overheard, "They are nearby."

The boys hold the wall while I hammer the last few nails. Mae is storing food. Etta and Elsa are on the second floor, knitting wool hats, stitching together what will be prized fur-lined leather gloves—when we hear the front door burst open.

The bark, a gunshot, and they storm in to shatter the seal of isolation.

I pull Mae and the boys into the hiding place and slide the thick board through the brackets to seal our secret room.

Our time came too soon. The four husbands who work for Jeremiah, their wives, and children were burying the last bolts of cloth. The basement dirt our hiding place for meat to buttons.

It is in the twilight before sunrise when the pack of the Colonel's wolves attack from the back door and front door, charge into the factory, everywhere in a moment, lanterns lighting their way.

The commander looks to be a general by the rows of medals decorating a regal blue coat. He smacks his club on the sewing tables and orders the women to march downstairs while his men bring the husbands up from the basement to join the line.

Ivan's wife runs into her husband's arms. The general smacks his club hard against Hedda's husband. Ivan is the youngest of the husbands and would be a warrior if not held at gunpoint, struck in the back by the General's guardians. Foot on his chest, "You know better," he stands over him with a smirk to seal the threat.

The General studies Hedda— the club pressed into her chest. Hedda is as Elsa, has the beauty of a German. The general enjoys testing a beaten man's courage, but his threat was made. The General turns, pressing his club against Mr. Balyarus, steering him into his office.

The beast postures as if the Czar himself, and sits in the leather chair, inspects the bare drawers. "No gun. Money?" More threats: "Each minute I wait, I shoot another."

"We are making your uniforms."

The Officer stares at Mr. Balyarus. "Yes of course, and then you will load the wagons with all you have, bolts of cloth, machines."

"What? Why? Better we serve the Colonel. Your soldiers need coats for winter."

"Not for you to question." Mr. Balyarus was convinced that making coats for the army earned him the safety of being useful. "But your men will need our coats?"

The Officer gets off the chair to face Mr. Balyarus, "Silence," and leaves the office. He points the club at the four middle-aged husbands, turns to his troops— "Take them to the basement and give them shovels. They know where to dig."

We hear him coming up the ladder and worry that my wall of wood scraps won't disguise our hideout. His boots stomp across the attic, pushing aside the broken crates. Our fate—shot as traitors or sent to the front lines, quarry, or some prison to labor. There's no court, no trial—guilty or innocent, our verdict is in the hands of the beasts.

I dare to peek and see him standing in front of the wall. Taps it with his rifle. A laugh, "Clever." Does he know? A soldier showing mercy? We hear him climb back down and breathe again.

I look through a peephole. Hundreds of soldiers, some police, a few Cossacks, the General flanked by two Officers, loud in giving command. All on the prowl, raiding the row of our neighbor's shanties, brutal in their mission, and watch as they load the wagons.

I hold the bar that seals the door of the wall, "Take a crate of wool and join your mother," I tell Mae, with a broken heart, "You should stay with your family and go north."

Mae turns to me, "What of you and my brothers? They'll be taken to lord knows where, and you'll be shot as a deserter."

The boys look to her, tears trembling. I take her hand, "If I'm to be killed, I'd rather be fighting for a free Latvia. No difference killing a German or a Russian." I turned to the boys. "We need to keep you safe."

Mae argues to stay here with me while Darius looks through the peephole. He suffers to watch his mother and the women being pushed to fill the wagons with the bolts of cloth, boxes of buttons and thread, and the soldiers carrying out the sewing machines.

Mr. Balyarus tries to reassure his people, "We are needed. We will be protected. We need to do as they say."

Mae knows the horror of staying in Riga and having to hide. "I can see only one path. It's too late to join. We'll stay here." She ponders, "My mother will be heartbroken." Turns to her three brothers. "You won't be safe here." She looks out the peephole. The women are still coming and going, carrying out boxes of supplies. Tobias trembles. Cries for his mother. "If we all stay here, we'll starve. Little hope of reaching the farm without trouble, nowhere to escape. They need to go with my mother!"

So much commotion. The vultures take all the sewing machines, tables, chairs, cloth, thread, boxes of buttons and needles, that we're not heard to slide the wall to the side, sneak down the stairs to the bedrooms. Mae grabs three dresses and tells her brothers. "Put these on." She needs to smack Tobias, "Don't be foolish," and lowers the dress over his head. "You'll pass." She puts a shawl over their head, laughs, "My little brothers, now my sisters."

Jeremiah is seated beside Etta on the wagon, his arm over her shoulder. She's sobbing, "What of my boys. What of Mae?"

He tells her, "Better the boys, Mae, Max, are together. Better Juska is free to fight for the farm without worrying about protecting you and the children. God knows what the Germans will do?" but as the line of women and soldiers continue to load the wagon—he looks back, and as heartache infects his mind, he sees three girls carrying out boxes—smiles, turns, and whispers to Etta, nods. She realizes the three girls carrying crates are her new daughters. She's beaming with thanks as they climb onto the wagon, "Thank god." Darius leans close, "Thank Mae."

"Is she coming?"

"Staying with Max."

It's an hour after sunrise when the soldiers lead the wagons away.

We watch through the peepholes as the procession of wagons leaves under guard by the Russians. Hundreds, if not thousands, were tasked with marching north to St. Petersburg in service to the Czar.

CHAPTER FIFTY – RIGA – 1916

Riga was gripped in madness. Men, women, children, and elders were all put to work in the forge making rifles and bullets, prisoners for any act of disloyalty. Prisoners are sent to the quarry, coal mines, the forge, and grueling labor at gunpoint, producing the war's blood.

Escape means joining the Latvian army. The battlefield will be as snipers. Taking shelter in abandoned shanties, tents, and cabins hidden by the wilderness. A brotherhood of friends and family, natives, tribal, townspeople, hardened into predators. War opened their eyes. Neither Czar or Kaiser will show them any regard for giving their life.

The Hasid and Orthodox hide in temples. They put their fate in the hands of God—Saints and angels as lambs.

Homes are shuttered or taken by the soldiers for barracks. The richer peddlers pay bribes to roam the roads.

Hiding in our nest, our love blossoms. We relive our journey. My truth comes easily, but the intoxication of bliss is sorely tempered by guilt, fear, and worry as the world burns. Our cocoon has two paces side to side. We survive on pickled vegetables and dried fish. A daily ration of cheese, thinner cut each day, a few days left. The sack of oats might last another week. Our nightly prowl is for water and burying our foulness in the basement dirt—comfort comes from a mattress filled with scraps of cloth. We dare a quick fire to cook a mush. Twigs at most. There are thieves, soldiers and vagrants coming and going from downstairs. We spend our time listening to their talk, always about the war, but lately it's been about taking down the Czar.

I got down on one knee. "I have nothing to give you but my love. Will you be my wife?"

Her smile melts in the warmth of our bond. "I take you with all my heart, all my love. I would be blessed to have you as my husband."

Our oath is sealed for the hundredth time. Five months sharing a cell in this prison, but our guilt is only that we are comforted by this bliss while the world around us shatters.

Mae takes my hand. Her warm brown eyes put me under her spell—"We either starve in each other's arms or join the Riflemen. The Latvian army at least fights for something we can believe in." She reminds me of Lina. "It is time we do something more than be selfish in our love."

I think of Mr. Dayan, Yitzhak, Jakob, and how their spark to the kindling of hate had fueled a war that now spreads beyond the taverns and factories to touch all lives. Marx wrote the bible. Lenin made the plan. His apostles lit the fire. Their disciples are the murdering, thieving soldiers of this Crusade. But it was a Kaiser, whose ambition had no limit, and a meek Czar, who was forced to be a warrior, that opened the gates to the castle and foolishly lowered an aged bridge over a shallow moat.

"We'll at least hear what this anarchist has to say." The decision landed on making our way to the outskirts and find a band of Latvian brothers, "Martyrs for the Cause."

Leaving our prison is the joy of a spring night's fresh air. Under the cover of night, we keep to the alleys we know. Sneak past the wolves and beasts. We're on our side of the river; their army is on the other. She keeps the small pistol her father gave her strapped to her thigh. I have a knife.

Hidden by shadows, we're plucked from the alley by three men. I know one, "Max," he takes me in a hug. "Abraham?" The boy who lived in the village down the path, the bond is as if kin. Trust. Know him. He doesn't let go. "This is fate. You must come."

He knocks on the door three times, waits, and then two more light taps.

There's a whisper, "Who?"

He says the password, "Liberty."

The basement is kept dark. The gatekeeper, a big man with a rifle in one hand, pistol in his belt, knife to the side, beside a sword. He leads us with a lantern. The path smells of smoke and the dim light shines against a low ceiling and stone walls that have me think this will be our death or prison, but when I hear the groans and cursing in Yiddish, Russian, and Latvian, from the room at the far corner, and from the lantern's glow I see Abraham smiling with a knowing nod, and I turn to Mae and breathe again.

We're huddled in a small room filled with tobacco smoke, where the vandalized furnace and empty coal bins make the room even smaller, but there are familiar faces among the forty or so who nod, some wave to those few Jews I know, but there's more Latvians: the shopkeepers, masons, and laborers who hold only a prejudice against Russians.

Mae is taken in a hug by two women hiding under men's coats. They confide their need for a revolution, but Mae wants all to hear that their revolution needs to include women. Crowded together, she braves the fear of being beaten for protest, and calls out—"Who suffers more than women? Who among you has been raped or forced into prostitution? We are treated less than a serf. A mother must suffer the heartache of hungry children who live in fear."

A tall man in a poor man's suit enters from the back door. A big man clears a path. All eyes turn as they cross the room, but he stops when he's beside Mae, takes the small woman's hand, holds it up, declares, "A true comrade. All must be liberated from tyranny," and then climbs onto a crate. "The Revolution has come to Riga!"

I'm in back, blocked from seeing Mae or this man who casts a spell on the crowd. There's something familiar about the voice, but a scarf covers all but the tip of a long beard streaked with gray. The peasant's cap hides all but the longest gray hair that covers his ears.

He waves his hands to bring quiet. Speaks softly, "We must be as the fox tonight, can't let the wolves hear our howl or bark," said in Latvian, and then with a nod to the Jews, he repeats in Yiddish, "German or Russian master, would it matter?"

His question is met by the stifled murmurs of an emotionally charged response, 'Not Czar or Kaiser!"

His eyes dart about. Studies his jury. His gravelly voice, the certainty to his preaching, and the posture of a messiah are an echo in search of a memory.

I sneak closer. Is it him? Can it be? Mae takes my hand. He looks down; we exchange a glance; he takes off the thick black glasses—and, in that moment, not ten feet away, a ghost has risen from the dead.

He avoids my stare, "The Germans are coming, the Russians are in retreat, the war is our ally, from their carnage we'll forge our path to independence, but you must be warriors."

The rest of the sermon was a blur. I was lost in my dreams of taking revenge on him for Mr. Joshua, Greta, my friends, my adopted family, and the countless innocents who were sacrificed as kindling.

German breeding flavors his tone. "Kaiser or Czar has sent millions to kill or be killed, for what—to defend *their* throne."

He wears the rags of the poorest serf to pose as one of them.

My anger wants to punish him, but I've seen too much of evil to convict him of being Satan. He warned me, "All is a battlefield. There will be no innocents. You must choose a side."

He's preaching to the converted. Desperation, hunger, and threats no longer penetrate shells hardened by war. "Lambs will be slaughtered."

Is it him? Or is this the spell of madness?

The murmurings become loud, but there is no army or police to fear. Riga is held in anarchy, with only predators and prey. The roads are battlefields. Thieves have little left to steal unless they are willing to kill the families who hide whatever is left and will defend their home with their lives. He waves his hands, "We fight for our freedom!"

His comrades push and shove in the fervor of rapture. Mae has taken him as her savior. Her tears show faith in his dream.

"Not Christian or Jew. Not noble or bourgeois. Not Germany or Russia—our empire! We will be the Master. Our time. No more kings posing as god!"

I haven't faith in anything. Doubt is the religion of my family. Only a fool would believe beasts could be tamed. Midas, Genghis, Caesar, Czars, kings, they resurrect and reincarnate. The beasts are greed and ambition.

He triggers memories: Yitzhak, Lina, Jakob, Ludwig, Michel, Joshua, and Mr. Moses Weinstein. This was Lenin's fault—his war. Leon and Julius argued for preaching, but the beasts do not surrender. Riga, Warsaw, Poznan, Berlin—prisons held by a king's madness. How to bring beasts to their end? Lenin would say, 'As the crueler beast.' There'd be no free Americans without bloodshed. Traitor or Patriot? The verdict was decided in victory. Lose the war, and patriots are hanged as traitors.

"We are Davids against Goliaths. The battlefield must be of our choosing, our time, our choice of weapon." Waits for quiet, "And when our war is won, no matter that your homes are in ashes—we will rebuild as free men."

He jumps off the crate and his bodyguard is helpless in fending off the crowd giving worship to the messiah. He retreats from a rabid flock needing a father's hug. He's pulled from idolatry by the bear of a man with a devil's dark eyes, thick black hair, thicker eyebrows, a Cossack's mustache, and temper.

The messiah stops at the door, "Arm yourself. Prepare for battle."

His scarf was pulled off. I'm close enough to see the scar. It's him. And once again, I'm forced to pick a side. But doubt about what comes after is lost to the war that is today. The beasts won't surrender.

Mae is under his spell. She holds me close, "Our path is clear."

I'm finally able to see Mr. Dayan's truth. No one is safe. Mr. Weinstein was a benevolent boss, but he was a master who lived in a palace, didn't know hunger, and kept his children sheltered in a cocoon. His temple sought to convert Jew to German. Berliner first. I had faith in that fable until the Kaiser took off his mask and took us prisoner.

I want to be a warrior, but as a fox setting the trap for a dragon. I am not one of them. They are wolves. Hungry to kill.

He's gone. Relief? Guilt? Either way, he's right. Fight the Germans, the Russians, a comrade, or as a Latvian?

I imagine the Cossacks waiting outside. No decision to be made. This will be our execution, but as I breathe in the chilly night air, the roads are barren, the streets are quiet. The silence is only broken by thieves and vigilantes. The Colonel and his army have retreated to find sanctuary further north. Most likely, he'll fight for a kingdom of his own. Riga is held under the laws of survival until the Germans take control.

Riga is a maze I know well—but as we turn the corner to leave the alley, I'm lost, which way to turn? To go back to our cell? Follow these comrades to bond as Latvians fighting for our homeland?

I hear a motor. Turn to see headlights bearing down on us. Trapped in the alley. I grab Mae and look for a doorway, an open window, anywhere to escape, but the motorcoach stops. The door opens. He leans out the window and waves for us to come closer.

"Max!"

Under the light of a full moon, the messiah manifests as Mr. Dayan.

I freeze. "That we meet again so close to where we began."

"It is you."

"Does my Trotsky still believe in preaching and strikes? You should know that Julius and Leon have converted to warriors."

We look into each other's souls through eyes that have seen it all. A father and son parted by opposite paths.

"Time to choose sides. Comrade or lamb?"

"You have always been a warrior, and I'm a lamb for having faith only in doubt." I've seen war. I've seen so much evil. I can't hate him. He was my father, tasked with teaching harsh lessons, beasts roam the wilderness. "My faith was held in the grip of doubt, but we're joined tonight by Lenin's truth; there are no innocents in war." There is no other path, "I'm a comrade."

He turns to study Mae. "Comrade or wife?"

Mae says proudly, “A wife first. A comrade will kill for a fellow man’s freedom, but a wife willingly dies by her husband’s side.”

His grin falls. He holds up his hands, nods to bring us closer, then shocks me when he wraps his hands over Mae’s head— “To die by his side for love,” his voice trembles, “The words of a true comrade,” and shudders, let go, turns away, as if taken by a great pain.

I look in the back seat to see if she’s there, but there’s only boxes and sacks of flour. I want to ask. My heart needs to know. Mrs. Dayan should be by his side.

But we’re pulled from sentiment by the driver, “We must go!” The devil tugs on Mr. Dayan’s arm, “What is this about?” his impatience announced in thick Russian.

I’m shocked, he takes my arm, “Are you coming?”

“Where?”

“St. Petersburg,” a smirk. The moment is frozen as I must choose between two battlefields—the Latvian Riflemen will fight the Germans and each other. That battle will be about survival.

Mae’s hand squeezes mine. She’s excited. “To die for purpose.” She knows about my pledge to Mr. Dayan. I had her respect for being a doubter but warned me that she’d have no respect for a coward. “Is this an invitation?” He nods. She gives him a hug, “An honor.” Mae has no patience for my doubt. She pulls me by my hand. “This is your Mr. Dayan.” I’d spoken of him too much for her not to know.

I blamed him for Lina, the brewery, the Weinsteins, but he taught me that to win this war, every place was a battlefield, and that everyone was a soldier. There are no sins for a soldier. The defense of a soldier versus a murderer—the unholy law of war—*What soldier is hung for the murder of a foe.*

Mae is my Mrs. Dayan for comfort and lessons, but she has the truest of a warrior’s soul. She’s Yitzhak, a Lina. I can’t lose her. I take the pledge for the second time, but this time in truth— “I swear as a comrade to give my life for the revolution, to die for liberty.”

He pushes the boxes over as we climb into the back. Seat pulled out to make space for boxes of Lenin’s missives and sacks of loot.

CHAPTER FIFTY-ONE - Comrade - Dec. 1915

The thunder of the German storm is days behind, but the path is certain—Riga is to be the war's next victim.

We leave under the cover of night. The driver knows a hunter's path through the northern wilderness to the tented village of Latvian Riflemen, but there's only a lone sentry.

"Gone to the city. A battlefield we know well. Better to fight as murderers and thieves."

We didn't talk of the past or the future; we slept until sunrise and then took on a path of ice, always in peril of sliding into a tree, ditch, or boulder. Nature's arsenal.

Mae and I are crammed between boxes filled with bread, beans, oats, cheese, and crates of vodka, and we're invited to share their bounty. Mae breaks off a chunk of cheese and bread, giving thanks over and over. "It's been so long in hunger, I'd forgotten food."

"The generosity of comrades."

The hateful driver whom Mr. Dayan calls "Joseph" tosses another empty bottle out the window before he demands another. His thirst for vodka is unquenchable.

Unable to keep to the forest, Joseph convinces Mr. Dayan to return to the road. They argue about how they'll negotiate passage against the anticipated shakedowns by thieves and soldiers, but Joseph has a way about him that ends a debate.

Midday, we come to a fence of thick branches stretching across the road. Mr. Dayan turns to us, "Hand me a loaf of bread, and cut off a block of cheese." Looks ahead to count the guards, "Two bottles should do."

A pile of bodies turned the snow red. Joseph grunts, "Estonians don't bow to wolves." Mr. Dayan's eulogy is said with respect. "I wager that there are more Russians in the pile than the hunters."

Four on horse, four more manning the gate. Rifles aimed. Joseph hands the weary Russian soldier a paper with the official seal. He shows it to the officer on the horse.

Mr. Dayan opens the door and hands the Officer the two bottles, bread and cheese.

A salute. We're waved on.

Mae whispers to me, "I'll prove myself by forging such papers."

Hours and miles spent in silence sliding over ice and snow, needing to get out every so often to push, but it's welcomed as the effort warms us from the cold.

He must know how badly I want the answer. Another test? What does he see in me? Why did he invite us along? He knows my doubts. Am I the reluctant comrade he needed to take the pledge to prove his truth?

I risk cutting the fragile thread that is our bond and dare to ask what I assume is obvious: "She's gone?"

He takes a moment, doesn't turn around, stares ahead. "Yes, Max."

His tone rings with sentiment that says more than his answer.

The road is cleared by the migration of soldiers and the thousands of innocents in flight from the oncoming storm. The Estonians have no choice but to accept the influx and serve as hosts in their seaside town, where there is a church, a tavern, a fort at the harbor's edge, and homes built with logs and stone.

Mr. Dayan slides a few coins over the innkeeper's bar. There are eight men, two boys, two girls, and three women who share in the meal. The Estonians are fiercely independent. Finns from Viking Norsemen by ancestry. A heritage as great hunters, able fishermen, warriors who fight, and don't surrender.

Tallinn is halfway between St. Petersburg and Riga. Two hundred rugged miles in either direction.

Mr. Dayan studies the mood of the twenty or more Estonian gentry. He preaches revenge against Russians. They toast Mr. Dayan's anger, hate, and frustration. "The Czar is a fool and a pig. His ministers are held by greed, ambition, and fear. Nobles have no soul."

The Estonians are a tribe of united warriors. Independence is their only cause. They cling to traditions from the Middle Ages.

A few miles from St. Petersburg, the Czar's letter is merely a pause before the bribes are pulled from the crate of vodka.

It's the Czar's capital. Roads are paved stone, wide boulevards, canals, bridges, and the last of the snow is trampled by the traffic of farmers and fishermen, traders, and merchants hauling loads.

Mr. Dayan pressed me to speak to a crowd of mourners as a test. For over a week we've shared little because we know enough of where we've been.

I consider what I'd need to hear. "This is a storm and drought, we must guard the fields, till the soil, plant seeds, and defend our farm, for how else will we reap the bounty of the coming harvest."

Back on the road, I find my voice and a possible path forward with Mr. Dayan, for he knows my truth: I could preach socialism, but I need to convince him of my value. "We no longer need to convince our recruits that evil will not be defeated by surrendering as lambs." But will he let me be a preacher? Am I to be his next Yitzhak? Mae is caught in the fever that we must be ready to go to war.

CHAPTER FIFTY-TWO – Petrograd – Spring 1916

Farms gave way to homes, homes to factories and mills, and we crossed a bridge that could only be manifested by a czar. Petrograd is greater than Warsaw by measure of its grandeur. More than Berlin.

Joseph knows his way. Keeps to alleys and side streets. Avoids the checkpoints set up along the boulevards. The city is a fortress of barricades—roving bands of soldiers, cavalry, motorcoaches with officials guarded with rifles at the ready.

He parks in an alley. Leads us up a narrow flight of stairs to climb five flights. Unlocks the door, flips a knob that turns on a lamp, and we enter a nicely furnished room—sofa, table, chairs, and a sink.

Mr. Dayan peeks through the heavy curtains— Joseph pushes Mae and me into a room and closes the door. "Stay here until I come for you."

The room has a toilet, sink, and tub. Tempted, both in need, we use the toilet. Sheets of soft paper. We laugh about taking a bath, but don't dare. A moment later he hands us a loaf of bread, cheese and ham. "Celebrate your honeymoon. Feast and bathe. I'll come for you in the morning.

We hear them argue. Then we heard strangers giving greetings. This went on through the night, but we were in our own heaven. The water was cold, but the bed was soft, blankets warming, and our love found a moment to express itself. A gift from Mr. Dayan that I couldn't begin to understand? When I tell Mae, "He's been reborn," she shakes her head, "We've all been reborn."

Mr. Dayan let us out the next morning. "You'll be taken to another apartment. We have a mission."

The couch and chairs are made of fine fabric and dark wood. I peek through the curtains to see a city of lights that turns night into day, but Joseph pushes me away to close the curtain as if to stop a ghost from flying in. He pushes me away and says in a strong voice, "Everyone is watching."

Mae turns from studying the books on the shelves. "What do you want us to do?"

Mr. Dayan smiles, "You are to be my spies."

Of course. He knew my skills—curiosity as my curse.

"I brought you here because you're trustworthy. You didn't betray me." He nods to the memories. "Gave the oath to Lenin himself. Trotsky and Leopold testified that your escape wasn't as a coward but as theirs, the bonfire was lit, better to move on and fight another day. Our humble life will be but a step on the path to communism, but I trust you have learned that to die for such a purpose is the greatest value to put on this trade." He's known me since I was a boy. "You're not a coward. You're a capitalist. You measure everything in profit. You are the smart student who asks questions because there's always doubt. But it is time to put doubt aside. I need you take the oath in truth."

I know what he's asking. "I am ready. Mae and I can't express our gratitude for you giving us this chance to prove our loyalty." I put my hand on his arm, look into his gray eyes, "On her life I swear that when the time comes, I will be Yitzhak."

We hold the moment as a flood of memories fill our hearts and minds.

"The Cossacks are the Czar's White Army. We are the Red Russians fighting for liberty. But regardless—white, red, Russian, Livonian, Latvian, or Polish, whether socialist or monarchist, the Germans have brought our small flame to a bonfire. The war will be won by the army that burns the longest. Many will try to seize the throne, but who can hold it? If your faith is tyranny, you do nothing. If you are a coward, you hope the armies will kill each other off. But you must be done with doubt, that this battle can only be won with a merciless revolution."

"I will serve as your loyal comrade."

Mae reaches for Mr. Dayan's hand, takes it, "I will serve as your loyal comrade."

Mr. Dayan pours the vodka into four gold-rimmed glasses and makes a toast. "To the Revolution."

The moment of bonding is shattered by gunfire. The explosions echo from the canyons of roads and streets between the mountains of towers.

"The battlefield is all around us. The government if fractured. Nicholas has the support of generals and the mercenaries who fight only to satisfy hunger. The Duma is divided by the Mensheviks who think socialism will magically appear. The hide inside committees spinning fables of a partnership with the bourgeois, nobles, and that they'll willingly share their treasure with the workers," he laughs. "The Bolsheviks speak the truth. We are the true party of the worker. We need a strong leader to break this never-ending swamp of debate and worthless laws that are no more than a dreamer's fable."

Joseph answers a knock on the door and steps into the hall. We hear laughter, and he returns with a sack, unwraps the newspaper, and holds up a thick sausage and jars of pickled vegetables. Another sack has four bottles of vodka.

Mr. Dayan reads the headline. "Victory in Warsaw. It's all lies and propaganda." He opens the paper. "This is the czar's paper. I know that the Germans have taken Warsaw." He reads further. "It says the Austrians are in retreat. They'll surrender to the Ukrainians." He goes to read from another paper. "Ah, yes, here! This one speaks the truth—Pravda, it is our paper. Comrade Trotsky and Lenin have their hands on their reports. France and Britain have put a wedge against the German onslaught. The Kaiser is running out of supplies, men, and time, but his U-boats keep America from mounting a decisive challenge. Their weapons are at the bottom of the sea." Mr. Dayan shakes his head. "The Russian farms are beyond the war. The greed of profiteers will keep those with means fed."

"More profit in vodka and ale." Joseph hands me the bottle. I smell it, take a sip. It's not worth the sickness of a poisoned escape.

But it's when I catch Mr. Dayan's knowing glance that I realize he knows of my inheritance.

CHAPTER-FIFTY-THREE - DEC 1916

I awake to a siren. Curtains darken the room. Mae is asleep on the couch. The bedroom doors are open. Joseph and Mr. Dayan are gone. I sneak a peek at the edge of the curtain, but blinded by the bright sun, I only catch a glimpse of the fire engine racing up the boulevard.

From our fifth-floor perch, the Czar's palace sparkles as god's heaven. St. Petersburg is not quaint, nor the random maze of Warsaw; the boulevards are straight and wide enough for giants. In the distance, a bridge of iron scrolls spans a broad river. A roadway of canals as moats. Corners and bridges are kept under guard—a masterpiece created by the unlimited power of a tyrant worshipped as God.

The nobles' estates are set amidst a paradise of island gardens that dot the harbor.

I'm warned by the key turning the bolt and step back from the curtain just as Mr. Dayan enters.

Mae awakens in a jolt.

Mr. Dayan draws us close to sit three across on the couch. In a quiet voice, as if the walls are listening, "We have much to do." We're shown a picture of a well-dressed aristocrat adorned in a suit embroidered with golf fringe and a chest of medals, white hair with a swirled mustache, an imposing pose; someone who believes in their significance. "Most mornings you'll find him at the cathedral," a snort, "not in prayer. It's where he conducts his meetings. Follow him. Tell me where he goes. Max, you still know how to draw?" We exchange a knowing nod, "I need a likeness of who he's with."

We watch from across the Czar's congress. A palace made from square-cut blocks of gray stone, given elegance by a blue and yellow fringe of carved molding. The Romanov dynasty is desperate, struggling to cling to its legacy. Too many lost battles, too many dead, the Kaiser within reach.

Mae and I pose as peddlers. Mr. Dayan gave us tins of sardines to sell. We inch closer. The guards are easily bribed with a tin. The politicians pass by cloaked in fine suits, fur coats, and high-polished boots, their trade is risking and reaping rewards, gladiators without shield or sword.

The Duma is infected from within by Lenin's Bolsheviks, arguing against the Czar's loyalists, while trying to convince a flock of Mensheviks that preaching mercy has run out of time. A web spun with greed and ambition, scrambling to find an alliance before the Kaiser seizes their empire, but finding brotherhood in a nest of snakes, wolves, and lambs hopelessly lost in a fog, with too many maps showing paths going in all directions, only to fade into an unknown future as dead ends.

The capital's headquarters teemed with soldiers, rifles at the ready, on guard, the last line of defense for the Czar's crumbling empire.

He is easily recognized. Two soldiers by his side. Two more following on horse. He wears the uniform from the picture, as does the fat man walking beside him. They argue with the tall and handsome noble.

We follow, keep our pose as peddlers, and I try to capture a memory of the other general with a chest of medals, and the noble in the suit of an aristocrat. After crossing the boulevard, they argue, and then go their separate ways.

Mae stays with them while I rush back to the apartment to scratch out a drawing that I know Mr. Dayan will mock, but I'll capture their identity by making notes with details of their size, hair, and the shape of their nose.

Mr. Dayan returns later in the afternoon. Mae arrived soon thereafter. I showed him the pictures, and she gave him the address of where he went.

He nods, leads us out of the apartment, and we follow him downstairs. We go to a nearby building, but enter through the alley, and down a long hallway to another flight of stairs. At the bottom, there's a door; he knocks, a pause, another two knocks, and the door opens.

We're greeted by Joseph, who gives me that stare that I've yet to earn his trust, but he leads us along a basement hallway crowded with men and women. Their arguing stops, respect is given to greet Mr. Dayan, but most turn away to avoid Joseph's commanding spell. He's larger than most, but it's his black eyes staring from between a thick mustache and black eyebrows that cast him as an imposing beast. I've learned it's best not to glance into his gaze. His stare is his power.

Mr. Dayan makes our introduction. "Comrades, Max, and Mae, his wife."

A low ceiling, the bare concrete walls dimly lit by bare bulbs dangling from a wire. Their shadows mingle through a cloud of smoke. Another reward of plunder is tobacco. All breathe through cigarettes and pipes.

We enter a room crammed by twenty comrades shuffling papers around a long table. There's a classroom blackboard, a chart of names with their titles, and different colored pins on the map.

Mr. Dayan taps the shoulder of two women. They turn from their study to stand and face him with regard. The women are tall and beautiful; one is blonde, the other has long black hair, and both smile with painted red lips that entice with seductive power.

He's immune to their powers, reaches between them, picks up a stack of photos, and shows me the man I saw. "Is this who you saw with the general?"

I recognize the portly man with long sideburns. "He was the one who argued without regard for who noticed."

"Gregorio Dimitrenko." He poses as a Bolshevik Minister but is a traitor. He serves the czar as his eyes and ears." He looks at my drawing and holds up another photo. Middle-aged, dapper, a noble gentleman wearing a fine suit and top hat. "Meeting with the generals to plead on Nicholas's behalf, to rally their troops and keep the Czar on the throne. "

"There'll be no armistice until the Kaiser and Czar are executed." I worry about Joseph. He's the cruelest of beasts. No soul. Where is Lenin?

Mr. Dayan goes to the map. "The war either ends in Riga, or we'll be facing the Germans in St. Petersburg. That's unless the Poles, Latvians, Estonians, and Lithuanians rise up for independence, but they'll need help. We must support their war after we finish our business here."

Josef boasts, "I'll finish this soon enough."

I overheard Mr. Dayan and Josef plotting the Czar's assassination. Josef boasted that he was the one who shot the Czar's Prime Minister, the peacemaker, Stolypin, murdered in 1911.

Mr. Dayan points to a map. "The Minister's Cathedral on Saint Issac's Square. They don't pray. They hold their meetings between pews."

Mr. Dayan looks past the women and the others in the room toward Mae and me. "Get close, sneak under the pews, or light a holy candle to hear what they're plotting." His mood goes dark. "If you're picked up and questioned, you are fools as peddlers selling sardines."

He goes back to the table with a nod to the two women. He holds up another photo. "If opportunity allows, you want to befriend him. Maybe you can lure him to our tavern on Malenkov." Mr. Dayan hands the two women four white pills," need to be a snake, coil, bite, and slink away. I'll have someone watching if you run into trouble. Poison is better than a bullet. Breeds suspicion."

Mr. Dayan hands me a gun and two clips. "You will follow Dimitrenko, but if you find an opportunity, kill him."

He hands Mae a telescope. "You will watch the palace from the top floor. There's a window in the attic." Hands her a photo of a ghoulish-looking man with stringy hair, the collar of a priest barely seen under the tangle of a sorcerer's beard. "This is who we seek." If you see him, find Mishka. She's here early and late in the day. You'll let her know."

We are moved to the attic of a four-story townhouse, where dozens of comrades live. They make it known we're comrades. Mae gets her wish to be treated as a soldier. She wasn't comfortable in the luxury of the fine apartment, or that he had so much food and drink. At the same time, everyone else is squeezed together in the basement and townhouse, with fish cakes and bread as the staple, and vodka and tobacco as the reward.

Mae is led by Mishka, the matron of spies, and climbs the four flights on a narrow stairway, then down a long hallway to an attic bare of all but a thin mattress and candles. Mishka hands her a sack. A loaf of bread, cheese, and a jar of dried fish. A soldier's ration. It's colder in the apartment than on the street. The wind howls through a missing pane in a window of sixteen small panes. Familiar punishment but given comfort with the reward of a fur-lined coat, layers of sweaters, two shirts, and two layers of pants.

Didn't find the General at the cathedral and returned to find Mae throwing up in a bucket kept in the corner.

I grab the bucket to empty it in the lone toilet on the first floor, but when I come back, she grabs it, throws up, and I worry to ask, "What's wrong?"

She tells me after taking a swig of ale, "Too much of this fish? or maybe the sausage? Don't be such a hen. Did you find the general?"

"I didn't." I can't confess that the thought of killing him has me in a nightmare. Mae spends her day looking through the telescope. Has an Eagle's view of the palace from our high perch. Winter softening, the howling and cold no longer inflict suffering.

The next morning, the general enters the church. He's under guard with three soldiers. I spy from across the Square, but before I summon the courage to go inside, he leaves a few minutes later. Stops at the corner newsstand. I pretend to buy a newspaper, but only hear him saying to the newsstand peddler, 'More good news,' as if a joke between the two.

On the fourth day, Mae spots the giant of a man with that scraggly black beard in front of the palace. He's lifting two pretty young girls onto a sled. Whips the horse to take a ride around the palace grounds.

That night, excited by the discovery, Mae tells me of the sighting. "I went to look for Mishka, but she hasn't been around."

Mae is still throwing up whatever she eats. I go to the basement and dutifully wait until late at night for Mishka to finally arrive and give her the news.

The next morning, I read the paper to pretend I'm not watching the general. I can't ignore the headline: "Germans take Estonia." Riga is their headquarters. German soldiers fighting against the remnants of the Russians, imprisoning natives as families trapped by fear, with few men and boys left as warriors. The German army gains another mile. Petersburg is their next battlefield.

Mr. Dayan comes for me, "You know what I ask."

"To be a soldier." But the very thought of killing tells me otherwise.

"To be a comrade. To be the warrior you've wanted to be since a child. To be the Cossack who rides at night without fear to take what he wants and burns what is left." He comes close, "Dimitrenko is a White General." Mr. Dayan has me in his grip— "This is your chance to bring truth to your oath. You will be the warrior who ends this pig's reign. An honor with purpose. Hands me a pistol. "Each clip has six bullets. Get close. Three for him, three for whoever comes to his aid."

He turns to Mae and hands her a gun. Mae studies it. She reaches under her dress. Holds up her one-shooter. Mr. Dayan laughs, "You couldn't stop a boy with that." She swaps it out for the new pistol.

Mr. Dayanis the patriot. Mae doesn't have Lina's temper. Raised with love, war has turned her into a warrior.

"There will most likely be guards and another Minister with him." He looks at me, back to Mae. "Kill as many as you can, take off your coat, should have a disguise underneath of another coat, change your hat, and then walk away—do not run, do not panic. Blend into the crowd as shocked witnesses. Return here only after you're certain you're not being watched."

She trembles, looks to me, whether to hand the gun back to him?

“He is the wolf.” Mr. Dayan holds the pistol in her hand. “This is how we win the war, not words—bullets. To do nothing is to surrender.”

I don’t confess that Lenin can’t promise that a Jew will ever find respect. What man is going to take orders from a woman unless out of love or in fear?” I’ll kill a general who believes he’s the patriot. I’ve seen his family, his loyalty to the Czar, and his faith in God. He meets in the church because he prays when no one is watching.

We climb down the stairs from the attic at sunrise. The other spies, assassins, and thieves are also heading out on their missions. I haven’t stopped trembling with doubt.

I go to the newsstand and buy the Czar’s newspaper. I read the story to Mae. “It reports that Nicholas II has made reforms. I wonder what more can he do?” I’m in shock. “He promises to abide by the Duma’s reforms.”

I look at Mae, “Isn’t this what we wanted. Isn’t this his surrender?”

I read further. “The Mensheviks believe they’ve found a compromise. The Duma has the power to set paths, and the Czar makes plans a reality, but they go in circles as committees debate every detail.

The Bolsheviks advocate for exiling Czar Nicholas. Lenin will guide the transition.

The Mensheviks call themselves Soviets. A promise to bless the people with fair treatment.”

I take a moment. Who will fight the Germans? The civil war between Russia as White or Red opened a path for the Kaiser to wait until we’ve killed ourselves, and then march in.

“This might change Lenin’s plan. A time for negotiation, not terror. Why threaten a chance for peace? We should talk to Mr. Dayan.”

“The Kaiser wants his cousin’s palace. I would ask who is going to lead the Russians into that war? Mr. Dayan? Lenin? Trotsky?”

CHAPTER FIFTY–FOUR Assassin - Feb. 1917

Deserting soldiers confirm the rumors of the German invasion. Stand behind the czar or risk the Kaiser's wrath. It's the miners, factory workers manning the hot vats of iron, feeding the furnace, pouring the soup, hell to feed, and only want the comfort of family and a warm home to take them through a peaceful night. Under the spell of war's honor, for three years they've killed too many brothers, sons, fathers, children, elders. All paths are dark, beast lurking. One day you're a traitor, next day a patriot, and by tomorrow, if there's a shift in the wind, your commander is gone.

"There are more deserters on the streets every day. Who will fight if the Germans attack?"

The few I befriend, sharing hours of life stories, childhoods filled with worry, no rewards, few coddled, most are also doubters that the beasts will never be converted, not by Moses, Jesus, or Mohammad. I take a risk. I earned the right to speak openly. "The price of war is dear, but it seems a lesson needed to be taught to all at the same time— The price of tyranny."

There's murmuring. "What code of law? Who will be the judges? The Sheriff? What will we teach? Where will we work?"

I had never seen this side of her. Mae's argument became bitter when we returned to the attic. She knew our master's temper well. "You know you make him angry. He's a strict and demanding father," Mae knows some parts about Mrs. Dayan but leaves that unsaid, "but you know Joseph. We'll be shot."

"He would side with me. The White army is at war against our Red army, skirmishes between rivals, but fear is driving all to madness as if a plague. What does it matter if we fight against the Kaiser and his Huns or the Czar and his Cossacks? You're right. Joseph will shoot us if we don't murder and steal. It's soon, one day soon, he'll want to blow up the palace. I don't know if I can do it." Her eyes close to a tightly wound squint.

The day was more of a trap than any before. Mr. Dayan will hear nothing of this regard for the Minister. "It is time for you to choose your side."

The guns are tucked under layers of clothes. We wear all we have. Her uncle's coat, the pants her father gave me. I hide in the heels of my boots twelve bloodied gold coins I've stolen from corpses. Reduced to a scavenger. Enough to buy escape?

We wait for our prey to leave his townhouse. Mae pulls me close to whisper. "Can we do this?"

I want to tell her the truth. Mae didn't hear Mishka boast that Josef shot Pietr after killing Rasputin. Is that our fate? To be shot so we don't talk. Josef has his own plans. I doubt his loyalty, even to Mr. Dayan. I think he'd shoot him if it served his purpose.

We wait on the bench. I watch the house from behind the paper. Small fires are scattered about the Square to keep the soldiers from freezing. The smoke hangs like a cloud to choke on. Women do whatever chore or degrading act of sin to last another day. The children run about like vermin. The soldiers reduced to sin, but loneliness and desperation bring on a fair share of desire.

A stiff breeze clears away the cloud of smoke. I spot our prey.

I hand the mother a paper ruble, look to Mae, "Charity," she nods, but by lifting her skirt, the woman thinks I'm asking for sex. A paper ruble would buy a loaf of bread. Mae steps between. I explain in Russian, "Charity."

It is almost 9:00. The large clock sits on a tall brass pole and keeps all to the same schedule. Her cheeks and lips are red from worry, and her eyes are red from tears, "We shouldn't do this?"

The wagons crowd the road. Soldiers are all about. All have taken to the street on this first day in months where the sun shines so bright it brings warmth, the sky so blue it brings hope, and clouds so perfectly shaped as to think you're looking at heaven.

He comes down the steps with three armed soldiers. Rifles held across their chest.

We follow our prey as they cross the boulevard. He salutes to roving bands of cavalry. Soldiers patrolling in motorcars. So many rifles, the forge and mills are massive factories as prisoners of no crime make barrels and bullets, everyone anxious and on watch.

I turn to Mae. "I love you."

"I love you." Mae squeezes my hand, the grin of sadness I can't move.

I ask her, "Doubt?"

"This is wrong."

The noble stops at a command post, the booth on the corner. We're two blocks from the Duma. He struts across the road. The prey comes to us.

My heart explodes as if a hammer hit my chest. I can't breathe. I squeeze Mae's hand. She's trembling. The General and his two Officers are not ten feet away. His pace is quick. I let go of Mae's hand and grip the gun in my pocket. My hand is sweating and slips on the metal.

He squints upon seeing my gaze and returns it with a nod as if to say hello to someone he knows. Could recognize me from following him all these weeks. His eyes are not evil—he's a father. I've seen his two grown boys. He's a husband. I've seen the elegant wife. He's a grandfather. I've seen his son's children. The Germans are coming. What war are we fighting? The Czar wants reforms. I look away. I surrender to Doubt, and pull Mae around the corner. "I can't."

She grabs me in a hug.

"We'll leave."

"To go where?"

"To someplace beyond this."

Our failure is not without notice. Mishka and Victor were waiting, watching us from the other corner. I search the crowd for Mr. Dayan. Josef? The Cathedral's clock strikes ten, Mishka and Victor pull rifles from under their coats, race down the street, rush past us, aim at the General, and start shooting.

Turn to see the General drop to the ground. His guards firing at Mishka and Victor. The dozens of soldiers on patrol, foot and horse, rifles drawn, a dozen mothers, children, and elders on the battlefield, but Mishka, Victor, and the General are the battle's only victims.

Our escape is a race between wagons, cavalry, and weaving motorcoaches, brought to a halt by gunfire.

We race across the Square toward the Cathedral.

Josef appears from the shadows of the church and grabs Lina's arm. Mr. Dayan is behind him. "Doubt won."

We're not shot, there's no sermon, but we're led back to the basement and locked in a small room filled with crates of newsletters and broadsides with Lenin's picture, and underneath are his missives on brotherhood.

Mae hadn't let go of my hand.

I search for words to bring her comfort. "I'm sorry."

Locked in isolation for at least four days, we lost track of time. Our piss and foulness wrapped on Lenin's face—thirst, more than hunger. We spend the painful moments arguing about our choice.

Exhausted by guilt, searching for absolution, Mae tells me, "I want to die at the same time. I can't think of watching you being shot."

The door is finally unlocked. We're grabbed by Josef and a bear of a man I've never seen. Joseph pressed his gun to my head. I glance over to Mae, "I love you."

Mr. Dayan walks in, looks at me, shakes his head, and then turns to confront Josef, "We agreed."

"They must die."

Mr. Dayan shakes his head, surprised by a smirk. "My reluctant comrade. You put too much value on life. A true comrade has faith in our destiny."

"Doubt infects me."

"You have proven what I told Lenin and Trotsky. There will be those who can't be warriors."

Mae takes a deep breath, "But the Czar surrendered. The Germans are coming, who is the enemy?"

"A true Marxist is born with the soul of brotherhood." Her lesson.

His face contorts. "You were the son she lost when he was two. Would have been your age, thirteen." Mr. Dayan is weary. He has none of the temper I thought we'd face.

It is Josef who stirs the pot. "I have earned my place as a comrade. I was with Lenin when he argued with Leon, Leopold, and Julius about a revolution needing preachers and teachers, engineers, and peddlers. I took the oath to Lenin himself, but it was to be a comrade, not an assassin. I have been your flint. I've earned my place as a true comrade, and Mae took the oath, but swore to you that she was my wife first. You know the meaning of that."

He grabs my shoulders. "You are a true comrade." He turns to face Josef. "Where is Lenin? Is he a warrior or a preacher? How many have Leon and Leopold shot?"

Josef shakes his head. He has asked the same question.

"I was there when Leon told Vladimir— "Jesus won a larger congregation than Caesar."

Josef raises his pistol, "Cowards will talk."

"What am I to confess. That this basement is our headquarters?" I've kept silent under the worst of torture. I had such hate for this man."

"I only ask that you kill us both at the same time. That would be my worst torture."

The spirit of doubt takes hold over fear of death. I feel free from guilt, free from the lie of my oaths, free by speaking my truth. "The path to revolution was a match to kindling, easy to blow up a brewery, a tavern, a city, but what about now? When the Duma is yours and the throne is Lenin's, who will convince the craftsman, shopkeeper, merchants, that their labor will be equal to that of a beggar? Will a miner be paid the same as a you? Communism has no god, and yet it preaches to God's commandments for brotherhood."

Mr. Dayan stares down Joseph. I've earned his respect. "Marx speaks to this. His answer was simple: "From each according to their ability, and to each according to their needs. I take this to mean that there's a place for those who are the shopkeepers, the factory owners, the workers, the leaders, the managers, the doers. To those whose sweat builds the temple, a fair share of the spoils.".

"Josef looks me in the eye, "Vlad said your vodka was the finest he ever had. Yes, I know where you've been. You have earned a medal for loyalty, never a saboteur, never a traitor. A coward, yes. But you have value." He confronts Mr. Dayan, "He makes the vodka," and leaves.

It's the grin of my adopted father, my master, my mentor, "You never betrayed me. I tested you," he nods with a glance to Mae, and then puts his hand on my shoulder—eyes probing mine, "If we're to win the war, we need a brewmaster," and Mr. Dayan's smile seals the deal.

I'm spared for my inheritance.

We drive past the bonfires of the homeless, hear the gunshots of another murder, need to swerve to avoid a battle between an army divided into gangs of thieves against warriors whose loyalty is unknown.

It is after he parks in front of the brewery, and about to open the door that I turn to him, "I will brew the finest vodka, turn potatoes into gold, and then when I've earned my freedom, you'll set us free. We want to teach the truth of brotherhood. Perhaps Leon has a school in mind."

CHAPTER FIFTY- FIVE - Tonic – 1917

I wake to Mae's moaning. She curls her knees against her chest and grabs my wrist. "Just a cramp."

"No, this is not just a cramp. What is wrong?"

She cries, "I wanted to tell you. I just could never find the right time."

"What?"

"We're having a baby," and Mae throws up on my lap.

She takes a moment, tries to wipe my pants with the bottom of her dress, but I push her hand away. I lift her chin to see my joy— "We're going to have a baby, " but the moment of joy lasts only for as long as the kiss, and then I panic. "How? Here? Now? When?"

Mae shakes her head. "I think it's been three or four months."

I cry, "I've been a fool," and hold her. "I know nothing of women. I thought you were sick. Why did you keep this a secret?"

She sobs, "A baby, now."

The battlefield is on three fronts: Lenin's Red Army of deserters and desperation, the ten-thousand-armed vigilantes led by Trotsky. The White Army is the Czar's loyalists, rallied by generals owing their fortune to victory, and the German armada, tens of thousands of hardened warriors, last seen somewhere between Riga and Estonia.

While everyone begs for a potato, I'm delivered sacks. The driver eyes me with a comrade's salute as he curses the Czar.

The steel kettles are large enough to fill a thousand bottles. I scan the shelves and tables for ingredients, and from yeast to barley, to potatoes, even sugar, I have all I need.

Mae can't sit idle. She helps with peeling, slicing, and lugging sacks of barley and potatoes, but as I'm overwhelmed by the task, it's her courage and optimism that keep me sane. Her inheritance was her father and mother's faith in their strength. "Being the eldest, maybe my father was mad that I wasn't a boy. He taught me to shoot when I was a little girl, and when the wolves or bears would come for the livestock, he'd lift me onto the branch of a tree, while he hid in a hole he'd dug, covered us in the scent of mud, and when they came, he'd yell for me and Momma to start shooting. My first kill was the second time this happened. Broke my heart when I saw the wolf lying dead, but his respect, pride, and celebration taught me that such is the way of survival against beasts.

Dimitri Petosky is one of Josef's most trusted and smart enough to learn my ways, but he admits that his first duty is to protect the brewery in case of trouble—the capital is a snake pit of vipers.

I let my mash settle, and two weeks later, drops of raw vodka leak from the pipe, but my first sip tells me that it needs Bubby's secret ingredient. Two days more of boiling and filtering, and having scrounged the marsh for dandelion, thistle, and feverfew, and it's good enough to make Josef smile.

Bottles are scarce. There are shortages of everything. Factories are pressed to make bullets, rifles, cannons, and shells, but Dimitri is a seasoned peddler, and he manages to 'find' a crate of tin canteens. Mae helps me fill seventy-eight.

Josef shows up with a band of a dozen thugs who finish off four canteens before passing out, all except Josef, who is seduced by the potion to take off his thug's mask and give me a hug that almost cracks my ribs. "Partner."

It takes only a day for the treasure to be exchanged for gold coins. Josef is in rapture when he drives Mae and me to see Mr. Dayan.

"You did well." He puts the money and six bottles in a suitcase. "Tonight, we'll give this treasure to Leon himself." He pours four glasses, "A toast to Max and Mae." We clink, a nod, "To Bubby's vodka."

My czar plots my future. "The farms to our east are far from the war. You will have enough potatoes and barley to fill our treasury."

We go downstairs, and Mr. Dayan puts the suitcase in the trunk. Josef goes to the front and cranks the motor. I press down on the gas pedal and open the choke.

Mae slides into the back seat.

I'm about to close the door when the rear window shatters, followed by another explosion, and a second bullet blasts a hole in the door, missing my hand by inches. Through the broken glass, I see Mr. Dayan standing tall, no retreat, but shooting at the two men running toward him.

I yell to Mae, "Get down on the floor." Another glance in front, past Josef, who was cranking the engine, but now has pistols firing from both hands, kills one, but there are two more. Not thieves, they have a silver star on their caps. It's the Czar's loyalists, Chekas, sheriffs, his White Army—a traitor in our midst. I warned Mr. Dayan that we'd be victims of greed to produce so much. That the brewery should be hidden, thought of putting it in the basement, but greed rules over risk.

Mr. Dayan falls to his knees but keeps shooting until I recognize that it's Dimitri. Josef appears beside my door, firing both pistols. I see the anger in Josef's glare as he kills Dimitri, then wastes no time to turn and go on the attack to chase down the two running from the alley.

Mae and I are hugging the floor, saved by the steel plates bolted to the inside of the doors and another plate behind the back seat.

In the silence of the battle's aftermath, Josef is rushing down the alley, Mr. Dayan is somewhere behind me, and I assume wounded or dead, but its not heartache or mourning his loss, it's that I suddenly realize I'm free.

I lean over the seat, "Mae, come here." I jump out, take a quick glance to see Mr. Dayan, dead, and yell to Mae, "Grab the wheel," and then tell her to pull the throttle, "press down slow on the right pedal," as I crank the motor, it turns over, and I rush to push Mae over.

Josef is at the end of the alley, sees me, shakes his head, aims the pistol, but I take the risk and hit the gas.

He's out of bullets.

Mae is in rapture. "What are we doing!"

"We're leaving."

Josef jumps to the side before I run him over.

I gather my wits to turn from the alley onto the busy boulevard.

"Where are we going?"

"Someplace beyond."

We argue about the plan. My only thought is, "Finland." Need to avoid the boulevards.

"Mr. Dayan is dead. Josef will kill us."

I pull into an alley, get out, open the trunk, and it's soaked in spilled vodka and broken glass, but in the suitcase is the purse of precious gold sovereigns.

Mae comes beside me, "What are we going to do?"

"We need to get somewhere beyond this hell."

"My family? The farm?"

I held Mae in my arms. Her bump is pressed against my belly. "The Germans are coming. The revolution is here. I don't have faith in either." I conjured our future somewhere far away. Your parents would tell you to save yourself and the baby. Maybe one day we'll come back, but we must try to escape."

She pulls me into a kiss that seals the plan. Her smile quivers. Her eyes are swollen with tears.

I look back at the Czar's palace. Its hundred lights were no longer reflecting on the river as sparkling stars but were blinded by the darkness of death in search of resurrection...

www.ingramcontent.com/pod-product-compliance
Lightning Source LLC
LaVergne TN
LVHW020704110826
845149LV00012B/2102

* 9 7 8 1 9 6 5 5 2 3 0 7 0 *